"*Provocative, gripping and masterfully crafted…*"

Caroline Brennan, Bookollective

"*The story draws you in and you always want just one more chapter…*"

Steve, Goodreads

"*Wild… but thoroughly enjoyable…*"

Mag.icalstories

"*The longevity of the themes of* The End of the Road *are most definitely assured, so is the book itself. Perhaps the legacy for this novel will extend beyond the written word and into film or TV format. It certainly has the capacity to translate.*"

Ash Jacob

"*A real page-turner with high intensity throughout the book, which makes it difficult to put it down. Great plot, well told, well written and careful in details…*"

Niels Erik Andersen

"*A tense rollercoaster of suspense and intrigue. The author writes with integrity and skill.*"

NetGalley

ALSO BY THIS AUTHOR

The Primary Objective
The End of the Road

Coming soon…

The Richness of Regret

THE
VALUE
OF LUCK

MARTIN VENNING

mvenning.net

Matador
Unit E2 Airfield Business Park,
Harrison Road, Market Harborough,
Leicestershire. LE16 7UL
Tel: 0116 2792299
Email: books@troubador.co.uk
Web: www.troubador.co.uk/matador

ISBN 978 1805140 337

British Library Cataloguing in Publication Data.
A catalogue record for this book is available from the British Library.

Printed and bound in Great Britain by 4edge Limited
Typeset in 11pt Adobe Garamond Pro by Troubador Publishing Ltd, Leicester, UK

Matador is an imprint of Troubador Publishing Ltd

You need a better proofreader!

PROLOGUE

HE WAS LATE FOR the meeting. Surprisingly, for a senior civil servant, time keeping was not his thing. He was a problem solver who could focus to the exclusion of everything else when he had a task to perform. It had been his assistant, a trainee, who had reminded him of his commitment, who held out his coat and umbrella as a respectful prompt to get moving from Horse Guards Parade.

Thrusting his laptop into a rucksack, he had muttered rapidly in acknowledgement and headed for the exit.

"Angela, can you get a message to this Marshall chap that I will be a few minutes late and he should start without me?"

His sympathetic assistant nodded, and he was gone.

Swapping the calm but regimented cloistered corridors of the department for the chaos of the drizzle-adorned street outside, where all of humanity seemed to be competing for their own momentary pavement space, didn't seem to worry him.

With hindsight it should have done.

In his head he was anticipating the encounter to come. He crossed the road in a hurry looking to hail a taxi coming the other way.

From nowhere, so it seemed, a motorbike suddenly arrived on his shoulder. The leather-clad rider pushing him to the ground in front of a No 458 coming the other way. There was no time for the shaken driver to avoid the crunching impact and the total confusion that ensued.

The motorbike roared away leaving pandemonium in its wake.

He was well and truly gone.

"Good morning everyone. Thanks for taking the time out to get together. We are here for a case review of Ciller Terzili with the potential for lodging a UWO – an Unexplained Wealth Order.

"For the benefit of all concerned, I would be grateful if we could just go round the table to make some brief introductions. I am happy to start. My name's Phil Marshall, Senior Investigator with the National Crime Agency."

He paused and looked to his left.

"Jane Clark, Monitor from Government Communications Headquarters – GCHQ."

"Oliver Watson, special investigations department, HM Revenue & Customs."

"John Smith, Cabinet Office – Corporate Intelligence."

"Thanks. We have another colleague, Hugh Fotheringham, from the Corporate Fraud Investigations Branch of the Treasury who will be joining us as well, but I've had a message he's running late. Hopefully you have all had the opportunity to review the file which I must credit Hugh for pulling together for us. This looks like it's becoming a complex investigation involving the use of international links and may extend beyond the present remit. I have to say, at present the weakness of our position is that although we have collected quite a lot of circumstantial evidence to build this proposition, we really need to fill out the picture to justify the resources we are committing to the case. Naturally this has to be kept secret until we can go to the Crown Prosecution Service.

"Let me summarise the present position as we understand it. Ciller Terzili – that's a woman by the way – is a Turkish citizen.

She runs an international trading company, Turhan International, nominally based in Istanbul but with representative offices in five centres across the world. She is single and a 'hands on' manager with an enviable grasp of detail on commercial matters. Turhan trades in virtually anything and everything, specialising in high-growth markets from commodities to pharmaceuticals. They are pretty difficult to track as they set up shell companies and single project joint ventures in places where either no one takes an interest or where they are untraceable via nominees. We got close to them about six months ago when they set up a major arms deal for the opposition in Mali, which for some strange reason they routed through Northern Cyprus via a single entity. It was sloppy by her standards, providing a short trail back to her Istanbul operations. The guy who set it up, Gemlik Canecale earned Terzili's displeasure for not covering his tracks so well and got involved in an unfortunate diving accident off the coast near Bodrum, shortly before we were able to issue an international arrest warrant. Unfortunately, with him went the evidence we needed.

"As you will have seen from the photographs, Terzili is considered visually appealing, perhaps attractive to some – so she's high profile and smart. We think she is running the day-to-day aspects of the business with or possibly on behalf of her father, Kerim. He had five kids, four who were pretty feckless and spent their time wasting their daddy's money. Ciller stood out because she liked making it and didn't give a shit about who she was prepared to step on to do it. She had an expensive education in Switzerland, but she's also smart in a streetwise way. Although she works hard she plays hard too. She is high profile because she supports a number of charitable causes including helping to fund Syrian refugee camps. Her commercial activities are less principled, however. There is anecdotal evidence of widespread 'below the line' weapons trades across the Caucasus region and beyond. The source of the supplies comes from Turkey, Bulgaria and Ukraine where her company has known agents and supporters.

"Intelligence suggests she is developing a new partnership to cultivate emerging markets, with North Africa thought to be a priority. This is particularly troublesome because potential clients will only be interested in procuring weapons they cannot acquire from state patrons, which means she will be looking to transfer either restricted products, technologies or embargoed materials. That's the big picture, but at this point, it is still conjecture. From our immediate point of view, Terzili has connections to a number of operations closer to home linked to criminal activity. Some are not that significant yet, such as procuring women for the sex trade via a network of nightclub partners and facilitating people trafficking into the UK. The family have dabbled in cocaine dealing from time to time but given the falling street prices their activities are not considered to be a threat for now. So, although they are players in these games they are by no means market leaders. It is their more brazen operations that are of more concern as they seem to demonstrate a consistency of approach – taking control of the market for doner kebabs through a nominee franchise, 'Izmir Barbeque' for example – which is estimated to sell one in four kebabs sold here, from a standing start two years ago. The 'Izmir' shops tend to be staffed by illegal immigrants and operate as late-night admin centres for fencing drugs and stolen merchandise. Dealing in the theft and export of high-performance cars to parts of the Middle East and Africa seems to be a growing area of business based on some of our most recent interceptions.

"But why should we be interested right now? Because we believe their core trades are fuelling a new spike in violent crime across the country. It seems they are becoming a major service provider to the serious criminal fraternity hereby helping them to launder many millions of pounds earned from robberies and other extortion rackets. Evidently, the Terzilis have hit upon a way of making their money disappear with their active support, which means they are getting it back in some way we have yet to discover and, like any other investments, probably with interest.

"We have circumstantial evidence that suggests Turhan has taken delivery of large sums of cash in recent months, so large in fact, there has either been a discrepancy in the reporting of major thefts or that some of the money relates to crimes committed over the past two years that the perpetrators have not known how to clean."

At that moment, a colleague entered the room and passed a note to Marshall. As he read it, the Revenue man took the chance to break Marshall's commentary.

"How much?"

"We can't be sure, but it looks like it is in the tens of millions, and we have no idea what has happened to it, so we need another line of attack. Remember our aim is primarily about recovering the lost wealth. If we are able to secure prosecutions along the way, that is a bonus. We need to establish whether Kerim or Ciller is running the show, but they've got some legit investments in the UK, some of the best real estate in London plus some interesting private equity in new, rising high-growth start-ups including a rural fibre provider Communi-Kate, HeadingtonMeds, the company that has patented the new virus jab and the Flit Hydrogen microcar amongst others. Interestingly, Ciller Terzili does have one major trading activity in the UK where she is not just a passive investor, Global Bus, a luxury international travel coach operation, running daily services from London to Istanbul with calling points in Brussels, Munich, Venice, Zagreb, Belgrade and Sofia. We need to take a closer look at all these investments and operations to see whether we can recover this lost wealth though sequestering some of these corporate assets. As things stand, Turhan and the Terzilis have access to what appear to be considerable funds, but we think she hasn't the ability to justify where it has all come from."

Jane Clark took her cue. "How are we going to deal with this?"

"We can only succeed with a multi-agency approach. My team in the NCA is researching the recovery of assets from criminal activity in the UK from the last couple of years. This will indicate a potential pipeline for her money laundering operations. I hope your people at GCHQ will target their electronic communications to pick up clues on their clandestine activities and networks. HMRC are putting any Turhan-linked trading operations in the UK under the microscope to check whether we have a full picture of their assets and corporate activities, and our friends here at the Cabinet Office have got the really big job, which is setting the international context. We need to know to what extent Turhan's operations are mirrored overseas and who is helping them. That means they have to get close to the family personally.

"Given her eligibility, Ciller Terzili has not been short of suitors, and our information says she's had at least four serious relationships that have all broken down when it came to money. Apparently she took the lead in bedding them and pulled the plug, one after the other, when she thought they were getting too confident. In each case, we don't know what happened to them. They just disappeared.

"So, as you will have concluded, the file is a better read than most crime fiction – I think you'll enjoy researching this assignment and it's clear there is much more to learn."

John Smith stared over his glasses. "Does she have any idea she's the subject of an investigation?"

Marshall responded: "I don't think we know for sure. She is certainly a cool customer – probably well aware that it would be dangerous to show nervousness with her business associates, but for all her cunning she only needs to make a slip and we'll have her on a hook. It could just be a coincidence, but our colleague Hugh, who really is the expert on the Terzilis and Turhan, has been run over by a bus in Whitehall, victim of a drive-by mugging on the way here. Colleagues from the Met are on the scene and if there is a connection we'll find it."

There was a momentary stunned pause as if the assembled company could not believe the turn of events. Even Marshall had been shocked by his own, almost casual, sharing of the news.

"How often is she in the UK?" asked Watson.

"Twice in the last year according to the Border Control statistics. On her last two visits she arrived from Monaco via Nice and she's always careful to observe the 90-day rule."

"But based on what you're saying, she's got people here working on her behalf?"

"This sophisticated operation will need lots of hands and good communication. We must assume she has intelligence to match."

"Where does she go when she leaves?"

Smith interjected: "Back to Istanbul. We have watchers in place covering her home and office, but they have to be careful. She has her own team of professional minders. Also, our Turkish hosts don't like foreigners operating solo on their patch on principle, and we can't tell them of our interest in case it leaks."

"So how are we going to manage in the future?"

"Our people will continue their day-to-day surveillance work, but we need additional resource on this. We have to get close so we're planning a honey trap."

Marshall felt the temperature in the room rise. Watson was quick to respond.

"What? We're sending in a guy to seduce her?"

Marshall glanced at Smith.

"Don't be so surprised – we have people practised in that sort of thing. After all we are not subject to the same rules in our conduct of international investigations."

"And how are we going to get close?"

"GCHQ has intercepted messages between her and a notorious Omani arms dealer in Dubai. She has a meeting fixed next Thursday at 16.00 at the Burj Hotel. This is our opportunity."

"You're going to bug their meeting?" Watson was in shock.

"In a way, but not by our normal operating practice. With the help of our Israeli friends, we have discovered that both this dealer and Terzili have booked office suites covering the period.

She seems to be having two meetings in the hotel that day before her appointment with the Omani. Given the sensitivities involved we are pretty sure he will not agree to the meeting unless it is in his own suite, and he will have had it swept first. It is also to be expected they will request a physical search on anyone entering the room.

"We have arranged for these two bookings to be accommodated on separate floors. Neither party will have met each other before, so our plan will be to send lookalikes to each."

"Are you crazy? We won't get away with it." The man was fidgeting at the idea.

Marshall conceded: "It's a risk, sure, but perhaps no more of a risk than any other method of eavesdropping, and the potential benefits are huge. We really need to get the inside track on what this Omani is doing in terms of defence procurement. He seems to have access to an *à la carte* network of unsavoury people. We must assume that is the reason why Terzili wants to work with him, instead of dealing direct. Also, we need to understand her capabilities.

"The Israeli secret service, Mossad, are supplying our two decoys and managing the hotel staff arrangements to ensure the right people are in the right place at the same time. We have the opportunity to supply questions they will incorporate into the briefings of their people. So the riskiest bits of this rest with them. Our piece is the honey trap that is being configured at the moment."

"Configured?" Watson was starting to wonder if he had entered a parallel universe.

"We are creating the opportunity and narrative to support the field officer. The Cabinet Office is selecting the individual to do the job."

"Whoever he is this seems like a big responsibility. We don't know much about her personality. What happens if they don't get on?"

It was Smith's turn to pick up the conversation.

"That is why we will be using someone with a proven track record of dealing with this type of assignation. You are right. He may not get anywhere, which is why we can't rely on this to deliver an outcome. The point is, if it doesn't work, we avoid leaving an incriminating trail in our wake."

"Why are the Israelis bending over to help us when our prime interest is recovery of public funds for the UK?" Jane Clark had tabled the question her bosses had already raised with her.

"Good point, Jane. Don't worry – we are not obliged to be exchanging any cyber intel you may collect. That is outside our arrangement. The short answer is human intelligence – the most valuable commodity there is and the hardest to obtain. Opportunities such as this are relatively rare and the subject of defence procurement in the Gulf is one of their hot buttons. It is true whatever intel emerges will be given to us second hand, but even allowing for that possibility, this is a good deal and may give us some compelling leverage to support our objectives."

"Who are we putting up as bait in this honey trap?" Watson was just starting to focus on the implications of the investigation. Marshall saved Smith from having to explain.

"That is a matter for the Cabinet Office and something we don't need to know, other than the fact this situation creates a separate opportunity for us which could produce results. It doesn't mean that we become reliant on this as our sole method for collecting evidence, but it may produce further lines of inquiry for us to pursue.

"So, to summarise the priority actions on this assignment:

"One, GCHQ will continue to monitor Terzili's communications and map their stakeholders and networks and will report on a needs basis as developments occur.

"Two, HMRC will continue to identify appraise and review fixed assets held by the Terzili family and associates in the UK.

"Three, the Cabinet Office, through department six, will be

responsible for managing the investigation into all international aspects of this case and, four, we at the NCA will act as the central coordinators who will be responsible for preparing the case for the Crown Prosecution Service and investigating all UK-based leads including this recent development with Fotheringham.

"Given the fact this case will have political undertones, speed and confidentiality are key requirements. In the event that one of you is unable to attend further regular review meetings you will need to provide advance notification to me, and any nominee will be subject to separate additional security vetting. Finally, securing this high-profile target will not only be a credit to our own individual organisations but we will all share in the success of demonstrating how public sector partners can work together for the common good. So the challenge is significant but so too is the prize. Thanks for your attendance just now. We are scheduling a review at the same time, same place next week. In the meantime, if you have questions or intel to share, contact me directly. Good luck."

Those assembled in the glass bubble of the confidential meeting room in the Ministry of Justice collected their coats and headed for the exit escorted by a stern-looking older office assistant, whose manner suggested she had been seconded from the Prison Service.

Marshall gestured to Smith to wait behind.

ONE

HAD SHE BEEN PRESENT at Marshall's meeting, Ciller Terzili would have been shocked listening to his description of her.

She considered herself ordinary, even if others might have thought her to be privileged. These 'others' would only be judging by appearances. Sure, she was arguably attractive, olive skinned, clear complexion, brown eyes accentuated with subtle mascara, a figure that, for someone approaching her thirties was trim and demonstrated the benefits of regular workouts. She considered her best quality was her smile which seemed to light up her whole frame and advertised her full lips and admirable dentistry.

Others' eyes would have probably been drawn to her dress sense – demure verging on the sober, in dark-coloured designer suits that expertly moulded themselves to her contours. And then there was her choice of scarves – only the best quality Chinese silks, gently patterned without being garish. Another mark of the woman was her ability to work a room, able to command attention at will but also with an admirable 'chameleon-like' ability to merge into the background when the occasion required. The result was that all too often, those meeting her underestimated her capabilities, especially in a business context. Of course her father had been a great teacher, not only instructing her on how to read a balance

1

sheet and understand the disciplines of profit and loss, but how to read and anticipate business trends. Ask half a dozen successful business people to recount the secret of their success and most will focus on 'luck' or 'timing' – knowing when to buy and when to sell. Considering his lack of formal education, her father had an instinctive grasp of this most fundamental aspect of trading, and it stood him in good stead over the years. With business success had come a degree of personal fulfilment – a number of properties including her favourite, now her home base, a traditional gated Turkish villa or *yali,* close to the Salacak district in Üsküdar. Located on the southern bank of the Bosporus, it commanded impressive views of the sea traffic against the background of the Maiden's Tower and Sultanahmet on the hill behind, the skyline dominated by the world-famous Hagia Sofia and Topkapi Palace.

Then the family had grown. Two brothers and three other sisters ensured domestic life was a constant battle to win attention and approval from her parents. She had enjoyed mixed success. For her siblings, their interest had always been on what she considered to be the frivolous things in life – the opposite sex, shopping and sport. No matter what they did, their mother was always understanding and forgiving. Her father less so. Having lived by his wits and pulled himself out of poverty, he was keen to ensure his children would have the best education he could afford and yet they had squandered the opportunity of training for a profession and enjoying the reputation benefit that would bring. Ciller's success had been unexpected. As her father's first child and a girl at that, it was probably true she was his favourite, and yet he had not encouraged her to seek the same high-profile career opportunities. She had always had a reserved disposition and some who knew her from school would have recalled a girl who had an air of melancholy and found making friends difficult. Looking back, she wondered whether her parents had just assumed they were creating an eligible young woman who would live a life of well-heeled domestic anonymity as the wife of some leading figure in the world of politics or perhaps the media. She was also the product of an era where the commercial success of women was politely but firmly discouraged. A Swiss school education was one thing, but attendance as a student at a leading university, either in Turkey or beyond was something else. As was the very idea of sex.

There had come a time in her life when her mother had to have that conversation about boys and intimacy. It felt odd because, although her parents had started to pick up on the interest of boys from her neighbourhood, personally she had been oblivious to it. The temptations of the flesh had left her cold and so the warning she could not indulge until she was married, did not bother her. She didn't feel particularly sensuous but privately had enjoyed the sense of intense pleasure and relaxation on her own in the fog of steam of their local hammam.

It didn't take long for the word to get around. The effect had been to further strengthen the relationship between father and daughter. Over time, she had come to watch him conducting business from his study and, once school was over, she started to help out at his office across the water in Besiktas, overlooking Yildiz Park and its contemporary sculpture exhibition dominated by the 30-metre tall, polished steel pin named the Value of Luck because it seemed to change colour depending on the position of the sun. Little by little, bit by bit, she started to get some understanding of the world of commerce. He had been impressed how quickly she seemed to learn and her liking for making money, not just spending it. Her demeanour contrasted with her younger brothers, whom most observers had expected to take on the family firm. She remembered how tired her father would get of their constant demands to fund their hedonistic lifestyles and their increasingly implausible justifications of their situations. Of course, nine times out of ten, the sons would get their way, but only because her father wanted to avoid the inevitable rows with their mother that would ensue. Her other three sisters were different again. For them, the prospect of early marriage and families was enough – their lack

3

of ambition would condemn them to lives of subordination and servitude, or so she thought.

For potential suitors who were perplexed by what they took to be Ciller's shyness, her father would instruct his security man to take them to one side to warn them very directly of the perils of hassling his daughter. She couldn't recall her sisters' prospective boyfriends being treated in the same way, but she had not spent so much time in Istanbul during her school days to notice – and even when she was home, they already seemed to be in relationships and consequently, there wasn't the usual opportunity for filial banter.

Two key events seemed to have shaped her destiny. The first was the death of more than half the family returning from a relative's wedding. They had travelled to the gathering at Fenerbahce on the coast some twenty minutes' drive to the southwest in a minibus. It was involved in a major collision at the start of the freeway just near to the football stadium with a container truck and fuel tanker. It wasn't clear whether they were killed as a result of the injuries from the crash, but the ensuing explosion of the fuel tanker took care of any possibility of survivors. Gone were her mother, her three sisters and one of her brothers. Both brothers would have been killed if one of them hadn't been away partying in Bodrum. The incident probably created the circumstances of the second key event.

Understandably, her father was broken by the experience. He became increasingly withdrawn and preoccupied. He lost interest in going to the office, his personal appearance, even eating. He developed a haunted look and, for a man normally focused and preoccupied by the detail of business transactions, he became a shadow of his former self. The family residence, for years the scene of noise and laughter became quiet, but she had not been forgotten. Gradually she started to receive out-of-hours calls at the villa from her father's business associates, some she knew by acquaintance, some she didn't. Generally, the approaches came out of curiosity noting the fact that it had been a while since they had heard from her father and enquiring after his health. Others had a far more nervous disposition, giving her the impression that whatever they were involved in, they had money out on the table. It was this group that would be the toughest to deal with. Ciller had to offer a general apology for the lack of contact, saying her father was a little under the weather, but if something needed fixing in the next couple of days, if they could tell her about it, she would see what she could do.

Although sincere, in the majority of cases her efforts were not well received – not least in the conservative business world, as these men did not like bringing a woman into their confidence.

The position had changed after she had sought the advice of whom she knew to be one of her father's closest friends, Repcer, the lawyer, possibly the only person to have an overview of her father's business activities. A veteran of Istanbul's legal community, Repcer had a reputation as a pugnacious defender of the indefensible. He was known for taking the cases others knew to be lost causes. It was a good trade to be in – a solid queue of instructions where guilt was never the issue, only the length of the sentence that had to be negotiated. No other performance-related criteria applied. He was known also to welcome the notoriety that came with it, often appearing on TV and in the papers. With his growing prominence had come a narcissistic trait. He had become a regular at the trendy barbers around the corner from the office, using a secret combination of dark oils to limit the emergence of grey and white, and started to invest in some of the finer, woollen designer suits not uncommon on the streets of Manhattan. By the shine on his pock-marked features from his desk lamp, he was clearly using some sort of moisturiser on his leathery skin. His bright ties contrasting with the sober tones of his outfits and, of course, being seen in the company of the great and the good all contributed to his personal brand. But his growing confidence was resulting in another less fortunate quality for a lawyer, carelessness, and the thought that no matter what he did, he would always succeed.

Ciller was not an emotional woman, but her meeting with Repcer, following her father's descent into depression was one she would never forget.

She had to make an appointment and travel across the city to attend his offices in the upmarket district of Nisantasi, in the north of the city, itself an awkward and time-consuming journey from her home and the family office. Although the meeting had been fixed for late afternoon on a Thursday, upon arrival, she had been surprised that his own support staff seemed to have left for the day and he was alone. It had probably been planned that way as she was sure he would have confidential information to impart. Sitting in a comfortable leather studded sofa in Repcer's oak-panelled office, she felt a strange, all-encompassing calmness with the noise and the bustle of the street outside effectively muffled. The lawyer had offered her tea, which she had declined, then came to sit next to her, a pen and pad in hand as he prepared to take notes.

"My, how good it is to see you, Ciller. I was trying to think earlier when it was we last met. I think it must be nearly a year ago when your father hosted a dinner at your *yali*. I have always admired the panorama of our city from that balcony and enjoying good food, and good company as well made it a truly memorable experience. And now look at you, so much more than a girl but a fully-fledged businesswoman building a career in the commercial world, despite, I am sure, the attentions of many eligible suitors no doubt."

He paused, looking at her intently.

"And how can I be of service?"

Having explained the circumstances that had prompted her initiative in requesting a meeting, she had been surprised that unlike some of his other business associates, Repcer had not been in touch to enquire about her father's health. Her surprise was increased by his apparent lack of knowledge about her father's business dealings and he didn't seem willing initially to offer the help and support she was counting on, until her stress gave way to her tears.

Instinctively she turned to him for comfort.

Instinctively he put his arms around her in what she had almost expected to be the sort of fatherly hug she had been missing. Through the flood of emotion, she became aware he was holding her perhaps a little more closely, a little more firmly, than was appropriate.

His hands moved from her back as he put his face in front of hers and started to kiss her. Now his hands had moved to her breasts which he was squeezing with some urgency. Her initial reaction was to recoil in horror, what was happening was unexpected and, as far as she was concerned, unwarranted. But he had her pinned to the sofa.

With hindsight she realised that what was happening could not just be dismissed as some spur of the moment thing but was premeditated. In this situation, this man knew what to do, how to do it and was careful enough to ensure there were no witnesses. With his body weight wedging her into the corner he was tearing away at the belt of her trousers whilst pressing her hand against his crotch.

She had felt the protests rising in her throat but with his mouth over hers there was little opportunity for sound to escape.

Her thoughts had now moved on rapidly from her father's situation to her own. Her interest was on saving her virginity. Now, freely, she unzipped his bulging breeches to release his phallus, madly massaging it in order to ensure she achieved a reaction before he was able to violate her. Although unpleasant, she had already decided this was the best course of action in her predicament and secured the result she had been seeking. His ardour now diminished, he relaxed his grip, allowing her to wriggle free, stand up and adjust her ruffled clothing.

"Oh Ciller, *sweetness*, you are truly a beautiful woman, be mine, and you will want for nothing. I am intoxicated by your beauty, seduced by your charm and excited by what we could achieve together. I will contact your father to ask for your hand in marriage. I understand you think a younger man can better provide for your personal needs but as you can see I have the appetite of a man half my age. My seed is high quality, I have satisfied many women and given them the intelligent offspring they seek."

What? She could hardly believe what she was hearing.

At this point, Ciller recalled thinking the lawyer was deranged – his 'high-quality' seed now had no home to go to having been liberally spread on the sofa, his trousers and fortunately only a little on her own. In this highly charged situation, Ciller knew she needed to turn this to her advantage and retain a cool demeanour.

"Well, Mr Repcer, you are a stallion in disguise. As you say there is potentially much we could achieve together, but perhaps there needs to be some proper preparation if you are going to discuss my hand in marriage."

Repcer, up to that point, had been entirely focused on his own base needs. He really hadn't fully grasped the potential of his victim becoming a willing supplicant or the possibility of what she might expect from a long-term personal relationship. He now focused on her with a new but different form of intensity. If the beginning of their meeting had been characterised by lust, the next part was clearly driven by avarice.

He too had smoothed out his clothing, taken a tissue to clear up the mess he had made and got a grip on his pen and notebook.

Hastily composed, he repeated his earlier question.

"Certainly. How can I help?"

"You will recall the terrible circumstance of my recent family losses. Although my father, one of my brothers and I have survived we have been changed by the experience. We are enduring a pain in our souls, perhaps as bad as if we ourselves had been involved in the accident. I am coming to terms with living with a heavy heart and a father who has regressed into a deep depression. We have many business deals not yet concluded and probably others

I know little about. I need your help in getting control of my father's business. I need to know more about his customers and what he has agreed to. For all I know, we could be facing several lawsuits that may put us out of business, or potentially even worse. At the very least I need power of attorney. I know from remarks he made to me in the past when I was helping out in the office that he made provision for all this in legally binding documents that you hold.

"Seek them out. Put me in charge and we'll get the company stabilised. If you are serious about making a future with me, you need to demonstrate what you will do to achieve it."

"What of your brother?"

"Adnan? What of him?"

"Won't he be expecting to take over?"

"No, I don't think so. He has a natural aversion to work and provided he continues to receive his allowance, he will continue to live the good life down south. He only turned up to the funerals on the basis he could get a day return air ticket. The business employs a small administrative team who have, in effect, already been taking instructions from me in the absence of my father."

The lawyer's brow furrowed.

"I will need to look into this further. After all, I have my own interest to consider. I too hold a modest stake in the business myself remember – *a sleeping partner* is one way to think of it."

A faint curl of his lips suggested some amusement at his own observation.

He continued: "If this is going to be worthwhile from all our points of view, we may need to think about reforming the business."

"What do you mean?"

"We may need to think about extending its activities to develop the profit base and justify our time. When I think back to when I first worked with your father we were just doing some straightforward deals, you know, the basics – leather clothing, carpets, ceramics, foodstuffs like fruit and spices – wherever he could get a margin. He moved on to commodities from the east outside traditional legal restrictions and scrappage where he still has some interests, but he was always a trader looking for the next deal. He never took a long-term view of his prospects."

"Was that so wrong?"

"I grant you the tactic has served him well – he made some money, but he never had a real strategic plan.

"When it came to raw commodities he was good at reading the markets. It was simple. He would buy a quantity of 'x' and sell it for 'y' with a clear profit 'z'. His skill was identifying the customer before he did the transaction and then fulfilling it faster than anyone else. Latterly he got into trades with longer capital-intensive timescales which required patience to unlock. The biggest thing outstanding is the *Hawaiian Sun*, a cruise ship that he bought for scrap. It's waiting to get into the breakers yard at Aliaga right now and he used other people's money to buy it. So for now, the ship sits offshore, the interest payments on the loans are ratcheting up and that deal alone going sour could break the business. I can tell you a number of investors who went into that one have been less than impressed and were threatening unspecified consequences if the business failed to make its interim payments."

"And was my father paying them?"

"I would need to review the exact position, but I do know he was keeping his creditors on the *Hawaiian Sun* happy by selling through opium consignments from Afghanistan to cocaine and heroin producers in Mexico. Ha! That was his skill – he was selling Afghan product to the Mexicans who were used to getting it from Columbia! I had to admire his sales skills, but really, if you tried to imagine a tactic that would piss off the big guys in Latin America, it would be that. From what I hear, they don't really give a shit about the money. If he was playing on their turf they would certainly come after him."

"Do you think that is why the family had the accident?"

"Who knows? It's difficult to tell. Commerce is a rough business. It's a game of winners and losers and these days there are more bad losers around looking to get even. The Afghans only liked him because they thought he was giving them an outlet when their usual supply corridors started to be broken up by the Americans. If his customers dry up, they will be annoyed as well. And there again there are the Russians…"

"Russians?"

"The Solokov family to be precise. When the old Soviet Union broke up, the Solokovs – aluminium oligarchs – decided to concentrate their holdings in Russia. Your father heard they were trying to offload a redundant iron ore mine in Uzbekistan and took it on without seriously looking at its future viability. He rented it off to a local workers cooperative who have got it working again and the former owners want it back. I can only assume they have decided the prospects are looking up, and maybe Uzbekistan is still safe for Russian investment. You're looking surprised? I guess he hasn't told you much about this?"

"When I was helping him at the office, most of my time was spent doing the administration for his tax returns."

Repcer's thin smile extended.

"Then at best you would only know about his pocket-money deals – spices, wheat flour, lamb, carpets, building materials and semi-finished clothing. Respectable but unremarkable trades.

"If you're serious about taking control of your father's business you will have to ask yourself some hard questions. Do you have the determination to complete the work he has started, quite a lot of which can either be regarded as controversial or in some cases contrary to prevailing law?"

Ciller picked up on the phase which, to her mind, was a euphemism. The implications were not lost on her either. Firstly, unwittingly, she had lived off and prospered from illegal earnings, so in some people's eyes she was already a criminal. Secondly, if she did take over the family business, she would assume control of some nefarious activities immediately that she would need to complete, even if her wish was to take the business on a different path. And yet there was a suggestion of hope in his words, perhaps some privileged knowledge which suggested some of the company's operations may come under the law at some stage in the future.

Listening to Repcer, she had already formed the opinion that her father had already set the direction of travel that she would need to pursue.

"How do you suggest we move forward?"

"You will need to review all Turhan's present assets and consider how they are managed. If you can't, you need to dispose of them. Second, you need to ensure you are working with the right people. Meet his business associates and decide whether you can work with them. Third, you need to set a strategic direction for the business. The point is, if you want to continue to make money you have to move from serving market need in the way your father did, by dominating and controlling the market itself. No one succeeds by being a jack-of-all-trades – the world has moved on. The winners are the specialists who dictate how business will be managed. Turhan is not big enough to do this. Once you have decided what the future for the business will be, you need to draw in partners by buying controlling interests. That way you can protect your cover, have some legitimate 'shop window' businesses and spread your risk.

"Finally, you need a small group of loyal advisers and partners around you who can help guide you through the stages I have set out here. Loyalty these days is a tricky concept. It is hard to earn and easy to lose. Of course, money helps to buy commitment in the early stages, but you need something more from them for the long term – a shared belief in your values and strategy. I am a good example; I do a good job for your father for the five per cent I take now. Just think what I may be able to deliver for twenty per cent."

"And what might that be, Mr Repcer, apart from your 'high-quality seed'?"

The lawyer momentarily winced at the barb but kept his eyes on the prize.

"My network is the best in Istanbul. We can agree how to develop the business and what skills we need. I can then go and get the people to deliver the vision, as well as continuing to look after your best interests."

"I will bear it in mind. Thank you for your candour, Mr Repcer."

"*Alper*, please…"

"I have much to think about. I must start with a conversation with my father."

"I wish you well, Ciller. I think when you reflect on what I have said, you will see the merits of what I propose. Do remember, as with any business, doing nothing is not an option. All that will happen will be that the vultures will gather and pick off the juiciest pieces as it suits them. It's a dangerous world. You have to be strong to survive. While you talk with your father, I will draw up some initial proposals for us to discuss next time. Have no doubt about it – you should seize the day – fortune favours the brave."

That much was true. The meeting with Repcer had sharpened her mind. Leaving his office, her father's driver, Osman, shepherded her into the family Mercedes and she settled down for the hour's drive back home. Repcer had both boosted her confidence and undermined it at the same time. Knowing she had the energy and drive for the task she also realised she would need friends, supporters who would get her through. Who could she rely on? The lecherous Repcer? Smart he may be, but based on that initial encounter not the most trustworthy. Her playboy brother (wherever he was)? Friends?

She felt isolated and alone.

TWO

THE HOUSEKEEPER, ASLI, HAD organised a light supper of mezes in the lounge behind the shuttered doors that led onto their balcony with that iconic view.

Her father had always loved that panorama, probably more than the *yali* itself, but since being bereft, the doors had stayed closed. When the family had been complete, the opportunity of the balcony had been there for them all to enjoy the constantly changing vista of the city. Since being on his own, he regarded it as a place where he would be on parade – gawped at by curious tourists or bored deck hands passing by on the water.

At one time he would have been proud to showcase his family and social gatherings to passing audiences, but in his grief, privacy, silence and darkness were his constant companions. Ciller had been wondering what to do to engage with her father. He seemed so difficult to reach. She had tried several different approaches – getting him to sign off the monthly domestic accounts, pay the staff wages, even suggesting he took a break with Adnan down south in the sunshine of the Aegean – all to no avail, but she did succeed in getting him to agree to have a weekly evening supper. Each time she made it her business to play some of his favourite music as a means of getting him to open up. To begin with he remained unresponsive, preoccupied, staring into the middle distance, nibbling in an absent-minded way. Ciller had kept up the conversation, making small talk about her day, her friends, even commenting on stories on the local TV news. Slowly she drew him out, sometimes deliberately avoiding acknowledgement of his answer as her way of celebrating the normality of his response. It had taken a month for her to make the breakthrough she had been seeking. This night she had selected the Borusan Philharmonic's uplifting interpretation of one of Tekbilek's most beautiful compositions – *Hasret*. It had long been a popular choice in the household in better times and her hope was it would in some way, inspire him to engage.

And briefly it did.

The breakthrough came in a casual reference to Repcer mentioning he had been in touch regarding a tax query.

"I have no interest in such matters anymore. If the tax authorities think I owe them money let them take me to a tribunal. Repcer can then deal with them and get me compensation if I have been wrongly accused."

"Don't you think it would be better if I managed the situation directly? You know how things are. If Repcer knows he is able to get an extra fee by spinning things out he will. If you sign the re-registration certificate attached to your last tax statement making me responsible for your affairs, I can take over the matter altogether and you won't need to worry about it."

"It is true I have grown tired of business. I am not interested in all these moaners chasing me for money or favours. I think I should be left to mourn my losses before I go to join the rest of the family in a better place. Give me the certificate and I will sign it now."

It was more than Ciller had hoped for.

Fortunately she had kept the relevant document close at hand with a pen for such an eventuality. All she needed to do was to countersign the form and get it in the post. She would have the corporate control she craved, her father would be able to live out the rest of his days in seclusion, comfort and peace.

Now she could begin to plan for the future.

The park bench in Whitehall Palace Gardens, closest to the mounted bust of Samuel Plimsoll, was the chosen location.

It was a favourite meeting place of John Smith's when he wanted to talk freely, away from the constraints of his workday four walls. Convenient in that he could get to the rendezvous in just under ten minutes from his desk, useful that he did not have to either send a meeting request or specify the venue.

All he had done was to draw a sketch of the symbol that had made Plimsoll famous on a notepad, taken a picture on his phone and directed it to the recipient via an anonymous government mailbox.

There was no reason for his guest to provide a form of acknowledgement.

His communication was not a request, but an instruction that had to be fulfilled within the hour. Duncan Matheson, from the Special Operations Directorate at 'Six', was assigned to carry out the order, arriving at the appointed place in a knee-length trench coat, the ideal attire for eating a M&S sandwich in public and deflecting the inevitable crumbs towards a couple of admiring pigeons looking for their own afternoon snack who were bravely approaching his feet. Considering his athletic six-foot frame, close shaved head and a light tanned complexion, which suggested he enjoyed the outdoor life, there was nothing remarkable in his outward appearance. He was a few inches taller than Smith and favoured roomy utilitarian off-the-peg suits; practical, easily replaceable clothing for someone who could be called to address a combat situation at short notice. Possibly ten years his senior, Smith was more carefully manicured, sober worsted pinstripe by Saville Row, Barker brogues and expensive haircut and wet shave from

Curzon Street to compensate for the heavy shadow on his chin. He had a steady blue-eyed gaze which seemed to communicate calm and control, suggesting an ideal companion to have in a tight corner. What the two had in common, however, was their gait, both moved with ramrod straight backs – testament to their shared military background.

"Ah Duncan – long time. Boys on the South Bank keeping you busy? Last time I heard they had sent you on some errand in Taiwan to secure some imperial treasures acquired by the Kuomintang. That could have got a bit sticky, but I heard you smoothed the whole thing out and got the offending material out of the theatre. How did you manage that?"

He paused, realising he had broken one of the unwritten rules of communication with this representative of the Department for the Black Arts.

"Better still, I don't think I want to know anyway," he added hastily.

"Don't go there, John – I'm not planning on going back for some time."

The spook changed the subject, replying in a Scots accent.

"Well, you've certainly succeeded in shaking our tree. Trust my luck I was the one who fell out."

"You make it sound like you were assigned by chance, when I understand you have a particularly relevant experience – 'skin in the game' as it were."

His guest ignored the question.

"Well at least I had the opportunity to take a top-line look at the file ahead of this meeting. Assume making contact in the UAE will be easier than in Turkey and you have people presently putting in place the necessary cover with our friends in Tel Aviv. Are you sure you aren't employing a sledgehammer to crack a nut?"

"Not at all. If this was just about sequestering assets, the whole thing would have been wrapped up by now. The intel prize is much bigger. Quite how big will be part of your job to ascertain.

Somewhere in this mess is a boundary between civil criminality and state-sponsored terrorism, but as we don't fully understand it yet we are not in a position to allocate the necessary resources. Terzili's networks could be the key to a treasure trove of information that may help in making the future much safer for millions of people across Europe."

"No pressure then. What I don't get is she must need a pretty big organisation to do all the stuff that she is credited for."

"I know. That is another reason why we have to get close. We're not sure how she's able to manage it or indeed whether she is really in charge. On the one hand, she is sufficiently engaged that most strategic decisions require her input, but on the other, she seems to keep most people at a distance. There have been a few who have got close in the past, but as you will have read, most seem to have disappeared."

"You mean they are dead?"

"I don't think we know for sure. I think it is fair to assume those who may be alive are in hiding somewhere as I guess they must have assumed they are targets."

"So really, I am being sent into this blind?"

"Sometimes it is the best way to be. If you have a skill or a connection she needs and you happen to come to her attention, your lack of knowledge may prove to be a positive advantage – no preconceptions and all that."

"So that's why we have agreed to work with the Mossad, and they are setting up the two sting meetings – why are they not doing my job?"

"Oh they are keen to take the whole show off us given the chance. They have a good line in likely Letharios, but if we give them that we will have no influence over the job and will have to rely on second-hand intelligence, which is considered to be unsatisfactory. Any other things you need to know?"

"Not really. The cover story seems solid enough. I am as ready as I will ever be. Who will be my field handler?"

"A logistics manager at the port authority – a guy called Brown. Yes really! He will be meeting you off the flight and has fixed up your accommodation and office facilities. Also, rather helpfully, he will be introducing you to some relatively low-level trading contacts, so that if anyone from the west coast of the Gulf is watching (or anyone else for that matter) it will all look OK. Brown will be monitoring Terzili's movements in Dubai and will advise you of the necessary interception arrangements."

The mercurial pigeons that had gathered at Matheson's feet started to lose interest now, all traces of his sandwich had disappeared. It seemed also to herald the pending conclusion of the discussion.

"OK, so I will communicate primarily through Brown if I need to and keep the back channel for any unexpected emergencies."

"Fine by me. Good luck and look forward to hearing of your progress."

The visitor muttered a farewell without making eye contact, tossing his sandwich wrapper into the nearby waste bin as he walked casually towards the park exit.

Given his security status, Smith would be the only member of the project team to meet Matheson. All Matheson had gleaned was that his boss on this assignment would be a man named John Smith from the Cabinet Office and he could be sure there were many who would answer to that name… or none.

Strolling back to his office that autumn afternoon, Smith reflected on the likely success of the venture. At best he thought it would be 50/50, although the worst of the downside was likely to be the plan would either be a no-show blind date or be exposed as an Israeli operation and would be unlikely to attract more than passing interest from the international intelligence community. He had satisfied himself of the knowledge and experience of his principal asset, but still felt a touch of nervousness about his overseas partners. He took comfort in the close relationship that had been developed between British and Israeli intelligence services in recent years, although it had been the Americans that had acted as the glue between the two parties. He had not worked with Mossad before and although their London station manager seemed like a regular type of guy, he was first and foremost a spook – so of course he was sure to like him. Similar to others in his profession he was a second secretary in their embassy's trade department, and relatively young in Smith's estimation, perhaps still in his late thirties. He had that 'Mediterranean' look that was such an advantage these days, allowing him to potentially present as a national of more than a dozen countries in the region. In Smith's book, there were a number of giveaway features, apart from the fact his name was Weitzman. One was his heavily accented English, another, his dark conspiratorial eyes supporting saggy bags, prematurely grey-flecked black moustache, and what he took to be his particularly sharp intellect. In Smith's mind, the idea for the double sting on Terzili and her contact in Dubai had come from Weitzman out of a casual conversation at a diplomatic reception to mark the launch of a new airline, *Shalom!* celebrating their inaugural route between Birmingham and Tel Aviv. As Terzili had been known to dabble in arms sales, Smith had enquired whether his target had 'form' in Israel, itself an active market for freelance arms traders. His enquiry had resulted in sparking an interest in Terzili which, it transpired, had been entirely new. It had been Weitzman who had turned up Terzili's interest in 'rogue regimes' after his people had intercepted an email she had sent via her lawyer's office in Istanbul to an Omani trader enquiring about 'procurement opportunities', and the response, suggesting a meeting in Dubai. Most conventional spymasters would have settled for bugging the venue to listen in on the discourse, but Weitzman knew this would be practically impossible to achieve, given the timescales. Also, as a first meeting, this would really be about setting the ground rules for future contact, especially as the cautious arms trader would want sufficient time to check Terzili out. Weitzman was excited about the prospect, although he could not be sure that there would be any follow-up. The fact that the Omani had responded positively to this approach was an opportunity not to be missed.

As a result, and without much help from Smith, Weitzman had assembled his own formidable dossier on Terzili, but his interest had not been on her criminal activities, but what he saw as her true potential for graduating into terrorism that would inevitably have implications for Israel. The Mossad man had shared Smith's concerns about her very close circle of contacts and the difficulty of predicting her actions. But on the subject of the Omani's contacts, he was far more eloquent.

"His name is Mohammad Sultan bin al-Harriri – he calls himself the Sultan. He made his name and earned his money working with the Iranians and his big buddy is their Dubai Trade Office Director, Muhammad Ruhollah Vehrani who holds the rank of colonel in the Revolutionary Guard and is a former Quds commander in Tripoli, northern Lebanon. Other than that, he seems to be a fairly opaque figure but enjoys all the perks that the privileged in the Emirate take for granted. He is often on the party circuit, has an eye for an available piece of skirt and has a habit of appearing at some diplomatic events from time to time. Seems to get on with the Germans best and has cordial involvements with Pakistan, Argentina and Turkey, so that may explain his apparent openness in talking to Terzili."

"Would he know about Dubai-based businesses transacting across the Gulf?"

"This is not just about traffic across the water. Do remember the Revolutionary Guards are much more than a military organisation. They are very commercial in their outlook and see part of their role to earn fees for the state – that is net of their own personal cuts and do remember their interest is much broader than Iranian import/exports. They collaborate in a variety of trades in places such as Myanmar, Laos, North Korea, Mauritania, Nigeria – the list is diverse."

"How do they get away with it?"

"They have always adopted the principle the end justifies the means. Vehrani opens the doors but it's the Sultan who walks through them. There are quite a few of their trades that move via Baghdad. There are plenty of freelancers either side of the line getting stuff over the border without documentation for a fee in US dollars. Paperwork is often created in Dubai, and few get interested in cargo issued from there. It is tolerated especially in food supplies and electronic goods where margins are relatively modest."

"What does the Sultan know about Terzili?"

"Well, it seems Vehrani organised for a junior trade counsellor to come up from Ankara to Istanbul to check her out and naturally we made it our business to help them to find out what we wanted them to know, so we have provided company references on her business, Turhan International, as well as a couple of obscure client references and pictures. I think the ones regarding recycled scrap for Sri Lanka and weapons for Tajikistan are those which we expect will have whet his appetite for a dialogue."

"And what about recognising her?"

"Finding a woman who looks the part took a little time, but we managed it. Our computer image assessment has got her to an overall likeness of eighty-five per cent, which is acceptable for this purpose. Given her obvious attraction we can be confident of getting the Sultan's attention. We have called her 'Bonnie'."

"Who will be your proxy official who will meet with the real Terzili?"

"That is a much easier task. We have substituted a member of al-Harriri's team who is away attending a family funeral. Our man will play the part of Reza Jalalabad, a second-level official counsellor. His name…"

"Don't tell me, is Clyde?"

"Spot on, John. I thought you would see the irony in that."

It had only been three days since Marshall had last spoken with Oliver Watson, yet he felt in need of an update.

"I should be flattered that you think we can move so quickly," Watson began, keen to dampen down his colleague's expectations.

"I think this may be slow work. Listing Terzili's property holdings in London is the easy bit. We've had a handle on that for the last couple of weeks and yes, when we can get together the case to present to an examining judge, getting control on that aspect of her activities will be fairly straightforward. There seems to be an erratic record of collecting rents – several injections of several million pounds made from a range of bank accounts, mainly in the Europe and the US. These may be legit, but if these are purely rents then they could be seen to be excessive.

"Scanning her corporate interests in the UK is a tougher proposition. First of all, Turhan holdings in the kebab business are limited to minority stakes in franchises and at last count there were 180 of these, most of which are held by individual traders and some of them are not up to date with their tax filings, so we can only monitor and chase over a period of time.

"The 'above the line' investments – Communi-Kate, HeadingtonMeds, and Flit Hydrogen – are all tidy from our perspective, with Flit even getting a research grant from the Business Department for a new engine design, but we will be sighted on any share transactions and dividends that may go their way. Then there is Global Bus – an interesting one, this. It is based in Serbia, with a subsidiary registered in West Drayton. Seems to employ around sixty people. Really seems to be about running an online ticketing operation and employing drivers and maintenance engineers. Global Bus also rents a shed on the Slough Trading Estate which appears to be for the servicing of coaches doing the run to Istanbul. Seems to be quite a big facility with room for six vehicles. In the event of us taking action, it looks like the only thing we could do with this is to impound any vehicles she would have in the UK at any one time. There's plenty more we need to understand but she will be needing quite a bit of cash on tap in London to keep things ticking over. We know of a transactional account at Municipal Bank on the Strand and an investment account at Dalabank in the City. There may be more but that's what we know. If you can get us some info on these stolen performance motors, we'll happily go after it."

"Any idea about the sort of money she's likely to have access to in the UK?"

"Impossible to say right now but the property assets alone will be in the forty million territory I would think. I will keep you posted on progress."

Marshall stared out of his glass-walled office on the 13th floor of his Canary Wharf office in the late afternoon sunshine admiring the snaking path of the river around the Millennium Dome and on past the Royal Observatory at Greenwich, towards the Thames Barrier and the sea. He would soon have to start work on his interim progress report on the Terzili investigation, which was already starting to feel like nailing jelly to a wall. GCHQ were reporting all was quiet from the comms perspective.

Yes, things were happening and overall, the prospect for success was reasonable. He would net the small fry for sure, but it was the bigger fish that he needed to hook. He knew the DG would be hungry for outcomes to take to the Perm Sec, and for now, he had more questions than answers. He knew the first line of criticism would be about the grounds for the investigation in the first place. How come this woman had become so influential in crime circles, yet no one seemed to know anything about her? More importantly, why didn't he know more about her? Perhaps overall the most positive thing he had to report was that Smith's man would be deployed in a matter of hours and shortly after, he would come to understand much more about Ciller Terzili. He might be late in the game, but he was fully committed to ensuring his intervention would be effective.

While he waited he would turn his attention to the kebabs.

THREE

IT WAS NOW REPCER'S turn to drive across the first Bosporus bridge to the Asian side en route to the Terzili villa. Whether he was liked or not, the lawyer was a wise old bird who knew that times were changing, and it was time to form new alliances to secure his own investments.

Having given the matter some thought, he had decided supporting Ciller's move to take control of Turhan International was not an act of betrayal of her father, a long-standing friend – rather a positive act of underwriting his client's fortunes and no doubt providing a fast-track route to increasing his own wealth.

The power shift was hereby being demonstrated by him bringing the necessary documentation to his client rather than merely granting an audience to a customer on his own premises.

He was confident he had all the qualities to impress – a revised company structure with new shareholders and ownerships, regulatory approval, bank authorisations and a business plan. What was there not to like? His car had a short wait at the main gate before it was recognised by the security camera and granted access to the grounds. The distance from the gate to the main entrance was relatively short but as the residence had been built in an elevated position, his car had to negotiate two tight bends on the driveway to deliver him to the front door.

Ciller watched his limousine approach from the covered balcony and waived her welcome as Osman opened the car door to direct him inside.

She remained on the balcony and listened as the lawyer's footfall grew louder as he climbed the stairs.

"Good day, Ciller. Already my day is brighter for seeing you."

Repcer had prepared well – new lightweight blue suit, freshly pressed white shirt, understated mustard-coloured paisley tie and a cologne clearly meant for a younger man.

"You are welcome, Alper. I am glad you found the time in your busy schedule to come and see me."

"My dear, the pleasure is mine. How is your father? Will he be joining us?"

"He continues to make some progress but has lost interest in commercial matters now. He still has a heavy heart."

The relief showed straightaway on Repcer's face, giving way to concern.

"I am sorry to hear it. Few realise grief is a disease like many others and when it strikes there is no telling how long it will take to recover."

"Indeed, before we start will you take coffee?"

She gestured to a tray with crockery and ornate pouring pot on a small occasional table by a wicker sofa and took a seat opposite.

This meeting was the start of a new era, and she chose to look the part. A black business pencil skirt cut below the knee, complemented by a black jacket with a high collar in the Indian style.

Her make-up was light, making full use of her natural contours, dark hair tied back, mascara and a patriotic red lipstick, the principal tools at her disposal.

The scene had been carefully orchestrated to present the opposite to the environs of Repcer's somewhat claustrophobic office.

Plenty of light, air and space.

The objective was to unnerve Repcer to make him slightly on edge so that she could better examine his weaknesses.

Coffee served, the lawyer comfortable, she deliberately paused before starting their dialogue, just long enough for the lawyer to feel he should intervene.

"Well, Ciller, I took some careful notes following our last meeting…"

"So did I, Alper. I hope you have acted on my wishes."

The lawyer put a small executive briefcase on his knee, clicking the locks open simultaneously.

"Certainly I have. Firstly, I have sought to restructure the business in line with your expectations. This means complying with the current law to have a minimum number of directors and splitting Turhan's operations between tactical and strategic investments. In view of some of your father's more 'experimental' trades, I have created a separate business called *Yilan* or Serpent.

"The new Turhan board and share ownerships are as follows: you, as chair and CEO, fifty-one per cent; me, nineteen per cent; your brother Adnan, ten per cent; and then three new directors: Asar Belgin of the Turkish Munitions Association; Duru Husni, owner of the Ottoman Breakers Yard in Aliaga and Ilkay Vahid, the CEO of PrivatPosta, the courier agency. All take ten per cent, all are clients of mine, all have specialist knowledge and interests in your areas of operation, all are… entrepreneurially minded. They understand they will provide active contributions to Turhan and will use their influence as we – you – direct.

"These appointments are strategically based to add value to Turhan, get creditors off your back and help build new collaborations to buy you time to reshape Turhan as you want it. You and I alone will run Yilan. The point is we can put those activities of Turhan's that do not comply with present statutory requirements into this pot. This will help us to strengthen the Turhan brand and allow us to earn additional monies, which in time, you may wish to cross subsidise. This will be a straight fifty-one/forty-nine arrangement and will benefit from separate accounting services provided far away in Trabzon, where no one will be interested. I have dealt with all the formal re-registrations for Turhan and aligned the banking arrangements. Yilan's money will be held in a deposit account at the local branch of Bank of Anatolian Commerce. It can only be accessed by personal authorisation from you as your father's representative. This is just a technicality but gives you a little bit of distance from any direct association. I will act as company secretary for Turhan and will manage all legal and accounting matters in line with your instruction.

"For now, I have put all our legally compliant activities into Turhan, with one-off trades and those requiring some sort of official sanction into Yilan. This means as of today the official businesses of Turhan International are commodities, travel, munitions and scrap metal processing – everything else will be secondary.

"The next thing is the business plan. I have prepared this in line with what I think your commercial priorities should be. As I said to you previously, the number one objective must be to generate cash to ensure all known commitments are covered. Then we can look at future investments and insurances, like what to do with the mine in Uzbekistan.

"I will get Hosni to sort out the credit issues on the *Hawaiian Sun* and then we can get your brother to sell the deals to the creditors.

"By the looks of it, you are carrying too much borrowing on Global Bus. I think we should look more closely at that together – the paper on this is pretty thin.

"Anyway, as you will see my projections and assumptions are set out for you to review. Once you have had the opportunity to consider these matters further we can, of course, review."

"Thank you, Alper. You appear to have done well. As you say, I must study your reports before making detailed comments but agree with your assessment that the future looks promising, even if the short term looks a bit shaky. Full marks for finding a suitable role for Adnan, I have always been aware of the need to have him in a role where I can see him, and he does not have the ability to cause problems. I will look forward to meeting your director nominees in due course and suggest you schedule the first board meeting next month here. Send me a separate note about your requirements and I will get it organised."

The lawyer was looking like an eager hound in need of continuous praise and possibly a cuddle. Ciller recognised the signs and, whilst wanting to show appreciation, was keen to avoid a repetition of their last encounter.

"I am already starting to see the potential benefits of our collaboration," she said. "And I am always ready to reward endeavour and show my appreciation."

"Ciller, don't worry about that. As you will have already noted, these plans more than double my income from Turhan and anything else that could come my way could only be a bonus."

His craggy features creased into a faint smile which allowed him to hide his nicotine-stained molars. Leaving the papers on the table next to the coffee, he closed the attaché case and stood to depart.

Ciller stood and touched his arm.

"You do know that I have great ambition for Turhan don't you, Alper?" she added.

She saw his brief quizzical expression before he rearranged his face.

"I will lead this company with determination and application. I will expect the same from colleagues old and new. Turhan will become an influential player wherever it operates."

"Of course, Ciller. I know this to be true. You seem to have inherited the energy and vision of your father. I can only hope to be of service to you in your future journey and as I think you understand, I will help you in any way I can."

It didn't take Ciller long to review the papers Repcer had left for her or for her to make immediate plans to fly to Trabzon. It was the first example of Repcer underestimating his client. In the same way he had assumed the regulatory authorities would not be particularly interested in an asset-rich small company based far away from the country's commercial heart, he hadn't bargained on Ciller wanting to review his provisional arrangements first hand. She had set up a day trip scheduling meetings at the Bank of Anatolian Commerce before proceeding to the offices of Mehmet & Ali, a local accountancy practice, recommended by Repcer as the company most appropriate to manage the affairs of Yilan Limited Sirket Company (YLS).

Her expectations of the Bank were fully met with the manager providing her with the reassurance about the privacy of their service and her providing the necessary identification to be able to facilitate their instruction.

The meeting at Mehmet & Ali, however, provided valuable insight about how the affairs of YLS should be managed.

She had requested the meeting on the morning of her flight to Trabzon and had taken the accountants by surprise. At first the receptionist had no idea who Ciller was and stone walled her efforts for a meeting at short notice. By the time she landed in Trabzon there was an apologetic message on her mobile from one of the practice partners, Yasmin Ali, saying she would be welcome that afternoon. Ciller had been initially pleased to hear that the firm had a female partner as well as the fact they had understood without further prompting who she was. Arriving at their cramped offices in Kunduracilar Street in the bazaar district some hours later, she was immediately impressed by the anonymity of the surroundings.

Miss Ali didn't disappoint either. Despite being surrounded by paper files and reports, her desk had an orderly look about it and the lady herself was cross referencing documentary records with references displayed on a computer screen. There was no plush reception area at this office, Ciller walked straight into an active working environment, with half a dozen others rammed into the confined space, all poring over laptops.

Ali was clearly focused on another matter when her guest arrived and seemed only to break from her task having registered the arrival of a new person out of the corner of her eye.

She jumped up immediately, removed her glasses and smoothed out her creased skirt, not just to greet the visitor, but in a desperate bid to scan the office for a spare chair.

"Miss Terzili, welcome. I am Yasmin Ali. We spoke earlier."

Her efforts to locate a seat failed, she instinctively pulled her jacket from the back of her own chair and stepped around the desk to shake hands.

"I am sorry you catch us in this confusion. We are approaching the end of the fiscal year and we are pushing to finish our clients' tax estimates. It will be more comfortable if we take tea at the café downstairs."

Ali was soberly dressed in a black business suit and cream-coloured blouse. Her hair was concealed in a green and red patterned *hijab* and she wasn't wearing make-up. Her complexion although clear was pasty. Taken together with her oversized thick-rimmed glasses, Ciller formed the impression she didn't get out much and the prospect of tea with a guest was something of a treat.

Ciller ordered a couple of glasses of tea and baclava.

"Well I'm sorry to arrive with you at such short notice, but I really wanted a chance to talk to you about my plans for Yilan while I happened to be in town."

"Yes, that is helpful for me too. I have had a chat with your colleague Mr Repcer already."

"I know. He provided me with a report. I don't want to waste time going through the main issues. Mr Repcer has set those out clearly enough. What I wanted to discuss was the private nature of the Yilan business."

Ali looked perplexed. Ciller continued: "I expect to be putting a significant amount of money through this business from a variety of sources, some international, others will be cash deposits. I want to be sure I can avoid making all unnecessary declarations as well as limiting the tax liability."

Ali nodded.

"I understand your requirement. I did suggest to Mr Repcer the possibility of declaring this business as a collaborative venture, similar to a cooperative, without the formal partnerships. All that would be required is for ten per cent of the gross earnings to be invested in public assets – either land or buildings each year. This is not about donations but loans. If you were to do this it would not attract undue interest from the authorities, but I guess you have decided it is not appropriate for your circumstances."

"No, I was not aware of that. Maybe Mr Repcer was not able to include it in his report. Do tell me, are there any limitations on share ownerships?"

Ali laughed.

"The main qualification is that the directors need to be alive! You only need a minimum of two and, as my client, either myself or my business partner Mustapha Mehmet could handle all the administration for you."

"That is very reassuring. One final point – I think I'm going to be very busy in the next few months. Getting to Trabzon for meetings is not going to be easy for me. If we get it organised, will you be able to attend periodic meetings with me in Istanbul?"

"Naturally, as my client and, if I may say so potentially one of my most important ones, I will be happy to attend as required."

"That is good to know." Ciller smiled. The time taken coming to Trabzon had been a useful investment.

"Please excuse me. I have a plane to catch. I will be in touch."

"Can I order you a taxi?"

"As we are at the bazaar, I think I'll be able to hail one around the corner. Thank you for your advice. I am sure we will meet again very soon."

She left a couple of bank notes on the café table and disappeared into the afternoon throng. Ali reflected on what she had thought an odd discussion.

Nonetheless, she had a sense their dialogue had been important.

Ciller waited until she had received the draft board papers for the inaugural meeting at her villa and then contacted Repcer once again.

"Alper, I need changes to the papers for the board meeting, meet me for lunch at the Four Seasons Hotel at Sultanahmet at twelve tomorrow."

Repcer knew he would need to be there and didn't wait to check his diary.

"Can you tell me now what you have in mind?"

"Let's talk tomorrow. I am getting to appreciate our encounters."

The Four Seasons was tucked away in the Old City behind the Hagia Sofia and was deceptively spacious, given its central location. Originally designed as a prison by Mimar Kemaleddin Bey in 1918, it was regarded as a prime example of Turkish neoclassical architecture, with an emphasis on pointed arches, ornate tiles, dramatic domes and towers. It was rare for Ciller to eat out by choice, and so when the occasion required, she preferred to be away from the main city restaurants that spanned the banks of the Bosporus. The Four Seasons was an inspired choice for lunch – good food, with a peaceful atmosphere especially at lunchtime with the tourists out sightseeing.

For all his years, there was something about Ciller that unnerved Repcer. Was it because he vaguely remembered her growing up as a child when, on more than one occasion, he had asked her father to have her taken out of the room when they talked business or perhaps he was unused to having his sexual advances rejected? He wasn't sure but what he understood was he would not be able to have a dominant relationship with her if they were to progress. Surprisingly he drew comfort from his belief that Ciller knew very little about legal and administrative processes so by complicating the presentation of these matters he thought it would help him to become indispensable.

Once again Ciller had prepared her line of attack. She had ordered champagne on the basis of celebrating the creation of the new Turhan. Once they had ordered, she fixed her guest with a cold stare.

"Now, Alper, I have had the opportunity to study your proposals in some detail. I must commend the speed with which you have brought the necessary documentation together and am sure your skill in bringing in the expertise the company needs will ultimately be rewarded but your plans are excessive.

"Under my father's tenure you have enjoyed a five per cent stake in all our activities, in effect for doing relatively little. The world, as we know, has moved on and now you need to make more effort for your fees. I am completely happy with your proposal to have nineteen per cent of the stock in Turhan, which I accept will be a just reward for your efforts, especially as you are introducing three highfliers to supervise our statutory businesses.

"Where your proposal overreaches itself is in relation to Yilan. Forty-nine per cent is unacceptable and, combined with your stake in Turhan, gives you much more control than is appropriate for your role, even accepting that you will function as my deputy.

"I think we must approach this differently. First, the role of Yilan should develop in parallel to Turhan. It has to operate in an opaque way and requires some distancing from our other operations. My stake will remain, as I will personally take responsibility for managing its activities. You will have a consultative role in the operation of the business and have a nominal stockholding that demonstrates your involvement with the enterprise. That will be set at two per cent. The other forty-seven per cent will go to Yasmin Ali in Trabzon. Yes, I have met her and discussed how the business should be run. Whereas I will take responsibility for getting the business, she will manage it on a day-to-day basis which will include making the necessary injections to Turhan operations as required.

"I understand you may be disappointed at my reaction, but I have had time to look at the figures and consider how we should progress. When you reflect on the implications of my decision you will understand how this will help to protect us all and maximise our new business operations. Finally, I am well aware of the value of your involvement going forward. You allow us to demonstrate confidence and continuity to our business partners, a quality I value highly."

Repcer sat back on his chair and took a deep breath.

"Are you sure this is the way you want to progress? You are risking the most sensitive part of the commercial operation to an unknown accountant, a..."

"Woman?"

"Well, yes."

"I am sure it is the right thing to do. After all you recommended her practice. She is clever and honest and frankly the breath of fresh air that will help us to influence government regulators. It is her very 'ordinariness' that makes her an attractive proposition."

"Does she know?"

"I will call her tomorrow, but the good thing is I expect her to combine these duties with her existing role in her accountancy practice. I expect to call her in for a separate meeting with us ahead of the individual new Turhan board members. Agreed?"

Repcer nodded his acceptance.

He knew this was not the moment for protest.

Marshall breezed into the NCA conference room to address his team.

"So, what do we know about Terzili's kebab business?"

A young South Asian woman in her twenties seated halfway along the meeting room table spoke up.

"Sunita Purewal, North West region, sir. Six Izmir premises have been successfully busted for employing illegal immigrants. We netted thirty-eight which we are holding at the Home Office processing centre in Cambridge and four of the owners are facing prosecution. Had we been able to coordinate more raids we would have found others, but unfortunately the word got around too fast and a lot of them melted away… for the moment, but we are keeping observation on a number of premises we think are the most likely to be of interest in the future. It is not always the case that franchisees run individual shops. Some do, but others own multiple branches – one we know of owns a dozen around Merseyside. One way or another they are all very good at coming up with a narrative to explain their circumstances. A lot of the guys we are holding are Kurdish and don't have much English language. Getting their stories documented is difficult and they are only able to make the most basic identification of suspects. They are full of shit about how they arrived. Most saying they paid some local mafia figure in northern France for a space on a boat across the Channel. It doesn't make sense to me. After all, if what they are saying is true, then they would have been picked up wandering around the streets of Margate or wherever, instead of the reality of them being efficiently collected and redistributed around the country. So far around fifty of the shops have been subject to health inspections with eight given warnings regarding their meat storage arrangements."

"OK, anything else from anybody?"

Another man in a T-shirt and bomber jacket next to Sunita joined in.

"George Wetherall, Central region, sir – there has been quite a lot of activity around drugs on about thirty of the Izmir shops but it's a bit flimsy. We've made busts but it's difficult nailing the crimes to the shop. Most claim they have no knowledge of their premises being used for this purpose. There are lots of instances where we pulled in the owners as well as the dealers visiting the premises but being able to prove it is the owners supplying is another matter. So far, I think we are only going to be able to make this stick in those shops where we have had sufficient visibility to get pictures. To my knowledge that has only happened in twelve cases at best."

"Thanks, George. I guess it's the same with the car jackings."

"Jimi Mwake, London South East region, sir – the car jackings are also a tough nut to crack, not because we are not aware the crimes are being committed but linking them to the Izmir Barbeque operation is harder. What we think is happening is that some of the shops fence the car keys for a chosen gang of thieves. The keys are then passed on to another group who take the vehicles to one of the quieter, small ports for shipping out of the country. Boston in Lincolnshire and Chatham are the most popular and we have been able to track where they go on from there. The Boston shipments go to Vlissingen in the Netherlands and transfer to Europoort for transhipment to Lagos. The Chatham run goes to Le Havre and on to Casablanca. The good news is we have mapped some of the people involved internationally but not in the UK. The UK guys are clearly organised, but the nature of the organisation means that those elements of the criminal logistics don't meet. No one seems to know anyone else, so until we can grip the domestic leg of the operation we are still allowing it to run."

"And the flow is regular?"

"About two a month, but we're not talking about your average Ford Fiesta here. These are performance motors – Lamborghinis, Bugattis and the like, each stolen to order with a book value of around four million."

"How are you closing this out?"

"So far we are building a dossier on the couriers, the ones who are moving the vehicles to the ports and are making enquiries to better understand their networks. Most seem to be freelancers contacted by mobiles. They are told to buy a kebab at a given branch of Izmir, come up with a designated password and get the keys. They drive to a designated point near the port, park and lock the car leaving the key on a wheel arch and then they get picked up and taken to the nearest rail station to get home. Another couple of guys pack it in a container, add some bullshit paperwork and send it into the port. We assume that when their appointed lift arrives the guys who have made the theft are also paid a cash fee but we haven't got the evidence to support that yet."

"But that sounds promising, Jimi."

"I think we are close, sir, but we might not be able to finish it for a couple of months. The question will be how wide we can cast the net on this."

Another investigator spoke up.

"Amalie De Jong, Central Corporate. I think I have a way forward on this. I am not sure if you are aware that Izmir Barbeque was the subject of takeover interest a couple of years back. Izmir was listed on AIM and for no apparent reason the stock started to move. The reason turned out to be an exploratory statement of interest from the US FizzyPop Corporation. They got as far as appointing advisers and starting due diligence on the operation. Their plan was to buy the network completely from the present owners, Turhan International and Unique Capital Partners, but then suddenly stopped without any explanation from anybody. What was interesting was at the time FizzyPop hired an adviser Ekrem Canecale, brother of Gemlik Canecale, who had the terminal accident in Bodrum after the Mali fiasco. It seems Ekrem was employed by Turhan to manage Izmir's franchise operations as well as taking a fee from FizzyPop and sold his shareholding in Izmir when the stock was at its height. He disappeared shortly afterwards but, unlike his unfortunate brother, his body has never been found."

"But that doesn't mean he is still alive…"

"True, but based on what we already know about the Terzilis, I think we can assume it would be in their interest for his body to be discovered somewhere as a means of sending a message to anyone thinking of stepping out of line. I think it is also fair to assume if he is still alive, he has taken a new identity. Records from his passport show he was well travelled, especially in Europe, but suddenly all that stopped and there was no trace of him after FizzyPop pulled out."

"I seem to get the sense the extent of criminal associations with the Izmir operation have increased since the decline of FizzyPop's interest?"

"I think that's difficult to tell," said De Jong. "The extent of their planning suggests the perpetrators are not amateurs and have perfected their routines. Maybe we have got better at detecting it or possibly they have become more careless, believing we can't make these cases stick."

"And what about the money?"

"We can only estimate what Ekrem was paid. Clearly we have no information from Turhan's records and haven't raised the matter with the Turkish authorities for the reasons we all know. But we have managed to find a source in the legal practice FizzyPop hired to prepare their bid. Protheroes in Lincoln's Inn. He has estimated Ekrem earned around a million dollars from FizzyPop and according to the share dealing service, he managed to double the money again shifting his stock. So he would have had enough to 'go to ground' somewhere secure."

"An interesting theory, but it needs some facts to support it."

"There is no doubt about the money. This issue is where did it go and who has it now?"

"Have we done a trace on the Canecale family?"

"The mother is thought to be deceased. Apart from Gemlik, he has two sisters, Cara and Ermine and they too have families. Cara lives on an island – Burgazada – outside Istanbul, Ermine at Rizokarpasso in Northern Cyprus and another brother called Bulent, whose whereabouts we have yet to confirm."

"Hmm, not the easiest places to go visiting, but useful intel, nonetheless. I will share with GCHQ; they might be able to eavesdrop on relevant communications. In the meantime, I think it is worth paying your contact at Protheroes another visit. I get the sense he might get us connected with an individual who can give us some leverage in this situation.

"Thank you everyone for your time on this investigation. Izmir Barbeque remains a high priority for the department. If you find you can link more cases to this investigation, please contact me directly."

Marshall was now starting to feel more confident about his report to his political masters. At least he had several strong lines of inquiry to pursue. He felt optimistic he would soon get some traction on the investigation and yet he knew timing was everything. Once he had shared his knowledge up the line there was no telling how it would be used and the biggest risk would come if information was shared too early with law enforcement agencies elsewhere, especially in Turkey. The fact was, he needed to be circumspect with the release of details until he had more hard facts and a strategy in place for arresting Ciller Terzili.

FOUR

HAVING RETURNED TO HIS office to start to put together the draft, his focus was disturbed by a call on his private line.

"Phil? It's Jane from GCHQ. Got some promising news in from Istanbul. Not sure where it fits into the story, but we have intercepted communications from a senior private attorney, Alper Repcer to Ciller Terzili with references regarding a pending reorganisation of Turhan International."

"Go on…"

"It seems we are only getting snapshots from an ongoing dialogue between Terzili and Repcer. Repcer has been the Terzilis' lawyer for a lot of years and has sent her a note that offers condolences and thanks to Kerim Terzili and refers to the restructuring of Turhan International and a board meeting. I didn't realise criminals engaged in board meetings…"

"Private enterprise can be malevolent as well as benevolent, so maybe we shouldn't be surprised. Do a deep dive on this and let me know if you find any more detail."

He closed the phone, frowned and stared at his blank screen.

The call put his report writing efforts immediately on hold. He recognised already that he might be in danger of moving too quickly. Clearly something was afoot that would have implications for the investigation. Not least, why was the lawyer sending condolences to his client?

Weitzman had flown to Dubai twenty-four hours ahead of the sting to review arrangements. Although he had sketched out the plan for the interceptions, he had seen no point in taking Smith through what he had in mind. In his experience, his partners would have little to add from the logistics point of view and he would rather recount the experience from a position of strength once the action had been discharged.

The recent diplomatic rapprochement between the UAE and Israel had certainly made life easier for Israeli businesses to engage in Dubai, and Weitzman himself arrived as a US citizen, Darrell Henry, from London, acting as a sales agent for a Haifa-based air conditioning firm, to be ably assisted by his two colleagues – 'Bonnie and Clyde', travelling on Jordanian passports from Amman. An introductory meeting had been scheduled with a leading local property developer the following day as part of his cover. He planned to make a hash of the opportunity, not least because he didn't want to find himself taking responsibility for a commercial order of which he had a very limited understanding. Afterwards the rest of the day would be free and he could be on standby to assist his colleagues if their assignations went wrong.

Their temporary base would be the Al Bandar Arjaan – a striking, upmarket ultra-modern hotel apartment complex with a prime waterside location on the north shore of Dubai Creek, close to the diplomatic quarter. This architecturally impressive property was just minutes by road from Dubai International Airport and close to several attractions including the Dubai Creek Golf & Yacht Club, Dubai Dolphinarium at Creek Park and the brand-new Rise Dubai Creek Harbour development. More importantly it was situated some seven kilometres north of the Burj al Arab – their target location – allowing them to arrive and depart easily without undue attention.

Weitzman knew Dubai to be an international trade melting pot and despite the new cordialities understood that his activities were likely to be watched by his hosts and quite possibly by the Iranians. His preparation was thorough, including buying three burner phones at the airport and charging them immediately following check-in at the apartment.

Bonnie and Clyde arrived two hours later, travelling separately but on the same flight with Royal Jordanian. Before arriving at the apartment they had no contact whatsoever. Weitzman was not overly concerned about Clyde. Playing the part of Reza Jalalabad, a low-level assistant to the Omani, was a relatively low-risk strategy. After all, in the outside world no one beyond his immediate circle knew who he was anyway. Comparing the reality in the apartment to the grainy image sourced by the Mossad, confirmed the likeness was good enough. Although resident in the Emirates, Jalalabad's family were Iranian, so Weitzman ensured his man was fluent in Farsi as well as Arabic, Turkish and English.

"You are clear on what we need?" Weitzman asked, when he had finished checking the brief with Agent Clyde.

"Sure, the file covered it well. I will have just returned from a family funeral and been asked to step in to represent al-Harriri at the last minute. My job is to ask some basic questions of Terzili about her organisation and why she wanted to contact al-Harriri. In effect I will be a conduit for messages. I have a business card for her use in the event she wants a follow-up meeting. I will be non-committal and explain any further contact from my side will be subject to al-Harriri being interested."

"Good. The phone and email is linked to our communications control in Be' er Sheva, so we can deal with anything that emerges. When you arrive, ask for 'Rafiq' at the concierge desk. He will take you to Terzili's suite, which will be on the fifth floor. A good tip for getting the most out of the meeting is to act bored, to challenge her to get to the point and fidget. That way she will have to work harder and may reveal more than she may have intended. You must keep an eye on the time and leave exactly one hour after the meeting commences. You have your UAE identity card and wallet with a picture of your wife and daughter plus five hundred US dollars in case you are challenged. Ensure you are careful on your return. It is possible you may be followed, so find time for a drink in the Creek Harbour before coming back here. I have a burner phone linked to an anonymous number purchased yesterday. If you think you are in trouble ring the number and ask, '*What's on at the movies?*' We will have a snatch team on duty if required in the lounge bar by the reception to get you out. But these guys are for insurance only. If all is going well you must progress on your own. Clear?"

"Got it."

Weitzman then turned to his other colleague, Agent Bonnie.

"I have to say the wardrobe team in the Caracal Battalion 33 have been thorough in their preparation. Your resemblance to Ciller Terzili is remarkable."

"Thank you, sir, but it wasn't such a big deal. I am the same dress size, and our embassy matched a couple of her outfits from high-end boutiques in Istanbul and although I think my assets might be a little more modest from the pictures I have seen, maybe the target will have more interest in what I have to say than the size of my chest. I am certainly pleased the state paid for my new hairstyle and provided me with better make-up than I would normally buy. I might even get to like it."

Weitzman looked at her intently.

"You are the star of this particular show, Agent Bonnie. You are playing the part of a high-profile character and your target al-Harriri will have certainly checked you out before agreeing to meet. You have studied the file and understand you might be asked questions about your background that they will already have the answers to. It could be anything to do with any aspect of your life from your favourite subject at school to the terrorist attack on your family. You will arrive in a pre-ordered chauffeured limousine, which our people are providing but will wait to approach the hotel security point until you get a call from Rafiq on the burner telling you that you are expected. You will not be required to show evidence of a reservation. He will come to the door to meet you and escort you to al-Harriri's suite. You are also aware, al-Harriri likes his women and is likely to make a pass at you, if only to judge how you handle such a situation."

"I understand what is expected of me and am prepared for any eventuality."

Agent Bonnie had an air of confidence that had already impressed Weitzman.

"As you heard me say to Clyde, you will not be going unsupported. The snatch team will be there for you too and can be alerted by the burner phone. In your case, the key line is '*Can you fix a round of golf in the morning and hire me some clubs?*'.

"How and when you leave your meeting is very important. You are impersonating someone who will be resident in the hotel two floors above you and may be out in the public areas of the hotel after her meeting with Clyde is completed. You must make every opportunity to appear anonymous when outside of al-Harriri's suite."

"I will have sunglasses and keep my hijab pulled forward and, as I will keep moving, I shouldn't attract undue attention."

"Finally do remember the security check at the entrance to the causeway leading to the island where the hotel is situated. The hotel security team tend to be light touch but will inspect the vehicles you arrive in as well as checking your passports and secondary ID. They record all vehicles leaving and entering the site so be aware that you should avoid hurried actions that will draw interest. When you leave you should walk across the causeway to meet your drivers. Your meetings are due to commence at 18.00. Clyde will arrive first at 17.30, Bonnie at 17.45. Your drivers will wait to collect you 75 minutes from dropping you off at the Jumeirah Road car park next to the Wild

Wadi Water Park. Let's aim to meet back here by 21.30. Take care! *Zol zayn mit mazel.*"

Weitzman knew he had done all he could to prepare, including putting an emergency snatch squad in place. As a veteran of such operations, he knew the secret was to find the planning 'sweet spot' – just the right balance between having the key elements of the arrangements nailed down but allowing his operatives a degree of flexibility to manage the situation as they found it. The fact that the operation had been progressed to a state of readiness was in itself an achievement. Notwithstanding the costs of putting the plan together, avoiding failure and the embarrassment that could potentially cause was of paramount importance. As he said to his British counterpart, the opportunity to get intelligence from this quarter at first hand was rare and needed to be taken, even if it proved to be a one-off.

He also had admiration for his two agents. For them the risks were much greater than a loss of reputation. This could be a life-or-death situation, and in the case of the latter option a more grisly and protracted end than that offered by an AK-47. He marvelled at their completive, quiet efficiency, reviewing their cover stories in meticulous detail and focusing on what they needed to find out. Clyde 'high fived' his two colleagues before being the first to leave the apartment. His was a formal Western businessman's style. A chain store light grey suit, white open-necked shirt, tan loafers and brown framed sunglasses which matched his heavy stubble. Part of the look included carrying a zipped leather folder with a plain paper pad and pens so he could be seen to be taking notes from his meeting. He looked just like half the men out on the street in the central district, the half not wearing the traditional Arabic *jubba*.

His car made short work of the Jumeirah Road freeway and was brought to a halt at the security checkpoint on the landside of the causeway. As predicted the Emirati security police seemed to only take a cursory look at the car – just another Mercedes limousine

– and gesticulated to the driver to open the boot. Registering the passenger's Jordanian passport there seemed no need to delay Clyde's passage to the Burj al Arab entrance where the passenger door was quickly opened for him. Breezing into the lobby he entered a world of organised chaos with tourists and businesspeople waiting to check in, trollies of luggage stacked waiting to be transported to the residential floors or out to the airport. Europeans and Asians asking how to get to the hotel's private beach and kids of what he thought to be several nationalities running around dodging people – just being kids. Taking the scene in he picked out the concierge desk and walked purposely towards it, targeting a uniformed member of staff who had just put down a telephone.

He drew the porter's attention starting the conversation as he approached the desk.

"Excuse me, is Rafiq around?" The man he had asked showed no surprise that a visitor seemed to know Rafiq's name and muttered something into a pager clipped to his waistcoat. He then said something in Arabic, staring unto the middle distance as if a state of mindfulness was helping him to cope with the seemingly endless and often facile requests coming from other guests. His disconnected gaze then focused on the visitor in front of him.

"Yes sir, I have called Rafiq he will be here in just one minute."

It seemed Rafiq had just been dealing with an account enquiry at reception. The message had alerted him to Agent Clyde's presence.

"Mr Jalalabad? I am Rafiq. I have been expecting you. Please follow me."

They moved to the elevator and joined a family group from Indonesia, (all eight of them) headed up the tower and exited at its first stop, the fifth of twenty-eight two-storey floors.

When Rafiq was sure they were alone, he said: "Madam Terzili's suite is right here. Please be aware, normally there would be a butler on duty, but Ms Terzili has specifically declined this. That door at the end of the corridor, next to the fire exit is to allow service access to the suite for our staff. It takes you through to a mini kitchen and then to the dining area. If you think you need to leave in a hurry use it. I have arranged for it to be left unlocked for the next hour. Are you ready to go in?"

Clyde nodded.

The door was opened by a thick-set, bald-headed man in a dark suit a size too small for him. Although clean shaven he had a scar on his left cheek which immediately gave him an air of threat. It was a quality he was clearly aware of as he instantly switched on what he thought was a welcoming smile which, to Clyde's eye, looked more like a scowl.

"Yes?" Rafiq managed the introductions.

"This is Mr Jalalabad for Ms Terzili." The bald-headed door keeper had guessed as much and nodded to Clyde to come in as Rafiq retreated.

It was an impressive room with thick patterned carpet, a mix of reds and crimsons featuring an Islamic design, ahead, a floor-to-ceiling window with a partially closed view of the nearby beach. Most likely one of the Burj's smaller suites, he thought. Designed with no bed it was clearly an anteroom.

As he moved further into the room he became aware of another figure, perhaps a little older than his bald-headed colleague engrossed in a video of a wrestling contest and clearly didn't want to be disturbed by the presence of a visitor. He glanced casually at Clyde but made no attempt to move. The bald one signalled to the guest to remove his jacket to be searched and took some interest in the leather sleeve although appeared perplexed by the virgin paper. He found the phone in Clyde's jacket and nodded to him to leave it on the occasional table next to the sofa. As their guest donned his jacket once more, the older wrestling fan pressed pause on the remote control and got to his feet. He went to the double door to the right of the monitor and tapped and waited to hear the instruction to enter.

"Madam, Mr Jalalabad is here."

"Thank you, Osman. Please show him in and ensure we are not disturbed."

"Mr Jalalabad, it is a pleasure to meet you, do come in."

Clyde's first impression was of a petite woman immaculately dressed and groomed, hair scraped back and dressed in a high collar, black trouser suit that accentuated a pearl necklace and matching earrings. He was reassured that his colleague, although slightly taller, could certainly pass as having a strong resemblance to her. Given all that he had read, it was surprising this well-presented woman was the target of Mossad interest. Strangely, in spite of her confident approach, he thought he detected a fragility in her body language.

He stepped forward and nodded his head.

"Madam."

"Please sit down. Tea? It is freshly brewed."

He sat down in an armchair opposite her and waited long enough for her to open the conversation.

"I was hoping to have the opportunity to meet the Honourable Mohammad Sultan bin al-Harriri."

"Indeed, Madam. He sends his apologies. He has many demands on his time and felt he would not be able to provide the level of attention you would expect at this point. I have been asked to prepare a briefing note on this meeting which he will consider for future action. I am asked to prioritise my report this evening, so perhaps we could get directly to the substance of your enquiry."

Theatrically, he opened his leather file, and took out the notebook and pen, and started jotting down the basics of a contact report.

Ciller started talking in a measured way, as though dictating to her guest what she was expecting him to note.

"I run a diverse trading company in Istanbul specialising in commodities and finished and semi-finished products."

"Yes Madam – we have completed our initial enquiries before agreeing to attend this meeting."

Ciller was irritated by his slightly dismissive hustling approach, but reminded herself, under the circumstances it was to be expected.

"One of my activities is munitions. I have been serving some diverse clients in the Caucasus region for some years now."

"We are also aware of this, Madam Terzili, but we understand these to be relatively minor trades in small arms, certainly no bigger than your share of direct sales in the Balkans."

"Well, perhaps compared to some of your trades, that might be the case, but the point is this business has been consistent and has successfully avoided international sanctions."

"That may be so, Madam. We don't do politics, just trades and revenue."

Ciller's annoyance was growing. Who was this upstart Jalalabad? Who was he to talk in this disrespectful way?

Clyde's instruction to 'smoke her out' was starting to work.

"If your business is good, why do you want to speak to the Sultan?"

"I am looking for a partnership."

"What do you have that could possibly be of interest to him?"

"Equipment and technology."

Clyde played his part well. He stopped writing and fixed Ciller with a measured stare.

"What equipment and technology?"

"Field equipment and energy-sourced weaponry, presently restricted to just the most sophisticated armed forces from the superpowers."

"Material not readily available on the darknet market?"

"Correct."

"Artificial intelligence?"

"That sort of thing."

"Forgive me, Madam, but this type of restricted product is problematic for us to procure. How come you can do it?"

"I have my sources which are private. This allows us to compete in the market."

"If you have this sort of access, with respect, I ask again why do you want to speak to the Sultan?"

"I have product, but not the right customer base. If I can sell to your customers we can all make money."

"So you would sell to us and we would sell on to our clients?"

"Alternatively, I can sell to your clients and pay commission to you at an exceptional rate."

"What are we talking about here?"

"Hypersonic missiles, guidance systems, high energy lasers, drones. I don't have customers with deep enough pockets for these items, but you do. I deal with individuals and companies; you deal with governments. Only governments can afford this type of product."

"In theory what you propose is interesting, but we would need to know much more about your operation before we could consider your proposal further. Like you, we value our customer relationships highly. We would have to be satisfied you could access the necessary items and we would need to bring in our own experts to validate their authenticity before we could discuss terms. I think you have some work ahead of you to prepare for a meeting with the Sultan. Anyway, Madam, I have to say my boss is a demanding taskmaster, I must take my leave. Here is my card. When you are ready to renew our dialogue, please get in touch. I will be happy to facilitate a further face-to-face meeting."

Clyde considered the meeting to be over and stood to leave. He smiled at Ciller by way of a farewell. As he opened the same door as he had entered, Osman and his assistant leaped to their feet ready to block his path.

"I'll just collect my phone." The bald-headed security man looked to Osman who nodded his approval.

"Not an impressive set for a man of your standing," Osman observed. "You don't seem to have any contacts programmed in."

"On the contrary, it is ideal for my purpose in case I happen to leave it unattended. I hope you got some fun out of it. The best game is called 'Jailbreak'. You should try it sometime."

Clyde took it firmly from the security man's hand and left the room.

He was well aware of the risks in leaving, not least that he could be jumped from behind.

His senses were heightened as he walked purposefully towards the elevator. If that had been Terzili's aim, it had not happened.

Back on the ground, he took a seat in the reception area, ostensibly to look through his jotted notes. In reality he scanned the space to see if there was anyone showing interest in him. After waiting ten minutes, he started out on the journey back to the heart of the city casually walking across the causeway. He was a good fifteen minutes ahead of schedule. As he strolled out into the cool of the evening, his thoughts turned to his colleague, somewhere in the tower behind him. Under normal circumstances, he would have remained to check all was well, but he knew Weitzman had already made backup arrangements and was pleased he had not required further help. As he walked slowly towards the agreed pick-up point at the car park near the Jumeirah Road he suddenly became aware of shouting from behind. This was not in the script.

"Mr Jalalabad, wait."

He turned to see Ciller Terzili running after him. For a split second he didn't recognise her because she had changed from her formal business attire to leisure wear – a pink silk blouse, white trousers, trainers and her hands were clasped holding a scarf in place over her hair.

She looked ruffled. There was no place to hide. He had to acknowledge the contact.

"Mr Jalalabad, I am so pleased I caught you. I half wondered if you were leaving by car. Look, thank you for your advice. I quite understand the Sultan's position. I just thought it would be a good opportunity to meet him and you did say you would be seeing him this evening…"

FIVE

IF AGENT CLYDE'S PLANS were starting to change, it was nothing compared to his colleague's experience.

Rafiq had set up Clyde's introductions and fifteen minutes later had done the same for Bonnie. Her assignation was in an even more luxurious suite on the 20th floor. The same basic plan was taking place, Bonnie was shown into an anteroom for the obligatory identity check and search. But this was even more thorough than Clyde's experience.

In this instance she had been met by two women and had been required to be strip searched. Her handbag and identity documents were checked. Her burner mobile phone examined, switched on and off again, but returned to her. Although the arrangement seemed appropriately formal, she had not been immediately aware that there was a CCTV camera strategically located offering an uninterrupted view of what was taking place. Upstairs in the suite, the Sultan was watching the feed, enjoying the impromptu show as if he was peeling an orange. Bit by bit he saw her disrobe every carefully assembled item and watched his female security officer scan her for any trace of metal. With the exception of a stylish gold ring on her right hand and a gold pendant, she was clean. He was impressed by her athletic figure, especially by her muscular thighs and neatly shaved pubes which suggested to him she must engage in regular sport. Was it his imagination but he thought his female security officer had been overly efficient in checking her out? That would be noted for discussion at a future performance review. He also observed the length of time his guest took to dress. In similar situations, ladies had not only been reluctant to submit to such a measure, but when it had been completed, had dressed with such speed they tended to look ruffled and less composed. This lady had an air of confidence which intrigued him to the point that when she had got dressed, she waited, spending a little time checking her appearance via the compact mirror in her handbag. Strangely, it was this final gesture that convinced him to meet her as arranged. He had failed to notice that the real purpose of the mirror had been for her to observe her surroundings, which included her noting the presence of the camera.

He looked to his butler.

"OK Hamid – show her into the library. Offer her refreshment."

Al-Harriri was old school. Despite technology he preferred to rely on his heavy gold Rolex Cosmograph Daytona to check the time. Part of the plan was to keep his guest waiting and to continue to observe her.

She was shown into the library with two walls given to leather-bound volumes arranged by language and subject. The butler had produced a jug of freshly squeezed lemonade. It was certainly one of the features that made the Burj special, fiction and non-fiction in six languages. Trust the Burj – relatively few hotels offered individual libraries within their suites. The colour scheme consisted of combinations of restful tones of azure, from a royal blue and mustard patterned carpet, striped Regency-style wallpaper and dark, velvet curtains with six matching scoop-backed chairs, grouped around the central feature, a lagoon-styled table. By the door, a large gilt-framed artistic photograph of a campfire outside a Bedouin tent. Once the butler had left the room, Agent Bonnie looked to take in her surroundings. From this elevation, the sea view and the coast slipping away towards Abu Dhabi was an alluring sight. In the period between late afternoon and early evening, the fishing dhows scattered at crazy angles at intervals across the seascape and the ant-like figures of sun worshippers deserting the beach, gave her a strange feeling of detachment from the outside world. It had a cosy feel she thought because of its lighting, which despite a typically glorious Arabian sunset, ensured that the occupants would be able to read in comfort. Given she was in the room alone, she was surprised by the silence. Apart from the restrained low-level hum of the air conditioning there was no noise to indicate activity in adjoining rooms. Inevitably, she was drawn to the books, especially the Arabic and English sections. Were the subjects on offer representative of the interests of the occupant? Given the exclusivity of the premises it was more than likely. She alighted on a famous example of romantic Arabic poetry, *Layla and Majnun* dating back to the 7th century – a tragic tale of undying love where despite an extended courtship, the couple never marry or consummate their relationship. Browsing the pages she recalled she had not seen this work since graduating from Tel Aviv University and, for a moment, took her back to a couple of her own doomed love interests at the time. But it was only for a moment, her private reminisces were abruptly interrupted by a single door opening above her and a figure wearing a teal-coloured *kandura*, head partly obscured by a freshly laundered, red-chequered *ghutra* appeared at the top of a flight of stairs. His embroidered jacket or *bisht* signified his status as a Sultan. She was impressed to see his dress tastefully coordinated with the library's decor.

He called as he descended, addressing her in English.

"Madam Terzili, it is a pleasure to meet you at last. I cannot understand how it has taken me so long to make your acquaintance."

Agent Bonnie looked suitably deferential as she looked up.

"Honourable Mr al-Harriri – the pleasure is mine. Thank you for taking the time to meet me."

"I hope you don't mind if we speak in English," he continued. "Unfortunately my Turkish is limited, and I guess you would have the same problem with Arabic."

Now he had got to the bottom of the stairs she was able to see his face more clearly. The Mossad reconnaissance team had done a good job. There was no doubt this was the man she had expected to meet. The loose style of clothing suited him, accentuating a muscular shoulder line, his figure was certainly trimmer than she had been led to believe. His features were classic of the region – brown, deep-set eyes, slightly hooked nose and a suggestive, almost sexy smile which drew attention to his most prominent feature, a broad expanse of expensively maintained teeth.

He gestured her to sit at the table where he saw the volume of poetry she had selected from the bookshelf nearby, followed by a brief frown.

"You read Arabic?"

"Only a little and some Farsi, but maybe the fact of meeting you will allow me more time to practise."

He nodded approvingly.

"So, Madam Terzili, I understand you have made a special trip to Dubai to meet me – I am honoured. Please don't think me rude, but I am asking why?"

"I think we have some shared business interests, and we could work well together."

His quizzical look remained.

"I deal in finished goods, not your specialism, alloy pressings. We both seem to have prospered very well so far without each other. What are we likely to achieve through collaborating?"

"New markets, my company Turhan International is well connected in Europe, especially through the informal economy, and for us, the opportunity to expand on a global scale, especially in Asia would be attractive."

"I am not sure I see the need for collaboration. Are we even in the same business? I specialise in technical products, most of which have a medical or military application. Expensive, but sought after by my clientele. Most of my customers are governments as well as one or two large-scale militias, so with respect, I cannot believe you will be able to introduce us to more of the calibre of partners we already have. But if you're able to assist us to improve our procurement practices in some of our more specialist areas of interest, I would think the case for buying out Turhan would make more sense. What would you think about that?"

Terzili smiled.

"What would *your* customers think? A buyout of Turhan would only give you a marginal return on investment. Collaboration could deliver more."

"Such as?" The Sultan's focus was sharpening.

"Credit lines for example. I understand some of your customers, especially those making high-volume repeat purchases, rely on underwriting from Qatari banks. Your friends in Ramallah, Tehran and Islamabad for instance. Some of the hottest spots in the world right now even the Qataris don't want to touch if they can't see the return – Moldova, Sudan, Laos, Myanmar, Eritrea, North Korea, Sri Lanka, Sudan, Zimbabwe. Although you don't need any help managing imports into Iran, helping them find outlets for their exports is getting tougher. I could offer more options."

"It is a theoretical point at this stage. You make a lot of assumptions about my business."

"I have done my research, as you would expect. I know how Vehrani has helped you to get established and how you have rewarded him."

"I do not know how you have conducted your research, but you should be careful of reaching conclusions without evidence."

"Evidence? That seems a defensive term in this context. Looks like my hunch is correct."

There was a moment of silence whilst the two locked sights, like two wild animals stalking each other before attacking.

Al-Harriri broke the tension with a smile.

"If there is any business for us to transact, we must get to know each other first. There is little point in doing that when, with all due respect, I have no idea what your capabilities are. You may not be familiar with Arabian traditions, but it is customary to bring your host a gift when you enjoy their hospitality. That gift should be something the guest knows will be of value and prized by the host. I think you should regard this meeting as part of your initial research. If there is a case for us to meet again, I would expect you to bring me something that would be difficult for me to obtain from other sources. That would tell me a lot about Turhan and set a foundation for us to develop a more meaningful relationship."

"Such as?"

"Come, Madam Terzili. A lady of your undoubted intellect can work it out. Restricted defence technologies are always of interest. I keep trying to acquire the leading-edge stuff but I am always left frustrated by the political nonsense it generates. Find me a route through the bullshit and who knows where our cooperation might take us?

"It is the end of the day. I have no wish to discuss commercial affairs further, but since we are here, and the night is young it would be my pleasure to invite you to join me for a private dinner right here."

"Thank you, Mr al-Harriri. Tempting although your offer is, I cannot accept. I have a full schedule of meetings tomorrow in Turkey and I need to review my papers tonight.

"I have found our meeting very helpful and have taken on board your observations. I shall review potential next steps and contact you again shortly."

She got up to leave as did her host. Almost by magic the library door opened, and Hamid stepped in.

The Sultan stood and took her hand. He learned forward and gently kissed it. It was his one gesture that had surprised Agent Bonnie, and beneath her professional training she couldn't help but be warmed by his action. She understood this man to be an enemy of her country but, perversely, she noted this was the behaviour of a gentleman.

"Please show our guest out," he said to his butler, who nodded his acquiescence, and with an outstretched arm pointed the way.

Having escorted her to the elevator, Hamid returned to the library.

"You have some homework to do tonight, Hamid. Check this lady out. Have her followed. Find out where she is staying and when her flight leaves Dubai tomorrow. Get me more on Turhan International. Who are they doing business with right now? There is something not quite right here and we need to run this to a conclusion."

Agent Bonnie sighed as the elevator door closed beginning her short journey to the ground. The encounter with the Sultan had gone as well as she could have expected, but she knew in this moment the danger she was experiencing was not yet over. If she had been subject to the level of surveillance she knew about, it was likely to assume there was more to come that would be new to her.

She had been surprised even with the obligatory security checks; how accessible the Sultan had been. She also knew despite his suite in one of the top hotels in the world, this was a location reserved for business meetings and his true lair would be someplace else, most likely in Muscat. Who else was working for him in Dubai would be part of Mossad's follow-up operations, but for now she would be blind. If she was being tailed, the watchers in reception would follow them so Weitzman would know what was happening. She was relieved to recall Weitzman telling her as a precaution he had booked six rooms in different parts of Dubai in the name of Ciller Terzili if the Sultan's people showed an interest. Rafiq had already reclassified the real Ciller Terzili's reservation to the hotel's private coded booking system for VIPs to avoid any random local check.

It was time to set her trail. Leaving reception she took a taxi to the city centre, telling the driver she was only in town for the night and wanted to see the sights before going to her hotel. Viewing the Palm Jumeirah, the palm-tree-shaped archipelago, glowing with lights, and the glittering yachts of Dubai Marina, her driver took her on, past the skyscrapers that border the 16-lane Sheikh Zayed Road to the spectacularly lit giant Burj Khalifa.

In the taxi she fiddled around with the lining of her bag to locate a spare SIM card for the phone. Although she had not used the first, it was possible the Sultan's scanners had recorded the detail and could intercept any subsequent call. She checked the time before texting Weitzman:

"Mission completed. Clear of target – may have company. An hour behind schedule."

Whilst Agent Bonnie sat back to enjoy the sights of Dubai by night, Agent Clyde was trying to escape the unexpected attentions of the real Ciller Terzili. The situation had started to become complicated, when having been unexpectedly approached outside the hotel by Terzili, he had reluctantly agreed to stop for a coffee from a street vendor close to the place he was due to meet his driver. The only logic had been to ensure he kept the real Terzili away from the Burj al Arab in the period where his colleague could expect to be leaving. He was aware of the need to strike a balance, by being approachable but not overly familiar. He didn't want to raise any suspicious thoughts from the unplanned change of events.

To help him manage the situation, he had picked a high-profile location where his driver would be able to see him and report the unscheduled encounter with a Western-dressed woman to Weitzman. The Mossad commander had instructed the driver to get a picture on his phone that would enable a positive identification of Ciller to be made.

"Yes, Madam, I expect to see the Sultan later this evening," Clyde replied as he emptied a sugar sachet into his espresso.

"It will be a normal review of our activities and I regret you cannot accompany me. Our meetings are commercially sensitive and other members of his network will be present. I am clear about the messages you wish to pass on to the Sultan, and once he has had the opportunity to consider your request, I expect I will be briefed to pass on his response. I'm afraid I cannot stop for long now as I have to prepare a full report on our discussion."

"Yes, Mr Jalalabad that is all very well, but I think there is something else you should be aware of before you leave."

He looked at her with a quizzical stare.

"I am looking to set up an operation in Dubai with or without the Sultan. Apart from my own unique expertise, I will need help from an experienced hand with good local connections."

She smiled and looked at him in a provocative way. She had a unique gift of making her brown eyes dance when she wanted to impress. She seemed to inadvertently nuzzle up to his elbow as she clearly attempted to give him a private view of the front of her blouse boasting the imprint of her erect nipples.

"You are clearly experienced at being a deputy, but I have not met many in your position who do not have ambitions to take the top job. We could work well together. I think our chemistry is good."

He looked at his watch.

"Ms Terzili, please forgive me, I really must go. Can I get you a taxi to take you back to the hotel?"

"Don't worry it's a short walk and I can enjoy the evening air. Think about what I have said, Mr Jalalabad. You know where to find me."

Ciller Terzili made the first move; it was part of her way of demonstrating she was in control. It suited Clyde to watch her depart, especially as he watched how her tight-fitting trousers seemed to mould to her backside.

He waited for a further few minutes and walked to the end of the causeway to check her progress. He could see her figure now sufficiently advanced towards the hotel to know that it was safe for him to leave. His driver was waiting patiently. He was satisfied he wasn't being followed.

Duncan Matheson had arrived in Dubai from London during the afternoon. As arranged, Brown had met his flight at the airport, provided him with his cover business documentation, a local mobile phone (the number already printed on his business card) and out-of-hours contact details and escorted him to a waiting car. He had to admit he liked this type of job, which, bearing in mind he was a specialist, didn't come up that often. Yet the opportunity bought with it its own pressures. He had just enough time to work out his own cover as Duncan McKee, a well-travelled commodity broker, originally trained at one of Hong Kong's most revered investment houses, when the British were in charge, but now independent, scouring the world for commercial opportunities to bring buyers and sellers together. Some trades were perfectly legal, others less so and one of the prerequisites of his business was to ensure both buyers and sellers had their own insurance arrangements specifically to deal with any overzealous customs or regulatory enforcements. His personal deals were simple – both sellers and buyers had to pay commissions to get him interested and those rates flexed depending on the level of personal risk he had to take. In the case of the sellers, their fee had to be paid up front and were non-refundable. Brown made small talk at they drove. Matheson was now McKee, and the chitchat was helping him to get into character. He had been given a tablet with a link to a website his masters had prepared for the assignment. Listings and search terms had been added to Google for the casually curious. Anticipating he would be explaining all this to his target as part of his cover, he needed to ensure his story held together. That meant Brown's job was to first show him his local office base, a room in a block downtown in Tariq Bin Ziyad Street, behind the Dubai TV studios, shared with a language school, travel agency and a small hot desk facility for British Council guests. It had always been planned that contact with Brown would be minimal, essentially for emergencies, so he decided to continue his journey alone to get a sense of the local geography, taking a cab south to find and engage his target at the Burj al Arab. Even this initial step would not be so easy in a hotel with a couple of thousand guests, and *then* he had to strike up a relationship with a person that he could not know whether he would have anything in common with. Yes, he had studied Terzili's file, so he was confident on her life story and was able to pick out a number of themes that he hoped would generate a positive response, but that was the point that science would have to give way to intuition. Before hailing a taxi, his first move was to memorise the route to the office and to eyeball the block. He used his well-honed powers of observation to note the building, stepping into the reception, noting the security arrangements, even checking the name of the janitor. He travelled light in a sky-blue linen suit and crushable bag which qualified as hand luggage with his business-class airfare. But his signature dress item were his Koio Capri Castagna sneakers, feel-good wear for feet and the obligatory bottle of his favourite cologne, 'The Night' by Frederic Malle, with its subtle notes of rose and saffron.

As the cab headed down the coast road to the Burj al Arab he started to get that uneasy feeling in the pit of his stomach. Despite his years of experience, he was still prone to 'first date syndrome' and knew it was time to fix his mind on Ciller Terzili. He looked hard into her picture as though branding an impression of her on his mind.

SIX

HE ARRIVED AT THE hotel a little after five and checked in to his fourteenth-floor suite. Although small by Burj al Arab standards he guessed, it was stylishly decorated in shades of green and brown dominated by a bed that served as a declaration of intent to any unsuspecting visitor. Like all new arrivals, his first action was to admire the sea view and play with the automatic control that adjusted the air conditioning, lighting, curtains and the Alexa device which welcomed him with some contemporary jazz classics. Yes, this is an ideal shagger's paradise – deep woollen carpeting, Krug champagne in the fridge and a bath he guessed capable of keeping four people entertained simultaneously. There was no doubt the office had reflected on his mission and had clearly gone to some trouble to ensure he had been provided with all the necessary paraphernalia for the job. But it was important he didn't get side tracked and resisted the temptation of exploring the TV entertainment system with its dazzling array of world TV channels, games, shopping and the rest. Having emerged from the en suite freshened up, he noticed a handwritten note had appeared under his door.

'CT booked for dinner 19.00 alone in the Al Mahara Restaurant on the ground floor. A table is reserved for you nearby. Rafiq.'

The venue proved to be ideal for his purpose, although entering through a gaudy silver archway reminiscent of a Moscow pole dancing club with mirrored walls and black onyx floor, a short passage led him to a suitably darkened, blue-tinged circular room housing a vast aquarium surrounded by two rows of utilitarian tables and crimson velour bucket chairs. The inner row next to the window on the undersea world were the larger tables set around the perimeter walls. This sub-aqua experience had an authentic, slightly claustrophobic feel – reflective steel ceiling, wave-patterned navy and grey carpet and grey flock walls (as far as he could tell in the dimly lit surroundings). Never mind, this was an experience and a great place for singletons who wanted an alternative to a room-service dinner where they could eat in relative anonymity, their meal *sensitively* illuminated by individual low-intensity table lights, bright enough to guide customers' eating utensils, but dark enough to retain the mystery of their plates' contents. Following the maître d' to his appointed seat, it was clear he had arrived ahead of the majority of guests, as there seemed to be a range of places he could have taken along the way. But he was here to make a connection, so he completed what he estimated to be a third of the circumference of the restaurant before being invited to sit, watched by a rather bored-looking croupier loitering with intent, clearly waiting to provide feeding-time entertainment for the restaurant's growing audience. He had to pass Ciller Terzili's table who, despite being accompanied by what looked like a well-travelled paperback novel published in English, was poring over an oversized menu.

She briefly looked up at his passing. She was stunning, big brown eyes, loose shoulder-length brown hair and a complexion only accentuated with minimal make-up. He nodded and smiled without breaking his stride.

The setting for this planned assignation seemed surreal, a bit like sitting next to someone in a cinema whose features were only illuminated by light from a screen. But the thing that made the whole scene feel odd he decided, was the strange Muzak which seeped out of the room's recesses. It was not unpleasant to his ear but seemed to lack a recognised melody and was liberally interspersed with the sound of oxygen bubbles and what he assumed to be the sound of whale or dolphin clicks and whistles. He couldn't be sure whether this was to add to the authenticity of the surroundings or some modern approach to sharpening the appetite or aiding the digestion. His seat was certainly strategic, facing in the direction of Terzili but slightly on the curve, providing a degree of privacy. Terzili may have the menu and her book; he had her on his menu and his mobile which he had linked to the Al Jazeera web page just in case someone passing had a view. He already decided to follow her lead in ordering a large bottle of Italian sparkling mineral water before the maître d' had departed and began to study the menu. Shortly, a waiter came with a tablet computer to take her order. It was time to engage. As the waiter turned to leave with Terzili's order, he called him over.

"Excuse me, I am tired and really don't want to waste my time trying to decide from all these dishes. What would the chef recommend?"

For a moment, the waiter looked perplexed.

"Sir – all our dishes are prepared to order and all are excellent. The chef doesn't have favourites."

It was now time to play to the gallery.

"That doesn't help me much," he said in a slightly raised tone.

"Tell you what, the lady here seems to have made up her mind, I'll have the same as her."

His show drew the attention it deserved.

Terzili had only just picked up her novel and this unexpected fuss just beyond her line of sight drew her attention.

The waiter nodded and said something she couldn't here, but she did hear his firm reply.

"Off the bone. Thanks, but I'll stick with the water."

The waiter nodded and disappeared.

Duncan was aware that Terzili's eyes were still on him. He pretended to be embarrassed and raised his eyebrows.

"Sorry for the disturbance. It's been a long day."

She smiled and returned to her book; he to his phone.

Presently the waiter returned with Terzili's meal – filleted Dover Sole with fresh vegetables and a hollandaise sauce. Vegetables were often given high status in Emirati restaurants because of their relative scarcity.

As her meal was served, he deliberately made a point of looking at it. As if he had invaded her privacy, she looked directly at him.

"Er, excuse me," he blundered.

"I thought I'd just see what the meal I had ordered looked like. It's great – I'm so glad I followed your lead. You seem to know the menu here. Are you a regular customer?"

The ice had been broken.

"No, but I think I had more time to study the menu than you did," she replied.

"I must admit it doesn't quite seem right, dining on fish in an aquarium, but I suppose we can't complain. At least we know it's fresh."

She laughed.

"Some of the ones we are watching get too much exercise, swimming around in circles. If they were coming from tank to plate, the chef must be picking the lazy ones who are overweight!"

It was his turn to laugh.

"Are you dining alone? As we are eating the same meal a couple of metres apart from each other, perhaps I could join you, if you would prefer not to be reading when you're eating?"

This was the point the whole operation could have gone horribly wrong. He didn't fancy getting on a plane back to London the following day without having achieved his objective. She seemed to hesitate for an eternity before nodding and putting her book to one side.

At that moment, the waiter was arriving with his food, so both of them had to tell him they would be dining together. The ensuing arrangement was hastily managed, Terzili waiting for her new dinner partner to be seated.

He continued: "We seem to have got this meeting arranged back to front. I'm having a meal with an attractive lady whose name I don't even know…"

"My name is Ciller Terzili. I am from Istanbul."

"Duncan McKee, from Edinburgh, Scotland."

He looked at the book now cast aside in his favour.

"An unaccompanied Turkish lady reading a Turkish book in English. Impressive."

"I am a single woman with an outgoing personality. I don't need the presence of a man to validate my business skills. I have had a privileged education. It is an opportunity for me to improve my appreciation of Turkish culture by seeing how different it is in a foreign language. *Madonna in a Fur Coat* by Sabahattin Ali, is a book I have read previously but the translation provides new insights. You knew it was Turkish?"

"Not really. Just an educated guess. What's it about?"

"A shy young man from rural Turkey who moves to Berlin in the 1920s, where he meets a woman who will haunt him for the rest of his life."

He wished he hadn't asked, but Terzili picked up the conversation, deliberately avoiding making her own enquiry about his family circumstances.

"Are you travelling alone?" she asked.

"Usually," he replied. "I'm a sort of international salesman, so I spend most of my time on the road. You?"

"Yes, I am alone on this trip, but I think I will be doing much more travelling in future."

"So you have had a successful visit to Dubai?"

"I don't know for sure yet, but I hope so."

"That's good to hear. I understand it can be difficult doing business in the Emirates for a woman."

"Really? I have not had that experience yet. I tend to think if you have the right offer you get the business."

"Up to a point, but you need to be right with the price and know what your customer wants."

"I couldn't agree with you more, Mr McKee. This visit has been helping me to research the market."

"And what line of business are you in, may I ask?"

"Alloy pressings. My firm recycles redundant ships to produce new sheet metal fabrications. I can see you appear surprised. Don't be. Mine is a family firm, although in the near future it will be restructured."

"So, these sheet metal fabrications are used for what, exactly?"

"Mostly machine components, piles for the construction industry, some finished and semi-finished products. We need to increase our production so I am obliged to find new markets outside Turkey."

"And your first port of call is Dubai?"

"Naturally I suspect I am here for the same reason as you. This is the international marketplace. Make the right connections and in the long run it saves so much time and effort."

"Couldn't agree with you more."

His first mouthful of Dover sole melted in his mouth.

"And what about you, Mr McKee? You said you were a salesman."

"Well yes I am. I spent the last ten years working for MacTaggart Johnston, the Hong Kong-based commodity traders. In essence I was selling all things British into China, from cars, high-end fashion and Scotch whisky to fire-resistant clothing for emergency workers. I had a lot of fun, but then the Chinese took over in HK and the fun went out of it. I got to learn quite a lot about the Chinese mentality from my regular visits to the mainland and knew for me it was time to get out. So I moved to London and set up my own operation, modelled on MacTaggart's but without the overheads. I was pretty well networked in the UK and parts of Asia and knew enough people who trusted me to get going.

Now I'm something of a niche player. I sell high-value products that are either difficult to shift or subject to complicated customs arrangements. The more complicated it gets, the better the fee."

His mother would have been proud of the way he set about demolishing the neat stack of green vegetables on his plate.

"I should imagine there is much you could teach me about international commodity trading," Ciller observed.

"I think the only useful lesson from my work would be to be aware of politics. The world today is so screwed up. It is only free trade that prevents wars, yet so many governments don't believe in free market economics, they slap tariffs and sanctions on individuals, product categories and countries in order to exert influence. It rarely works, just encourages buyers and sellers to look for alternative means of trading."

"And that's where you come in?" Ciller prompted.

She had already noted his ability to eat and talk with speed and dexterity. At that moment he was savouring his final mouthful and deliberately avoided a direct response.

After a general appreciative 'umm' sound a glance at the aquarium and then back to her, he suddenly looked shocked.

"Miss, Miss Terzili, I am so sorry. You came here to have a quiet dinner and instead have met some mad Scot boring you rigid about business at the end of a working day. Forgive me. I suspect that bad-tempered monster in the water tank would have been better company. At least he wouldn't answer back. I have to say your English is excellent and I shouldn't have just assumed you would follow everything I said. As you can see, years of solo travelling have not made me better mannered. It's just nice now and again to have a chat with someone who…"

He paused. Now it was her turn to be finishing her final mouthful. She nodded her head as if to invite him to finish his sentence. Her brown eyes seemed to be mocking him.

"Someone who doesn't know me or need to know me, but is both beautiful and engaging," he muttered.

He remembered his mother saying he should have taken a career on the stage. It certainly impressed Ciller Terzili.

"Have you time for a coffee?" she asked.

He kept up the pretence, now knowing he had her on his hook.

"Er no, no. I think I need to get going. Got some serious business on in the morning so I need to prepare tonight. Look, thank you for spending some time with me. I really enjoyed it. Don't worry about the dinner, I'll tell the maître d' to charge it to my room."

He stood up to leave. She started to stand but he gently touched her arm to stay seated.

"Please, don't disturb yourself on my account. I am sure the fish will keep you entertained over coffee."

"At least take my card," she said. "Istanbul is a halfway house between London and Dubai. If you can spare the time, I would be pleased to show you around some of the places tourists don't get to see – you could even stay at my villa."

He reached into his pocket.

"I'd like to make the same offer to you if you happen to be in London. But if you are coming, give me some notice. For all I know, I could be back here when you call."

They swapped smiles as well as cards, a sort of unspoken contract that said they would meet again.

For Duncan, this was still going to be a matter of timing – soon enough to build on the contact but sufficiently far ahead as not to raise suspicions.

Bonnie had found the most useful piece of equipment she had taken on this mission had been her compact mirror. Sitting in the back of the taxi, apparently checking her looks, her eyes were trained on the traffic behind, trying to pick out the detail of any cars that might be following her. Even at this hour, the roads were pretty busy and her task was not the easiest – not helped by the number of other cabs on the road. Having passed the Burj al Khalifa, she instructed her driver to stop at the metro station, not aware that the station which shared the tower's name was itself more than a kilometre away – a point her driver made after a minute noting his passenger's apparent unease. When they arrived, the driver pulled in, awaiting a further instruction or ready to take payment.

"I want to wait here for a few minutes," she told him. Seeing his surprise in the rear-view mirror, she held up her mobile.

"I am waiting for a call before deciding where to go."

Suddenly, there was a knowing look on her driver's face. His customer was one of those 'scarlet ladies', not an uncommon phenomenon in this part of the world, especially at this time of day.

In reality Agent Bonnie was waiting to check for any unannounced followers. She watched the meter tick on, her driver fiddling with his radio to find some upbeat music.

After ten minutes she decided it was safe to move on. She hoped that the duty Mossad team had been watching her back and that any suspicious activity would have been dealt with.

"Oh I have heard from my friend," she suddenly announced. "I will leave you here."

She thrust a wad of notes over the driver's shoulder to amply reward him for his time.

"Thank you for showing me the city lights."

"Are you sure you will be alright, lady? Can I take you on to your hotel?" he asked.

"No, no – I will be fine from here. Goodnight."

She climbed out of the car. She saw the driver count his fare which was obviously to his liking as he waved before setting off back into the city traffic.

She in turn watched him depart before entering the station to get back to the marina.

Her driver meanwhile had informed his control the location where he had dropped his passenger and the cab company called

Hamid with the news.

When she did arrive back at the apartment, she found Clyde and Weitzman watching TV. It was clear they had no real interest in the basketball game they were watching but at least it had been a distraction as they waited. They exchanged high fives, and her boss offered her an impromptu hug. She went immediately to the bathroom to shower and to change her hair to match her Jordanian passport. They vacated the building five hours later, leaving the key in a small plastic bag buried next to a yucca plant in the ornamental garden outside. The clean-up team from back home would arrive to ensure there were no forensic traces left, in the event others were on their trail. Certainly there should be no possibility of anybody checking in the near future as his booking still had 72 hours to run. Weitzman and colleagues had made their own separate trips back to the airport, each taking separate routes out of the Emirate, one travelling to Athens, another to Cairo and their boss to Rome. When the Dubai apartment booking expired, Weitzman was sitting in a coffee bar around the corner from City Hall in London.

It was ironic, at the same time his team were passing through the airport, Duncan McKee was driving to Muscat. He had left the Burj early, not least to ensure he would avoid another chance meeting with Ciller Terzili and he had been right to do so. After a leisurely breakfast, she had decided to go to a local mall to go shopping because her Istanbul flight was not until early afternoon.

Prior to checking out, she asked after McKee as she had intended to suggest meeting again before she travelled home.

She was disappointed to learn he had already left but resolved to ensure their paths would cross again soon.

Marshall was starting to wonder if he was working too hard. Long office hours, the commute west of the capital and a couple of beers at the wrong end of the day was starting to cause him restless nights. He was even starting to dream about kebabs. How could a humble snack be causing him so much angst? It really was time to make some serious inroads into the Izmir Barbeque company. He smiled to himself as he realised the process of bringing the business to book would need to be handled in 'bite-sized chunks' and would have laughed out loud at the irony if one of his colleagues had made the observation.

He had been studying his investigator's case files.

Whoever had set up the business in the UK had known what they were doing. Every stage of obtaining information was difficult. The franchise operation had an office address that was a rented first-floor unit in Ilford High Road. Companies House had the name of just one director, one 'Mustafa Ismail', a dual Turkish/British national, apparently resident in the UK, but a visit to the registered office had drawn a blank, with just a mailbox with no matching identity for the director found on any of the standard security databases. The published micro accounts were sketchy too with the barest of reporting information supplied. It suggested that the business made a £30.7 million profit in the past financial year but there was nothing to suggest how. The company seemed to have an unusually small asset base and, according to the record, an updated confirmation statement was due. Enquiries through several of the detained franchisees had established the business supplied premoulded lamb spit rolls and point of sale materials – menus, posters, stickers for closing food service trays, but that was it. The rolls themselves were normally purchased for cash from a pool of five halal butchers in different parts. Orders were accepted by phone and only fulfilled when money had been transferred via a branch account in Green Lanes in North London. Attention was being paid to finding out who managed the account. Once again the name 'M Ismail' emerged with the address as the registered office, but interestingly, the name of Izmir Barbeque was missing from the record. The problem of dealing with the illegal immigrants was not only one of language, but relationship. The first line of defence had been to claim each was a brother of a relative already living in the UK. Most claimed to have an extended link either brother or cousin to Mustafa Ismail, who according to their statements had residential addresses in East London, Birmingham, Liverpool and Glasgow. In each case these addresses turned out to be short-term lets, and the landlords had no record of a tenant called 'Ismail'.

On the drugs front, there appeared to be some better news. Collecting evidence that implicated a small number of the franchisees in drug dealing had proved successful when raids had been initiated, resulting in prosecution for possession, but making some causal link to Izmir Barbeque was elusive. Reviewing the pre-trial statements, Marshall had to give some of the suspects full marks for creativity. In answer to the question, where did they get 'the gear', the answers seemed to fit a pattern. Most made reference be some random local who they had seen in the shop 'a couple of times' previously (most thought to be minicab drivers) who had left a scribbled note of a mobile phone number, suggesting the server behind the counter could make some extra money selling on to customers waiting for their favourite late-night snack. Most said their acquiescence had come from the thought that the stuff was hot and it was better to get rid of it quickly with the added bonus of cash in the back pocket, rather than handing it back – with most saying they couldn't return it as they didn't know the person who had given it to them.

The news got better when he reviewed the stolen luxury car trade, which Investigator Mwake was leading on. In amongst the detail of the heists, progress had been made in identifying the network managing the thefts. Mwake had spent months watching and in some cases following the merchandise out of the country. Although he had not received budget approval yet to follow any consignment to its ultimate destination, he had succeeded in identifying three people connected with the trade. What two had in common was they were members of known criminal gangs, the Leery Boys and the Screamers, one based in Tottenham the other in Croydon. The Leery's operation used Boston with the Screamers the Chatham route. Each gang appeared to have learned from each other and had a similar *modus operandii*; each having a coordinator whose role was to personally supervise the transfers and according to Mwake, that person was charged with managing the transactions, products and cash. Utilising ANPR cameras Mwake had established vehicles registered to both men were in the local areas when the thefts had occurred. Although Mwake had observed the trades and gathered the evidence, his investigation was far from complete, but the fact he had confirmed the identities of the two UK-based fixers was an important step forward. Abel Kotobi, a thirty-eight-year-old mechanic from Enfield was the Leery Boys man, Celik Abou, thirty-two, unemployed from Streatham was managing the Screamers. Helpfully, both had criminal records for handling stolen goods, but that was it. The penny had dropped in Marshall's mind. Had Mwake stumbled on to the connection that clearly linked Izmir Barbeque with organised crime? True, at this point, the evidence was limited, but at last there was something to go on. Pictures showing car keys being handed over the counter at five different Izmir Barbeque shop locations close to the time of thefts of high-end cars. He had been preoccupied by the type of car being taken, not just a typical Mercedes or BMW, but Lamborghinis, Bugattis, Aston Martins – the type of high-profile 'collector's item' that would only appeal to a small but nonetheless affluent market. Given their rarity, Mwake had been able to obtain pictures of each, sourced nominally from the dealer concerned. All looked like racers, the sort of vehicle that might get stopped by police anyway for novelty value. And that too was a point. The value. Most cars depreciate over time, but these handcrafted engineering masterpieces defined their value in rarity and uniqueness, like a painting by a grand master. Mwake's notes suggested an average second-hand value of one of these, even with questionable acquisition was in the region of $3 million for the 'right kind' of collector, considerably more than even Marshall had thought. This being the case, he was also surprised to note the number of such vehicles registered in the UK. These seemed not just to be the preserve of the footballing elite, but owners included Middle Eastern expats, City grandees, and a few of Britain's wealthiest landowners. The potential for this trade was significant and within it there was a clear but limited role for Izmir, but it suggested to him those involved would make the best use of their time with other areas of collaboration. No one had yet joined the dots between the supercar thefts, drug distribution and people trafficking.

It would be important to cross reference all this activity by geographical location and timing to see if there was a clear pattern emerging. Marshall scribbled a note to himself to follow this up. But he was not done with Mwake's reports yet. The final point to draw his attention was an identification of the recipient of one of the cars in Vlissingen from Interpol, a Turk called Bulent Canecale, listed as running an Amsterdam travel agency. Now that was unusual. Was it possible Ekrem had a relative they didn't know about? It was becoming clear that the Canecale clan could be holding the keys to unlock the mystery. He was impressed with Mwake's work to date and could already see links with De Jong's enquiries. He would talk to GCHQ to arrange additional monitoring for Kotobi and Abou as well as talking to Mwake and De Jong about the next stages of their investigations.

He also needed to check up on Oliver Watson's review of Terzili's UK assets. More 'notes to self'. The pace of the investigation was now starting to develop its own momentum. Then his private mobile lit up.

SEVEN

"PHIL? IT'S JANE FROM Cheltenham. Got some more intel on what Repcer and Terzili are talking about. I think I owe you an apology. There was an error in translation in the intercept received when we last spoke which talked about condolences and suggested Kerim Terzili had died. It transpires that five members of the Terzili family, including her mother, were recently killed when returning from a wedding. They were in a minibus that exploded on a local motorway. Turkish police had put a news blackout on it while they were investigating, and it seems Kerim Terzili had instructed the lawyer, Repcer, to put the pressure on to find out what happened. Repcer is reporting he is getting stonewalled. Further from his dialogue with Ciller, apparently Kerim is no longer dealing with family business and that she is in charge. With Repcer's help, she is restructuring it and bringing in outside assistance to strengthen it. Repcer is talking about Kerim remaining a non-executive chairman, a sort of figurehead, but Ciller is holding the cards. What she is arranging is a first formal board meeting for Turhan International which will confirm the new organisation structures and appointment of directors. We can't say what has caused these actions to take place, but it seems it's moving quite quickly."

"Do we know who these other directors from outside the family are?"

"We don't have anything like that yet. Repcer is charged with putting all the paperwork together and so far, he has not used electronic means to circulate. My sense is we won't know that in advance of the Turhan board meeting, but we will probably get hold of it when Repcer lodges the requisite corporate reporting information on the Turkish government's company registration portal."

"OK. Anything else?"

"Look, I'm not sure how relevant it is, but based on what we know so far, Repcer seems rattled by something. You get the impression in the past few weeks he has had to do more for the Terzilis and Turhan than may have been required of him in years. Repcer, in public at least, is a high-profile and confident figure, but it's not the way he comes across in the dialogue with Ciller Terzili. He sounds slightly nervous – almost expecting a push back from Ciller."

"Hmm, interesting..."

Marshall was chewing gum as he reflected on Clark's report.

"So when is this board meeting?"

"Tomorrow at four o'clock local at the family villa."

"Any chance of being able to eavesdrop?"

"Without getting one of our own people in there, virtually impossible. According to satellite imagery, their place is in private grounds with a high walled boundary."

"Can we get something in to Repcer's document case?"

"Very difficult at short notice. We have no idea about what equipment or staff he'll be taking with him, and we also know nothing about security arrangements at his office."

"So if we need any help like this in the future, it looks like I will need to talk to John Smith?"

"That is for you to decide – from our point of view we can continue to follow events electronically. I have already put in place the additional arrangements you asked for on members of the Canecale family as well as these two chaps, Kotobi and Abou. Of course when I get more on Terzili and Repcer, I'll let you know."

Ciller was tired when she got back home from her brief trip to Dubai. It had seemed like a lot of effort for very little, but she was optimistic. After all, she was trying to get a position in a market where she had no track record and given the sensitivities involved, she was unlikely to achieve her ambition without help. She had made two potentially important contacts in Jalalabad and McKee and was confident about engaging with them both in the future. Her exchange with Jalalabad was the least satisfactory. He had given the impression that he had only engaged in a dialogue because he had been instructed to and didn't seem to demonstrate more than a passing interest in what she had to say. Her somewhat fortuitous exchange with McKee somehow offered greater possibilities. Here was a widely experienced trade negotiator operating in some of the same challenging markets that interested her. She could see that having a man like McKee fronting her operation in Dubai could give her vital leverage and perhaps attract some of the Sultan's key clients. She resolved not to share her experiences in the Emirate with Repcer yet and Yasmin Ali, potentially her greatest confidante, was too new. The immediate focus had to be bedding in the new company structure and then she could set the necessary wheels in motion. Whilst she was doing that, she would arrange to make some further enquiries into Mr Duncan McKee.

Notwithstanding the business agenda, her first concern had been to check on her father, Kerim, who seemed to be in a more positive frame of mind than when she had left. At first she had just assumed it was because of her safe return, but there was something else that suggested more. Gently quizzing the old man, he told her while she had been away he had received a visit from an old friend from out of town, Mersut Canecale. When he first told her she missed the significance of the name, and he just said it had been some years since they had last met and they had spent an afternoon taking tea and reminiscing about old times. Kerim seemed to become more animated as he recalled some of the exploits he and Canecale had been involved in over the years, most of which involved his friend becoming his 'gofer', a sort of international representative. Many of the tasks had involved managing transactions that Kerim had organised where some sort of personal element was involved to manage the transfer of money or goods. Needless to say, such transactions required discretion and trust, two qualities that had governed their friendship ever since they had met as rival traders in the city's Grand Bazaar forty years previously. Ciller's interest was sparked by the timing of the meeting. It seemed strange that such a casual meeting had taken place at this time. Canecale lived near Izmir so it was understandable that an old man could not travel freely to Istanbul, but why not speak on the phone? Stranger still, despite their long years of association, Ciller never recalled her father speaking of Canecale as a friend. He was an 'associate', a business colleague, and entirely divorced from the family's social circle, mentioned only in the context of getting tasks done. And handsomely paid at that. Ciller knew that whenever Kerim called Canecale, he would be on hand to do his bidding, even if she didn't know exactly what he had been asked to do. Maybe given his present absent-minded condition, Canecale was just a distraction – here to cheer him up and give him some focus. However odd it may appear, if that was the outcome, she would judge it to be worthwhile, but it didn't seem to make sense. When she tackled her father on the subject, he casually batted the question away, choosing to recount a story when he sent Canecale to represent him on a disastrous blind date with a belly dancer which he had set up – long before he met her mother, of course.

The following days were always going to be a challenge.

Within forty-eight hours, the new team at Turhan would get together for the first time.

Despite her bravado, Ciller was apprehensive. She had sketched out her plans with her brother Adnan on the phone and had received the support she expected. After all, her plans provided him with more money and greater status in return for less responsibility. He would arrive at the family villa in the morning and offer her all the practical and moral support necessary to ensure the legal restructuring would go through smoothly.

Playing on the importance of ensuring the family's influence was maintained, she had confided in him about her caution regarding the new directors. These key players were not people she knew personally – all had been identified by Repcer and could already have allegiances to him, despite her understanding the logic about why they had been approached to become involved. Adnan had listened carefully, recognising his sister may have inadvertently given him some extra leverage for the future, whilst pledging his personal support.

In some ways, she drew strength from the fact that she had kept Repcer distanced from the Yilan project. If the purpose of the Turhan restructuring had been to bring new dynamism and respectability to the business, the real financial power she sought would come from the opaque 'non-statutory services' Yilan would provide. Yilan was, for Ciller, a sort of insurance policy, a tool she could direct without reference to formal decision-making structures. The appointment of Yasmin Ali was hers alone and one of the decisions the new board would take would include rubber stamping her appointment as executive finance officer to Turhan, providing her protégé with a ringside seat to observe the operations of the new business as well as helping her to run Yilan.

For the rest, her strategy was clear. She had allocated an hour to each of the directors to discuss how they would manage their respective business units of Turhan.

There was a balance to be achieved here. She would have to start demanding loyalty based on her position but knew that would not be enough to sustain their commitment in the long run. If they were going to deliver value to the balance sheet, she would have to stand back and give them the autonomy they would expect. She would be meeting each director in the morning and confirming their appointments that evening. And if that wasn't stressful enough all these meetings would be taking place under the same roof as her presently distracted father. In fairness, she had tried to discuss her plans with him at the private suppers, but in his grief following the family funerals, he seemed to have lost interest in business matters, merely telling her to do what she thought best. In the unlikely event of him being in the same part of the house when her business guests were being entertained, Adnan would be on hand to distract him.

Her timetable moved forward at pace.

The next day, Adnan arrived at the *yali* an hour before Yasmin, and Repcer had sent a courier with the board papers, together with a long-winded note explaining the papers had also been issued to the prospective board members under non-disclosure agreements ahead of their formal appointments.

Ciller had welcomed her houseguests and suggested they took the opportunity to get to know each other over tea before a family dinner in the evening, at which she planned Repcer would attend. The purpose was to review plans for the following day and ensure Kerim, as head of the household, was involved.

Whilst Adnan and Yasmin took tea, Ciller retired to her study to review Repcer's papers, double checking he had fulfilled her instructions. She had already received full biographies on her prospective new colleagues. All were capable individuals with impressive track records.

She had to admit Repcer had done well to get them on board. She would get her first sight of them in the evening over an informal supper.

The afternoon had proved enjoyable for Adnan. He was impressed that his sister had scheduled a period alone for him with a clearly attractive lady from Trabzon. He wasted little time informing her that he was the inspiration for the reform of Turhan and how, as his father's favourite son, he was well placed to play an increasingly influential role writing the next chapter in the firm's future success. He congratulated her impending appointment as Turhan's financial officer and looked forward to inviting her down to his place on the coast, 'to get to know her better'. Yasmin smiled to herself as she recalled Ciller's description of her brother – pleasing on the eye in a sort of raffish manner, but certainly not the sharpest knife in the box.

Dinner on the balcony was preceded by the arrival of the new directors, each wanting to make an impression with a grand entrance. Ciller sensed competition in the air, each wanted to be the first, but the drive from the main gate to the front door meant only one vehicle could approach, drop off and leave before the next, with the inevitable result two would be left waiting in their cars at the entrance to the grounds. Repcer was on hand to make the introductions, Adnan and Yasmin to escort the first arrivals to the balcony to be greeted by Kerim.

The competition to arrive first was won by Duru Hosni, owner of the Ottoman Breakers Yard, who politely explained he had travelled from out of town and the traffic had been unusually light. Ilkay Vahid from PrivatPosta & Asar Belgin of the Munitions Association were delivered to the door shortly after, the last to arrive having the additional benefit of being escorted upstairs by Ciller. The gathering, on a warm evening against a background of the twinkling lights of the city and passing Bosporus shipping at dusk, was an occasion in itself, even for Adnan. Ciller had hired some local performers to play a soft medley of some of her father's favourite Mevlevi music for tambur, flute and violin. Mayflies provided the cabaret, dancing around the increasingly intense balcony lights as if following the rhythm, A seemingly endless supply of mezes ensued but the main feature was a serving of *Mantı*, a ravioli type dish of boiled beef and lamb dumplings served with yogurt and butter, accompanied by a range of spices. Kerim had been heartened by the appearance of Adnan, but reminded all concerned the meal was a private occasion and any talk of business would be for Ciller to deal with in the morning. He had made it easy for his guests to comply as he announced his decision to retire for the evening early once the meal had been finished. Then the music stopped, the players taking their cue to depart.

The assembled company stood in respect as Kerim retired, accompanied by Ciller who said she would return presently.

The absence of their hosts encouraged those remaining to move from making small talk to observing their new colleagues at close range, weighing up their potential against their own private enquiries. Whatever concerns they had, would for now, be unspoken. They were here for three reasons, greed, opportunity and a strange faith in Repcer, a man not liked by many, but respected by all, nonetheless. And it was the lawyer who set the tone for what was to follow.

"Tomorrow is a big day for Turhan. The company will write a new page in its history," Repcer observed. "Up to now, Turhan has been all about one man – Kerim Terzili, who has achieved remarkable success, but it had no future, as a one-man band. The world has moved on. The scope for his personal brand of entrepreneurialism is now limited. To survive takes energy and commitment, and it is tragic to see his drive and motivation sapped by such personal sorrow.

"What seems like just a few weeks ago, I thought I was facing presiding over the winding-up of Turhan as the prospect of bankruptcy was real. I sought a meeting with Kerim but ended up meeting Ciller instead. Since then, I have worked with her not only to save Turhan but to put it on a growth trajectory that even I could not be certain of being able to deliver. I have to say even for me, this experience has been exciting, invigorating… something I am proud to have helped create. As a result, I have developed a new respect for the new Madam Terzili, who has demonstrated to me she has all of her father's commercial acumen and mental agility. For us who have chosen to join her on this journey, we have much to look forward to."

Smith had to hand it to Weitzman. The Israeli seemed to have the knack of finding some of the best 'out of the way' places to meet in central London. Today's venue was an inauspicious café in Old Quebec Street, round the corner from Marble Arch tube station. The venue was a favoured breakfast stop for local builders and tradesmen, churning out a standard generously sized 'full English' and mugs of coffee and tea with enough content to drown a man with a heavy cold. Although Weitzman personally dodged the bacon and sausage on offer, he made the most of a plate of scrambled egg and smoked salmon.

"Good spot this," he began, "with a good vibe. To me, this place sums up what workday London is all about. It's a great place to 'people watch'. You get to see a real diverse range of characters in here, perhaps some of what I would imagine to be the last real cockneys. Builders, cabbies, shop workers, motorbike couriers, one or two smart City types – all of life is on show." They had managed to get a table by the window.

"Half an hour ago they'd be queuing out of the door. That's why it's best to come a little later when the rush has passed."

Smith was starting to understand what Weitzman meant by a 'good vibe'. There seemed to be as many plump women serving behind the counter as customers in the shop. It was noisy with the sound of local commercial radio blaring pop music and traffic reports, as well as the group of women making up sandwiches, working the cooker and coffee machines. Food orders were being shouted in several obscure European languages as well as English. The air was thick with the fumes of burning fat and steam, creating condensation on the window to obscure the view of the curious who might wish to look in to observe the organised chaos.

As they reached the halfway point in a stack of toast, it seemed the right moment for Smith to focus on the reason for the meeting.

"So how was Dubai for you?"

"The best, my friend – Bonnie and Clyde did very well. We picked up far more intel in the time available than any analysis of bugged conversations could have given us.

"Firstly, we have confirmation that al-Harriri is, amongst other undesirable customers, supplying weapons to the Palestinians on behalf of the Qatari government. Although we had suspected it previously, now we know for sure. It secures his place on our target list and means I continue to get funding for his future elimination.

"Secondly, we know for sure that Terzili wants to expand on al-Harriri's turf, initially through collaboration but ultimately taking over from him.

"So this means he can be liquidated and Terzili can be identified as the perpetrator. That will save us a diplomatic incident with the Emiratis just at a time we are trying to build good relations.

"In time, al-Harriri will know that he has met an imposter but by then it won't matter. For you it is good news too. Terzili told *my* man Clyde she needs someone to establish her Dubai presence – she meets *your* man McKee that same evening who is perfect for the task. Once McKee gets to grips with Terzili she will lose interest in our Mr Jalalabad. And you potentially have control of a major asset in the region. So yes, I am satisfied – I am, of course, assuming McKee performed as expected?"

"It's too early to say for sure, but I think there is cause for optimism. The introduction was made according to plan, and he has been invited to visit her in Istanbul."

"And he didn't have to sleep with her? Not bad for an evening's work, John. Looks like our respective masters will be giving us a pat on the back."

"I think we have some way to go on this. There's still a lot about Terzili's operation we need to understand. I'll call you when I have more. Do me a favour in the meantime – don't rock the boat with al-Harriri just yet. I don't want him out of the picture until an alternative is in place."

"Don't worry, John, I've got to clear my lines with Tel Aviv. Even we are a bit more careful how we go about these things than we were. For now, time is on your side."

Smith nodded, stood and headed for the door.

On this occasion, he was happy for the Israeli to pick up the tab.

Duru Hosni cut a dapper figure in a grey linen suit with a lime green tie on his return to the Terzili villa the following afternoon. Ciller knew him to be in his early sixties and his full figure and disproportionate waist suggested years of gratuitous indulgence. His receding hair line and long jaw gave his head an unusual oval shape, accentuated by deep-set brown eyes which seemed burdened by the weight of the puffy bags below.

"Madam Terzili… *Ciller*, I must thank you for your generous hospitality last evening. It was a good way for new colleagues to get introduced."

He had the advantage over the other new directors having been personally acquainted with Kerim and Repcer for several years. He had also met Adnan on occasion as well, and even recalled meeting Ciller as a child when she accompanied her father on a visit to the breakers yard, many years ago. As customers, his relationship with her father had been cordial until the money he was due started to run out. As the strains began to tell on both sides, Hosni had been obliged to weigh up whether it was worth suing Kerim for breach of contract, or taking the informal approach used by Kerim himself in the past to recover debt – sending a couple of his workers round who were owed wages. In the end, a third option had emerged that promised him the opportunity of recovering the value of the contract with a debt swap and share deal together with control over Turhan's entire breaker's business. Maybe a few months ago, Hosni would not have countenanced such a proposition but the opportunity to underwrite his existing business supply chain for the next ten years could not be overlooked. Any remaining doubt was removed by Repcer's skilful presentation of the Turhan accounts which, although low on profits, had some respectable turnover figures. He had negotiated hard with Repcer, not only over his stake in the new business but also a 'golden hello' and a three-year escape clause. Repcer had only gone along with it because he knew Hosni was potentially the most dangerous adversary Turhan could have, and his entire plan for the future of the Turhan business depended on securing his involvement.

It was a point not lost on Ciller. Hosni was a well-known figure in the shipping industry. His involvement would give Turhan instant credibility in the markets.

"You are welcome, Duru. Thank you for taking the time to meet me privately. I wanted the opportunity to be reassured we could work together."

"Dear lady, I had the same thought myself, but Mr Repcer has provided me with all the reassurances I need. The new structure means we can look forward to solid growth and new financing which will allow us to realise our potential. I am happy about the prospect of working with Adnan too, provided he understands who is boss."

"Adnan likes the good life. He will do what he is told in order to retain it. All you need to do is to accelerate productivity of our reclaimed steel by thirty per cent this year so we can strengthen our position in the international munitions trade."

"It is certainly possible, provided I can run the division without interference."

"That is why we want you, Duru. With my backing you will not encounter problems."

Hosni seemed satisfied with that and departed to the balcony to take tea with Kerim and Adnan.

A very different discussion ensued with Asar Belgin.

Belgin was different to Duru Hosni in every way. A formal suit wouldn't have looked right on him; jeans and a black leather bomber jacket were his signature clothes. A former special forces captain from the Turkish Army he was some ten years Hosni's junior and with his close-cropped hair, dark stubble and muscular frame, gave the impression of still being on active duty. Repcer had recommended Belgin because of his present connections with the military and his knowledge of military hardware. This man knew what equipment the military wanted and where to get it.

"Your plans are certainly exciting, Ciller. Potentially we could control the Turkish munitions market if you can produce the right quality alloys that are light and durable."

"That is the point – if we can produce the right products, at the right volumes and drop our material prices perhaps by as much as half, then we have a truly ambitious business model."

"I will need to see the quality of the product and we will need to do some test pressings."

"You don't have to delay. We have some of the right graded sheets now so you can produce prototypes. Assuming they work as we expect, we will be able to test them in live market conditions and that will help us to bring in the volume of business we need. All you need to do is to tell me what material is required, when and where it needs to be delivered and you can get on developing the products with complete freedom. *With my backing, you will not encounter problems.*"

Ilkay Vahid was the youngest of the new board and potentially someone in the mould of her father. He was tall and thin with a blond, curly fringe and thick, black-framed spectacles. Although suited he preferred not to wear a tie and at first sight, Ciller thought, could have been mistaken as some north European academic, not the skilled Turkish trader who has succeeded in becoming a key figure in the Government's main international trade agency.

Once more, Repcer had been the one to identify Vahid and Ciller had been immediately impressed with his detailed knowledge of international trade rules and logistics.

"Vahid has the ability to move any product, anywhere at any time, legitimately or otherwise. If Turhan is going to sell product in unregulated international markets you will need his expertise to make it happen," the lawyer had explained.

"I've heard a lot about you, Ilkay, your background is impressive. After PrivatPosta you could go into the Trade Ministry. Why do you want to work with me?"

"I think we are the same, Ciller. I get the impression from Repcer you like making money, a lot of it. Working with you, I will make more than is ever possible in government. Besides I am an expert in my field. There are not so many of us around. It is quite likely in the future the government will get themselves in the shit and then they will need my help, irrespective of whether I'm working for them at the time. If we are working well together, they may have to negotiate with you to acquire my services."

"You know some of our trading operations will be controversial?"

"The law is a blunt instrument when it comes to trade. In the end, there are only buyers and sellers. We are just the glue that brings them together. Glue is a useful commodity – few care how it is made, providing it sticks. If we are to succeed, I need the freedom to be agile. Take decisions and act."

Ciller smiled. *"With my backing, you will not encounter problems."*

EIGHT

AS MARSHALL HAD ANTICIPATED, this whole investigation was assuming multi-faceted political dimensions that would, in due course, attract critics and supporters. Right now he faced pressures from several quarters. Number one, and always number one, his bosses' constant thirst for news, outcomes, arrests, asset confiscations. Number two, the need to protect his team's own vulnerability – yes, some solid lines of inquiry were starting to open up, but there was still pretty thin evidence to support any potential convictions, and all could be lost through unauthorised leaks.

On the domestic front, there was a head of steam emerging with prosecutions for drug offences, but these were small scale and had not much more than circumstantial links to the kebab trade and his ultimate target. People trafficking followed a similar pattern. The luxury car theft business was definitely showing signs of promise, and he could be confident that the Revenue would get the necessary authorisations to look into Turhan's London banking arrangements.

It seemed his prospects depended on three factors – finding this 'Mustafa Ismail', exploring the links of the Canecale clan in Europe and using the McKee factor to leverage the rest.

The strategy would have implications for the structure of the investigation with Smith's role in the Cabinet Office becoming more important. As the senior investigating officer and client, Marshall would retain overall decision-making authority, even if he judged it necessary to use more international resources. Logic dictated he should now be opening up a formal connection with Interpol, but he remained cautious – all too aware that information could not be controlled when shared outside his circle. The real challenge would be avoiding the danger of alerting the Turkish authorities, who themselves were well networked with the relevant agencies across the continent, not least because of the pivotal role they were playing supporting a number of terrorism investigations. There would come a time when he would need to formally request their assistance, but now was still too soon, especially when he was still unclear what resources he may need. He had been staying in close touch with the key UK investigation stakeholders – GCHQ and Revenue & Customs, but to an extent their roles were the most straightforward. GCHQ could only play a monitoring role to back up and fill out any intel gained from elsewhere, and Revenue & Customs could formally kick off the process of sequestering assets, but would, in all likelihood, achieve little in the short term beyond alerting the targets to the ongoing investigation.

Marshall was aware Smith had succeeded in 'selling in' McKee but patience would be required before he could expect any return. For now he would need to double down on Mustafa Ismail and Bulent Canecale.

Purewal and Wetherall would focus on Ismail; Mwake and De Jong on Canecale. He would have a separate discussion with each.

His instruction to the first team would be the most challenging as there was so little to go on. Ismail appeared not to have a passport or driving licence, and there was no geographical or age-related information to work with.

Wetherall seemed particularly despondent.

"Geez, we could be chasing our tails on this a year from now," he moaned.

"Based on the records we can find, there are around eighteen and half thousand Mustafa Ismails who would fit the age profile, and at least half of them are 'ghosts' with no traceable tax, or medical records. We haven't even got a pic to work with."

"A good result will be to narrow the possibilities, start with civil records and take a closer look at some of the extended family networks. Check with Border Force records about relevant arrivals over the past two years. Then bank accounts, land registry, etc. – you know the drill.

"Purewal – take another look at some of the statements from those trafficked – see if there are any common denominators relating to their arrival here. Any descriptions of the individual, distinguishing features, odd habits. It's possible there could be some clues to Ismail in there somewhere.

"Try starting to visualise the character we are looking for. What personal behaviours do we expect him to display? What sort of people will he be mixing with? Does he use social media? If so, for what purpose? Has this Ismail suddenly come into money? Does he have a woman stashed away from friends and family? Quite a few of his sort do and go to some trouble to keep it secret from the family. My sense is if he thinks himself to be successful, or his peers think he is he will want to show off in some way, then he is vulnerable. Find that vulnerability."

The brief for Mwake and De Jong was more specific, but no less challenging.

"It seems we have a real prospect of success on this one. The first thing you need to do is to liaise with GCHQ. Make sure you are following Kotobi and Abou's phones and social media. We need to find out who they are talking to in the Netherlands and, if we get lucky, that could take us straight to Canecale. We need to understand what happens to these hot cars once they get into Europe and find out how the money that holds these transactions is managed. The two gangs clearly have responsibility for getting the merchandise out of the country. My hunch is they're not easy bed fellows and are probably eying each other up for future expansion. We already think we know where their embarkation centres are, so let's ensure these are kept under observation. Remember at this point, we are in the business of gathering evidence, so it's important to be low key for now. Follow the trail as you need but be careful if you think it takes you outside UK jurisdiction. If that becomes a possibility, you must have my personal authorisation. This is not yet an Interpol matter and it won't help to stir up the locals until we know for sure we are on to something."

Oliver Watson's lines of inquiry were moving in an unexpected direction. With GCHQ's help he had been able to access the bank accounts of interest with relative ease, and although he didn't need their assistance in requesting the information, it was still important at this stage to avoid alerting his targets. Much of the information discovered was not that unusual. Communi-Kate, HeadingtonMeds, and Flit Hydrogen were conventionally structured businesses (Headington even listed on AIM in the previous year), their boards filled with regular if dull luminaries of apparent relevance to their market interests with Ciller Terzili listed as a non-executive director, remunerated with generous-looking dividends. Not much else to say from the record – the tax and treasury operations were tidy and up to date. The Terzili's properties showed rental income was being fed back to a holding account in Turkey, but what had caught his eye were regular and substantial payments going out to an entity called Global Bus in Slough which seemed to be logged as 'servicing costs/charges'. A closer examination of the accounts had showed payments had started three years ago and had risen from £250,000 to £2 million. Quite what these monies were buying was not clear. Global Bus appeared to be incorporated in Belgrade, with no registered UK subsidiary.

Further investigations lead to an account at the Enterprise Bank branch in the town, with a signatory of one Michael Abraham. Abraham's recorded address was the same warehouse that Global Bus was renting. The company's costs told their own story. The business paid rent on a warehouse, paid the wages of a dozen people, seemed to buy random vehicle components, web hosting and a series of one-off 'consultancy' payments – a year's business rates were outstanding.

At first sight this did not present as a typical small business – a multi-million-pound turnover, yet consistently posting losses with no apparent assets. What was Global Bus's business and why would a Serbian-based business set up a loss-making operation in the UK? Watson's efforts to learn more would inevitably be frustrated as there was no law enforcement collaboration arrangement in place between the UK and Serbia. It was clear if he wanted to know more he would need to get up close and personal with this Mr Abraham and his colleagues and would probably need the support of Marshall's people to do it.

The corporate restructuring of Turhan International had occurred as choreographed by Repcer, with the only unexpected element the renewed enthusiasm of Kerim Terzili, who somehow seemed to be invigorated by the loss of executive responsibility to his daughter. She in turn was happy that what she considered Turhan's legitimate shop window was now in place, managed by three senior experienced professionals and allowing her the oversight she had sought to focus on Yilan. Yasmin would have an increasingly influential role as a 'go between', ensuring Ciller's wishes on day-to-day matters were fulfilled and giving her space from the attention of Repcer. The new structure looked neat. From an operational perspective there was only one direct interface between the Turhan businesses and the more opaque family concern of Yilan, and that was the vehicle servicing operations of Global Bus at its three service centres at Slough, Venice and Istanbul. In every other respect there was distance between the two entities. The reason for the interface at Global Bus hadn't been explained to the new boss of the business, Ilkay Vahid and it was possible be had not picked up on its significance when viewing the accounts, but there was no point in having that discussion unless Vahid chose to bring it to the table. For now Ciller's strategy was to let the businesses and their new managements settle and consolidate. For now her focus would be to get a grip on some of her father's more lucrative and 'unregulated' activities, as this would provide the pipeline of funds to expand the group's legitimate investments. But where to start? Much depended on persuading her father to at least talk about what he was involved in but, based on her efforts to date, that was going to take time. She also knew that the way of getting her father to open up would be tricking him into making disclosures, and to do that she would need just enough knowledge to use as bait. It would be a tough ask – her father had a dislike of paperwork at the best of times, and he would have been unlikely to have left a trail. Kerim kept the detail she needed locked up in a cabinet in his head. She had long since discounted the value of Repcer in providing the insight she sought. Although she knew him to be no fool, his knowledge was limited to contractual and regulatory matters, not the form of person-to-person barter Kerim preferred. There were some levers nonetheless. The most obvious being the old man Canecale, perhaps the other being the Solokovs.

She would start to make some enquiries.

Then there was the matter of the Scottish trader she had met in Dubai.

"If we are going to get some traction on this situation in the near future we're going to need something more than just traditional gumshoe detective work," Marshall concluded as he briefed his boss, the director general.

"What did you have in mind?" Madam Boss was multi-tasking – simultaneously speed reading his report on her laptop and listening to the senior investigator providing an informal commentary on the story so far.

"The fastest way of getting to the right people will not be following their tracks but engaging them in business."

He decided to fly his political kite.

"…Which would be illegal, of course," she responded dryly.

"Only up to a point, depending on how you chose to look at it. If we are not directly involved and those working on our behalf are not presently employed by the state, I think there is an argument to be made. Supposing we parted company with certain members of the investigation team and they set themselves up in a new high-margin enterprise? We might not know about it directly and we could use informal communications to share intelligence and get to the people we are targeting quickly."

"You would be sailing close to the wind. We have already reached out to the Cabinet Office and other arms of government to assist us in the grey zone."

"True, but if we are serious about nailing this bunch across multiple crime fronts, we need a new MO that gets us on the front foot. Assuming we are successful then we can rehire them when we close the investigation. That way we are all happy."

"No, we won't be. I won't be. Apart from potentially exposing us to flagrant breaches of employment legislation, you know this will get us all into trouble if this gets near a court hearing. I can see a defence lawyer screaming entrapment from the outset."

"Well I think there is some merit in the saying the 'heart will not grieve over something it has not already missed'. My job is to get a result out of this sooner rather than later. I can't risk getting the investigation closed down early by the Perm Sec because we crashed our budget."

"How are you planning to do it?"

"The team are tied down by the OSA so I will tell them what I propose and get the HR team to fit them up. The easiest way of doing it is for me to decide they have failed with the case so far, damaging the reputation of the organisation. They can leave quietly with a golden goodbye to help things along and then, well, it will be up to them."

"It's a bit of a risk isn't it? You are then at the mercy of your investigators."

"It's no bigger risk than all the others we are handling right now. Frankly, compared to the other problems likely to emerge if this doesn't work out I think it's rather a good bet. Personally I regard this action as an investment in their personal development, a sort of sabbatical – giving them the opportunity to engage with the criminal mind at first hand."

"Who will be in charge?"

"Who knows? If I dictated that to them, then I would be guilty of going even further beyond my remit. They are all bright people – they can organise themselves – I will just keep in the background to oil the wheels with some disbursements here and there to help them on their way."

"...And while you're playing these undercover games, what will happen with the day job?"

"I will continue the investigation but position us as the client for the GCHQ and HMRC elements. That way we can report progress 'above the line', but it just won't be at the same pace we would have liked."

"What happens with the contribution from Six?"

"Again, this is an intelligence product which we can continue to buy incrementally. I am talking about adding value to our outcomes. The base mission here is to collect evidence to sequester UK-based assets based on an Unexplained Wealth Order. If we can use our investigation to bring additional criminal prosecutions, against significant smugglers, be they dealing in drugs, people or whatever you, 'we' will be credited and that will benefit the reputation of the department as a whole. Given this approach we may even be able to show some useful cost savings along the way."

"You're asking me not to probe your work diligently as a line manager would normally do, accept whatever update reports you choose to share, and plead ignorance if the Perm Sec or the Minister or even some MP raises a question in Parliament?"

"Yes – this is about trust. Trust me as I trust my investigators. Let's face it, none of us are here for the money. We do this job because we believe in putting the bad guys away. Sometimes we need to play their game to win. I can't see that we won't be able to deal with questions as they arise. After all, they can only come from sources with privileged information. If we control the sources then it will be OK."

"So if the Perm Sec chooses to raise with me why suddenly four leading members of your investigations unit have been fired what would you have me say?"

"I think the usual would cover it – internal reorganisation to ensure we deliver improved performance – better outcomes, lower costs."

"If this goes wrong it won't just be your head on the block…"

"I know, but this is a much bigger case than we thought. Not only do we need a new strategy, but I can't document this for obvious reasons."

"OK. Granted: I can't worry about what I may not know but you had better make sure your regular written reports are exemplary, even if they have been creatively edited."

"So you'll back me?"

"There's no such thing as a blank cheque – especially in our world. You had better think very carefully how you manage this, Phil. To date, your career has been exemplary which is the only reason why I have even discussed this matter with you. Get this wrong and be clear I won't support you because in truth I will be trying to save my own skin. Let us just say you are the editor of your own future. I will be studying the words you put in your reports very carefully. Very carefully indeed."

Back in the NCA briefing room, Marshall was laying out the strategy to his senior investigators.

"Look at this as creating an administrative framework to get this job done. I understand the frustrations this investigation is raising, and I have no doubt, in time, you will get the breaks you need to bring this investigation to a conclusion. But the fact is we haven't the time to wait for that. We must force the pace. By cutting your ties with the department and setting up an independent business you can engage with the targets directly. When it's all over you can rejoin the team, just like you had been on a sabbatical – in fact, it will be a learning experience that could improve your knowledge and skills."

Marshall had thought he had sold the idea to his team well when Wetherall, the one person who had been the most critical of the investigation so far, became the first to show his support.

"I get it. What you're doing is letting us get on with the job without all the procedural crap we are expected to go through. I'm up for that."

"You are expecting us to take a lot on trust, sir," added Purewal.

"Not really – trust is the only basis for us to work together anyway. If we didn't have that we wouldn't be an operational unit."

"So we get shuffled out and left to make sense of the situation as we find it?" asked De Jong.

"Not quite. You need to get organised; I'll give you the plan and provide the resources. You can get on with it and keep me posted from time to time. You'll be directors of a small market research business. It will give you the cover you need to get involved with our targets."

"Who's in charge?" Jimi Mwake asked casually. He was trying to think through how the arrangement would work in practice.

"That's you, Jimi. You need to bring the different strands of the case together, I can only have minimal contact, so you need to be the one who provides me with the progress reports."

"So I'm coming back to the office?"

"No, you're finished here for the time being. I will expect a monthly call from you. If I have a problem or we come up against the unexpected I will call a meeting in the field. Your instructions will be sent to you at a new email address next Monday. Today being Wednesday you can regard it as your last official day. There is an envelope for each of you with a P45 and a statement of a one-off payment in lieu of notice. I'd like to thank you for your service to NCA and look forward to engaging with you again in the near future."

He handed each an envelope, rather like a head teacher dispensing prize day awards to his senior prefects before departing.

The four were left to absorb the news and their new-found situation.

"What can we do that we're not doing already?" asked Purewal.

"If it was down to me, I'd tap up some of those scrotes we know are in touch with Ismail and offer them a big deal to bring him out of the shadows," said Wetherall.

"Which scrotes? What big deal?" queried De Jong.

"We have a list of around eight people – '*bigwigs*' – whose names have come up in different parts of the country with established drugs connections. We haven't pulled them up because assembling all the evidence we need and the lightness of conviction from prosecution hasn't justified the time. What they have in common is skin in the game. Those lower down the food chain who we have fingered for local police intercepts have suggested each one of them has a connection to Ismail and each uses a connection with one of the kebab shops to get their supplies. They also help out distributing illegal immigrants into local back-street businesses such as late-night takeaways, nail bars, barber shops, halal slaughter houses, clothing sweatshops, massage parlours, cleaning, personal security services and the like. All we have to do is to pay one of them a visit, tell them we are working for one of their competitors and suggest they go into retirement. Forcing them out of business will be a bigger threat than any rap the CPS can come up with. We can say we are helping Ismail by slimming down the supply chain. The first thing that will happen is one of our targets will call Ismail to ask what's going on…"

"The second thing that will happen is you will then get your bollocks blasted off," said Purewal.

"I don't think so. Ismail has worked hard to keep a low profile. He will be curious about who is out there and will have a meeting. He will also be suspicious about who we are claiming to work for or whether this is a plan to strengthen the position of the so-called retiree. I think we go and explain it to one of the eight and tell them we will represent their interest. We don't have to lie. Just tell them we are ex-cops out to build a pension and that we have enough evidence to put them out of business anyway. All they have to do is to broker a meeting with Ismail for us and they can carry on and potentially double the size of their trade. If they don't respond, we say we'll pass our dossier over to Scotland Yard. What we are doing is conning them into believing we've got more on them than we actually have – and let's face it, we know what they're up to. The problem has been the burden of proof."

"These guys aren't stupid. It's not going to work," said De Jong.

"I'm not so sure," Mwake replied. "They a are bit more sophisticated than the gangs we're dealing with over the performance car thefts – these bigwigs have got to where they are by having diverse supply chains, some of them have taken years to establish. They are the type who need respect in their local communities. This is a reputation thing – an ego trip. They are not wanting to look dumb in front of one of their most important customers. I think it depends on us finding the weakest link. In other words, which one looks like being the most vulnerable – the biggest ego and the smallest brain. Think about it over the next couple of days and we'll talk about it in our new office… wherever that will be."

"So how are you going to crack the performance car trade?" asked Purewal.

"By comparison that will be straightforward," said Mwake. "We know who is running it – just need to collect the evidence."

De Jong looked surprised.

"We are going to hijack one of these cars en route in Europe and bring it back here to resell into the system. This will allow us to zero in on Canecale wherever he is. Once we have Ismail and Canecale in our sights, we will have the keys to our Turkish connection."

NINE

"HELLO, IS THAT CILLER Terzili? It's me – Duncan McKee, from Dubai. Remember?"

"Mr McKee – how could I forget?"

"I did say I'd look you up when I was passing through Istanbul, so that's what I'm doing."

"You are here now?" He detected surprise in her voice.

"Well almost – at the airport but heading into town shortly, once I have fixed a hotel reservation."

"Most people who visit tend to send an email in advance," she cautioned.

"Well, I'm not '*most people*' and, as I have a couple of other meetings while I'm here, I thought I'd call on the off-chance to follow up on our conversation at the Burj a couple of weeks back."

"If you recall our conversation as clearly as me you'll also remember that I invited you to stay at my family home as my guest, and I like to keep my promises."

"Even at this short notice?"

"I will text my address – show it to the taxi driver so he can bring you here directly."

"Are you sure?"

"I would not suggest an arrangement I was not happy with. I look forward to welcoming you in a couple of hours."

The line went dead.

McKee smiled and headed out of the arrival's hall.

Ciller's estimate about the drive time from the airport proved accurate, even allowing for the inevitable traffic jams on the approach to the city and crossing the first Bosporus bridge to southern suburbs on the Asian side. It was early evening and his taxi had caught final knockings of the city's commuter traffic. As his taxi came to a halt on the quiet tree-lined residential road outside the walled property, McKee reached for his phone to announce his arrival. At he did so, the iron gates to the driveway opened beckoning him inside. If ever he had cause to doubt whether Ciller Terzili was the real deal, this imposing, twisting elevated driveway to the villa's front door, sent a message of power and privilege to the first-time visitor. The increasing dark shadows of the trees against the streaked orange sky at dusk seemed to add to the grandeur of the setting as he saw the outline of the ornate three-story tiled palazzo-style lodge come into view and his host waiting by the oversized double entrance doors wearing a vivid blue one-piece dress, which seemed to have been perfectly crafted to accentuate her full figure.

As the car stopped, a uniformed man stepped out from behind her to open the car door before Ciller stepped forward to greet her guest.

"Mr McKee, welcome to Istanbul and to my home."

Instinctively, he took her hand, kissed it and bowed in a slightly exaggerated way that seemed fitting for the occasion. It certainly set the right tone with his host.

"My friends call me Duncan, and I hope you are happy for me to call you Ciller."

She nodded and smiled her agreement.

"Please follow me. My assistant will take your bag to your quarters, I will show you around and then you will have time to freshen up before dinner."

He followed her into the marble hallway, dominated by a grand staircase, with oil painted pictures of turbaned men on horseback galloping into battle armed with swords and spears.

She caught his gaze.

"My late grandfather started to collect pictures from Ottoman history after the Second World War. You will find items from his collection all over the house. It is one of the largest collections in private hands these days. In order to keep it we have had to agree to only sell the entire collection to the Turkish state in future, so you could say we feel we are custodians of a small part of our country's heritage."

"Your family must be very proud," he ventured.

"Yes, they were… *we are*," she said hesitantly, "it helps to know that we always have a bargaining chip for the future with the tax authorities."

Duncan let her remark rest while he took in the opulent fixtures and fittings of the first-floor landing.

Hand-crafted wooden furniture, giant tapestries, stuffed bears and deer (hunting trophies), glassware, ceramics and several gilded clocks all attested to the history of the villa and its occupants.

"Your home feels like a palace," he said.

"Yes it was of sorts. The building dates from the reign of Mahmud II, the 30th Sultan, when it was built as a hunting lodge, a convenient base to have south of the city. Towards the end of the 1920s anything then regarded of value was either taken by the state or sold off. The rest was left to ruin through neglect during the war years until it was bought after the war by my great-grandfather who started to spend money on refurbishment and artefacts which has made the place what it is today, a museum of Ottoman relics and family memories. If you look from here, you can see we have a direct sightline across the water to the Topkapi Palace; an essential characteristic to ensure the nobles of the Empire staying here would be able to keep themselves informed about developments at the Imperial Court.

"Anyway, I know you are not here for a history lesson and there is plenty more to see in the grounds but it's too dark now. Perhaps I will show you tomorrow."

He noted a slight sadness in her voice.

She continued: "For now it is a tradition in Turkey that guests meet the head of the household – in this case my father, Kerim. He will join us shortly for tea on the terrace."

McKee could not have been happier about the prospect. He was already absorbing valuable information.

"I hope it is not too late to meet him and the other members of your family," he ventured.

"My father is my family here in Istanbul, I have a brother, but he lives on the Aegean coast, near Bodrum."

She noted his quizzical expression.

"I did have a larger family – another three sisters and a brother, but they were killed a couple of years back together with my mother in a road accident."

"I'm so sorry…" he opined.

"Not to worry, it is still painful, but I have got used to living with it now. It is just one of life's burdens we have to carry."

"It must be difficult for your father."

"Yes, much more than me. It has changed him from an outgoing character to something of a recluse. He doesn't leave the house and most of the family's business interests have passed to me to control."

"He must have been a good teacher for you to be in the position you are today."

"He didn't spend time teaching me, just allowed me to accompany him to his office and join some business trips. He spent a lot on my education, so I think he always expected me to work it out for myself."

"So he was right?"

"Up to a point – he has a trusted friend, a lawyer here who helped me fill in the gaps and get organised. We have recently completed a major restructuring, so our business today is very different. I'm not sure my father recognises the scale of change that has taken place."

"This is Turhan International?"

"Yes, we are now an industrial conglomerate. We specialise in marine scrappage, ferrous fabrications and diverse trading activities."

"Which is why you were in Dubai?"

"Which is why meeting you was a happy coincidence. You call it serendipity I think?"

At that moment a raised voice came from behind, they turned to see the man who had collected McKee's bag, now helping a white-haired old man with a walking stick emerge from the hallway towards them on the veranda. But we have time enough ahead to talk about all that," said Ciller. "First, can I introduce you to my father, Kerim?"

McKee smiled his greeting at the stooping figure who nodded his acknowledgement in return.

"Father, this is Mr Duncan McKee, a commodities trader I met in Dubai. I have invited him to stay with us for a couple days. I think he will be able to help us secure some new contracts."

"Welcome, welcome," Kerim muttered and gestured him to sit in a nearby armchair.

"How can you help us, Mr McKee?"

"I hope this will be about how we can help each other. I think we share common interests. Like you I am a trader in high-value premium products and like you I have customers and contacts. I am sure we could both benefit from collaboration."

"What sort of items do you sell?"

"Components for hardware products, personal protection equipment, defence industry supplies… all sorts. What they have in common is they are big-ticket items by scale or quantity and, as a rule, it's only governments who can afford to buy. As a trader I make it my business to find out what my customers want, then go and source it. Sometimes what customers want is bespoke – then I have to get it manufactured to their specification. My business is quite transactional – it's cash on delivery so it keeps everything tidy."

"I understand. I built my business on commodities – everything from fruit and vegetables, textiles and other agricultural crops and then diversified into metals. I am sure Ciller will tell you all about it."

"Of course, but not just now, Father. Mr McKee is tired and wants to relax. We have all day tomorrow to talk business."

Kerim seemed satisfied.

"Very well. I hope you enjoy your short time with us in Istanbul – this is truly a great city. If you have not visited before, take a trip to the Hagia Sophia. It will be the perfect introduction to our history and culture and will demonstrate why this is one of the world's great commercial centres. Please excuse me."

Kerim climbed stiffly to his feet and was escorted away by the butler.

Ciller sighed as he left.

"He is a shadow of the man he once was before the family accident. Had I not witnessed it myself I would never have realised how destructive grief could be."

It was the first time in their short acquaintance McKee had seen a vulnerable side to her personality. It was an observation that would be noted along with everything else when the time came to report to London.

"It seems unusual for a family to loose so many members at the same time," he ventured.

Ciller sat in the seat vacated by her father.

"I would agree. Highly unusual to the extent it becomes harder to regard it as an accident."

"But that's what it was, right?"

"I don't know. The police are still investigating after two years. Even by our standards you could at best call it inefficient. I have tried to find out more, as has my lawyer, but we haven't got very far."

"What happened?"

"The family had travelled to a wedding. Only my father, brother and myself could not attend. Everyone else was in a minibus. On the return journey, a truck carrying cement smashed into it. They were killed instantly."

"Tragic."

"It's more than that. If you saw the location where it happened in Fenerbahçe you would understand that it would be difficult to create an accident like that on a slip road especially at the speed the truck was going."

"So you think this was premeditated?"

"In our world, Mr McKee, we all have lots of enemies, but we can't always respond in this way to personal grudges. If we did, we'd be no better than the Mafia."

"But that is what you think?"

She nodded.

"Have you enemies capable of such action?"

"Not many – perhaps one or two."

"Have you approached them?"

"And give them the pleasure of seeing how much pain they have caused? No. In due course, the family will take action to resolve this matter, for now we have our businesses to consolidate. But first, let's have some dinner here on the veranda. You can tell me more about yourself and we can enjoy the view of the city lights."

It was the perfect opportunity for McKee to get down to business. The food and wine came a distant second to the company of the beautiful woman in a thin aquamarine silk dress who had become his host. The setting was magical, the air infused with jasmine fragrance, soft Western jazz played in the background; even the cicadas seemed to follow the restrained beat of the music. McKee was used to working under much greater duress than this and their conversation seemed effortless as they talked about everything other than business and her family.

It was always this stage of the entrapment that was the worst. Focusing on targets that he didn't like was easier than situations like this. He was starting to like Ciller Terzili. This was the point where temptation could cloud professional judgement.

As dinner finished, he reached the point of conversion.

"Thank you, Ciller, not only for your generous hospitality but wonderful company. It is sometime since I last had such an auspicious and, may I say, beautiful host. I have a meeting with an associate tomorrow lunchtime across the water, but I hope we can take a couple of hours before then to discuss business."

He stood to depart. Instinctively her hand reached across the table touching his.

"It's been a special evening. Thank *you*, Duncan. It is a long time since I have enjoyed the company of a gentleman without worrying about his motives. It's been a long time, but since we met in Dubai, I realised I needed a man in my life. You know, it's just us here. It doesn't have to stop now."

She stood from the table but retained a firm but somehow soft grip on his hand and pulled him towards her, locking her other arm around his waist pulling his body close to hers. Her breasts were hard on his chest but the rest of her seemed malleable to his touch.

He offered no resistance as slowly, she looked into his eyes and offered him a languid kiss, her mouth soft and giving.

Already she could feel his undivided attention against her abdomen and sensed the excitement of releasing him into her secret world of passion.

"There is much you still have to learn about me, Duncan. If we are to work together, you have to give me what I want when I want it. Tonight you will share my bed. I will fuck you and if you measure up, tomorrow we will do business."

She took him by the hand and led him away from the balcony to her private suite. The conversation had finished. The interplay had begun. She seemed to fall out of her dress with such ease he wondered if her disrobing had been premeditated from the start. She released the knot in her hair which fell forward masking her large brown areola. She knelt before him. This was the consummation of their relationship.

Their bodies entwined. The night hours turned to minutes of personal chemistry energised by bursts of electricity, her body writhing on his, her erect fulsome breasts rolling to her rhythmic thrusts on his rigid form. It didn't take long for him to lose his control in their intimacy, but the urgency of her attention continued, prolonging the conclusion of their love making.

The songs of the nightjars started to give way to the sounds of cuckoos and thrushes heralding the start of the new day before an overriding sense of calm prevailed.

Duncan felt the elation of the moment, a deep personal sense of satisfaction as well as that of professional fulfilment. His partner in passion lay curled at his side.

He had come to understand the intensity of the emotion she had been living with and the opportunities it presented for the future.

"Good morning!" Watson shouted across the garage as he walked into the rented warehouse on the Slough Trading Estate.

At first sight nothing seemed out of place. To his right, three Neoplan double-deckers lined up over services pits, radios turned up loud, boiler-suited mechanics checking inventories on racks of components running around the walls. In the centre a heavy-duty winch in front of a temporary builder's cabin which appeared to be serving as an office. To the left – eight cars, presumably owned by the mechanics – all non-descript mid-market saloons, nothing flash and a space with plenty of soapy water on the floor and industrial roller brushes.

One of the boiler-suited brigade responded to his call and walked purposely towards him.

"Oi mate, this place is private – we don't welcome visitors," he said as he approached.

Watson ignored the implied threat.

"Oliver Watson, HM Revenue & Customs, Customer Service. This is the premises of Global Bus?"

"Yeah, this is our service centre. We got another office at West Drayton for dealing with customers *and that*. They may be able to help you, or you can go online."

"Thanks, but I need to talk to someone now. It's important. Who is in charge?"

"When the gaffer is away, me, I suppose."

"…And you are?"

"Jeff, to my friends."

"OK, Jeff, perhaps you can contact your gaffer and tell him I'd like a word."

"You mean Mr Michael?"

"If that is Mr Michael Abraham, that would be great."

"Alright, if I do that you got to do something for me. We have a strict rule about visitors here – we don't allow them. Health and safety and all that. I'll give him a call but only if you wait outside."

"Don't worry, I'll sit in my car."

Jeff accompanied Oliver outside and watched as he returned to his car and made the call. His eyes remained fixed on him as he spoke. Closing the phone he walked over.

"Mr Michael is coming over to meet you, but you'll have to hang around. He says he won't be here for an hour or so."

"Thanks – I'll wait."

If Jeff's message was designed to make him lose interest it failed. Watson wanted to meet Mr Abraham however long it took. In reality it only took half the time and when he did arrive he was well briefed. Like Watson he chose to park outside the warehouse. Not only was he conspicuous where he parked but arriving in a black Range Rover with designer alloy wheels he was used to attracting attention. Climbing out and walking towards him, Oliver was at first unsure whether this was the man himself or just another of his assistants. He was younger than Oliver imagined, clean shaven, albeit with a heavy shadow, oiled hair, of South Asian appearance with a neat style of dress – white open-necked shirt, sand-coloured chinos and highly polished, natural leather designer Oxford boots.

Watson came out to meet him.

"Hi Mr Oliver?"

"Oliver Watson, HMRC." He offered his card.

"I'm sorry, Jeff isn't very good with surnames. I'm Michael Abraham. You got lucky catching me. I was working from my home up the road in Buckinghamshire today, so I was able to get to you quickly. I am so sorry for keeping you waiting. How can I help?"

"I'm from our customer services team. We're the new friendly face of the tax system. Instead of chasing citizens with demands and summonses we are now into client management, which means we offer our assistance in understanding how we calculate our customer's bill and offer flexible payment terms. It's good to meet you, Mr Abraham. We think you are getting a little behind on your paperwork – NI contributions, corporation tax and the rest, so we just wanted to check you weren't experiencing difficulties."

"You guys are sharp. It's true, we've been experiencing some problems – I've been without an accountant for several months now. Just can't seem to find the right person for the job, you know how it is."

"I'm sorry to hear that. Based on your last return nine months ago it certainly looks like you're having a topsy-turvy time of it – great turnover but making a loss."

"Yes, it's a very fickle business, but at the end of the day we offer a service so we have to schedule our trips to a timetable that our customers can believe in. As you know we are foreign owned, and our backers are in for the long term."

"I understand. Presumably backpackers are seasonal trade."

"We are not about backpackers. For that part of the market there are plenty of cheaper alternatives. Our customers are the premium variety who want a better-quality overland experience – table service, entertainment, even private meeting space. You forget that although our busses look big, our customer count is more modest, but is steady. We get a lot of repeat business."

"And just the two sites in the UK?"

"A sales office in West Drayton and this maintenance base here, which is one of three, the others are outside Venice and Istanbul. We have daily services in each direction and expect to increase the frequency on the northern leg, Venice to London next month. Here in Slough, we do the technical maintenance of the coaches for the journey to Istanbul, prior to collecting customers at Victoria. You will have seen online the stopping points on the route, all cities with affluent catchments that need our service. Some of the fleet will do a straight run end to end, others require a break in Venice, so it is a more complicated activity than you might imagine."

"Based on what I've just seen, your vehicles seem to take a lot of wear and tear."

"Yes, I'm sorry I can't show you around. We have strict health and safety and security protocols to observe. At any one time we may have around a million pounds worth of spares in this unit, everything from a replacement chassis upwards."

"I did see the giant winch when I arrived. I assume you have a lot of money tied up in that."

"We don't need to use that too often, but it is a required capability that we call upon from time to time as well as the specialists to operate it. But we are fortunate. To save you checking our records, we don't own anything here. So there are no depreciating assets to worry about, just some chunky rental and insurance costs."

Watson had got all he was going to get for now and closed out the conversation.

"Alright, Mr Abraham. This is not an investigation as such. Just a friendly reminder to prioritise your tax records by the end of the quarter. Do this and I'm sure our conversation will not need to go any further, but please be aware, we will be watching."

He offered Abraham a brief smile as an alternative to a handshake.

TEN

SUNITA 'SUNNY' PUREWAL HAD arrived early on her first day at the new rented offices of Four Musketeers Research in Colindale, north London.

Ahead would be a frustrating day of organising their IT links and transferring records, casually downloaded onto her laptop before leaving the NCA offices the week before.

The new premises was already equipped with every service they needed to start work immediately, but she had arrived, carefully nursing the pot plant that had been a fixture on her desk at Canary Wharf.

Arriving early had proved useful in another sense as well, providing the opportunity to meet the concierge and post room manager in the foyer.

"I'm pleased to meet you," he said, "I was wondering what to do with this parcel that arrived by special delivery half an hour ago."

Fleetingly, he noted her surprise.

"Oh, I didn't realise anyone had our new office address…"

"Perhaps it's an office warming present," he replied. "Do you want me to bring it up?"

Purewal, already weighed down with her handbag and a pot plant, offered an apologetic smile.

"Thanks. I've certainly got my hands full."

Arriving at the office door with her new set of keys, she fumbled with the lock, before the concierge stepped forward to open it. Following her inside, he put the parcel on the nearest desk and withdrew.

"Toilets are at the end of the corridor and the coffee machine is opposite the lift," he said over his shoulder.

She repeated her thanks to his departing back and sighed.

The others would arrive shortly, but for now she stared around her new quarters.

First floor, glass fronted with one general office room and a separate small interview space. The desks were facing each other. She would have first pick and opted for the one already bathed in the early morning sunlight. Time to check out the coffee and facilities, but first to look at the anonymous parcel that had been delivered. Her training had made her cautious, but she was somehow reassured by the notion that very few people would know of her new company or office address, so there was no need to imagine it was anything sinister.

It looked pretty normal. Typed label, central London postmark, but no information that might have allowed the mail service to return to the sender in case of non-delivery.

She took her car keys out of her coat and broke the seal on the box.

Prizing open the first flap she got the first clue to what was inside. A faint smell of scented nail polish the unmistakable indicator of the parcel's contents. Continuing to open it, although with more caution than before, she uncovered a series of tightly packed plastic packets of a white powder.

Although instinctively she knew exactly what it was, stabbing a packet with her key she put a small amount on her finger and then on her tongue. The bitter, slightly peppery taste told her all she needed to know. Hastily she closed the box, consigning it to the bottom draw in her desk.

What was happening? The first day at work in a new company in a new office and a special personalised delivery to her – a box of cocaine, at street value more than enough to finance her for the rest of her days.

What would she do with it? Who had sent it? What did they want in return? These and other questions were racing through her mind. Whatever the answers, she would need to get rid of it quickly.

Right now, she needed a coffee, grabbed her keys and headed for the door. At that moment it opened anyway. Wetherall and De Jong arrived.

"Hey this looks a bit better than the pigsty we used to work in," Wetherall observed. Both had already brought their takeaway coffees in from outside.

De Jong read Purewal's expression.

"What's up Sunny? Still worried Marshall has diddled you out of your pension? I'm pretty sure he's gonna want us back soon and we'll have more money to show for it."

"I've had a surprise delivery," she said.

"Don't tell me – a bouquet from an admirer wishing you well for your new career."

"I wish. Try a box of cocaine."

"From whom?" The unexpected remark came from De Jong.

"Well, I would have been surprised if they had sent a greetings card as well," said Wetherall, "maybe it's golden goodbye from the NCA."

"On the contrary." Mwake had just walked in.

"Just regard it as a temporary loan from the NCA asset library. Marshall fished it out of a consignment due to be destroyed over the weekend. He guessed you guys were going to need some product if you were going to start dealing."

"So he just put it in the post?" Purewal looked amazed.

"Courier actually," Mwake replied matter of factly.

"What about the risk of it being discovered?"

Mwake shrugged his shoulders.

"Certainly a risk as it would not have been insured, but it's here and we all know on occasion it's best to hide something in plain sight."

"And what do you mean 'loan'? Are we expected to return or repay this?" She was still unhappy.

"Perhaps not a loan as such, but we will need to account for it in some way. The key thing is to do as much as we can to prevent it being used. Besides if it helps us to get to the big guys I'm sure we won't have a problem with the paperwork."

"What happens if we get caught with it in the meantime?"

"That is an operational risk. We have no special protection. We will just have to be careful in how and when we move it and where we keep it."

"OK, so how will we do that?"

"A safe deposit box in Hatton Garden. The registration arrangements are set up for you, Sunny – the address is on your phone. I'd take it there straightaway but keep a couple of packs out for you and Wetherall to have as bait."

The morning after the night before and Ciller and McKee had returned to the villa's veranda to take coffee and pastries. As McKee looked out on to the Bosporus, it seemed the shipping traffic of the previous evening had intensified, and to his way of thinking looked only slightly less congested than the vehicles on the bridge when he had arrived from the airport.

"It's true you can't get bored sitting here – there is always something to see."

"Your father must appreciate that."

"He tends to come here in the afternoons. At this time of day he goes walking in the grounds as he prefers the shade. But never mind him, I am sure you will see him again later on. I recall you saying you had a meeting over lunch today in the city."

"Yes, I have to meet a banking associate of a Russian mining oligarch who is looking for a new international sales agent. We're having lunch at the Asitane at midday."

"Sounds interesting, what will you do?"

"What I always do – bring buyers and sellers together and take a commission. That is good business for me. I only get customers by arranging the trickier sales they can't manage themselves."

"And this deal is tricky?"

"I have no idea, but the fact that he wants to talk tells me there is something where my special skills and networks will come in useful."

"Sounds interesting. You know Turhan has extensive smelting operations here in Turkey. If his business involves any refining maybe we should talk about whether I can be of assistance."

"Worth knowing, Ciller, but I'm not sure he is interested in supply chain collaborations. If he's talking to me it will only be about straight sales."

"Who is he anyway?"

McKee sounded deliberately vague.

"Just your typical oligarch really. As far as I'm aware, he took control of a network of mining interests when the Soviet Union collapsed in faraway places like Kazakhstan, Uzbekistan and somewhere else – Azerbaijan I think. Quite how he managed it I'm not sure, but he's made a lot of money since. Keeps a flashy cruiser touring around the Black Sea and the Med so I think he has brought it into Istanbul to do business. The name is Solokov."

"Seems strange he is staying on his boat but coming ashore to meet you..."

"Not strange at all. We are playing by my rules. I don't know the guy. I think we need to get acquainted on neutral territory before I start visiting his lair. Besides I want a chance to work out just how good this piece of business will be."

"I've got a great idea. Men like that like to show off their wealth. If you are not going to meet on his boat, he will want to show you he is a player. I bet he turns up with some expensive arm candy, just to see how you react. Why not play him at his own game? Take me. You know I can dress the part. I was good enough for you last night and if he sees me draped around you, it will convince him of your credentials."

McKee laughed.

"If this wasn't a first meeting then yes, maybe, but for now he has to know that I'm hungry to do business and it won't be a good idea to upstage him. But who knows? I'll have a friendly chat and we'll see where it takes us. Anyhow, I am making it my business to be free mid-afternoon and wanted to take you up on your promise to see the sights, and then we can get down to talking about your own aspirations in the Middle East."

"There's a café called Hafiz Mustafa opposite the Hagia Sofia. I will meet you there at three. We walk and talk then."

McKee wished John Smith in London could hear all this – the plan to build a relationship with Ciller Terzili was already working well, but the Solokov connection still required more preparation. He had been aware that the Russian's vessel had moored on the Bosporus from the beginning, but certainly hadn't got as far as arranging a lunch appointment. Nevertheless he still had a couple of hours to change all that.

"Great – can you fix me a taxi to get me into town?"

"Yes, but from here it will take time. I'll get Osman to take you across the water in our motor launch and you can pick up a taxi from there."

The boat dropped him close to the ferry terminal by the Radisson Hotel at the base of the hill leading to the Sultanahmet, perfect for the taxi to take him across town to the Golden Horn shore where some of Istanbul's most eligible leisure boats were docked. It didn't take him long to find Solokov's craft. It was clearly the biggest and newest. Its name, *Oddessy*, confirmed he had found what he was looking for and, conveniently, he was pleased to see a gangplank in place that would make boarding easier. Unfortunately there was a sullen-looking deckhand blocking his access – certainly not an obstacle he had expected to encounter.

Approaching, he called to the man, "Is the skipper about?"

At first the man, apparently in a world of his own, ignored him but as he drew closer and realised he was being addressed shook his head and gestured for him to move on.

McKee dutifully ignored his warning and persisted.

"Can you get me the captain? My name is McKee for the Marine Insurance Syndicate in London. I have been sent by my office to make a routine inspection? This is a required condition of the insurance cover. Under article 5 paragraph 4 of the policy we can make the inspection at random at any place in the world."

McKee had deliberately spoken in a loud voice, not because he feared the deck hand didn't speak English but was hoping someone else on the boat would hear.

His luck was in.

The deckhand was considering taking physical action to deter him but was prevented by a shout in a language he did not immediately recognise and followed by a smartly dressed woman in a white uniform coming down to meet him.

"Please excuse my colleague, he doesn't speak English and he has orders to deter visitors. When we come to a port we usually attract unwelcome attention."

"No worries. I guess you heard about my enquiry?"

"Yes. Can I see your identification?"

McKee showed one of many he kept for this type of meeting.

"OK, I don't know about the insurance situation and any visitor to our vessel requires authorisation from the captain."

At that moment another voice called from the deck.

"Tatiana – let him on board."

The woman and McKee looked up to see a blond-haired man in a garish yellow Hawaiian shirt smiling down.

McKee's path was immediately cleared and he went aboard.

"Good morning, I am Valentin Solokov. This is my boat. Can I help you?"

McKee ran through his cover story once again.

The Russian frowned slightly.

"I didn't know about these random insurance inspections."

McKee countered: "It's a relatively new thing, an anti-fraud measure and happens at random only because we don't have the manpower to do it regularly."

He smiled. "Well not to worry, we are here for a few days and I'm happy Tatiana shows you around. I'm having a day off today, so be sure to stop by before you go. I would like to be reassured that everything is in order."

He nodded to Tatiana.

"The maritime crew are on a break so we will start on the bridge and work our way down." She smiled. "Follow me."

Solokov watched their backs as they moved across the deck before pulling out his mobile.

"I think I have found a target car for us to follow," said De Jong.

Fresh from sending Purewal and Wetherall off to organise their clandestine drugs bank, Mwake had been thinking about the logistics for stealing a car from a criminal enterprise, a high-risk strategy considering he didn't yet understand who he was dealing with.

"What have you got?" he asked, scrutinising his colleague's screen.

"It's a Koenigsegg Jesko 2020 edition, a 5 litre Twin-Turbo V8 9-speed multi-clutch transmission, yellow, owned by a Ravshan al Lailani, some playboy living in Belgravia."

"What makes you suspicious about it?"

"Apart from the fact it's a racing car? The owner had gone to a Mayfair restaurant and parked on the street outside. He was there for a couple of hours, and it was gone when he came out.

There were no signs of it being broken into, no glass in the street or anything like that, and it was parked between other vehicles, suggesting that whoever had taken it knew how to drive it. No casual bum from Brixton would deal with that. Besides, in yellow, it's not exactly discreet. It is likely someone would have seen it in the area."

"Any reports?"

"Nothing so far but the Met are following it up."

"What are our friends up to?"

"Don't know – guess you'd need to check with Marshall. Now we are on the outside, we won't be getting our usual feed from GCHQ. But this is clearly a collector's item, so it won't have been blagged casually. Someone, somewhere, will already be a customer lined up for this one."

"Michael Abraham is an unusual fellow," Oliver Watson concluded as he reported back to Marshall.

"When I went to Global Bus they didn't exactly roll out the welcome mat for me and when I did get the chance to look into the garage, I was surprised by the amount of heavy lifting equipment, winches and what looked like welding going on, in what is for all intents and purposes, just a servicing depot. I'd like to study the routes they use across Europe because, all things considered, they seem to suffer from a great deal of wear and tear."

"Well I suppose that's understandable. I would assume the quality of the roads deteriorate when they do the southern European stretch."

"If that was the case, I would have thought they would do their higher-level maintenance in Italy not here."

"We can't possibly know that. We don't know enough about their scheduling operations."

"I would have settled for that, but this Michael Abraham makes interesting reading. He lives in Beaconsfield in a £4 million mansion which it seems was bought with cash a couple of years back. He is a director (in name at least) of twenty-two different companies here, a couple in the Caymans and one in Rotterdam. The Dutch business seems to be the biggest payer, he took just over a million from that source last year, but that is only the piece we know about. We are following up on his banking records just now."

"Is he linked to the Terzilis?"

"Again, I can't be sure but there is a Turkish connection through Rotterdam. One of his fellow directors is a guy called Ilkay Vahid who has just joined the board with some other bloke called Bulent Canecale, who is an Italian citizen of Turkish decent. I'll let you have more when I get it."

"What are your doubts about Global Bus?"

"It's very frustrating. There's nothing obvious but something doesn't add up here. They have relatively new equipment, but it seems to be high maintenance, their operations seem above board. Their drivers' tachographs are in order, but their load factors fluctuate erratically. This doesn't have a steady pattern of sales you would expect to find in a transport business of this type, so we've got to take a closer look."

"What do you have in mind?"

"I think I should take a return trip to Istanbul with Global Bus to get closer to how it's run. I assume you can approve that?"

"On the basis that you are making a return trip. I don't want to have to answer for paying for an impromptu holiday break."

"OK, you'd better get on with it. Keep me informed in the usual way."

"I trust you have seen everything now?" Tatiana used her best smile to great effect.

"Yes thank you – I have really appreciated your help."

"I know Mr Solokov wanted to say goodbye before you left. He is by the pool at the aft first deck, please…"

McKee followed, keeping up a running commentary into his phone about features of the boat that would help maintain his cover.

"Mr McKee – good to see you again. I trust Tatiana has shown you everything you wanted to see?"

McKee smiled. "Almost. She has been a most charming host."

"Delighted to hear it. You picked a quiet day to visit, so it has worked out well. I didn't realise my vessel was insured with your company."

"As you know, Mr Solokov, value can be a subjective thing. My colleagues understand important customers such as yourself expect to be engaged with the minimum of fuss, they sell on elements of the risk to limit their own exposure to potential claims. That is what your insurers did for my company which would explain why you may not have been aware of my firm's interest in this matter, but it is not an unusual practice in our industry."

"And who are our prime insurers?"

"At the moment they are Belagio Risk Mitigation on Guernsey, Channel Islands I believe."

The Russian nodded his head.

"Thank you for reminding me. Insurance is very important in my business; I tend to overlook its role in protecting my personal assets."

"It's not unusual, Mr Solokov. People only think about us when something goes wrong."

"Indeed so. I am pleased to know all is well, Mr McKee. You are welcome to stay for lunch if you have the time. I have a number of assets with potential contingent liabilities that I would be interested in your opinion about."

"That would be nice, but I have another appointment to keep in the city. I'm sure you will understand. When I am sent overseas I am normally given too much to do. But I tell you what, I know of a good restaurant close by that does excellent Ottoman-style food. It's on the way to my next meeting but perhaps we could have some mezes there? It's not ideal but it would give us a little more time together."

"OK, I'll have Tatiana get my driver to take us there. Do you have an address?"

Ciller Terzili would not have believed the impression Duncan McKee had made on her. Although she couldn't help admitting to a schoolgirl-type attraction when they had first met in Dubai, seeing him on her own turf had only increased his appeal. It was not just his athletic build and model looks, but his natural air of confidence. This was a man at ease with himself and comfortable in what, for a foreigner, was an alien environment. That same confidence had been applied in her bed as well as in her early commercial exchanges with him. She was starting to conclude the meeting with McKee was in some way down to fate. And yet there was still a reserve in her. This looked too good to be true. Her research, both online and through her representative in London had checked out, but she still needed to be sure he could be trusted. He had not taken her bait of joining him for lunch with Solokov but still needed to be sure he was doing what he had said. Her man Osman had been told to follow McKee to check his progress and report back. She knew McKee had visited Solokov's boat, but couldn't understand why, when the night before he had denied his intention to go there.

As instructed, Osman had watched McKee and Solokov leaving the *Oddessy* and followed their car to the Asitane.

She resolved her planned walking tour of the city's most famous sites would be the right occasion to talk about the serious collaboration she had in mind.

ELEVEN

THEY HAD A TABLE outside on the sun terrace next to the Byzantine church of the Holy Saviour in Chora.

"I always try to fit in a visit here when I come to Istanbul. It's so much more relaxed than the places downtown and it's in a great location if you need to get across the city quickly."

Solokov raised an eyebrow.

"Is it possible to get anywhere quickly in Istanbul?"

"I guess everything is relative."

Waving away the offered menus, McKee ordered mezes and pomegranate juice for two, before taking a direct approach to his guest.

"So, Mr Solokov, I am intrigued to know why a man such as yourself agrees to an impromptu lunch away from their home base with someone they had met only two hours ago, who is male and an insurance salesman."

Solokov smiled and stared into the middle distance.

"I am curious, Mr McKee. You are clearly a man with a hidden agenda, and I wanted to find out more about you."

"More?"

"I had you checked out while you were touring *Oddessy*. I was interested in the responses to my enquiries."

McKee was concerned but knew this was part of a test that he was certain to meet at some stage of his mission.

"And what did you learn?"

"I have concluded you must be the best paid insurance agent in Europe if your employers have sent you from London to Turkey to check my boat out. I hear also that you have other business interests which also makes me believe you operate for your employers in a freelance capacity. For example, you do a lot of deals out of Dubai I understand."

"Well, we are all traders at heart – that's what makes the world go round wouldn't you say?"

"So why have you targeted me?"

"I think you are the type of customer I need for my business. You are asset rich; your income comes from corporate deals, and you are well connected. But most of all, you are not weighed down by all this corporate governance shit. You know what you want, and you go and get it – which is why we are here?"

The Russian raised an eyebrow quizzically.

"You have a proposition to discuss and think I might be the man for the job."

His guest nodded.

"Possibly. In my world there are great opportunities, but great risks too. As I get older I grow increasingly tired of lawyers and contracts. I like to keep my business simple. I look someone in the eye and decide whether or not we can do business. If I think we can and it happens, I am known for my generosity. If it doesn't work out I tend to leave things tidy and terminal. I am sure you understand."

"So what do you have in mind?"

"If you have checked me out you will know that my wealth comes from mining interests in the former Soviet republics in the east. In recent years people have assumed that to be fossil fuels, to keep factories going in Russia. But that is a lot of work for relatively little reward – global commodities like copper and aluminium have better returns, even when you include smelting costs. Most of my time these days is not taken up with supplying what is a volatile market but actually controlling global supply, so I am buying up mining assets and cutting production where I can, to drive up prices. So that is time consuming for me. I have pressures that I cannot yet control but I must start to influence. Firstly, I need to slow down the trade for metals recycling as they weaken my price position and I need to diversify into other forms of extraction. And this is the reason why I am here in Turkey. Apart from its growing importance as a world trading centre, Turkey is a leader in metals recycling and more state resources are being committed to growing its position. I intend to be a player in this market and have identified a business that I want to acquire here."

"What makes this business special? From what you are saying there must be a number of firms you could buy."

"That is true, but there is one that has a special relationship with one of my home markets – Uzbekistan."

"Oh?"

"Yes, a bit like you, I came across them by chance. When the Soviet Union collapsed I had the opportunity of taking options on a portfolio of around fifty mines, but a few had inflated production statistics and there were poor reports about the quality of ore they produced. I reviewed them and decided to take on thirty, which forms the core of my portfolio. The others I let go; some closed and others were bought by other businesses. One of those who became active *after* I had made my move, was a Turkish entrepreneur who acquired a mine at Nurata, in the middle of the Kyzylkum desert in Uzbekistan, a long way from any recognisable transport connection. Its performance was shit and it looked more like a state job creation scheme on its last legs. I confess I stopped paying attention, until I heard they were running trucks of semi-treated ore, completing the smelting, then exporting it here. Believe me, in my world this is an expensive operation and not the type of logistics trade that even high-grade copper would justify. I started to investigate and discovered some of the metal being excavated was gold and the business was being managed by this Turkish outfit. When I reviewed my documentation (originally issued by the Soviets but guaranteed by the new independent government), I found that I had a case to reinstate my option on the basis that the information in the prospectus I was given was wrong. There was never any mention of gold. I contacted the Turkish company with a fair proposition. I would take over the option and pay them a third above the market price. It was against my better principles but I decided to do it to secure a quick deal. It was rejected. I tried to contact the entrepreneur concerned to negotiate directly.

"He told me to *fuck off*, which I thought disrespectful. I warned him that he should be careful in his dealings as I would be looking out for him and that was as far as I got. I sent him a message predicting an event that could become a personal tragedy which I understand has come to pass. But he is either a tough old bird or a fool. He doesn't understand my capabilities and the fact that one way or another I will take him out. But there is still more I need to know before I do that. Firstly, although I have reliable reports about the volume of gold he is taking out of the mine, I don't know what he is doing with it and suspect he is exporting. He will certainly be stockpiling some to ensure price stability; but where and how he is selling it, I don't know. If I did, I'd shut them down. I want you to act as an agent for me. Find out how and where he is selling gold. I will provide the resources to allow you to make some minor purchases that I will need as proof of his dealings, plus…"

It was McKee's turn to offer a quizzical gaze.

"This guy's firm is a major player in metals recycling here. He breaks ships, smelts metals into sheets and sells to munitions manufacturers. Buying a position in that market is very attractive to me, so you can understand why I am thinking meeting you has come at an opportune time."

"I assume you are talking about Turhan International?"

"That's right. You have come across them before?"

"Only by reputation I have some knowledge based on a couple of contacts in the Turkish munitions industry."

"So here is my deal. I will deposit a million US dollars in a bank account of your choice. Get me samples of the Turhan gold, where they store it and who their customers are within a month. Do that to my satisfaction and you can expect a generous success fee. Should I not hear from you, I will send one of my security teams to find you wherever you are in the world and will liquidate our relationship. Here is my card, contact me on this cell phone number with your bank details in forty-eight hours.

"Now, Mr McKee, you will understand, you are not the only one with a full diary of commitments today. As you invited me to lunch, may I thank you for your hospitality. I will leave the bill with you."

Abruptly he got up to leave, his driver opening the gate of the terrace to the car park.

McKee remained reflecting on what he had heard. The news from Solokov was unexpected but could mean the potential prize from his activities would be that much greater if he could nail a Russian oligarch alongside a Turkish crime syndicate. There was also a possibility he was being set up. An organised gold smuggling operation from Uzbekistan to Turkey would require a level of organisation that he didn't know the Terzilis had, only because he was certain Turhan would not be directly involved given the risk to their legitimate operations. He would need to find out more before deciding what to do.

"Got any more on that Koenigsegg?" Mwake asked.

"Not that much," De Jong replied, "but my mates at the Met said they'd appreciate any help they could get."

"The guy who owns it is some playboy from Dubai who is related to some big cheese in the business world there called Mohammad Sultan bin al-Harriri. Apparently, he's gobbing off about the inefficiency of the police and that his father is going to make some complaint to our ambassador in Oman."

"Never mind that, do we have any eyewitness reports?"

"Only one that looks interesting. Some girl was babysitting at a mews flat around the corner said she saw a yellow sports car loaded on to the back of a flatbed and wrapped in a tarpaulin. Apparently that is not an unusual sight in those parts. A lot of people have swanky motors which may look good but are unreliable. When something goes wrong with one of those babies it takes more than a visit from the local AA man to sort it out."

"Anything from CCTV to back it up?"

"The Met are doing that now. Have you heard from GCHQ?"

"It's a pain in the arse, but now we are outside the family, any intel we need has to come via Marshall. I've put in a request but not heard yet."

"What do you reckon? Leerys or the Screamers?"

"Probably our Irish friends the Leerys – shifting a car like that is less likely to be noticed out of Boston than Chatham. We've got watchers out in the meantime, so we can follow up as we need.

"More importantly, if this is the car we are going to recover, we need to think about how we will organise our own carjacking. Don't forget we can't expect to get help from the Dutch authorities on this, we will need to use freelancers. You'd better start to make some enquiries, so we are ready. If I were in the thieves' shoes, I'd want a high-profile vehicle like that off the patch asap, so we must be ready to move quickly."

Mwake's phone flashed.

"Talk of the Devil – it's a message from Marshall. According to GCHQ, the Leerys have it, so it looks like we're in business and we have probably got forty-eight hours to get our plan in place. I'll check with the gaffer and see whether he has any more on how the European end is going to be managed."

"What about the Met?"

"It's too soon to bring them in. Suggest you let them know we are making our own enquiries and will alert them if we uncover anything useful. We need some hard evidence of our own first. Better make sure you have put the watchers on standby as well. If they are expecting a delivery at the warehouse, there will be extra activity going on. We need to make some more positive identifications, so we can get the complete picture."

Philip Marshall was aware making progress on the Terzili case meant working at the very edge of his authority, if not beyond. He had already done enough to justify a reprimand from the director general and still not had the quality of evidence needed to justify his actions. Without arrests and convictions, at best he could look forward to an early retirement, at worst he may be replacing some of his quarry in the dock at the Old Bailey. He had a sense that his colleagues understood the chances he was taking and were motivated to get the result, but could any of them really understand what it might take to get results? In due course, he would need to take Smith's advice about what actions could be deemed officially as covert. This would help him through the trickier legal impediments of entrapment and misrepresentation, but that was not the most immediate priority – getting some traction on the investigation came first. Watson's team seemed confident about the approach to the Unexplained Wealth Order which could at least result in the sequestration of the Terzili's property investments in London but reflecting on their conversation, the Revenue man had seemed more interested in this travel company, Global Bus. He knew if he reported that up the line, the response would be forget about it and concentrate on the property. That would result in getting hold of the assets and cash for the Exchequer but wouldn't assist in a criminal prosecution.

He was the lead on the investigation for the NCA. The job of the NCA was to nail major league felons and this was where his effort must be directed. Outside of the potentially questionable tax position of Global Bus's director, this Michael Abraham, he wasn't sure what Watson thought he was on to, but the fact he felt he could justify his time investigating this business gave Marshall the clear impression there was more to come.

To him, the other investigative enquiries looked stronger. Smith had seemed confident enquiries in Turkey were on track and Mwake's team were making progress on the luxury car thefts and the drug dealing, so the best thing he could do for now was to wait, knowing his real job was to keep the big wheels of government off his back. He would only succeed if he kept up with the intel being provided by GCHQ, especially as they were not allowed to speak with his investigators now they had officially left the service and focused on analysing its value.

Jane Clark had been particularly helpful providing regular high-quality reports on their targets. Marshall was continually amazed at their ability to source high-quality information but knew best not to enquire into their sources.

On the basis of digital interceptions (he assumed) GCHQ had come up with a list of the top ten kebab houses implicated in drug transactions that would be the focus for Purewal and Wetherall's enquiries. She had already pinpointed the two gangs dealing with the cars. But the real win would be to find links between the gangs, the cars, the drugs, the people trafficking and the kebabs. The cherry on the cake would be to make a clear connection to either Terzili or Turhan, but it was important not to get ahead of himself and ensure solid steps were being taken.

Purewal and Wetherall's investigations had taken them to Leicester, to an unassuming location in the Oadby Road to a branch of Izmir Barbeque. It was approaching two in the morning on a Thursday night. They had been watching the comings and goings for the past three hours, taking pictures of vehicles and their occupants visiting the premises. That in itself told a story – a succession of quality cars – the majority German, their occupants dropping by for a late-night snack, although most left without the obligatory bags of food. The surroundings didn't look affluent, and the impression was that most of the customers were not local. Although most people would be tucked up in their beds at this hour the immediate surroundings of the Izmir were busy.

"God could you imagine living next door to that," Wetherall ventured as they sat in their car a short distance away.

"Funnily enough I could," Purewal replied. "I guess if you worked in a place like that, living nearby would be an advantage."

"But the smell?"

"That depends on the time of day. Now it's pretty appetising. At ten in the morning probably not, and if you are here all the time, I bet you don't notice it at all."

"You talk from experience?"

"I do. I grew up living over my dad's Indian restaurant, so cooking smells are part of life to me. Have you seen anyone that might be of interest?" she asked in hope not expectation.

"Not really – apart from the 'beamers' – just the usual array of shift workers from the clothing factory around the corner, a couple of ambulance crews and some yobs who look like they've been kicked out of a bar down the road."

"So who are those others over there?"

"Just taxis."

"Do you really think taxis are gathering here to get passing trade?"

"You need a taxi to find this place. Taxi drivers have to eat like the rest of us."

"So that must make this the most popular kebab joint in town. There are others open in the city centre at this time that aren't half as busy. I think we had better introduce ourselves."

Without waiting for agreement, she got out of the car and walked towards the restaurant, Wetherall following.

Inside, the premises didn't look the cleanest, but nonetheless she continued: "Two doners with salad mix please."

The manager smiled his welcome.

"Do you want special sauce?"

"Only if it makes a difference."

"Izmir sauce is what makes our doner the best in town. That's how we have such a loyal group of followers."

"Is that right? OK, let's give it a go."

"Please – you will have to wait a couple of minutes – I think you may be our last customers tonight."

Purewal nodded to Wetherall, who moved to drop the lock on the front door.

"Thank you," said the manager. "You've saved me a job. Do you want Coke?"

Purewal looked surprised.

"Diet or normal?" he added quickly.

"Just water. Thanks. I was a bit surprised you asked if I wanted Coke…"

"A lot of people like it with a kebab. I think it's too gassy… makes me fart!" He laughed.

"I've not had that experience – I find it makes me high," she added with a smile.

The manager laughed again.

"You mean drugs… you may be right. I wouldn't know. You look like police to me. Your mates are always in here getting food. If anyone was doing stuff here they would know."

"If we were police we'd have nicked you ages ago."

The manager stopped laughing and looked nervously at the open door at the back. Two muscular South Asian boys appeared the other side of the counter.

"Look we keep our noses clean. We don't want no trouble. As you can see I have my own security here."

It was Wetherall's turn to join the conversation.

"Two big lads chucking a nice couple out of your shop looks dodgy don't you think? Especially when we can go straight round to the cops and make a complaint, when my wife here can claim

139

you threatened her with one of those sharp meat cutting knives of yours because she turned down your offer of coke." Almost casually he took out a small plastic packet of powder and waived it like a teabag under the manager's nose.

"What do you want?"

Wetherall continued: "I hear you have gear for sale. In fact, based on at least half a dozen of the dudes who have been in here in the last couple of hours, I think you have sold more lines than kebabs. You know, you really should ask your customers to keep quiet about it. Once they are off their heads they start talking and you know what that's like. Once they start they don't know when to stop. Bet your supplier is charging you loads to provide this sort of service. We can do better supplying more and better quality."

"Whatever you're being told it's bollocks."

"So, if I get a driver from Hotcars to take me out tomorrow night and tell me where I can buy a line, you are pretty sure he won't bring me here?" Purewal put the pressure on.

"Hot cars? We have nothing to do with that," came the strange reply.

"I'm talking about the local taxi company," she added.

"If a driver brings you here for a score it will only be because you told him."

They noted the manager's terminology.

He put wrapped packages into a paper bag and put in on the counter.

"This is what we do. Two doners, two salads, two waters – £20."

Wetherall put a note on the counter. The manager snatched it and held it up to the light before putting it in his back pocket. One of his security people had moved to unlock the door.

Purewal had watched the manager closely during their dialogue. He was clearly nervous.

She studied him with a critical eye, noting his white, fat-stained hat and name badge.

"OK. Selim is it? Nice to meet you. My name is Sunny – this is my friend, Joe. You have been very helpful. I will be back to collect my coke order tomorrow night. I will compare it to our stuff, so you know we do quality. I don't want cans or bottles, just a couple of little packets, know what I mean? Don't forget my name. I have written it down on this £50 note". She left the folded note on the counter.

"Don't let me down. I hate being disappointed."

TWELVE

"HOW ARE WE GOING to lift this motor, Amelie?" Mwake asked De Jong, staring across their conjoined desks.

"There is a tramp out of Boston, heading for Vlissingen the day after tomorrow and the Leerys have arranged a container, reference RX 2428 to be aboard. It will only be one of thirty, the majority going across are just empty returns. According to the detail Marshall has picked up from Cheltenham a guy called Bulent Canecale will collect it over there tomorrow. He will see the container onto a low loader with two drivers for its trip south. Interestingly this consignment is bound for Malaga and not being moved through a French port. Canecale is going to meet up with the merchandise before passing it on to his customer there."

"So Canecale is not travelling directly with the merchandise?"

"According to our information, no."

"That must mean either the drivers have no idea what they're carrying, or they work directly for him."

"I think that's right. I have the sense it's probably the former. Once the container leaves the port, there is no reason for it to be stopped while it is on EU territory. This Canecale guy will probably have a tracker on the vehicle and, in the unlikely circumstances of it being stopped, it will be much better if the drivers act natural, so they won't be able lie about what they're carrying."

"And your plan?"

"I've got a couple of watchers lined up to see the collection and will attach our own tracker. They have the resources to manage the hijack. They will stop the truck here in a forested area at Onnaing just off the A2, transfer the vehicle to a new container, put the drivers in the back, and take it to Dunkerque for the night-sailing to Sheerness. I will arrange the collection from there."

"How many hours will it be in France?"

"We think Canecale is based in Rotterdam. If the consignment stops close to the A2 there will be nothing sinister in that for an hour or so. He knows his drivers have a long way to go.

"I think from the time of the interception to him realising there is something wrong is going to be about two hours. In that sort of time frame, our guys can have the cargo back to the coast. Besides, the consignment will be swept for trackers, so at short notice, he won't know where to go looking."

"How do you know he won't find our tracker when he collects?"

"At the pick-up in Vlissingen, Canecale will need to sign a customs declaration. He will be presenting an import exemption document which will be inspected by the port authorities. Our guy has access to the holding area where the container will be collected, so that will be the time to get the tracker in place. Because he has already hired the transport, his tracker will be in the cab of the truck carrying the container."

"OK, assuming it all happens as we want, how do you expect this to pan out?"

"Canecale will be under pressure to keep the deal he has already arranged which will be COD. His first move will be to find it. His second thought will be to blame those who know about the transaction. It is certain the Leerys would not be paid until Canecale makes the handover in Spain. Their communications at this time will all be monitored by Cheltenham then we can go for arrests and return the merchandise to its rightful owner."

"Happy with that. Your guys in the Netherlands are good?"

"Some of the best, ex-military. Their fees are in line with my projections. All you need to do is complete the billing arrangement with Marshall."

Tea and cake at the excellent but congested Hafiz Mustafa was not to be missed, although being at a table so close to the kitchen made the type of conversation McKee was expecting difficult. Maybe that could wait until they had set out for a walk.

For now, the conversation focused on catching up on the day's business.

"How did it go this morning?"

"Oh, fine. I really appreciated Osman taking me across the water. It stopped me being late for my appointment."

"And that was successful?"

"We will see. We discussed terms. He's thinking it over. No doubt I will hear from him soon if he wants to do business."

"How much do you know about him?"

"Not that much other than he has a lot of money which was probably earned in some sort of dishonest way, and he wants to clean up his act. Many of my customers would tell a similar tale, and if they didn't have 'baggage' of one sort or another, they wouldn't need the services of someone like me."

"Don't you worry about these sorts of people?"

"Not really. I'm not that interested. All I need is to be confident I can do what is asked and that I get paid."

"How do you stop getting ripped off?"

"That is an occupational risk, but my terms are always fifty per cent up front, the balance on delivery. I don't let any outcomes pass back to the client until I know settlement is in the bank. True, not everybody likes that way of operating so they can go elsewhere if they like. I put my terms upfront before taking on a project. That way my customers know I'm not making up rules as I go along. Now I have told you this you will have a chance to reflect before discussing your own project with me."

"What did this Russian want from you?"

"I should have also said that when I talk with a client it must be completely confidential."

"What would have happened if I had come with you this morning?"

"That would have been personally agreeable but professionally inappropriate. He and I would have just gone for a stroll together – a bit like you and me this afternoon."

"You are a mysterious man."

"Possibly – but not a liar, I have retained my wealth and health. Not always easy to do in my line of work."

A few minutes later they were strolling through the Gulhane Park towards the Topkapi Palace. Ciller spotted a bench in the shade and invited McKee to sit beside her.

"So now I think is the best time to talk," she said hesitantly.

"Better than at your villa?"

"Certainly. No prying ears here."

She smiled.

"It seems so crazy for us to meet so soon after meeting in Dubai," she began.

"I invited you to my home and to my bed on the strength of my intuition. I am not sure I have ever done such a thing before, and it is very out of character for me. I am involved in a complicated situation and need help to sort it out. I think you may be the person best qualified to assist."

"Why?"

"You are experienced with dealing with governments and businesses in the grey zone, between what is legal and what is not. Turhan is finding itself in this territory. I am clear what I need to do, but less sure how to go about it."

McKee nodded sagely, understanding that so far, his host was not making a lot of sense.

She continued: "Turhan was my father's business. He started out like we all do, buying and selling products and commodities and taking a margin. As a young man he was smart and he and his oldest friend built the business and his reputation as a successful entrepreneur and fixer. Of course, in the early years he did a lot of illegal trades – mainly smuggling, money lending and bidding for public contracts, bribing politicians and meting out punishments and worse to rivals who got in his way. Most of the smuggling was weapons and drugs, the money lending was always to other businesses with assets that he would acquire by forcing those he had lent to repay their debts early. He kept up a veneer of respectability, getting married, buying our *yali*, the family home and having five kids whilst mixing in influential business circles and keeping an office around the corner from here. He then decided to become legitimate by buying up a breakers yard on the Aegean about a couple of hours away. This facility enabled him to accept redundant ships for recycling, effectively dismantling and smelting the different metals into sheeting used in construction and the military. So Turhan was earning big money disassembling ships and selling the recovered metal to make armour for tanks and a new generation of Turkish weapons such as bomb casings, rockets and machine guns to the government. For a few years all was well. As his eldest (and I think his favourite) I was sent away to an international school in Switzerland, but the others stayed here. So much happened whilst I was away. He kept the family separate from business. But I think he started to get bored, or else something in his past wouldn't let go of him and so despite his growing acceptability, he still kept dealing with the illegal stuff. He got into mining and money laundering, building connections with criminals across Europe and the former Soviet bloc that wanted outlets to finance their corrupt activities. Somewhere along the way he and this business partner acquired what he thought was an iron ore mine in Uzbekistan but instead started producing gold which somehow he kept secret but used it to ramp up the money laundering. He became preoccupied with it to the extent he ignored the need to plan the future of the breakers yard. I can only assume it became too complicated for him to manage and the returns were not as good. The result was that the ship contracts started drying up with the inevitable knock-ons, staff wages cut and layoffs. Production of the alloy composite sheets went down, losing government contracts. Yet at home, we didn't feel the effects, as the gold kept coming.

"When I turned eighteen he saw something in me that was different to the rest of the family. I started to accompany him to the office where he let me sort out the filing and assemble the tax records for our family lawyer to send to the authorities. Little by little, I started to understand the business. I would overhear conversations with his business partner when they discussed the need for enforcements against people who owed money. My father never did any of that stuff but would give the instructions and it was his partner who would get his hands dirty.

"I returned to my studies abroad, so there are still some gaps in my understanding, but I used my time to get a business degree and gave my father the certainty that in due course I would succeed him."

"Why you and not your brother? Isn't it unusual for women to have such high-profile roles here?"

"Traditionally that is so, but it is changing here as elsewhere in the world. Besides, my brother wanted to enjoy the benefits that wealth brings without understanding the need for hard work. He moved south on the coast to become what you would call a playboy."

"Then what happened?"

"The family tragedy. My mother a brother and three sisters were killed returning from a wedding when a minibus they were in exploded, apparently as a result of a collision with a truck on a motorway slip road. Although the police investigated they have never arrested anyone as a result and the circumstances are a mystery. What we know for sure is that the collision is credited with causing the explosion, but it seems unlikely in that scenario an explosion would have been the result. Perhaps without it, one or more of them would have survived.

"Whatever the circumstances, the result seemed to accelerate the decline of my father. Not only was he ignoring the needs of the breakers yard and the metal sales, but even his illegal activities with whatever obligations were forgotten. Looking back, it seemed strange that despite his achievements, all day-to-day matters still depended on him. He became a shell, consumed with shock and grief. His friend and business partner, who you might have expected to be supportive, became more distant. We started to receive more visits from our lawyer. Although always courteous, it was clear he was having to spend time fending off a host of demands from government and businesses for payments.

"Looking back, for different reasons, we turned to each other for help. He needed a family member with power of attorney, I needed to understand what was going on.

"Together we forged a plan to restructure the company, bringing in new management and revitalised the business. My father remains as non-executive chairman, but I now run the company. I have given a minor directorship to my brother to keep him out of trouble. We have been able to take on new loans and create an order book for the breakers yard, securing new sales for the recycled metals business. Finally, we have set up a new trading company that is looking to manufacture recycled components for cars and using 3D technologies to produce weapons, including our own microwave gun for the military. It will also look after a range of smaller investments that we have which are not core to our business such as Communi-Kate, a fibre network firm, HeadingtonMeds, the company that has patented the new virus jab, Global Bus – a travel concern, and the Flit Hydrogen microcar amongst others. We will sell these in due course."

"It all sounds very positive, and you seem very organised. I still don't see why you need someone like me."

"I need to get out of all the illegal businesses my father is involved in, in fact, I'm not even sure I know what they all are yet. Everything I have found that doesn't look right I have put into a separate trading company, called Yilan with a separate management structure. I have no idea the status of these. I have used Yilan assets to secure some short-term loans for the main businesses while their order books recover. The mining assets are there as well plus all unidentified cash holdings. My intention is to clean the lot and manage disposals. I need your help in several ways.

"Firstly, our trading division needs new customers especially for armaments like the new laser and microwave weapons that have the potential to be industry leading. These are most likely to be Middle East governments. This was why I was in Dubai. I was seeing one of the region's best-connected arms dealers who could open up that market for me, but he is suspicious and won't deal with me unless he needs to. You could fill his role by acting as my sales agent. Secondly, I want to understand more about my father's illegal trades. I can't work out why he won't talk to me about it. Whether he has forgotten, or just refuses to discuss it, I can't tell. I think there may be a ghost network of criminals he is involved in which I need to get the family out of. The only other person who may know is Mersut Canecale, my father's friend and business associate who, until only last week, had disappeared."

"He came back?"

"Yes – out of the blue he turned up at the *yali* to see my father, who didn't seem surprised. It was like he was expected. I wanted to talk to him, but he left without seeing me. But at the centre of this is the gold trade. I am certain it is being used to launder drug money. I don't know how it is being moved into Turkey or whether some is being stockpiled, but I need to find out. Through your connections, can you help me find him? I think the mystery of the death of my mother and sisters is linked to this in some way."

"I am sure your connections in Turkey are better than mine."

"That is the point, the answers to my problems are outside Turkey. Turhan needs new arms sales, the Terzilis need justice. I need someone with the experience to find solutions to both. Now I know your terms, you had better provide me with your bank details. I am ready to make a down payment in the morning."

There had been a lot to absorb. McKee was starting to realise Ciller Terzili was an unlikely international master criminal, but someone struggling to get control of her own destiny. He was already beginning to understand how the Canecale family, which seemed to be connected to the Terzilis, may know much more about the criminal activities being conducted in Turhan's name. Also, he knew his bosses would be interested to know Mersut Canecale was alive and at least one other significant player in all this – Solokov – was aware of the family's gold trade. Understanding this gold business was probably the key to the whole investigation and must take priority.

And what was that about a microwave weapon? What to do? The entrepreneur in him saw the opportunity to take fees from both the Russian and Ciller for doing the same job and Smith would want to know all about this as well. He needed to accept both commissions. The solution would be to make sure Smith was warned about the arrival of funds in his HMRC arranged cover bank account. No doubt when this matter was settled, whatever he had earned could be credited to reparations for the recovery of criminal earnings. It was moments like this that made him realise he was glad not to have trained as an accountant, especially one working for Six. A report to Smith was his next task, but first he would need to think through his recommendations for the next steps.

Purewal and Wetherall were driving back to their hotel after their first encounter at the Izmir Barbeque. The smell of second-hand kebab was obliging Wetherall to keep the driver's window open.

"Happy with that?" he asked.

"It's a start. I think we can say we've laid the groundwork. I expect Selim will have reported to his masters by now, so we'll see what happens tomorrow. I won't be surprised if we get an audience with his dealer. Whatever we get we can get it analysed, see if we can relate it to any known operators on our database. I want to use the time tomorrow to check out that cab company, Hotcars. Think he knew he'd dropped a bollock over that. Again, there could be an angle for us. You have got those registrations of customers we can pass back to Marshall to run through the PNC and we can find out who owns those terrace houses near the shop. There were people in and out of there all the time we were on station. I just wonder if any of these addresses are accommodating some of the smuggled brothers we would be looking for? I know it's a pain, George, but this lead from GCHQ may be one of the strongest. It's worth us checking this out fully before putting our heads over the parapet. You know as soon as they think they're in trouble the whole show will just shut down."

Despite her Dutch heritage, De Jong had been surprised by how quickly and efficiently her countrymen had planned for the repatriation of the Koenigsegg, to the extent she had poured over the arrangement in such detail to cover off the unpredictable snaggings that may occur. The security team he had hired looked to have been thorough in their preparation and clearly had an eye for detail, but it wasn't going to be cheap. This was a labour-intensive assignment requiring teams of watchers and electronic surveillance. The contractors had signed a confidentiality agreement and had been security checked by Interpol, but that was the matter that De Jong had overlooked. Establishing the necessary clearance had produced an unintended consequence – a notification to the official Dutch state security service. Ordinarily this would not have merited particular attention, hundreds of such requests were notified daily, but this one stood out as it involved 'a person of interest' Bulent Canecale and had come from an unknown British private company – Four Musketeers Research of London. The Dutch authorities had placed an amber notice on this request requiring De Jong's contractors to offer full cooperation whilst keeping them informed of developments.

The communications intercepts had ensured Mwake and De Jong knew when the Koenigsegg was being sent to Boston, so surveillance was routine. Intelligence had suggested that given the value of the cargo no effort would be made to disguise the vehicle other than the removal of its registration plates and engine serial numbers. It was being moved on an HGV low loader, wrapped in a giant tarpaulin. It would be transferred to a container at the port before its sea journey.

As expected, Abel Kotobi was in charge of the operation and had driven ahead of the consignment to ensure its load.

Mwake and De Jong had been following the transporter at a discreet distance up the A1 and onto the A16, heading for the Lincolnshire coast. The senior investigator at the wheel, his partner studying his mobile.

"Are we going to pick Kotobi up once he has made the delivery?" asked De Jong.

"And spoil the party so soon? You forget we are trading in our powers of arrest to take this assignment on. If there's going to be some action like that we have to get Marshall to sort it." The reply seemed to mock the question.

"Anyway with what we've got so far, we've not got enough to go on. We know where he lives, we know what he does and fortunately, because he doesn't know we are on to him, his behaviours are nice and predictable. We must use the opportunity to understand his network better. I want to know as much as possible about who he talks to and what he's talking about, so let's leave it with GCHQ for the moment. For now, a clean set of pictures of the departing merchandise is what we need and then your countrymen on the other side can take matters forward while we go to Sheerness to supervise the return. I am counting on the fact that Canecale will be panicking when the Koenigsegg goes missing and we should then be able to collect all the evidence we need. This is undoubtedly our best chance to plug him into our friends in the Netherlands."

They drove on; low-level music from the radio interspersed by messages from local police contacts picking up and passing on their targets, Kotobi in his black BMW and the vehicle transporter. According to the chatter, Kotobi had now arrived at a warehouse on St John's Road on the approach to the port and had parked outside. Researching the address, the premises was on a short-term lease that could easily be verified and Mwake was pleased to learn the main entrance was wide open, providing the casual observer a clear view of the interior. It was late afternoon, and the investigator didn't want to miss the expected show. Confident about its destination, Mwake now drove ahead of the transporter with around ten miles to go. He had noted the vehicle and its driver were likely to be on a one-trip hire and would not know anything about their cargo, other than where it was delivered.

Evening was approaching. He wanted to see the transfer before it went dark. He need not have worried. Arriving at the warehouse the interior was still wide open and bathed in light from sodium arc lights overhead. Inside were just three men, two in boiler suits he didn't recognise, together with Kotobi engrossed in conversation and oblivious of their arrival. The scene was dominated by another truck facing inwards with a container with open doors and a ramp leading to its interior. On the basis of this evidence, loading was unlikely to take long, and given the likely course of events would not allow for the warehouse doors to be closed.

And Mwake was not disappointed. This operation was well planned. The merchandise arrived. Kotobi met the driver, signed the receipt on a clipboard and the driver removed the protective covers and winched the car on to the kerb. One of the boiler-suited mechanics climbed in and it started first time with his colleague helping him to guide the vehicle to the ramp.

"Well that was easy – thought it would take them longer than that to get it started," muttered De Jong.

"It's simple if you have the right security code and hacking the software on one of those babies is not that difficult if you know what you're doing," her boss replied.

Once in the box, the steering wheel was removed, the protective covers were put back in place and stabilisers attached to ensure damage in transit would be avoided.

"Like their personal approach to security – are they keeping the steering wheel as a souvenir?" De Jong observed, as she took pictures of the proceedings.

The irony wasn't lost on Mwake.

"Looks like they've learned from experience. A car without a steering wheel is just a collection of parts and won't attract customs interest at the other end. Whoever receives the container can just re-attach it to the steering column. For a mechanic who knows what he is doing, it's no big deal."

Kotobi climbed in the container, presumably just to check the fittings were secure and then jumped out gesticulating to his assistants to seal it for the journey to come.

As if playing to the gallery, he reached into his coat pocket and pulled out a thick roll of banknotes and passed it over to the boiler-suited pair. All the action had been caught on film.

Then things started not to run to script. The truck with the container reversed out and headed towards the port gates. Mwake had expected Kotobi to wait but he returned to his car and drove away, heading back to town and the main road. The other boiler suit switched off the lights and locked up the warehouse.

"Are we following the merchandise or the man?" De Jong asked.

"Always the man. There is only one sailing out to Vlissingen tonight, only one ship capable of taking it in the dock anyway, so we don't need to worry about that. I think we should know where Kotobi is going in such a hurry."

THIRTEEN

MCKEE HAD TOLD TERZILI he would act on her behalf in Dubai, but first would assist in straightening out her father's business affairs, if only to be sure he could operate with credibility as an agent on Turhan's behalf.

Given his encounters with Solokov and Terzili, the only matter that seemed clear was that the route to solving the case lay in understanding what was taking place in Uzbekistan.

Oddly for an asset the Terzilis claimed to own, their management of the mine appeared to be arm's length. They had employed a local – one Ammar Jalolov – to take care of day-to-day matters. Ciller herself had not visited and she seemed not to know whether her father had ever undertaken an inspection, but apparently Repcer, their attorney, had sorted out the deal and managed communications with Jalolov.

There would be a time to talk with Repcer but there were still critical gaps in his knowledge which needed to be filled in the meantime.

Considering it was a corporate acquisition, McKee had been surprised the Terzilis had not invested further in the operation, especially as it was producing a significant return. Was this because of the disputed sale from Solokov? Did Ciller Terzili understand her father's dealings in the matter? What role (if any) did Canecale have in the business? Although it was likely Canecale was still in Turkey or nearby, running a trace on his whereabouts would take time he didn't have and, even if he was successful, could be a wasted effort. From what Ciller had said, McKee had the impression Canecale was not so much a formal partner, but a sort of fixer to be called in as required – employed to implement instructions, not think through strategy. When Ciller had explained how Turhan was being run, she had not mentioned him at all. The matter of Canecale would wait for another day.

Ciller had responded to McKee's request to put him in touch with Jalolov which had required her to brief Repcer. She had used the fact that she was planning to have McKee run a Turhan office in Dubai that would oversee its operations across Asia. McKee wanted to visit the Uzbek mine as part of his diligence preparations. Repcer had agreed and provided the contact.

Jalolov would meet McKee at his hotel in Tashkent in 48 hours, at the end of his first day in the Uzbek capital.

Dressed in jeans, brown check shirt and a sports jacket, the grey-haired Jalolov looked to be in his late 40s. He had deep-set brown eyes with several bags below which were testament to either a lack of sleep or stress.

"Mr Mac from Turhan in Istanbul?"

His opening gambit seemed like he was attaching a title to the face in his mind, rather than a greeting. His expression wasn't giving much away.

"Repcer asked me to look after you while you are here. I am at your service."

"Good – do you know a place outside where we can get a beer?"

"There is a café in a park downtown about ten minutes' walk – you can get a hot dog as well if you like."

They started to walk and talk as they left the hotel, passing by the impressive façade of the Navoi Theatre and turned left on Zarafshan.

"I understand you want to know more about our mining operations, Mr Mac." Jalolov stared at the ground as he walked, avoiding the uneven paving stones and treacherous open drainage ditches at the side of the road.

"Yes, I'd like to have a look around and find out about how the business works."

"I am not sure what you know about my country, but don't be fooled by the attractions of Tashkent. The mines are far from here, about a six-hour drive into the Kyzylkum desert. If you want to see the facility you will need at least three days. If you haven't got the time, I will try to answer any questions you may have."

"I think we should do both. I am assuming you are staying in Tashkent tonight, so we can drive out tomorrow."

The Uzbek nodded, looking nervously to his right as they walked by the police intelligence building and on towards the Amir Temur Square.

McKee couldn't be sure about Jalolov, but so far he had given the impression of being reserved and, despite his good English, uncomfortable about dealing with a foreigner. Perhaps it was because he was being asked to collaborate with a stranger who, although sent by Turhan, was not Turkish and he could not know his agenda.

Their destination turned out to be a café in a small park in Sayilgoh Street, where they took a table under a cypress tree. An almost imperceptible nod from his host resulted in a couple of cold Sarbast beers arriving within a minute. He signalled for his guest to take a bottle and clinked his against it as a greeting.

Normally in such a situation the host would start a conversation, yet here he said nothing, leaving it to McKee to break their silence and open the conversation.

"It's a nice spot here – thank you for bringing me. When I arrived this morning and started to look around I didn't walk in this direction."

"We have little parks all over the city. If you want to see how people here live, they are the best places – families, children, lovers, skateboarders and the rest all come out at this time."

He pointed. "That's why over there some come to have an informal market selling trinkets, pictures that sort of thing. It gets people out of the high-rise apartments most live in on the edge of town. You may have seen some examples on the way in from the airport. Unfortunately this place is still haunted by the ghosts of the Soviet era."

"You think many Uzbek people miss it?"

"A few. Many are starting to wonder what all this talk about freedom was after independence. You have to remember, one of the crowning glories of the old Soviet Union was that most had plentiful cheap food and a roof of sorts over their heads. Modern life means we may have the freedom to make and keep our money, but many others have lost out. We were never rich but in those days you never used to see homeless people or have begging on the street."

"You live nearby?"

"I have an apartment on the other side of town. It's small but comfortable – warm in the winter. Nice to come back to when I get my alternate weekends off."

"And the rest of the time?"

"At the mine, life is a bit more basic. I have my own room, but the majority of workers share a dormitory and canteen with a TV and video recorder. Mobiles work fine here but out there..." He shook his head.

"How long have you worked at the mine?"

"Around thirty years. I started as a trainee at the state mining school before being allocated to a job. I slowly worked my way up through the state structure during Soviet times, then the mine was taken over by the Solokov family who brought some people out here from Moscow; but they pulled out when we exhausted the iron seam and faced closure. Solokov did some sort of deal with

Turhan and here we are. As the senior member of staff on site, I'm still around as I'm part of the fixtures and fittings."

"Why would Turhan buy a clapped-out iron ore mine?"

"Solokov did what all the new breed of Russian businessmen did – he got it and many others for nothing, fattened the asset and then started bullshitting about its prospects to anybody who would listen. Outside Russia, Turkey has always seen itself as a power here and links with Turkish business are good. I guess he thought Turhan were just the most gullible, although I had heard a rumour Solokov had some long-standing money racket running with them and basically giving them the mine was a way of writing off a debt, but who knows?"

"Is your family living at the mine?"

The Uzbek snorted.

"You can't know much about life out there. It's no place for a wife and kids. Life is tough and we're constantly battling the elements – sun, heat and dust, blizzards in the winter. The guys are all given a weekend off each month so they can go someplace else to relieve the tension. You understand?"

"Yeah I get it. What time will we leave in the morning?"

"I will collect you from your hotel at nine-thirty. I will have loaded my pickup with extra provisions, but make sure you eat a good breakfast. We will break the journey at Nurata which is the closest settlement before we head out to the facility. Do you need me to escort you back to the hotel?"

"No, I'm fine. Don't worry about me. If you need to get away to prepare, I will understand." McKee had noted his host's discomfort.

Jalolov immediately stood, nodded his farewell with a fleeting smile and walked off in the direction of the Timur metro station.

McKee pulled a wad of local bank notes out of his pocket to work out how much he owed for the beers.

In a strange way, McKee was enthralled about the prospect of taking a trip into the desert, but this was no tour by camel train over rolling dunes of the type found in the Sahara. The journey out of Tashkent to Samarkand and on to Navoiy was on a standard tarmacked road you would find anywhere and, owing to the limited number of routes out of the capital, drivers could only proceed at a leisurely pace due to the congestion. To McKee's eye, there seemed to be more people on the road than he had so far encountered in the city. Perhaps this was because there appeared to be few junctions or intersections for travellers to turn off for those headed out of town. He had started to take a passing interest in the diversity of his fellow travellers as the scenery of undulating hills started to become more barren, flat and featureless, save for the sporadic clumps of bluegrass and thorn bushes in the endless expanse of sandy loam which appeared to bleed to the horizon. Unintelligible music with a rap meter blared from the radio.

Although it was mid-September, the heat of the day was establishing itself in the cab of the pickup. He had the window open and had been pleased to take Jalolov's advice to wear a protective scarf to complement his sunglasses to guard against the hot wind, sun, sand, and fumes. For him, as a result, conversation was difficult, but Jalolov seemed immune to the discomforts of the road and the rising temperature and was becoming more animated than he had been the previous evening.

"If you were travelling this road four months ago you would have seen a panorama of wild poppies in this empty scrub, like a red carpet," he raised his voice above the din.

"Somehow they manage to grow. I have never understood how. There is not much rain here, but they seem to get moisture from the air and perhaps deep underground in places. This area suffers from heavy fog in the spring which is not the result of industry or other man-made factors. The poppies attract bees who pass through heading for the cotton fields in the east, and people come out of the villages to tend hives and collect honey before the summer heat strikes and the flowers wither away; but now the summer is passing and the winds are rising, creating sandstorms and soon the temperatures will fall below zero. This is an unforgiving land."

"Does anyone live here?"

"Nomads pass through when the seasons change, when they do, you get to see their colourful yurts which lift the empty brown and beige landscape. Generally, it is too hot or too cold for people to live here all year round. Anyone tough enough to stay here is in Navoiy or Nurata as these are the only settlements with regular access to water, power and communications. Navoiy is a vibrant trading centre because it is on this road that runs to Turkmenistan and services the travellers on this route. Ceramics are what the town is known for. It is also one of the few intersections before the frontier and as you will see, the road becomes smaller and rougher as we turn north. It's not the sort of place you want to drive an expensive saloon car around.

"Nurata, where we are headed, is the nearest habitation to the mine, but still a ninety-minute drive away. It owes its existence to a local *wadi* called Chashma, the only source of naturally occurring fresh water in these parts. It is a historical anomaly and dates from before the time of Christ. Archaeologists have found the remains of fortifications built by Alexander the Great nearby. The Romans were the first to use the waters to irrigate the immediate surroundings by laying a local network of underground pipes and in those days, the ground was fertile as a result. Today most of the houses here rely to some extent on this network, but the flow isn't strong enough to support their further development."

Since leaving the main highway heading for Nurata, McKee started to feel the sense of solitude which no amount of conversation or radio output could mask. They had stopped for a pee and some green tea the driver produced from a flask. With the engine off and no other vehicles around, the silence was deafening. Resuming their journey, McKee gazed at the monotonous steppe only occasionally demonstrating motion by the varying thickness of thorny bushes and gnarly saxaul at the side of their track or the sight of a bleached ox skull illuminated against the grey ochre of the stony ground. A look in the wing mirror showed a cloud of dust seemingly chasing the pickup as if to convince the driver there was nothing behind worth turning back for. No sign of life here, no birds or animals, no cars, houses or signs of cultivation.

Just a void, an area of leftovers following the creation of the world.

And then, without warning, out of the timeless desolation a collection of about 30 single-storey, whitewashed buildings arranged in a haphazard way, defying the viewer the possibility of seeing an organised road structure.

"Nurata." Jalolov pointed.

McKee's surprise was that, although small, these houses appeared to be well maintained, some with patches of green grass next to them.

Almost as casual as the siting of buildings were signs of community life – a general store, three trucks and as many four-by-fours and people, women hanging out washing, children playing football.

Jalolov noted his guest's surprise.

"Uzbekistan is a land of contradictions. When I described Nurata as remote, I didn't say it was poor. The folk who live here are hardy and live with purpose."

"How do people earn a living?"

"Quite a few are our people, travelling out to the mine either in excavation, smelting or logistics, some others work for the military who have a training base about thirty kilometres east of here. But given where we are in the desert, Nurata is the supply centre for the region. It's where we get our trucks refuelled and serviced, where we can stop for a beer and a meal and stay in a clean room with a bed. It's got a small school, pharmacy and a cinema. If you ever come here again it's worth exploring, the locals are very welcoming and there is a good local bakery."

Despite having sold the virtues of the town and its heritage, Jalolov showed no signs of slowing on their onward journey.

"Not far now," he smiled.

It was with a sense of relief when they arrived at the Nurata mine an hour later. Given the pressures of the journey he understood why Ciller had not made the trip. There had been no warning of their imminent arrival. After what had seemed like an age, the pick-up negotiated a shallow ridge and straight ahead was a fenced complex with two large five-floored buildings and a vast corrugated warehouse with two tall chimney stacks, one at each end. It didn't help that the buildings seemed camouflaged, built from breeze blocks that had assumed the colour of their surroundings, showing evidence of being pummelled by the elements.

As they passed through the main entrance gatehouse, McKee noticed two poles with the flags of Uzbekistan and Turhan stretched in the wind. The security guard recognised his boss and waved him through the checkpoint.

"This is our administrative base which contains accommodation blocks, security, medical centre, gymnasium and canteen for the workers. Next to that is our garage where we service our dumpers and commercial transporters. Over there on the far side is our smelting plant, hence the chimneys and next to that is our firefighting equipment. At the other side, as far away as we can manage is our ordnance section where we store our explosives and detonators. As you can tell, working out here, we have to be self-sufficient. I am sure you are tired. I will have the housekeeper show you to your quarters and explain about meal arrangements. I hope you will excuse me, but I have to review the day's production figures. I will collect you at nine-thirty in the morning, give you the tour of the site and deliver you back to Tashkent."

Jalolov's demeanour had softened a little on the journey, but it was clear he was still cautious about McKee and why Turhan had sent him.

FOURTEEN

MCKEE HAD WOKEN WITH a start to the low rumble and momentary shaking delivered by the early morning explosions at the mine. With few distractions and an intermittent mobile signal, he would not be late for breakfast and his third encounter with Jalolov. McKee had noted, apart from the housekeeper, his host made no effort to introduce other members of his management team as he might have expected. Not that the Uzbek was being unhelpful or unhospitable. He either lacked social skills (understandable based on the environment and the responsibilities of the job) or wanted to ensure as little was known about McKee as possible and avoid subsequent questions from colleagues about the purpose of the visit. Perhaps some of them had contacts of their own in the outside world. Jalolov had decided he would do no more or less than Repcer had asked and relieve himself of this additional burden at the earliest opportunity. This day, Jalolov arrived in a reefer jacket and hard hat, and had spares in the cab for his guest.

"Please put them on. Site rules. No exceptions, even though you will not leave the vehicle during the tour."

He noted the surprise on McKee's face.

"I am going to take you to the best surface level vantage points. It would take too long to get you down to the operational interfaces.

The air is shitty with dust and all you will see is excavators loading dump trucks for the journey up here. You can see all of that from up here with binoculars anyway."

"Our workings are either side of us. Iron ore to the right, quartz to the left. These are vast terraced open cast pits presently thirty-five levels down from the surface with a diameter of three kilometres wide. It can take a truck two hours to get down to the rock face. Normally we set explosives once a day at four and five in the morning which gives time for the boulders and dust to clear before the safety trucks and excavators move in from eight and nine respectively. Iron ore deposits are loaded straight into transporters to a low security crushing plant the other side of the pit. This is stored outside the base until our customers place their orders. We then take it to Jizzakh on our private route north through the steppe for processing.

"Transporting of gold-bearing quartz rock continues to sunset when loads are brought to the crushing shed before being taken by conveyor to the smelting facility. During the first stage of the smelting we add the coagulant that extracts the gold from the rock in the form of a course powder, 'gold dust', which we then reheat for moulding, either as ingots or in the case of Turhan, machine parts or components."

"A big job for your security people."

"Yes and no. Nobody works here by chance – all have specialist training and that includes security. Of course, the most secure area is over at the bond warehouse where our product is stored for trans-shipment. But do remember, this mine is so out of the way no one comes here unannounced, and no one is able to leave without our assistance. Moving the product off site is a major undertaking. We are a working community here. We have all the resources we need to deal with an incident or even a theft, but we try to keep it low key, especially as we have the military as neighbours if we need them."

"The changes of ownership at the mine must have been worrying for local people," McKee observed.

"Not really, there wasn't much change until Solokov decided to sell out. Once he took over, production volumes declined anyway. He'd sent a couple of geologists here from Moscow who ordered us to start excavating in a new area. It was a waste of time, money and energy. We knew that, but the bosses wouldn't listen. It was that failure which led to the sale to Turhan. They took a different approach and listened to us. We told them that although iron ore was declining there was still enough to be viable for our domestic customers we thought for five years. Repcer came and agreed to back us but required a twenty per cent reduction in operating costs. We reduced smelting operations by ten days a month and cut our staff. Some people who had come to Nurata left and moved away and we had to think about our own futures which are dependent on keeping the mine open. That was when we had an idea to start prospecting for gold, copper and other metals that are often found near iron ore seams."

"And you got lucky?"

"Given the amount we discovered – yes we did, but we were always confident that there was some there."

"So, Turhan now owns a gold mine?"

"It's not as simple as that. Technically Turhan retains ownership of the iron ore mining deposits. Under Uzbek law, all gold mines are state assets and cannot be owned by the private sector or foreign owners. We have had to register our gold excavations as a separate mine, whilst in a neighbouring cut we continue iron ore extractions on behalf of Turhan."

"Seems a complicated arrangement."

"Yes it takes some managing. Turhan subsidises iron ore production in exchange for one third of our gold-carrying quartz aggregates. The other two thirds gets smelted into ingots and collected by the military for registration, stamping and storage at the national treasury. I have a monthly quota to meet. Unstamped ingots are flown to Tashkent for the local military airbase. Internationally, the gold has no market value without the registration and stamping process, so there is little risk. Our government record our production reports that only show the volumes of quartz mined for them, therefore they don't know about the Turhan arrangement, so they pay us for what we produce when they receive it."

"And Turhan's cut?"

"Normally it is formed into casings for machine tools. These are flown out to Istanbul as machine parts. As components they are not checked by customs here so there are no problems.

"The arrangement keeps everyone happy especially all who live and work at the mine. Our wages have risen. We can live better and have the ability to save for our old age as we control the production ourselves."

"Where does it go?"

Jalolov smiled. "I would have thought Repcer would have told you. Turhan use an agent, a middleman called Canecale. I've never met him, just get told to ensure the consignments are sent to him. Probably some tax dodge – I don't know. Anyway I assume this is part of the arrangement you have been sent to make."

McKee knew he had been invited to comment but countered with another question.

"What does Solokov know about this?"

"He sent some investigators out here a few months back to check out the gold story and wanted to know how we were still managing to produce iron ore. They wanted to see our production records. I may not have told you, but I am also in charge of security here. I had them thrown out."

"Presumably he will know you are now producing gold?"

"Yes, but not the quantity and if he wants to get his hands on it he has to deal with our government. I am sure they would sell if he was in the market, but our advantage is we control production and report the records as necessary. We can create fluctuations or anomalies in output when it suits us, so unless he could intercept one of our deliveries to Istanbul which are sent anonymously via a shipping agent he will have nothing to go on."

"How does Turhan know it is getting its fair share?"

"They don't, but we have some trust. I regard it as a cross subsidy. They make regular cash deposits into the mine holding company that I run, and they have a minority holding. We send them gold roughly equivalent to the prevailing market value of their financial deposits."

"Who runs this for Turhan?"

"Normally Repcer, but recently he has taken more of a backseat, and has introduced a new contact who is coming over soon, this Mrs Yasmin Ali. But if I have a problem or am unhappy about something, I go to Repcer."

The afternoon journey back to Tashkent seemed shorter even though Jalolov took the same route.

What conversation McKee had in the pickup changed to a subtle interrogation from his host.

"So, big changes are happening at Turhan, I understand," Jalolov opened.

"You know how it is, business is always responding to changing circumstances."

"Repcer says Turhan is being restructured…"

"That may be true, but I am an adviser to the company so have only a limited understanding of what's going on."

"What are you advising on?"

"Sales and marketing mainly. Investigating new markets, opportunities, customers – you know how it is. I have to say I am impressed about how you have gone about re-inventing the mine. You seem to have gone from being a contractor to a major supplier."

"Thank you for making the observation. I think we have a little more influence than before. I have to say I like working with Turhan – the business relationship is simple and straightforward. Solokov might have done better if he had bothered to establish a relationship with us rather than sending some of his goons to order us around."

"Do you think he will come back to cause trouble?"

"Probably, but I'm not sure what he will achieve. His only way back into the game here for him is to repurchase the asset he sold to Turhan, and based on how well we are working, I can't see that happening."

Back at his hotel preparing for his return to Istanbul, McKee reflected on what he had seen and heard during his visit. Now he had some firm leads to take the investigation forward. He would update Smith before discussing his findings with Ciller Terzili.

It was the following evening when he made it back to the *yali* south of the Bosporus. Dinner was preceded by a shared visit to the property's *hammam* in the basement. It had seemed strange to McKee considering how long he'd been in Istanbul he had not had time for a Turkish bath, but Ciller had recognised his need and came with him to administer the aromatic cleansing oils. Alone, there seemed little need for renewed formality, and she slipped out of her dress and into a towelling robe to join him in the steam.

As he relaxed, he recounted the news of his whistle-stop visit to Uzbekistan and what he learned about the gold mine and the connections to Turhan. As she massaged his shoulders, he observed: "I'm really hoping you're not wasting my time, Ciller; you must have known about the regular payments being made to subsidise the iron ore mine."

"Yes, as a company asset I knew we were investing in it, but I left the details to Repcer, who has been an authorised signatory. He presents me with a schedule of payments from time to time and I just sign them."

"Do you know what your money buys?"

"Not really. I assume it is to keep the mine solvent and subsidise the commodity price?"

"In part maybe, but a lot of it pays for unregistered 22 carat gold, sent to Canecale here in Istanbul. So what is he doing with it? If you don't know. It's time you did, if you don't know where he is or what he is doing I'd talk to your father or Repcer. It's clear there is something going on that you should know about."

"What else?"

"Solokov knows about the gold and thinks that your father cheated him out of a share. He wants to get the mine back or failing that take over Turhan. He's had investigators working on it in Uzbekistan."

"And the deaths of my family members?"

"He knows about it certainly, but there doesn't appear to be any direct evidence about his involvement. He seems pissed off about some dealings he had with your father and thinks he's been disrespected but doesn't seem to know about your restructuring. I think I should keep in touch with him and see if I can find out some more."

It had been a long day – a tiring few days in fact. Time to forget business if only for a short while. The effect of the steam and incense, together with the prospect of dinner and another night of lovemaking with his host made him reflect the travails of the day had produced their unique reward.

It wasn't until they got the far side of Grantham that Mwake guessed where Kotobi was headed. He called ahead to Wetherall with the vehicle's details and asked him to take up the surveillance from the superstore at the junction of Melton Road with the Leicester ring road.

Once he had passed on the tracking responsibility he continued heading south to the office and then on to Sheerness. Wetherall followed the black BMW conveniently to the Izmir Barbeque on Oadby Road. Anticipating the contact, Purewal had split up earlier in the evening. She was already stationed near the kebab shop ready to document the arrival of Kotobi. It was relatively early, just before ten when he turned up and business was quiet. The scene didn't look good. Kotobi had parked relatively close to the shop and his body language looked like he was preparing for trouble. As he walked in, he flipped the 'open' sign to 'closed' and dropped the lock on the door. It was clear that Selim recognised Kotobi, and three other workers then emerged from the back. Their conversation was animated and concluded with Kotobi leaning across the counter and grabbing Selim by the scruff of the neck. Under normal circumstances the others present might have been expected to have intervened to help their boss, but even at a distance they looked petrified and frozen to the spot. Having made his point, Kotobi released Selim who nodded to the others who in turn seemed to busy themselves preparing a takeaway. Kotobi reached into his pocket, produced an envelope and planted it firmly into Selim's hand, his animated dialogue continuing, as Purewal continued to record proceedings.

Wetherall had been watching as well a little further down the street and called Purewal.

"You got all that? It's not often these guys make it easy for us to observe their business. I guess they are confident about their prospects."

"We'll see what response we get when we go knocking at closing time," she responded.

Because Wetherall knew he had now got evidence of a connection with the Izmir Barbeque, he hadn't bothered to follow Kotobi when he left Oadby Road and stayed put. He really hadn't been interested about where his target was going and had assumed he would be returning to London. It was his first mistake. Had he stayed with him, he would have noted he was using his time well, checking up on other neighbouring branches. With half an hour to go before closing, Wetherall was alarmed to note the return of the BMW. Ironically it had parked three cars behind him, that being the closest spot available to the shop given the increasing flow of late-night customers. Wetherall called Purewal further down the street to look out for Kotobi again, but although he had left his car he walked to a nearby terraced house. He hadn't announced his presence by ringing a doorbell and entered quietly suggesting he already had a key. Again, he reported it to Purewal: "Make a note, we need to run a check on the owner of number 34."

"OK. The taxis have gone. Looks like they're cleaning up for the night. Think it's time to pay Selim a visit…"

"Negative. If Kotobi is still around it could be dangerous."

"What's there to worry about? I'm a customer. I'm sure he won't complain if I'm buying."

"It's too risky."

"This is what we're here to do. Keep an eye out and let's see what happens…"

It was ten minutes before closing.

Before Wetherall could respond, Purewal finished the call and climbed out of the car heading for the kebab shop.

"Hello Selim – remember me? I've come for my gear."

She could see Selim was in two minds – whether to blank her request or comply. He still had her fifty pound note in the pocket of his overalls. He chose not to speak but went to the backroom. Kotobi came out.

"I am told you are interested in some merch," he began.

"If you want stuff, don't deal with Selim – his business is strictly kebabs. For people I approve of he has my authority to be a post box. You know – give him money one day and collect from him the next. Like what you tried to do last night. But that had one problem. I don't know who you are or whether your credit is good. Know what I mean? So who are ya babe? I know your name coz you write on the banknote. Just coz you do that doesn't mean you get them back, you know?"

"No. I just want a good service – I have a lot of friends who need looking after too."

Kotobi laughed and came round the counter, putting Purewal in an arm lock.

"Now I'm getting confused darlin' – are you a would-be

customer or a competitor looking to set up deals on my patch? If it's a service you're lookin' for, I'll take you round the back and we can get to know each other."

"No need for that, friend," Wetherall came into the shop behind Kotobi and put the barrel of a pistol in his back.

"Let go of the lady and she will search your pockets. Understand you might be feeling frisky but don't read anything into it – she just wants the gear, any cash, weapons, your mobile and the car keys. The lot. Thank you. Now, if you're half the people I think you are, I don't think you'll be calling the police about this, so let's just all go home quietly. And you, big man, can tell your boss that you met 'Joe' from the Screamers. You can also tell him I know other places you go dealing and may decide to have a nibble at your business… they do say that competition, makes the service better. OK, got what we need?"

Purewal nodded and left the shop.

"So all of you, down on the floor, face first. Chill out. Some people round here are trying to get some sleep. By the way I'd give it a few minutes before you move, anyone who tries to follow will get a bullet."

Her car pulled up outside. It was time to go.

FIFTEEN

THE TRAMP SHIP DOCKED in Vlissingen just before ten the following morning, convenient for allowing Mwake and De Jong to check on the live feed supplied by their colleagues in the Netherlands. The collection was made as expected, the container transferred onto a low loader and away towards the Belgian frontier, with a brief stop at a warehouse nearby at Sluiskil for a personal inspection by Bulent Canecale and the reattachment of the steering wheel before the trip south.

As arranged, the interception was made at the forest near Onnaing over the French border, with the merchandise transferred to a fresh container and rerouted north to Dunkirk, the hapless driver tied up and deposited in the back of the old container, the truck left at the side of the road, conspicuous with its hazard warning lights on. So far so good. De Jong had received copy of the consignment dockets online to facilitate the collection in Sheerness. Mwake was confident the local police would not need alerting as Canecale would investigate the reason for the transporter being stationary in due course.

The Dutch team had been meticulous in their preparation and left no unexpected traces as they left the scene. The hijacked cargo had been scheduled to leave within two hours of its arrival at the French coast, the timing fitting neatly with Canecale's arrival in the Raismais forest. The occasion provided some light relief for the two investigators – not only was the stolen item being returned to them with the added bonus of forensic evidence attached, but with Marshall's help, they were able to intercept the subsequent phone call between Canecale and Kotobi. The call from Canecale had been as unexpected as it was unwelcome to Kotobi, following his embarrassment at the Izmir Barbeque in Oadby Road.

"Abe – it's Bulent – you Leerys have fucked up big time bro, the merch has been nicked."

"What?"

"You heard. The transporter was hijacked in France. Somebody was waiting for it, and it was a pro job, the driver didn't have time to call and reckons there was about a dozen of them armed and dressed in black."

"Why did he stop?"

"There were barriers and flashing lights – he thought it was a random police check. I've got my people looking into this, but understand, I will find out who knew about the consignment, and I will come after them. Know what I mean? If I don't get the cargo back, you don't get paid and I'll send all my gear to the Screamers and if I find you've been talking or trying to double cross me you'll be a dead man walking…"

"Maybe it was the driver…"

"Fuck off man, he was just an agency guy hired to do the driving. I personally resealed the container before sending it on its way. He could have no idea what he was carrying. No – something must have happened your end. Whatever it was I will find out and when I do you can be sure we will be meeting…"

Listening to the short exchange, De Jong was puzzled.

"Bloody hell, I didn't realise they were supplying the Leerys with drugs as well. That's huge and it probably means Canecale is helping to move illegal immigrants as well as supplying the

Screamers. Now Kotobi will be feeling the heat and thanks to Wetherall I guess we are going to see a turf war."

Mwake frowned. "Maybe not. If Canecale is supplying them both he will want to achieve something more than punishment. He'll want greater control. If people smuggling is involved as well, it's safe to assume he's paying the Leerys and Screamers to move them on round the country once he has put them on the beaches. I would think he's been paying them in drugs, so it's triple jeopardy for Kotobi – not just losing a big fee for the motor, but a steady supply of gear and the prospect of losing his customers to a rival as a result. It looks like Marshall's tactics to get some traction on this investigation are working – we have got more evidence linking the cars and drugs to the Izmir Barbeques in the past couple of weeks than we've been able to get in months."

"What happens now?"

"We watch and wait. Let Kotobi and Canecale make the next moves – whatever they do will increase the body of evidence. Purewal and Wetherall will be reviewing other Izmir shops to see if they are involved. That might force Kotobi's hand. We'd better keep an eye on Celik Abou so we can follow any reaction from the Screamers. I will ask Marshall to give us a contact in the Border Force. The big challenge will be to make a link from Canecale to people smuggling."

"What about Canecale himself?"

"I understand he is outside our jurisdiction, but apparently Marshall has a separate intelligence source active on that."

At that moment, Marshall was indeed taking stock of the situation at his Canary Wharf office as he briefed his project team colleagues.

"I am pleased to report that we have made progress following the outsourcing of the investigative team. Firstly we have established a link between a London based crime syndicate specialising in bespoke vehicle theft and drug smuggling, and a Dutch-based travel company where a Turhan International director has a minority shareholding. Further, the London-based syndicate is supplying a number of Izmir Barbeque premises with drugs. We are still investigating the scale of this network, but it looks like it is significant.

"We also know this Dutch company has a similar arrangement with a rival London crime group which we think they want to integrate into a single network. We don't know how the syndicates are paying for their supplies, but it seems to be a barter arrangement, whereby drugs to the value of the price of the vehicle are supplied, but we don't know for sure yet. There is an assumption that the drugs are being delivered along with consignments of illegal immigrants coming across the Channel but that is something we are going to be looking at.

"At the moment the two connections to the Terzilis comes from the aforementioned Dutch company and the Izmir Barbeque chain, but I think there is more to come. Oliver…"

Watson picked up the story.

"Thank you – HMRC is concentrating on two issues for now. These are the trading structures for Turhan International and Global Bus. Turhan owns a number of prestigious properties, mainly in Belgravia which is benefitting from substantial rental income from sources that appear not to relate to known tenancy agreements. This is odd because this money appears in the UK subsidiary accounts as rental income. If we can show this income comes from other sources, we are well on our way to securing an Unexplained Wealth Order against Ciller Terzili – the key focus of our work, but Global Bus, another business with a minority Turhan shareholding is also attracting our attention owing to the inflated running/maintenance costs of this business. As of now, we have not yet identified any illegal activity, but we still have some work to do to understand the connections."

"The support from GCHQ on the comms intercepts has been excellent so far. Anything you want to add, Jane?"

"As you were saying we are monitoring communications from

Bulent Canecale that link him to the cars and drugs but have not yet got evidence of how he works with Turhan, but it is only a matter of time…"

"And how is your man in Istanbul getting on, John?"

Smith was more downbeat.

"I must admit I am getting more concerned about this case as it progresses. He seems to be uncovering a line of activity that is bigger than this investigation originally envisaged, and we will have to decide how to manage this case as it progresses further. In essence, we have established Turhan is a sophisticated business with a mix of legal and illegal activities. It appears the new management of the company led by Ciller Terzili, may not be aware or in control of everything being done in its name, but there is a new entity, a 'company within a company' called Yilan which seems to be syphoning money out of Turhan, Yilan doesn't appear to hold any assets in the UK.

"Ciller Terzili seems to be calling the shots with this as well, but the admin is being handled by an out-of-town accountant called Yasmin Ali who we know nothing about. The most important result so far is the confirmation the company is involved in the commercial smuggling of gold mined in Uzbekistan and has somehow got access to unconventional military technology that it is seeking to sell. Clearly, there is much more to come on what's involved. Now we have an operative embedded over there, we have decided to extend his commission until further notice. I will, of course, keep you informed of developments."

Marshall summarised the position.

"OK, you will all be pleased to know that we have recovered one of the stolen cars exported to order by the Dutch company and it has provided a good track of evidence to support the prosecution case. It seems Bulent Canecale is a key player and will be the focus of my attention in the coming weeks."

"An Italian of Turkish extraction running a business in the Netherlands? What do we know about Canecale?" Watson could always be relied upon to expose the weakness of their position.

Marshall was on the backfoot.

"Not that much. His company in Rotterdam is called Pionier, located in Kruisstraat near the railway station and is listed as a travel and logistics consultancy. Looks tidy at first sight taxes and rents up to date, if anything it's a bit nondescript. Apart from Vahid representing the Turhan interest, the only other director listed is one 'M. Ibrahim' who is marked as 'overseas'. Canecale is a minority shareholder, along with Ciller Terzili in Global Bus, and he is the youngest son of Mersut Canecale, a long-time friend and business associate of Kerim Terzili. Our ambition must be to unravel these relationships and understand the implications. No doubt your man will help us fill in the blanks, John…"

Smith nodded his acknowledgement of his colleague's public 'nudge' and would send Matheson instructions within the hour.

McKee's relationship with Ciller Terzili seemed to be going from strength to strength. Despite his absence in Uzbekistan, his return to the family's villa in Istanbul was starting to have a regular feel about it. He seemed to have achieved a rite of passage. Sleeping with his host had become a given and talk of his departure had faded from their dialogue. He had formed the impression Ciller was heading an enterprise made up of people she was either getting to know or didn't trust. She confided in him precisely because he appeared to be an outsider with no obligations to anyone in her circle. Why had she freely engaged in a sexual relationship with him? Was that her way of exercising control to keep him coming back or because it was a more reliable incentive than money?

Although he had informed London of his impression that she may not be in control of her situation in the way that the scant documentary evidence presently available to his masters suggested, it had produced a predictable response. If the story of Ciller Terzili was wrong he had better get a new credible narrative in place.

With this in mind, he knew he needed some space and time.

At breakfast on the terrace of the *yali* the next morning, McKee announced his departure.

"Ciller, I have been thinking hard about what we discussed about your situation especially during my time in Uzbekistan. It seems to me you need to know more about some of the people you are working with and perhaps review those activities you have undertaking on the basis of personal advice. I am sure I can help you, but I can't find all the answers you are seeking. You must start with your father, find out about his relationship with Canecale. And then there is the group's weapons sales. What are you selling? Who is buying? And what is this microwave gun thing all about? I asked a couple of my business associates about this, and it seems nothing of that sort is out on the market right now, so you could have a real game changer on your hands. Most of my clients like tech weapons and it seems to me if you want to sell conventional stuff in volumes having a credible hi-tech story will be part of that."

"Where are you going?"

"Unfortunately, I've got a couple of urgent pieces of business to do in London and Dubai that will take me out of Turkey for the next ten days or so, but if you find anything out call me."

"Are you going to see Solokov again?"

"I think it is quite likely but not in the immediate future. I need to work on a pitch for him first."

She leaned across the dining table and put her hand on his. He became aware once more of her sweet scent and absorbed her beauty as her deep brown eyes connected with his.

She said softly: "I don't want you to go. I like having you around. Stay here. I can't think of any commercial activity that you may be involved in that you can't run from here. Even better if you are able to do it as part of Turhan International."

"It's too soon for us to think about that right now. Remember you were interested in hiring me to be your agent in Dubai? How can I do that from Istanbul?"

She withdrew her hand and sighed.

"Now you have had me and heard my story, are you sure you are going to come back?"

"Of course and perhaps sooner than you might think. We have money to make…"

"And…?"

"Maybe more – we will have to see what the future brings."

McKee was gambling that the potential of a longer lasting affair might be her motivation for finding out more of the privileged family saga he needed to understand.

She nodded with what he took to be a sense of resignation.

"I will have Osman run you to the airport."

Mwake had picked his moment well, spotting Marshall at the bar in the Lincoln Lounge next to King's Cross station.

"Make mine a pint while you're there," he called as he approached. His former boss nodded to the server, who in the absence to the contrary went to the nearest tap.

"Missing me already?" Mwake said with a chuckle.

"You're doing well my friend. Makes me realise I should have got rid of you a long time ago. How are you enjoying civvy street?"

"It has its moments. You know how things are. I get to travel to faraway places like Boston, Leicester, Colindale; but still keep hold of old habits like my strict diet of takeaways…"

"Bet you're looking for a bit of variety. I heard you can only eat so many kebabs."

They shared the joke.

"The powers that be are pretty pleased with the progress so far. For the first time in months there is some real momentum now. Your work has got HMRC and the Cabinet Office stepping up to the plate."

"Pleased to hear it. Does that mean you won't moan when I put in my account?"

"I'm sure it will be fine. In your situation we don't pay overtime anymore."

It had been a good time to meet, a little before five, ahead of the traditional arrival of the first phase of office workers. They moved to a table in the alcove away from the rest of the assembled drinkers and the tone of their dialogue became more serious.

"You know, Jimi – as always we have some challenging expectations to meet. We need to achieve arrests and against the clock. Don't get me wrong, I have no doubt you couldn't have collected more evidence than you have secured thus far, but we've got to keep it going and the stakes will only get higher.

"As it stands, we can make a series of low-level prosecutions that will only stop the problems we are trying to solve for the short term. We must get the 'big fish'."

"I thought that was what the Cabinet Office were doing."

"Only in part. They are dealing with the international dimension. We need to link it up on the home front."

"What do we need to do?"

"We need to link Canecale and his Pionier directors directly to criminal activity. GCHQ is monitoring Canecale's communications to secure evidence that he is discussing the hijacking of cars and people smuggling with Vahid and Ibrahim. We do not have numbers for them at the moment, so it is important that Canecale doesn't think he's under investigation and feels free to call."

"What happens when he finds out who stole the car back?"

"I'm counting on the fact that will take him a while yet, even if he is in the market for buying the information."

"So if you have got GCHQ on the job what else is there for us to do?"

"Two things – on the drugs front, I agree with your contention that Canecale, for his own reasons, is trying to merge the Leerys and Screamers into one structure. It's ambitious but quite possible as he is controlling their supply. You need to keep Wetherall on the case monitoring Izmir Barbeque operations. But the big one for you is to infiltrate their people-smuggling operations and you need to approach it in two ways.

"Firstly, from a corporate perspective, you have to approach Pionier as a client, letting Canecale know that you have a pool of paid-up travellers that need moving across the Channel. You have to find a way of agreeing terms in a way that will give us hard evidence. Second, and separately, you need to get one of the team undercover in Calais to join one of the crossings he has already organised so that we understand how he is doing it and who is helping them. I want you to put Sunny on this as she is less likely to draw attention."

"And De Jong?"

"Keep her in the background for now. If we need to mobilise further resources quickly in the Netherlands we will need her ready to go, especially if we have to pick up Vahid or this Ibrahim."

"Do we know where they are?"

"I'm assuming Vahid stays out of range in Istanbul for now. If GCHQ confirms it, we will need a strategy to bring him into Rotterdam or London and at the moment we don't know who this Ibrahim fellow is, so all this still has some way to go."

"Any guidance on tactics?"

Marshall appreciated the irony.

"As you are aware, for now, you are out of the service, out of my control and on the edge of my personal influence. With the progress you're making, I don't want to limit your options. I don't want to know how you do it, I don't want to know how much it costs. Just get this done and concluded soonest. We can get the washing-up done later."

Mwake drained his glass, nodded his understanding and headed out into the rush-hour traffic.

He had plenty to think about ahead of his own team meeting at Colindale in the morning.

SIXTEEN

MCKEE HAD TAKEN A short flight to Cyprus and took a two-hour drive north to the small town of Rizokarpasso in search of Ermine Akdeniz, eldest daughter of Mersut Canecale. He had tracked her down thanks to some dogged detective work by colleagues in the Cabinet Office in London, but despite clear instructions about how to find her house, things looked more complicated on the ground.

The town was the most northerly on the island and as such had an air of frontier lawlessness about it, about as far from a centre of authority as the island could provide. Although located in the Turkish controlled sector, there were still a minority of Greeks living locally in properties more recognisable through their exterior fortifications – clearly designed to ward off the casual visitor. The town centre was strangely quiet for the time of day, which McKee put down to the hour of his arrival – siesta time. Coupled with the absence of people, four local pet dogs sat in what little shade was afforded from a gnarled eucalyptus tree near a well. The few essential shops and bars were shuttered, and, to his eye, there was no sign of a tourist hotel to attract vacation spenders.

The most likely location for the Akdeniz residence appeared to be a smallholding on the south side of town, surrounded by olive groves, just off the Karpaz Anayolu. The property had the benefit of a spacious yard set back from the road, occupied by a rusting Citroen van and a good number of hens which dashed for cover to escape the dust as his hire car ground to a halt.

Switching off the engine and climbing out, he was immediately struck by the tranquillity of the scene. Again, if this was a working farmyard the owners were either away elsewhere or in their beds. Having been on the move most of the day this was the first time he had become aware of the midday heat and the intense UVA, obliging him to return to the car to collect his sunglasses. As he did so, a brown, pock-skinned man in a worn check shirt and breeches stepped out of the house carrying a shot gun.

"Excuse me, I am looking for Mrs Akdeniz?" he ventured.

"I am from an insurance company in Istanbul. I have some news about a policy that names her as a beneficiary."

The man did not move or speak, keeping the shotgun trained on him.

At that moment, a woman, perhaps in her late forties, in a dark blue boiler suit and red patterned scarf came out and shouted something in a local tongue that McKee didn't readily understand. The gun was lowered but its owner didn't move.

The woman spoke up.

"I am sorry, we don't get many visitors here, especially people dressed as smartly as you. Those who come are usually from the prefecture seeking money. I am Mrs Ermine Akdeniz."

McKee shook her hand.

"My name is McKee. I am an international insurance broker based in Istanbul. My company held a life policy on one of your relatives, now sadly deceased, Gemlik Canecale. My instructions are to get this policy closed which means making a payment to the next of kin. Our research suggests you are that person."

"Really? How much will I get?"

"I can't say yet as it depends on the circumstances of Mr Canecale's death which I understand was a couple of years ago now. I am here because my company was expecting a claim to be made. In these cases where we are not approached, after a set period of time we are required to investigate the matter personally – but to answer your question maybe up to a million Turkish lira."

At this point, she gripped his arm with one hand and waved away her shotgun-toting husband.

"You must come in out of the sun. Will you take tea?"

She led him to the nearest door which proved to be the kitchen. It was simply furnished, peeling white stucco walls, earthenware tiled floor which seemed slightly uneven as he walked across it, wood burning oven, wooden dresser, table and four chairs. There was a kettle gently boiling on the hob, so the promised tea was quickly produced. Despite this, the spartan scene offered some respite against the heat of the day.

"So you want to know about my family?"

McKee nodded his encouragement.

"A few years ago, had you approached me on this matter, I would have let my husband do his worst, but since we moved here from the city, we have had a quiet life."

"It must be very different from Istanbul."

"Yes it is. We were lucky we got the chance to come here under a government resettlement scheme which paid for the property. Since then we put our money into planting fruit trees. They take time to cultivate so we have made a living from livestock. We have chickens, sheep and goats."

"Was it just the money that helped you make the decision?"

"No, but it helped. Being a member of the Canecale family in Istanbul was not always easy. You see we are a family of traders in the best Turkish tradition. We buy and sell and haggle over merchandise, but we do it better than most and so there are many who didn't wish us well."

"You were threatened?"

"Not so much personally. Me and my sister, well, we were never really involved. Some of the family's business associates occasionally threatened us as a way of getting to my brothers. Sometimes it produced unexpected outcomes with them going to visit the perpetrators first. Occasionally there was violence."

"So what was their business?"

"Commodities – spices, fruits, cotton in the main. My father, Mersut and eldest brother Gemlik would visit farms in the east, buy their products and bring them west to market. They were good negotiators and because they paid suppliers well, they had some loyalty, which was important when others started to take over their trade."

"Then what happened?"

"Dad teamed up with another trader they met in the bazaar, Kerim Terzili. He had some big ideas about how they could make even more money. He had started out selling carpets. Like them, he would go east to buy but went further, going to Afghanistan and Uzbekistan to do trades. He got them thinking. They would only go east to buy stuff and then bring it back to sell. Terzili took products with him when he travelled, so he was selling on his buying trips. At the time, he found there was a big market for guns, so he started buying cheap Russian-produced weapons, taking them to the warlords. At the same time he would charge them for taking drugs consignments back to Turkey and selling them on. I think a lot went to Bulgaria for onward distribution in Western Europe. But Terzili couldn't do this alone, so they worked together. They loved it – they had never made so much money in their lives. But they weren't as smart as they thought. Terzili took on a deal – his first I think in Africa – supplying weapons to a resistance movement in Mali. He got the contract through a Russian middleman, but a condition of the arrangement was the supplier had to ensure the Turkish authorities were not implicated. Gemlik hit on the idea of fixing it through Nicosia.

"Anyway, the deal went wrong. The goods were collected but the payment somehow went missing. Kerim was furious – he had lost face with an influential customer, but the middleman said he would kill him. As I said, the family were used to these kinds of threats and thought no more about it. A couple of weeks later, Gemlik, and his then girlfriend, went on holiday to Bodrum and drowned when they got trapped while exploring a shipwreck. The authorities recorded it as an unfortunate accident, but my father understood it was a message."

"But no evidence of foul play was discovered?"

"No – the authorities took the view it was misadventure, and they should have taken precautions. After that, Kerim decided to stop gun running, and Mersut thought he was next. He retired and moved out of the city and shares a villa with my sister, Cara on Burgazada island."

"I have another brother called Ekrem. He had a big fallout with Dad and left the country. I think for some reason, he blamed Ekrem for Gemlik's death, but I really don't know why. In fact, my father refuses to talk about him at all."

"Is he dead as well?"

"I don't know. But my youngest brother, Bulent, moved to the Netherlands to run a travel agency – he may know more than me. The men in our family are not great communicators especially not with their sisters or wives."

"So, listening to you it seems your dad is still working with Kerim Terzili?"

"For sure, as some sort of paid adviser to Terzili's company, Turhan, but now it is probably more of an honorary arrangement. He certainly doesn't travel beyond Istanbul anymore for his own safety and he has never expressed any desire to come here. I think our life in Cyprus is too tough for him," she laughed.

"When did you see Mersut last?"

"I go shopping twice a year in Istanbul. We normally meet for a meal then. But why the interest? I thought you only wanted to know about Gemlik?"

"Yes that is true. But it is useful for me to know the background to his case, especially the fact that the authorities have decided he was not murdered. I have to report to my bosses but according to our rules I see no reason for payment to be withheld. I consider myself lucky with this enquiry. I had to interview at least one member of this family and you were the first person I tried to trace. All I have to do now is to contact your father and Cara on Burgazada before I finish the paperwork. Thank you for your time – you have been more than helpful. I will be in touch."

"It was a pleasure. Living here I don't often get the chance to have visitors, Mr—?"

He interrupted her as he got up to leave.

"By the way, do you remember the name of this Russian you mentioned? It could be useful…"

"It was a long time ago…Vladimir? No – Valentin – I think."

Smiling, he put on his sunglasses and stepped out, back into the heat.

Returning to Istanbul, he hired a car. His intention was not to go straight to Burgazada, but to an industrial estate at Odayeri, an address he'd picked up from Jalolov. Although he knew he needed to check it out he wasn't entirely certain of what he expected to discover. Located close to the motorway and only 20 minutes from the airport terminal, it had been easy enough to find. It was simply a warehouse operated by a local general haulier, Marmaris Logistics but big enough to swallow a couple trucks, complete with containers. The frontage was wide open, giving a clear line of sight inside. It all looked pretty tidy as though the tenants had either just moved or were moving out. Conveniently, the sign over the entrance had a contact telephone number. Calling as a clerk in the bulk goods receiving department from the office, he said he was due to receive a consignment from a Mr Jalolov of Kyzylkum Mining in Uzbekistan for a Mr Mersut Canecale and that he was calling to say it was delayed. The woman who had answered at Marmaris Logistics sounded suitably confused and flustered, saying they had not had any new instructions from Mr Canecale, but she would check. It was odd because Mr Canecale would personally come to the depot to sign the receipt for the goods at their premises. Did she know where Marmaris would be sending the consignment? She was not sure but assumed it would be going to the same address as the last delivery, which went to Turhan Smelting in Gebze, south of the city. Was he sure she didn't want her to call Mr Canecale to enquire? Not yet, but he would call again when the shipping note arrived from the airline.

It was more useful intelligence. *Why was Canecale taking receipt of a consignment of gold machine components from Uzbekistan at a freight forwarders before passing it on to Turhan, when it could just be taken direct?* At least he now understood what Turhan would be doing with it, but still needed to know where it was going after that.

It was the first time the Four Musketeers had been in the office in Colindale together since they had moved in, and Sunny Purewal was pleased to see the premises was at least big enough to provide each of them with their own desk.

Mwake summarised progress on the investigation to date and his last meeting with Marshall, concluding with his observation about the momentum the team had given the investigation.

"You'll be pleased to know that my next job will be to send an invoice for the work to date for Marshall to sign while he is well disposed to us."

"In other words, so long as we don't fuck up he's not going to worry too much about our expenses," Wetherall observed dryly.

"It's more than that, he's under pressure to bring this to a head sooner rather than later, so we are expected to push on as far as we can, so we should be able to chart the extent of the Izmir Barbeque drug distribution network. Remember from his point of view he is looking for quantitative and qualitative cases for prosecution. The more cases we can set in place, the more flexibility we get. So Izmir Barbeque will give us numbers, but we still have to get after the big fish, so we need to see what happens between the Leerys and the Screamers. We think they are getting their drug supplies when collecting illegal migrants off the beaches for distribution around the country, so that must be the focus for the next stage of the work. Marshall is trying to get more intel from GCHQ on what Canecale is doing on this. I will pass on any news as and when. In the meantime, we need to get the inside track by infiltrating one of us into their people-smuggling operation. The key is linking the dispatch of immigrants from the continent to Canecale."

"How will we manage that?" asked De Jong.

"I'm not sure yet, but this looks like a job for you, Sunny, if you are up for it."

"I should have guessed," she replied with a mixture of irony and resignation, "I suppose you'd say I look the part."

"So do I," Mwake was quick to point out. "But you look more vulnerable, and I can't be away for an unspecified time as I need to report to Marshall. Besides – before we do anything we must devise a credible cover and approach that fits the situation, and a sufficiently big cash bait that will pull him out of the shadows."

Marshall had been pleased with the progress of Wetherall's work, creating friction in the apparently smooth running of the Izmir Barbeque drugs and people-smuggling operation. For him the greatest achievement had been in the sowing of mistrust between the two rival criminal gangs responsible for sustaining it. He had been delighted with the latest news from GCHQ detailing how one of the leading protagonists, Kotobi, had sought a 'clear the air' exchange with his opposite number in the Screamers. It was clear Mwake's repossession of the Koenigsegg, timed to coincide with a programme of disruption and raids on selected Izmir targets, had created the dynamic to plant the seeds of mistrust and destruction of the criminal enterprise.

Each intervention was accelerating the evidence base necessary to build the prosecutions, and now at least there were clear signs one of the main instigators was feeling the heat, his moves being closely monitored from Cheltenham.

SEVENTEEN

THE ALBERT MEMORIAL IN London's Hyde Park in the start of a weekday morning might seem a strange place for two of London's leading gang bosses to meet, but for Kotobi and Abou the landmark was regarded as neutral territory. For two men whose working lives were spent primarily in the shadows, the timing of the encounter at the start of the working day provided them with some protection from a possible ambush. The fact that such a meeting was convened at all was something of an achievement and had taken a week to organise. Kotobi realised without some sort of valedictory contact, a destructive and ultimately self-defeating turf war would ensue. Suspecting Abou had already fired the first salvos in the dispute, Kotobi didn't want his action to be misunderstood by his rival and seen as a sign of weakness, so he had made initial contact with Levi Gardiner, a tropical fruit importer in Bethnal Green. Gardiner was the ideal man to manage this exercise in underworld diplomacy. His family was second generation East London, but his roots and networks stretched to Montego Bay, where Kotobi and Abou had their own family connections, and the two protagonists represented territory north and south of the river. For this, a meeting of players who made their living breaking the rules, terms of reference had to be put in place. The meeting would involve the two men only, Gardiner acting as referee to ensure fair play. No guns, no hangers-on, open ground. Gardiner personally would check each of them out before moving away so they could talk directly in private. Neither wanted to be early or late. Both arrived in private cars, Kotobi a BMW, Abou a Range Rover. Both vehicles were conspicuous in black with darkened windows, inviting the attention of curious but unsuspecting passers-by on South Carriageway Drive and had pulled in as close to the memorial as they could get. It was clear neither expected the meeting to take long as engines were kept running with hazard warning lights on. Such a sight in the locality so close to a number of diplomatic missions was not unusual and would be unlikely to attract the attention of predatory traffic wardens. The only matter the occupants were interested in was spotting Gardiner and awaiting his signal to come and meet him. Even the exit from their cars had to be choreographed. Kotobi would leave the protection of his vehicle first, aware that his short unaccompanied walk would be covered by marksmen from both camps, with the proviso that his men would keep their weapons trained on his rival's vehicle, until their principal started his own walk to the memorial. Given the circumstances both men approached the meeting place at a steady and deliberate walking pace. Each shook hands with Gardiner who responded with a perfunctory bear hug, come frisk. The tension in the air was palpable, even their exhaled breath captured in the morning chill was directed away from each other to avoid the risk of sharing.

"OK boys, good to see you're being grown up about this. I am going to stand over there by the edge of the plinth – out of earshot. Say what you need to say. If you need my help just signal. Otherwise let's get this done and we can all be on our way."

The protagonists nodded their agreement as Gardiner moved away. For this prize fight, there was no tapping of gloves before the sparring began, just the locking of eye contact.

Kotobi spoke first.

"It's funny we've known about each other for so long and managed to do our business without pissing each other off, know what I mean? Suddenly things start to change, your people are moving onto my patch with gear and incentives."

"Incentives?"

"Threats, you know? Then I get a message from Uncle across the water, he's pissed off with me for placing my business with you and saying we should merge into one organisation – which is bollocks."

"I understand you may have problems managing your business but my people haven't pissed on your post yet. If you're getting ripped off on any of your deals, it's not the Screamers. I'm busy enough with my own stuff. Maybe one of your own people is doing a bit of overtime to eat your lunch and Uncle is just squeezing your balls. Your point is?"

"Uncle doesn't know how trade here operates. He doesn't give a fuck. All he wants is payment for the gear and a home for his people he sends over. We're both doing that fine without any problems. Tell him we are OK as we are and let things settle down."

"What if I disagree?"

"My guys won't work for you. All that will happen is we'll both do a lot of *tit for tats* all over the place and whilst were doing that, some new player will come on the scene. What I am saying is if we don't keep a lid on things, our respective businesses go belly up."

"You know, one of the reasons I agreed to this meeting was to short circuit the process. I have two guys with telescopics who will take you down with just a nod from me. Your problem, Kotobi, is that you fucked up not just on a drug deal but on the other merchandise you were sending to Uncle. It is because of that he has said he wants one organisation here. He already thinks the car deal you fucked up was a sign of intent from a new player. The way I heard it, he doesn't want to deal with a third party in the UK. Business is complicated enough. He's fed up with the alternate monthly collection arrangement changes between our people and yours. He wants one point of contact for the drugs, money and people and he's decided on me. Remember, the real difference between you and me is I have a Turkish mum and we Turks stick together when the shit starts flying. I've got the lingo. He's a good guy at heart – he could just have cut you off, man, and left you to deal with all the shit from your customers, but what he is saying is you should work for me, and what I'm saying is you can manage all the people distribution thing for us both, and I'll do the rest. I think it's a fair offer."

"So you've talked?"

"Just a routine chat as we do from time to time."

"I think it's bollocks – if Uncle wants a new arrangement here, he can come and discuss it face to face."

"Don't be a fool. Uncle is in charge of this show. He don't need to parley with you. He controls the supply, man, and what he says is the law. If I were you, I'd take the offer I've made, even if you won't be making the same returns you used to. Tell you what, I can see you're pissed off. Go away and think about it. My offer is open for the next couple of days. If you're up for it, call me on the number on the back of this card. We can meet again and work out how we run things… but if I don't hear from you this week, I guess you and the Leerys will have to get back to what you do best… whatever that is."

Abou turned away and walked back to the car. Two of his men climbed out, hands to their jacket breast pockets, ready to draw at the first sign of trouble. Seeing Abou depart, Gardiner returned to Kotobi's side.

"Happy?" he enquired.

"Anything but," the chief Leery replied.

"Abou's a lying bastard. He claims his people are not ripping me off, but then admits he's been talking to my supplier. He says he's too busy to involve himself in my business and says my supplier wants to change the delivery arrangements on my deals. He's so full of shit. I'm not going to get pushed out on the say-so of a supplier who leaves all the problems with me and walks away with the money. He's not the only one who can call the shots. There's going to be a reckoning. It starts now. I'm gonna kill one of the Screamers who comes on my patch. That will be the best way of telling Abou and Uncle to get out of my face."

"Be careful Abel. Celik keeps some scary acquaintances. His Turkish connections are strong. If you start a war with him you must be confident enough to see it through."

"This is the world we live in. We're always on the edge. Sometimes you have to fight for what you believe in."

Abou's Range Rover had now departed. Kotobi started back to his team waiting in the BMW. Gardiner watched him go with a real sense of foreboding in his heart. Growing up in Jamaica, he understood how destructive the drugs business could be. He would have his own choices to make – to walk away or continue to play peacemaker.

Smith recounted the latest news from Matheson to Marshall with a certain satisfaction. He had to hand it to his man, he was starting to get results and uncover a web of international criminal enterprise. Yet it was frustrating, as soon as one question was resolved another emerged. He was already concerned about the escalation of the case and the role of the investigator's alter ego, McKee. The present situation was making it harder to bring Matheson's role to an early conclusion. On the more positive side it was becoming clear that the intelligence flow was growing, and its potential value to other HMG outlets or perhaps potential friendly foreign governments was growing. Further, although his agent had to retain a cloak of anonymity, he did not, and would be able to take personal credit for perhaps unmasking some high-level villains in due course.

Marshall was impressed as he summarised his understanding.

"So we know for sure Turhan is smuggling unregistered gold into Turkey from Uzbekistan via this Mersut Canecale, who seems to act as an intermediary before passing it directly to a Turhan smelting plant. We don't yet know what happens to the gold after the smelting, or where it goes after. What's Matheson's hunch?"

"He seems to think Turhan is keeping it somewhere because Canecale will not have the facilities to do that."

"Turhan must be paying Canecale a fee for acting as a middleman? Why could that be?"

"Because the goods come into Turkey as components. The metals or alloys are never tested. Their customs people are not interested because they're exempt from import fees. Technically, the gold disappears off the radar. If it went directly to Turhan it would mean that they would need to complete customs declarations and state its ultimate destination, which is what we don't yet understand, and until the gold is officially hallmarked it doesn't exist. Whatever Turhan is doing, they have to be getting it registered, somewhere, and will have to do it slowly so they don't undermine future prices by putting a glut out for registration. So they will be stockpiling and exporting steadily. There is a criminal market for unregistered gold but it operates significantly below present market levels maybe by as much as forty per cent, so Turhan must manage their position carefully. Matheson needs to find out where they are storing it and how they are exporting. Because of this slow release of gold it can only be one profit centre for their firm, their sheet metals and armaments businesses will still need to perform strongly. In short, he has to follow the supply chain out of the smelting plant."

"And what about Turhan's links with the drugs trade?"

"We still haven't got clarity on that yet. There is plenty of historical evidence on Kerim's activities, but nothing definitive about their present trade. Matheson will be looking at that as well."

Sunny Purewal had always been attracted by the variety of law enforcement assignments she had been involved with, but this latest challenge caused her to be more apprehensive than usual. She found herself walking towards the seafront from the main railway station in Calais with just the clothes she stood up in and a backpack with what appeared to be all her worldly possessions. She was a British South Asian woman, but part of a white European street scene. She was conspicuous and felt out of place, like she did not belong. Passing the collection of restaurants clustered along the Rue de la Mer, she saw to her left the marina sheltered from the sea by the promontory leading to the beach. This was the picture postcard side of town between the ferry terminal and Channel Tunnel terminal to the west at Coquelles.

It was the Calais of old – the quaint historic French coastal town, which today so few travellers stopped to admire. It was also that part of the local metropolis without the chaos of the commercial port and the squatter camps of the thousands of migrants seeking to stow away to a better life across the water to the north. She had deliberately stayed clear of that outlying area, known as 'the jungle', to avoid both the risk of arrest by gendarmes or mugging (or worse), by members of the itinerant tented population, but nonetheless, her objective was the same. Intelligence supplied from Marshall suggested Canecale operated a premium travel experience for illegal immigrants that guaranteed their safe arrival in Britain, for a higher fee than was charged to the average occupant of the rubber dinghies set adrift in the narrow and unpredictable sea lanes that divided France from its neighbour. Her first problem was to make a connection to arrange her passage. She had reckoned that if Canecale wanted to conduct this trade in a quiet and efficient manner, he would site it close to, but away from where the majority of his competitors were based, not least because he would be unable to satisfy the insatiable demand. Hours spent studying local maps suggested such a service would probably be provided by a sailing yacht moored at one of the marinas along the coast. If she was wrong, she had also surmised that she might meet someone who would know where such a service could be accessed. Calais marina was her first target location. Marshall had picked up some intel that one of the duty managers had a criminal history for embezzlement a few years back. Her sense was criminality was a bit like smoking – a difficult habit to break. The chances were even if this character was not involved he would know someone who was.

For the uninitiated, visiting a marina could be a strange experience. Although often appearing to be deserted, many of the boats were occupied by people relaxing in their mini home from homes or doing one of the myriad of maintenance tasks required of seafaring vessels. In fact, given her appearance on the quay, several occupiers of moored craft made their presence known as if assuming she had arrived to stow away or perhaps steal their pride and joy. Their body language did not encourage dialogue. She smiled nervously at those she had been unfortunate enough to make eye contact with and kept up her steady pace. Her immediate problem was the end of the jetty was now in sight which would oblige her to return the way she had come, which would serve only to heighten the suspicion of those already watching. As she was about to turn to retrace her steps, a voice called out to her in English: "Hello? Are you lost? If you are looking for the town centre it's over there."

He pointed back the way she came. It was the statement of the obvious but at least this had been the first vaguely friendly encounter she had experienced.

"How did you know I spoke English?"

"I didn't," came the reply, "but most of your sort who come round here do – certainly more than those who can speak French."

Purewal had felt her hackles rise at the casual insult, but knew this wasn't the time or the place, instead responding: "I didn't expect to find any of *your sort* speaking English."

Her accoster chose to see the funny side and the two exchanged smiles.

"It's true there's not so many of us round here, most of us tend to hang out further along the coast in Normandy or Brittany. This isn't my boat, it's owned by someone in Lille, but they've hired me to come over and do some running repairs. I normally come here for a month for so in the summer – a sort of working holiday. I'll be taking the ferry back home tomorrow night assuming I get finished in time."

"What are the local hotels like?" she asked lamely.

"Didn't realise you were here for a vacation. No idea. I'm camping on board. It's a bit basic, but OK for a sailor. I do treat myself to a dinner at one of the local restaurants before I settle down. You looking for a bed for the night or a billet across the water?"

He saw her hesitate and belatedly decided to introduce himself.

"Hi. My name's Tony. Sorry didn't mean to be rude, but even in the few days I've been here, there have been a few folk wandering around looking for business."

"I'm Anita. What sort of business?"

"Oh anything I think – providing there is a prospect of getting a lift over the water."

His tone had become more serious – or so she thought.

"This isn't a great place for a woman like you on be on her own. You got friends here or are they over at the jungle? You need to be careful. Periodically the cops come round to clear out anybody they think is up to no good."

He paused, then answered his own question.

"No, I guess you would have come with others if you could. They say the jungle is a bad place for an unaccompanied woman."

It was a moment to be brave. She knew what he was suggesting.

"I am travelling alone – I have access to money and want to buy a passage to England. Can you help?"

The man looked at her as if weighing up whether she was serious.

"I'd love to help you if I could, but I only work here. The big car park across the dock, close to the restaurants, tends to have a few motorhomes stopping overnight before heading for the early morning ferries. But you will have passed the warning signs coming over here. Most are securely locked overnight so your chances of sneaking in the back of one of those is limited. Besides they are the obvious target for searches at the dock. Tell you what – I know one or two of the owners who do go to sea – I go drinking with them sometimes, I'll ask them if they have any ideas. You're on your own. You say you have money. Are you in trouble with the law?"

"No but I am escaping a difficult domestic situation."

"You got a passport?"

"No. I travelled with my husband from the UAE to Germany where I left to make my way here."

"OK. You can stay on the boat with me tonight if you can't find anywhere better. Otherwise come back and see me tomorrow at eleven and I'll tell you if I have heard anything. But remember, I'm going home myself tomorrow night, so if you want to hear what I have been able to find out, make sure you find me."

Sunny nodded, smiled and pulled the hood of her anorak around her head. The wind was getting up and the rapidly gathering clouds were looking threatening. She walked away towards the beachfront in search of a bed and some hot food. A modest hotel less than 10 minutes' walk met all her requirements, and the receptionist was happy to ignore the formality of passport identification in return for a cash payment. She checked in before calling Mwake to update.

Rested and fed, when the clock struck eleven and most normal people were catching up on sleep, Purewal set out to retrace her steps from earlier in the day. The promised rain had now arrived landing in squalls created by the blustery wind. Walking by the moorings she crossed the Henri Hernon bridge on the way towards the town centre. Immediately ahead was a café bar bathed in purple light with thumping dance music blaring out for anyone facing the misfortune of seeking rest in the vicinity. She paused at the bus stop directly opposite the entrance to take some shelter from the elements. Based on the proximity of the marina and the relative distance from the main drag of cafés and restaurants that made up the town centre, she realised this bar was the most likely place where her new friend, Tony had gone drinking. Despite their brief conversation hours earlier, Sunny had fixed the contours of his round face and tousled hair in her mind. The bar had a glass front and was half empty, meaning its windows and the view inside was not hampered by condensation. From her position she studied the occupants to see if she could see him. Perhaps under normal conditions after dark, her effort would have been rewarded, but the purple light made any positive identification difficult. She went for the next best option opened her anorak to the weather and put down her hood and walked along the frontage of the bar to at least give the occupants the best opportunity of seeing her. It took three trips of walking outside along the bar's frontage before she succeeded in drawing attention. The shout came from behind.

"Hey, Anita? Is that you? It's me, Tony from the marina. I thought we'd said we'd meet in the morning? Come in out of the rain."

Although Purewal followed the instruction, she saw Tony was with two other men and what seemed like a battalion of empty beer bottles on a nearby table. The pulsating music made any conversation impossible. Tony had realised that his invitation into the bar, although well intentioned was not a good idea. Instead he grabbed his coat, waved to his companions and ushered her outside.

"Get yourself wrapped up – you'll catch a cold. Look, don't think I'm being forward, but there aren't many places to go around here at this time of night. Come back to the boat. At least it's warm and fairly quiet – I've got a bottle so we can talk."

Purewal had gone looking for the conversation but not the proposed venue. She had realised one would not happen without the other. They made it to his boat without getting soaked to the skin.

"Sorry it's a bit of a mess. I was going to put it straight before I left tomorrow. At least there is a heater here to dry off your coat. Anyway what were you doing there?"

"Looking for you. I worked out if you were going drinking nearby there were relatively few choices."

"But we'd said we'd talk in the morning."

"I realised when I left you I may not have time tomorrow. I think my husband has people looking for me. If it's 'no go' here I must try elsewhere."

They sat either side of the dining table in the forecastle, a bottle of Irish whiskey and a couple of shot glasses between them.

"OK, well let me cheer you up," he continued, launching into a rambling tale about his recently concluded divorce, before realising she wasn't really interested. He returned to the business in hand.

"One of those guys I was drinking with has put me in touch with a bloke in the Netherlands…

"Do I have to travel there?"

"No, no. He's got a meeting along the coast in a couple of days with an associate from England who happens to be sailing over. Apparently, he doesn't do this type of business because of the risk but has said if you haven't got a current passport and can pay fifty thousand pounds into a UK account, he'll take you across."

"Fifty thousand?" She knew Mwake would be expecting a high price but was already anticipating his reaction.

"Well lady, based on what I told him he's put two and two together. A woman from the UAE travelling alone? You don't want to become another statistic in a capsized dinghy out on the sea at this time of year. The people who do this sort of thing have a lot of overheads. Assume you do internet banking? You'll have to pay fifty per cent in sterling to the UK account before you go. This guy will get you across safely and securely and will arrange onward transport to any city in the UK, but you must pay the balance when you arrive. In fact they will stay with you until they have the confirmation of payment."

"How come you're suddenly an expert?"

"I'm not, but I've been drinking with someone who is. You remember those guys you saw me with? The long-haired one is called Pascal. He's one of the operations managers at the marina. He's the one who's got the connections."

"Why didn't you introduce me?"

"He's a dodgy dude. Not someone I'd want as a friend, but unavoidable for me working here. There's something else besides..."

She looked at him, prompting his answer.

"Er... I will stay on and take you to meet them."

"Why would you do that?"

"Look, although I don't get paid after tomorrow, the owner is not out here until next week. My ferry ticket is flexible and ideally I could use a bit of extra time to get this place looking shipshape... you could help me. I'd like to meet this bloke anyway – seems like he could be a good client for me to cultivate for the future... besides, having made the approach they will probably expect me to turn up with you anyway. It will give them confidence especially if they're not used to doing things illegally."

"And you also thought you'd find an easy fuck..."

Her host spluttered into his whiskey.

"I... I didn't mean that. You are welcome to stay... no strings..."

"Is it because I told you I had money?"

"Not really. But I think you're different. Most of the people trying to cross the water are doing it, not because they are refugees escaping persecution at home, but are economic migrants trying to make money. I don't hold with that. They are being exploited by criminals. I wouldn't want to add to the problem. I can identify with you. I'm here trying to forget my messy divorce, which is why I'm doing this kind of work. I needed to get away and get my head together. Maybe when you get to England safely you'll remember me, but for now, I'm just a guy trying to do somebody a good turn."

"You know, in my life I have met many bullshitters most of whom were employed by my former husband, but in your case, I believe you, or to be precise I believe you think you're doing the right thing. I have to trust someone in this situation, it might as well be you. So what's the plan?"

"Help me tidy up on board tomorrow, then the day after I will take you to meet the person who will take you to England."

"*Aye, aye, Captain.* I'll drink to that." Sunny smiled clinking her glass against his. "I'm just starting to warm up. Can I stay here tonight?"

EIGHTEEN

IT MAY HAVE BEEN the result of the drink, but when she woke a few hours later, she had little recollection of her late-night chat with Tony. Fortunately her clothes were still intact, although she seemed to have been rolled up in a smelly quilt cover that had a faint odour of dog about it. There was no doubt she felt shit and probably looked as good. Reason enough for her new 'best buddy', Tony, not to try his luck, she thought. Looking across the cabin she saw he was still out of it. Surprising considering their situation, but he looked quite sexy in a strange sort of way... now she knew she wasn't feeling good. Struggling to her feet she found her trainers and slipped out into the fresh air – she needed a hot shower and a pee.

Returning to her hotel room a short time later, she called Mwake with the update.

His reaction was just as she'd anticipated.

"Fifty thousand? Marshall's gonna love this! Is he buying a collar? OK, OK, I'll get this set up and text you the details and pass codes. If they try to get you to come up with more, say the fifty thousand figure is the max you can withdraw from the joint account without secondary authorisation from your husband. As soon as the first payment is made, we will have a banking trail to follow might allow us to get the police to move in and make some arrests. Be careful, Sunny – if Canecale is wrapped up in this, you will be in danger until we can pick you up the other end. Amelie will look into this guy Tony and speak to the French about Pascal. Call when you get more."

Purewal returned to the marina with coffee and croissants for Tony.

Marshall had only just got to his car for the trip home after a fraught day in the office, contemplating how his investigation was gathering pace as well as increasing in cost. Although it had succeeded in recovering the treasure chest of forensic goodies provided by the Koenigsegg and pipeline of middle- and lower-level arrests tied to the Izmir Barbeque business were reasons to be cheerful, he was suffering the new stress of providing a further fifty thousand credit line to Mwake. He hadn't been pleased to hear of the new strand of the investigation being undertaken by Sunny Purewal either. She was walking into clear and present danger without proper backup. No matter Mwake's claim that to be authentic, she had to be vulnerable. This was a step too far. Had she still been on his books, he wouldn't have sanctioned her task, but Mwake, although himself a talented investigator didn't always draw the distinction between consulting and informing. There was no doubt the investigation had real momentum now, and he was reconciled to taking it to its conclusion before answering for the consequences. Whether it would mean promotion, or a forced early retirement was still not clear. His thoughts were interrupted by his phone buzzing as he prepared to fire the ignition. It was Oliver Watson.

"Phil – just picked up an interesting transaction from Turhan UK account – six million for 'services', paid from an Isle of Man account, Abraham Associated Investments, I'm running a check, but it looks like the boss there is called Michael Abraham. Global Bus has a lead director, who I met recently who goes by the same name. Fancy that!"

"Good, see if you can find out what services Turhan is supplying in return and where their money comes from."

"I'll keep digging but getting info like that takes longer than in most other places. Banking secrecy is only given up in rare cases and normally requires political intervention from Downing Street. It might be quicker to get Jane on the case."

"Let's see what progress you make first, Olli – think I'm starting to run out of favours in Cheltenham. I've not been refused anything yet but have received the amber light when she reminded me they had other pressing assignments that needed her time as well."

As far as Matheson was concerned, the investigation had gone well so far. He had uncovered new information that would help the investigation into Turhan and was enjoying the experience. This case was complex with multiple strands and the solution required an unorthodox approach to get leverage. Normally, engaging in a personal relationship with the principal target of the investigation would be frowned upon in a legal context, but as he continued to make discoveries he was increasingly confident that Ciller Terzili was either not fully aware of events taking place in her name or not in control of them, but others close to her must be involved. It was a challenge to pursue the enquiry without the backup of colleagues, but as he was starting to realise the case was evolving in a way that could not have been anticipated. He was not yet ready to return to the Terzili family villa for the inevitable update that Ciller would be seeking. He had sent her a text saying his other business was taking longer to resolve than he had expected and that he would be back in a few days. In the meantime, he set off to the Turhan smelting works at Gebze.

Arriving at the run-down, edge-of-town site, his first impression was the level of secrecy at the plant, the exterior surrounded with heavy corrugated, razor wire topped fencing, recently painted, contrasting with the decay of its immediate surroundings. The roof of a long warehouse was just discernible above the fencing from the approach road, together with two defining thirty-metre chimneys emitting a steady volume of white smoke. He knew he had found the right place as there was a large sign outside announcing the presence of the Turhan Ferrous Smelting Company together with a strange warning in English – 'No Admittance'. Access seemed to be controlled from within, as the main gates were opened automatically to receive trucks and were closed immediately afterwards. Other than cameras strategically located at intervals around the boundary, there were no other obvious signs of security. He would have to be patient and observe the comings and goings before working out how to get inside. Before that, he drove around the perimeter to check for alternative entrances but found nothing. Based on the size of the compound and what he estimated to be the building it contained he assumed the location could accommodate delivery trucks and the cars or busses of site workers. Certainly based on the general sounds being generated – shouts, sirens and ground-shaking crashes – it was a hive of activity. Professional curiosity told him he should be more interested in the vehicles coming out than those going in. That, or maybe the boredom of not much movement outside the fenced-off area for the nearly three hours he had been observing. So when a different tone of siren and flashing lights appeared at the gate clearing the way for two articulated trucks to depart, it was something of a no brainer to follow. Clearly fully laden, one followed the other onto the motorway network by passing the city centre heading north in the direction of Edirne and the Bulgarian border. As he followed, he made a note of the vehicles' identity details in case they were due to pass into European Union territory. Having recorded the details on his phone he was surprised to see both vehicles leave the second intersection and approach a, what looked like, newly built logistics park. At first sight this appeared to be a secure truck stop for drivers who needed to rest and refresh before their onward journey, but then out of the corner of his eye he saw another two warehouses next door, fronted by a big sign with the logo of a firm called 'Global Bus'. As good as its name, outside, a double decker Neoplan passenger bus was parked a short distance from a car park, used, he assumed, by workers at the site. One of the two hangars had its front doors wide open and the first truck drove straight in. The second parked up next to the Neoplan, its driver waiving to someone back at the hanger he couldn't see before getting in the cab of the coach and driving back the way he had come, towards the motorway. Compared to the smelting works he had just come from, security here was relaxed. The boundary protected by a wire-mesh fence, although still topped with razor wire, and had a guard house at the entrance, keeping an eye on comings and goings. Looking across the site, this place had the feel of a service centre for the busses with a stack of tyres, refuelling, emissions testing and cleaning facilities. A closer look through binoculars into the shed with the open doors revealed another Neoplan bus parked alongside where the first truck had stopped and already the truck's tarpaulins had been opened, and it looked like a forklift was starting to remove the cargo, although, frustratingly at the distance he was at it was too far away to be able to tell what the cargo was. Although he would need to get closer to understand what was going on, he had, in the moment, established a connection between two of Turhan's businesses which he had thought operated independently. What seemed to be happening was that components for the bus company were being supplied directly from the smelting works. If he was right at the very least there would be safety transgressions as well as potential fraud and counterfeit activity in progress.

He made the short trip to the truck stop; parking close to the boundary with the Global Bus depot. Going into the café he bought a meal, sitting in a position where he could continue to observe what was happening. Whilst his attention had been diverted buying breakfast, activity was continuing apace at Global

Bus. The second truck parked outside had had its tarpaulin opened and appeared to be being loaded with large-scale steel frames, the sort that were used to secure vehicle bodies onto chasses.

These items were big enough in themselves not to allow for more than five to be loaded at any one time and when he returned to watch what was happening, the third was being loaded into place. Without seeking to attract attention, he surreptitiously took pictures with his camera as the loading proceeded. A short time later, with five frames on board, the canopy was reattached, and another driver appeared to take the truck away. Interestingly, as his eye followed the departure, he saw the truck take the first exit at the motorway intersection, heading north away from Istanbul, towards the border.

Matheson was getting a hunch about what was taking place but knew he would need more than that to deliver to his boss.

Getting into the Global Bus depot to see at first-hand what was happening would be an essential requirement. He decided to pass the time at the truck stop, buying a book and a pot of tea and sending his pictures back to London. As time was moving on he went to fix a bed at the onsite hostel. He had filled the time easily and now with dusk approaching it was time to pay Global Bus a visit. First he decided to take a shower and used the opportunity to acquire one of the occupant's boiler suits, conveniently left out on a peg in the changing rooms. The navy-coloured covering, whilst not offering camouflage as such, was a reassuringly dark colour to use during the cover of night-time.

Going out into the lorry park, he surveyed a few of the parked vehicles to see which seemed to have occupants. Finding one seemingly deserted, an examination of the trailer revealed a toolbox with a clip lock; inside – pliers, ideal for cutting chain wire fencing. Keeping to the shadows he found his way to the perimeter of the Global Bus site which was still operational. Lights were on in the guardhouse and in one of the sheds where the door was only partially closed. Reassuringly, the offices had closed, the lights were off and away from the buildings there was no illumination, providing a contrast to the sodium floods covering the truck stop next door.

He had moved to the back of the property where he cut a tear in the fence big enough for him to slip through and moved towards the shed where activity was taking place. As he approached the noises grew louder. Dance music was playing on a tannoy and there was the unmistakable sound of pneumatic drills, winches, welding, shouting and heavy machinery. He arrived at the door and stared inside. It was as he had thought – a servicing base for coaches and one of the Neoplans seemed to be in the process of being stripped down with its engine cowls open and what looked like the replacement of part of the subframe across the second back axel. With a team of at least twenty or so he estimated no one was paying any attention to the stranger at the door which was helpful because at that moment the engine at the rear was being taken off its mountings and put on a bogey while the subframe alterations were made. Three of the technicians were in a pit below the vehicle attempting to fit a new structure, which appeared to be assembled as a single part. Interestingly, two more copies of the same structure were still on the truck he had followed from the smelting works. With so much effort being focused on fitting this one part, nobody was paying any attention to the mouldings left on the delivery lorry, so it provided an opportunity for him to approach the vehicle and hide in its shadow. He was as close as he dared get to the works and was able to record the scene on his phone, but there was a final task to perform. He needed to have his suspicions confirmed that the subframe mouldings were in fact gold. To this he would need to get a shaving of the metal from one of the mouldings as evidence. His initial idea was to use a knife to scratch and collect the shavings for analysis, but close examination showed he would be disappointed. The frame exterior looked like normal steel and was not worth the scratch, but on the far side of the truck opposite his hiding place, two of the mechanics were arguing about the fitting. Even in his limited Turkish, he got the sense of their dispute. The moulding they were trying to fit was four millimetres too wide and it would need to be cut by two millimetres at both ends for it to fit. A foreman was called over to mediate and agreed that the part should be shaved with a cutting tool. The two mechanics got to work straightaway with their heavy-duty saw performing the necessary procedure. Being so close, the noise was deafening but the outcome could not have been better. Dropping to the floor and seemingly ignored was a thin cross section of the moulding that fell tantalisingly close to his position. Looking at it he saw it was exactly what he expected – the moulding was gold wrapped in a steel casing, a job that could only be produced by a professional smelting operation, surprising then that the smelters had failed to produce an accurate specification. It was getting late now but the general hubbub continued. Again, Matheson thought, because the team needed to get the coach back into one piece and operational, perhaps as early as the following morning, they were being sloppy and looking to cut corners. He was right, as one of the mechanics walked by where the cutting had taken place, instead of sweeping up he kicked the piece of metal out of the way and under the truck where Matheson was hiding. This seemingly throwaway gesture had given him what he needed.

Together with the pictures he had taken, he now had a vital part of the hidden Turhan story.

They had arranged to meet at the summer house in the dunes at Saint-Gabriel Plage, a couple of miles to the north of Étaples. The location was ideal. It was close to a marina on the Canche river with fast access to the Channel and adjacent to Le Touquet airport. Being on the very edge of the hamlet and set back from the beach, the setting was quiet – out of sight of casual walkers on the shore – and benefitted from occasional security patrols checking for illegal immigrants.

Abraham had brought his motor yacht over from Lymington and was using the long weekend to mix business and pleasure – a VIP passenger to take back plus the chance to discuss face to face the recent concerning developments in his shared business enterprise with his continental business partners.

He had arrived twenty-four hours earlier to check that his caretaker had opened up the house and freshened up the rooms. Also because he planned to pick up his associates the following day from the airport. He had planned a casual day reviewing their shared business interests before taking them back for their homeward flight, then he was expecting his VIP package to arrive. They would set sail later the same evening. It was always best to sail at night if you had a vessel with an expert crew and equipment as the chances of interception en route were greatly reduced.

Abraham had prepared thoroughly, setting out the dining table like a boardroom with an agenda for the day. Given the nature of their activities, he was conscious many of their decisions were taken on the run and recent events had demonstrated the importance now and again of getting face to face to plan their activities strategically. This was even more important now as it was clear to Abraham at least they were in a process of transition which if they failed to influence the future, their existing business model would fail.

The dynamic of the group would be key. There were just three of them. As individuals controlling the vital elements of revenue generation, but each slightly uncomfortable about their interdependencies, not only with each other, but the wider world. Abraham oversaw the biggest revenue generator the group had, controlling supply on the London commodity exchange, his partners took responsibility for distribution and logistics. Despite this he was apprehensive about his colleagues arriving together, imagining what they had been discussing before meeting with him. Although their operations were not limited to the UK their focus would be on that territory as it was the shop window for their

European operations, enhancing their reputation among their competitors. Their agenda would cover a broad range of subjects from speciality car exporting, drug running, people smuggling and money laundering.

His two partners, Vahid and Bulent Canecale arrived on a private jet from Rotterdam. They looked an unlikely trio to control a multi-million-pound business. Both were dressed more smartly than their host who had arrived in a stripy T-shirt and shorts. Vahid was the more conspicuous in a business suit and tie, Canecale, perhaps more aware of the location, chose more casual attire – chinos and sports shirt. The smart-looking one also appeared the most impatient, fidgeting and looking at his watch. It was clear he didn't want to be there and wanted their meeting to be concluded as soon as possible. Abraham was pleased – he and Canecale had worked together for some years and, although not exactly friends, they were confident in each other's company. Vahid was the new man – an unknown quantity. The body language told Abraham he would not be disadvantaged in the discussion.

Seated at the dining table, he took control of the proceedings.

NINETEEN

"SO THIS PIONIER BOARD meeting is now open. What's new?" he began.

"Things are changing in Istanbul, and I am part of the process," Vahid explained.

"Turhan is going through a change of control, Kerim is getting old and has lost his mojo. He's becoming a liability but is still trying to run things through his daughter, the one who survived the assassination. She's bright and has set a new direction. Wants Turhan to get rid of its sub-legal activities, get out of our prime business activities and sees me playing a leading part in that. The problem is she has no idea how much money we make."

He turned his attention to his fellow traveller.

"Meanwhile Bulent, your father, Mersut, is still helping out managing the imports and transfers from Uzbekistan, which with Ciller's support I intend to take over myself. Mersut has also been helping Kerim's son, Adnan, manage the import of cocaine from Afghanistan. Trouble is the boy is lazy, spends too much time chasing women and drinking. He's not interested in the business, just taking the cash and I'm pretty sure his sister doesn't understand how little he's doing. I'm worried he's getting careless or cocky and he'll make a mistake with his deliveries, which in turn will give us problems with our customers and impact on our own reputation."

"What does he need to do?" Bulent was annoyed.

Vahid continued: "He just needs to do his job properly. His role is simple. He receives deliveries organised by your father, stores them until the stock reaches the correct transfer level and then delivers to Global Bus for me to deal with. And for that minimal responsibility, he gets his fat fee."

"But he's honest right?" Bulent persisted.

The irony was not lost on Vahid.

"If you mean his deliveries tally with Mersut's casual record keeping? Yes, but I don't need to tell you about how he could be cheating. For all we know he could be running his own selling operation and probably is, albeit he won't get anything like the uplift in prices on the domestic market. Again, we need to stabilise this by taking control."

"How?" Abraham was now becoming concerned.

"The most effective way is to take him out. An accident off the coast in that part of the world is not an unusual occurrence. That way we can step in to ensure continuity. It will further weaken the Terzili's grip on our business. Right now, while I am sorting the problems in our supply chain, I want to know more about what is happening in England."

Abraham nodded and summarised the position.

"We've got issues as well. The good news is imports and transfers from Global Bus. We're doing well. If ever there was an activity able to manage long term within the law, it's that. The gold recovery, transfer and laundering is going well although I am looking for more storage facilities before going to market, and we have paid in six million pounds to the Turhan corporate account for cleansing.

"We've got problems with the import and distribution of people and drugs from our Izmir Barbeque network. We work through two contractors who used to be working well managing the distribution of customers and product, but now it looks like rivalry and a turf war is developing. Either they have an informant or they're hitting on each other. The result is the police are making arrests and we are losing capacity. The cops are showing a greater interest in our staffing at the shops, so it is getting harder to place migrants in our workplaces unregistered. Again, I think the solution is to be looking to take this work in-house so we can take a greater control and weed out those who are hampering our efforts. I spoke to Bulent about this already because what we have been doing is sending cash payments to our contractors when they have been collecting customers from the boats. The risks of this going wrong are growing considerably. I would prefer we take the drugs and cash element out of the people business and leave those paying the base fee to manage for themselves when we dispatch them to the other side. We can use the Global Bus operation as an alternative. We're already working on a plan to merge the two contractors into one operational unit."

"And what about the car business? That's not going so well right now either?" Vahid observed.

Canecale showed a flash of irritation.

"It has been progressing well until recently. Our skill has been picking the right orders to supply. In essence – not too many, just four a year and picking the right orders to fulfil – rare, high residual value marques. Nothing below the two million sterling baseline. It's even better that the majority of the vehicles we target are in London and the south of England, and we have our associates available to manage the process."

"Presumably that arrangement is threatened by your plan to force the merger of your two contactors…"

"Let's get this straight. For the first time ever, our process was interrupted a few weeks ago with a vehicle we were supplying hijacked whilst in the process of delivery. It was a professional hit and I'm investigating exactly what happened. So far, it is clear that our contractors in the UK didn't do it – not least because they haven't got the resources, but the crew who supplied it probably have a leak in their team. Those who took it planned meticulously. They had to have known when the consignment was shipped."

"So, at the moment, you don't know who is responsible?"

Canecale stared into the middle distance, then at Abraham.

"No. But it is because of this situation we took the decision to merge our UK contractors."

"Shouldn't you have talked to me about that first?"

"Well, I took the view you were too busy at home to engage with the problem. The two of us are closer to what happened, and we are a majority on the board."

"It's still not clever. If you had contacted me I could have told you what happened. The owner of the car, a Koenigsegg I believe, is a London-based relative of Mohammad Sultan bin al-Harriri, a Dubai-based arms trader Turhan is looking to do business with. I think you can assume they had the resources to track and intercept your delivery and that is reason enough for you not to pursue your enquiries further."

"How do you know?"

"Ciller Terzili has hired an agent to build up arms sales in Dubai. He knows al-Harriri. Apparently the subject was mentioned in passing when they spoke about doing some deals. It would explain how the intercept was managed so professionally and why no one is talking. You know what the Emiratis are like. They don't give a fuck about the goods themselves but care about their reputation. They don't want to look like mugs."

"So you're saying we write off over a couple of million and piss off one of our best customers in Africa on the hearsay of some agent the Terzilis have?"

"No, just use a little charm. The reason why the subject came up this guy is a Brit and al-Harriri started moaning about London taking over from Moscow as the home of international criminality. Your deal will be delayed until you can source an alternative. When you do, the transaction can go ahead. Buy yourself some time and let things quieten down a little and then you can get on with it."

There was a momentary silence, then Vahid continued.

"I think we will have to meet more regularly. We have more challenges to face in the months ahead than perhaps the business has faced in the last two years. From now on, we take decisions about the future of Pionier together – the three of us, so we make better decisions. If an outsider looked at what we were doing, they might conclude our position is not the result of bad luck or unfortunate coincidence. Perhaps we have a new competitor trying to bring us down. I could be wrong, but maybe we should be working with the possibility that the reverses we are suffering may have a common link."

Reflecting on his initial perception, Abraham had started to understand Vahid's apparent impatience to get the meeting over. The Turk was clearly a class act who had quickly grasped an understanding of their underlying operations. The rest of the meeting's business had been relatively uneventful, centring around agency sales service agreements for Global Bus across Europe, but the highlight was Vahid's presentation of the firm's profit and loss account – a true work of fiction good enough for the Dutch tax authorities, but no one else.

The day had now come for Sunny's return trip across the Channel courtesy of the criminal fraternity. It had been something of an achievement, despite the funding, she had obtained access to a passage so quickly. She had no expectation of how the crossing would be managed. At least she knew she had found her target through the identification of Pascal Kimmerlin, Tony's drinking pal from the purple bar next to the Calais marina. Kimmerlin had been identified as an associate of Bulent Canecale, by French police, the two having served a prison sentence together some three years previously.

In the past hours, Sunny felt she had got to know Tony a bit better. After all they had spent a day bonding, cleaning out his client's boat. In the time they had been together, they had swapped stories of their previous lives (the fictitious version in her case) and to his credit, despite having the opportunity, he had not come on to her at any time. Was he a true gentleman, naïve, gay or just worried that she might scream 'rape' and land him in a whole lot of extra trouble? She had concluded he was damaged by his recent divorce and probably had enough of personal relationships for a while. Or perhaps he was shy as she knew some of the best available men often were. Conjuring with these thoughts was a welcome distraction for the seriousness and danger of the task now facing her. From now on she would not have any direct contact with Mwake and the other 'Musketeers'. She had to hope they had her back. This morning was the second time she had brought breakfast to the yacht in the basin where Tony had been staying, but this time, instead of climbing aboard she found him on the quayside fiddling with the moped.

"So where are we going?" she asked.

"An hour or so down the coast from here."

"It looks like it's going to be good weather – I quite fancy being a passenger on the back of the moped."

"It's not the most comfortable ride, but it will do the job."

"When do we go?"

"After breakfast, I'll lock up and leave the key at the harbourmaster's office."

She looked at him with a smile.

"You know, Tony, I must thank you for helping me out here. I don't know what I'd have done without you."

"Tried your luck in Boulogne, I guess."

"I still don't know why you're helping me."

"That's easy. First off, I didn't know I could, until Pascal sorted the arrangement out. He says once I have delivered you to the guy who's taking you across, I'll get paid a cash fee for my trouble. Finally, well I can tell you, it's OK for me, but there's some dangerous people about around here. It's no place for a woman on her own and I wouldn't want it on my conscience that I didn't take the opportunity to get you somewhere safe. Besides, once I have dropped you I have time to get back here and get on the ferry tonight like I had originally planned, so I guess the arrangement works for us all."

Sunny considered herself to be a good judge of character. She thought Tony was on the level and fervently hoped she was right.

"What time do we need to get there?"

"Four this afternoon. I have a number to call before we arrive."

"Great, so we can make a day of it, why don't we stop at the market get some cheese and wine and have a picnic along the way?"

Tony clearly lacked social skills and hesitated before agreeing. Sunny thought it was because he couldn't think of a reason for refusing. The weather had been a factor, it was a classic blue-skyed summer's day.

Sunny was not used to riding pillion but soon got the sense of travelling by moped. It was noisy and slow with the occasional backdraft of fumes but, against that, strangely liberating. She hadn't known whether a safety helmet was required on French roads, but her driver didn't seem bothered so neither was she. The feeling of freedom as the breeze ripped through her hair was exhilarating, neither did she need to make conversation, just hold on to him and enjoy the ride. They pulled in at the Place Dalton, parking up by the St Nicholas church in the old town and spent the next half hour touring the stalls, which were jammed, cheek by jowl in the cobbled square, surrounded on all sides by quaint restaurants and bars. For a short time, this was a chance to live in the moment and absorb what most visitors would regard as a quintessential Gallic scene. Heading south out of town they continued to follow the Côte d'Opale south for a few kilometres before taking a right turn down an unmarked service road to the beach.

Arriving at the edge of the dune, set back from the shore, Tony killed the engine.

"Nice find," Sunny called. "How did you know where to come?"

"I didn't," he replied, "got the route from my phone."

"I can't believe you have found a bit of beach that's deserted."

"Don't be. We are a good fifteen minutes' walk from the nearest village here and most of the migrants you would expect to find are north of Boulogne where the Channel is narrowest."

"So there are no police patrols here?"

"Who knows – I've not taken an interest myself. Besides, Pascal was telling me they're doing most of their patrolling with drones these days so they can eyeball what's happening relatively easily."

Tony got a rug out of one of the panniers and set it against one of the elevated edges of tufted grass which acted as a convenient wind break. He passed Sunny a knife for the bread and cheese before finding a plastic glass for the wine. Both seemed intent on keeping busy to avoid being the first to speak.

"Cheers." They nodded at each other as they sampled the wine. After what seemed like an age, Sunny opened the conversation.

"Are you OK, Tony? You seem a bit... distracted."

"It's nothing – just thinking about all the stuff I have to get done before I go to the ferry tonight."

He offered her a nervous smile.

"Are you worried about the meeting you're taking me to?"

"A little," he conceded. "I've not met the guy I need to take you to. He could be a bad lad. All I have is a number and a name. I have to call him before we arrive. You will have to wire him twenty-five thousand when you arrive via your web account. Once he's got that, I get a thousand by way of commission and leave. That's it."

"And you are worried about me?"

"I told you I don't want something bad to happen as a result of what I've done."

"Would you be happier if you were able to meet me in England?"

"Don't misunderstand me, but yes. Even if it was just a coffee and we then went our separate ways."

"Then it's a date," she laughed. "Has it not occurred to you that I have already faced considerable danger to get to this stage? I am capable of looking after myself."

"I know, but you haven't been in a situation like this. You won't be in control. I've come over to work here every summer for the past five years. It's never been as dangerous as it is now. I'm glad I don't have to live here all the time."

"I am sure with your help and advice I'll get through it. Now I think I'm a good judge of character and have chosen to put my trust in you, so we have got to this point. I guess now is the time I should ask if it is reciprocated."

"Reciprocated?"

"Yes. Do you trust me?"

Tony nodded blankly.

"I am asking because on top of everything else you've done, I still need a little more help."

He looked at her in surprise.

"You see Tony, I am not a wife on the run from a vengeful husband without a passport. I am an investigator, a sort of secret agent working on behalf of the British government, and I am looking into an associate of your drinking buddy, Pascal, who is a major people smuggler across the Channel. Whoever you are delivering me to this afternoon is connected with this man and I am here to collect evidence, in fact, you could say in a few hours from now I will be part of that evidence."

"Who are you?"

"I can't tell you that. As far as you're concerned you can continue to call me Anita, Anita Berri from Dubai."

Tony was transfixed.

"But all that stuff about your husband and escaping from Germany…"

"Don't give it another thought. I am sorry I had to lie to you. Unfortunately, it's an occupational hazard."

"How come you targeted me?"

"If you remember it was you who first spoke to me. I knew nothing about you. But I checked you out. You're Mr Tony Moroney, known as 'Bony' to your mates – I assume because you are relatively tall."

She tried not to laugh but hoped she had lightened his mood.

"You have a first-floor flat at 22 Cromwell Road in Southampton," she added.

He averted her gaze, staring at the horizon and the calm sea and seemed to be gathering his thoughts. He retained his focus on the waves, gently breaking on the shore.

"You do understand you have put me in a difficult position. I have lied on your behalf to get your passage to England booked. You arrest anyone that I have introduced you to, and I will be a dead man. These guys have connections everywhere, they will find me in England."

Tony's face was a knot of tightened muscle and deep worry lines.

Sunny tried to ease his fears.

"It may not be that bad. We knew of them before I arrived. We didn't know where they were which is why we had to dangle the carrot of a fifty-grand fee to bring them out. We would have found them ourselves eventually, besides, you've not provided us with any evidence against them so there's no risk of you meeting them on a future date in court."

"That won't matter to them. They will put two and two together. They trade off fear. Pascal has silenced hundreds of punters who complained about being ripped off, sending them out on flimsy dinghies to drown. I've heard he's cut a few of his own people who for one reason or another didn't follow instructions."

"But you don't work for Pascal."

"No, but it won't make any difference. I have his trust. In bringing you here I have broken that trust. Although I'm going home tonight, when all of this becomes known I won't be able to come back."

"Forget it. By the time you are ready to return, he'll be the one who won't be coming back. As far as you're concerned, all you have to do is deliver me to your contact in an hour from now, take your money and go."

"So you let me take a fee from them for bringing you here and then bust me for taking a payment?"

"No. I don't need to know anything about that. That's cash in your pocket."

"But you said you needed more help?"

"Before I leave you, I will give you a stamped addressed envelope. Take it back on the ferry and drop it in the nearest post box when you get to the other side."

"That's it?"

"Nothing else. As far as we're concerned, you can forget we ever met. If anyone asks you all you have to say is you followed the instructions you were given, and you don't know anything more."

"How will I know what happens to you?"

"That is not your concern."

"But I'd really like that…"

She looked at him, trying to work out how serious he was.

"Tell you what, if you do as I have asked, I will contact you when all this is over and maybe we'll meet for a drink or something. Is that a deal?"

She smiled and held her hand out to him in a high five.

He returned the compliment, and they packed up ready for the final run in.

It turned out the address Tony had been instructed to go to was in the dunes, but to get to it they had to retrace their path back to the main road and drive further south before taking a track back towards the shore.

TWENTY

THIS ROUTE WAS NOT like the previous approach to the sea. On this route there were houses spaced out at intervals in a random way. If they had been grouped together the casual visitor could have called the collection a village, but in this case the properties were spread out without boundary definitions. At short intervals, Tony stopped and checked the satnav on his phone to identify the property that would be his final destination. When he found it, he gestured Sunny to get off and laid the moped down on its side.

"It's that one over there with the blue Peugeot outside, but we're early. I suggest we wait here out of sight, and I will make the call in half an hour."

Sunny nodded her agreement, taking the rug out of the moped pannier and sitting in a sandy hollow below the surrounding tufts of grass. In her mind, she was calm knowing that events would take their course in the hours ahead and all she needed was patience. By chance she had sat with her back resting against a hillock with their target behind her. It was the perfect position to take advantage of the sun without being exposed to the sharp sea breeze. Her companion was less relaxed, sitting up to watch for activity.

As she reclined she reflected on their earlier conversation and knew that despite his odd ways, her companion was a good guy and she had been lucky in more ways than one to find him. Given she lived in a world of subterfuge, it was refreshing to meet someone who was just ordinary, uncomplicated. Maybe this was the type of man she needed a relationship with, if only to keep her grounded. Maybe she would follow up on what she had said – meet him when all this business was over and get to know him a bit better.

Maybe.

These were definitely questions for another day.

As arranged, Tony called the number he had been given at the appointed time.

The conversation was short.

Sunny looked at him with a questioning expression.

Tony replied: "The bloke says to come to the door in thirty minutes. He's got a computer and internet connection. Says you need to be ready to do the money transfer when you arrive."

Ten minutes to go and Sunny was checking she had all she needed in her backpack. She emptied it out on the ground before putting the random items back. Tony couldn't help but notice the underwear and various toiletries which were the first items to be loaded, together with a bottle of water, some protein bars and an apple. Just as the items disappeared, Tony drew her attention.

"Look there's movement at the house, three guys putting bags into the Peugeot."

She fiddled with her phone.

"Get a picture."

Tony was about to comply when one of the men pointed in his direction.

"Shit – I think they've seen me – one is heading this way."

"Get a picture!"

"I've got the guy coming towards us."

"Get the others as well – *here*."

Sensing the danger, Sunny stood up, her back towards the approaching figure and peeled off her sweatshirt, revealing her sculpted torso and ample breasts, dark oval areolas and erect nipples.

"Take my picture now and don't use the zoom. The point of the picture is the *background*, not me."

Tony followed her instruction.

She turned to face the man approaching, squealed and rushed to Tony making him drop the phone and instructively pull her close, shielding her nudity.

The action had the desired effect, the man stopped, nodded and smiled and walked away. His two colleagues had stayed by the car watching the scene.

"You missed a sight there," Canecale called to the others as he returned to the car. "There's a guy there getting it on with some chick in the dunes. He's obviously playing away and didn't look like he wanted to be disturbed, and I'm not sure if I'm ready to appear in his dirty movie on Instagram or wherever he's going to put it."

The other two laughed and got in the car and head off down the track towards the main road.

Tony had not yet released his grip on Sunny, and she could already feel the tension in his body.

Gently peeling herself away, she picked up her top and the mobile, and whispered: "There's no time for anything like that now. You'd better save yourself for when I get to Southampton."

She deftly opened up the mobile and removed the SIM card, putting it into an envelope and passing it back to Tony.

"OK – you know what to do with that when you get to Dover. Now I assume we are just waiting for the driver of that car to return."

It was her turn to experience the adrenaline rush. This was the moment of no return. The Peugeot had only been back five minutes before he took her to the door.

"Anita? And you must be Tony – do come in. My name's Mike – 'Muzzy' to my friends."

There was not much in the way of small talk. He got to the point.

"I will be taking you across to England shortly, but first we need to get your deposit arranged. I have a computer ready for your use in the front room – the account details are on a piece of paper next to the keyboard. While you're doing that, Tony and I will be in the kitchen having a beer – this sea air gets to you after a while."

Once in the kitchen, Mike's tone became more conspiratorial. He pulled a wad of banknotes out of his back pocket.

"Here's your fee, Tony – I hear you prefer sterling than Euros, and here's a bonus. I like it when people just do as they're told, which reminds me, you can *fuck off* now."

"What about the girl?"

"What would you care? I will deal with her. If she pays her fees on time she'll get to where she wants, no problem. If not, well I'll just have to come up with an alternative way of recovering my investment in her."

"Can I say goodbye?"

"Don't tell me you fancy her? You randy old goat. Answer's no. You're just the delivery man on an errand that is now finishing. All you need to do is to follow my car to the jetty down the road. I will leave the keys and you can return it to the renters' compound in Boulogne on your way back. Your scooter will fit in the trunk. Let yourself out."

As Abraham turned to leave his phone lit up to confirm the twenty-five thousand pound fee had been deposited in his account. It was time to start the return journey to England.

It was time for McKee to start to fill in the blanks of his knowledge about Turhan International. From what he had discovered so far, there was a confusing mix of legal and 'out of scope' activities.

'Out of scope' covered a range of activities that were either internationally illegal, partially legal but constrained by sanctions in some parts of the world, and activities that could be argued as legal in Turkey but not elsewhere. The overall picture was messy, but at least he had started to sort it out.

The illegal gold trade had been identified and passed to London for further investigation. If there was more for him to do he would be told in due course. That was likely to be the highest value trade Turhan was undertaking, but Turhan's arms business may be of greater concern politically, even if it wasn't illegal. He didn't need to wait for the instruction from Smith. He needed to get close to this Asar Belgin, the pugnacious ex-soldier running the arms trade to understand what was going on. This should be relatively easy to fix via Ciller Terzili, he thought – after all, her original request to him was to help her find new customers for this trade from Dubai.

He had promised to return in ten days, but here he was, back at the *yali* a week after he had left and as his greeting from Ciller Terzili confirmed, he had been missed.

"Now your business affairs are under control we can have more time together," his host observed.

"Yes. It's rare to bring business and pleasure together, so I have given myself another week familiarising myself with my new client," he responded carefully, hoping to manage her future expectations. He continued: "If I am going to improve your commercial prospects, I need to get some focus on what you have to sell – volumes, timescales, prices, credit terms, export licence procedures and most importantly, capabilities – so you need to get me plugged in to your defence company, so I can get my head around the details."

"I had already anticipated your request and briefed our divisional managing director accordingly. He has told me that getting you up to speed will be a priority and that I am to send you over to meet him at the earliest opportunity."

"Tomorrow then?"

She nodded.

"Leave your hire car here and I will have Osman take you over to their base. It's a twenty-minute journey."

The trip took him northeast towards Elmali to an anonymous compound secluded in a narrow valley and concealed by a dense blanket of stone pines. Approaching along a narrow track for around five kilometres, the setting looked more appropriate for some tourist adventure activity centre than a munitions factory. Its true purpose was only conceded by a small sign next to the road, around 100 metres from the entrance and would only be visible to those who had persevered past regular warning signs announcing, 'Private Property' and visual images of snarling guard dogs in the vicinity. The site itself appeared to be fortified with two-metre-high sections of solid metallic fencing, painted dark green to merge as much as possible into the surroundings. There was a wide gap, big enough to accommodate a 4x4 between the fencing and the trees which had the benefit of CCTV pylons at regular intervals.

The gate looked like the standard access arrangements that would be expected at any military facility. Checkpoints, barriers, an elevated watchtower and strategically positioned concrete blocks that would oblige all vehicles to follow a chicane to move in and out of the compound. Although security outside appeared unobtrusive, at the entrance were guards with semi-automatic weapons and dogs. Osman was clearly expected. Their Mercedes, one of Turhan's fleet McKee assumed, was waved through without enquiry, and its driver knew exactly where to go on arrival.

They came to a halt by a utilitarian administration building that was next to a warehouse; itself in front of a large concrete platform with half a dozen items he estimated to be the size of construction waste skips neatly laid out in a line, covered by tarpaulins. Beyond the platform, in the distance there looked to be a small firing range and in front of it what looked to be a pen with four sheep in it. Considering the heavy security presence at the entrance there was little sign of military activity of the type he had expected to see – no sign of tanks or other mobile armed vehicles, but he guessed these were likely to be out of sight of a visitor.

A moment later, a solidly built, tall, tanned bald-headed man with sunken eyes, tattooed forearms and the nose of an unsuccessful boxer came out the office building to meet him.

"Mr McKee, welcome! I am Asar Belgin."

His host noted his surprise.

"You were expecting someone older? Perhaps dressed in a suit? Your reaction is not unusual. I don't do suits and I don't like offices. Fortunately, in my line of work it doesn't matter. I spend most of my time with fighting men as I am sure you would understand. I have heard much about you from Ciller. She seems to think you can help us to build our arms exports. I will be interested to hear how you intend to do that. Business in our field of activity is often… complicated.

"Today I have been asked to give you a briefing on Turhan's arms businesses and to explain something of our future strategy."

Again, Belgin was reading McKee's reaction.

"Don't worry Mr McKee, this is one of our test sites, and considerably the smallest, but given you were in Istanbul is the most convenient to access from the city. You should know, I also don't go in for boring computer presentations – there's a team of people in our main admin office who do that sort of stuff. I am going to tell you what is happening on the ground, and I like to do that as I walk, so please let me show you around."

McKee nodded and Belgin set off, he nodded to a nearby guard to remove the tarpaulins on the platform.

"Ciller will have told you about my background," he continued.

"Ex-Turkish special forces, former army surplus trader, secretary to the Turkish Munitions Association and now here, boss of Turhan International Armaments. One way or another, my life has been shaped by the military, the fifth largest in the world, and they have given me a good career. I think I have been successful by understanding change and responding to it, before being dictated to by circumstances."

McKee could sense that although Belgin appeared to be talking off the cuff, he had clearly thought through what we wanted to say and that he should hear him out before initiating a dialogue.

Belgin continued: "Now is such a moment, Duncan. I hope you don't mind my familiarity? The world is changing fast and with it the nature of managing conflict. The traditional alliances of yester year and competing ideologies is gone. Today's battles and those of the future will be around the control of resources – the essentials of life – oil, gas, minerals, drinking water – perhaps in the longer term – even food. In essence, whereas we may never face a world war again, because that would result in mutually assured destruction, the scope for regional and localised conflicts has increased and countries need to be better equipped to meet this new challenge. In the future, armies cannot define their effectiveness in terms of numbers of soldiers, tanks or guns. In fact, even today, the secret is not in numbers but capability and agility. Having the right people, the right equipment in the right place at the right time. Forces need to deploy at pace and withdraw as quickly. What does this mean for us? I think it means we need to produce high-tech weaponry. Artificial Intelligence or AI will define the conflicts of tomorrow. It will cost more, that's for sure and customers won't buy so much of it, but for those suppliers who can meet customers' aspirations the future is good."

Belgin paused to observe his guest's expression.

"Why does this matter to Turhan? Our business has been supplying recycled small-arms personal protection equipment and components (including ammunition casings) from re-engineered alloys and we have done well as one of our military's principal suppliers. But for us this business is a volume trade. Soon even the numbers in the Turkish armed forces will be cut and correspondingly our market will shrink. Where else will we be able to sell this equipment in bulk? There are parts of Africa and the Americas that may take it, but certainly not at the margins our business needs. The Chinese and Russians keep on spitting out the same old stuff and their command economies mean their supply chains are protected and can undercut anybody. We need a new offer in the market, and you can help make it happen."

"What is the offer?"

"The big opportunity is with drones, like the ones you see here. We have six models with surveillance and bombing capability that are already acknowledged as internationally market leading. We got that opportunity thanks to our president agreeing to supply a test squadron to the Azeris in their most recent struggle with Armenia a couple of years back. Most observers acknowledge they won this round of their ongoing dispute so emphatically the Armenians agreed a peace treaty after just two weeks. Personally, I was surprised. Our product, which was based on a design we managed to acquire from the Israelis was OK but not particularly sophisticated. I would have expected the Armenians to bring them down in short order, but they were clearly unprepared and lacked the technology to do it. There is no doubt they will be ready next time unless we improve. We also have a critical logistics drone which can lift up to fifty kilos of essential supplies up to two hundred km at an altitude of two km. Given its airborne characteristics, that too is difficult to bring down and can be particularly effective when deployed to jam radar. Missiles also, have always been a competitive international market and all the talk in the industry is about hypersonics that can avoid ground-based defensive radar, but in reality there is a limited demand for this given the infrastructure required for its operation. Our approach is a new intelligent shoulder-launched product that can be guided to a moving target from a control unit the size of a mobile phone. Under test conditions, this has a range of around five hundred km and is probably the best in class at the moment. But AI is not just about what we can do in the air. A big prospect for us is the small, unmanned tank. We have a product here, complete with three weapon options, no bigger than a Fiat 500. Utilising Turhan's latest titanium alloys for protection, these vehicles are lightweight, fast, highly manoeuvrable and capable of rapid firing, better than the Russian T-14 *Armata*. More importantly they can be controlled from an operational centre potentially the other side of the world. Our plan is not only to be able to sell the hardware but also offer the command-and-control technologies as well."

TWENTY-ONE

MCKEE COULD HEAR THE understated excitement in Belgin's voice as he spoke.

"Of course, all the products I have discussed with you are in production now, but what I really wanted to show you is new technology where we believe we have a world first. For some years now we have been experimenting with electronic systems which we tend to run from this facility. Our original expectation was we were looking at improved jamming technology that we have perfected but, as a biproduct, and working from an Israeli blueprint, we have developed a new weapon. It is so new we haven't given it an official name but it is, in reality, a sonic gun. It can kill a target silently by directing a concentrated microwave signal over a distance of ten metres. It can lock onto the target before firing and has the effect of creating an embolism causing instant death and leaves no trace. Although the power of microwaves have been known for some time, the challenge has been to focus it, in a concentrated form over a set distance. At present, I am not sure anyone else (including the Americans, Russians and Chinese) have been able to do that. Certainly we have discovered this by trial and error so it is likely others will follow our path once news gets out. Think of the business potential for Turhan from this alone."

"How come you developed this piece of high tech?"

"We didn't really. We acquired some classified research papers from a source in Israel that included a 3D printing specification before I took charge, so I don't know much about the circumstances. Kerim took care of it. A professor at Istanbul University, one of his contacts, adapted it to get a research project from Teleturk, the mobile company, to propose how broadband coverage in the centre of the country could be improved quickly and cheaply. He came up with the idea of trialling directional pulsar signal boosters on existing broadband routers closest to the areas not presently served. This was originally proposed as a short-term fix rather than building new masts. It worked for a while, but then reports came in that people living in the properties affected were getting sick with headaches and other cerebral symptoms such as loss of concentration and dizzy spells; some of the worst cases resulted in deaths from blood clots. An investigation took place that resulted in the gradual removal of the pulsar units as they were replaced by masts. It was all hushed up as neither the university or the telecom company wanted to be nailed for compensation."

"Let me be clear, are you saying the sickness and deaths were caused by the electrical pulsar boosters?"

"According to the university tests there is a direct link. And we know that the same understanding has been reached – by the Russians in particular. You see, this technology is driven by microwaves. Microwaves are particularly important to electronic surveillance. We think the Russians have been siting microwave boosters around US diplomatic facilities to intercept communications and to create illness amongst diplomatic staff, who in many cases are retained on spying duties. We think this is happening right now in Ankara. Stories about this are starting to appear in media around the world – I am sure you have heard of Havana Syndrome?"

"Vaguely, but I hadn't linked this to your work. If I understand you correctly then you have applied the pulsar booster technology to create a weapon that concentrates the microwave on the target to create a blood clot?"

"That is correct."

"But surely that takes time?"

"Yes, according to our tests to date, we think it takes between two and five minutes to work after exposure depending on the physiology of the target."

"You have tested it on humans?"

"Our military is always engaged in operations against illegal migrants. Getting hold of a supply of people to test is not an issue. After all, we don't keep records of individual identities, just the outcome of the tests."

"If it takes so long to take effect, what relevance as a weapon does it have?"

"Firstly we are experimenting with the level of charge we can put through the gun. There is an assumption that the greater the level of charge, the faster death will occur. But that is not proven. What is more relevant for now is the fear this weapon can engender. It allows us to eliminate people without them knowing at the time they have been exposed. The ability to create fear is the best outcome that any military tool can create."

"But nobody knows you have this prototype…"

"No – but we must plan to patent it and then news will leak, and no doubt rival products will be created. We plan to perfect the technology first, go into production and only then register the international patent. We think that can happen in the next two years, the ideal window for you to generate orders from foreign governments in advance."

"How did Terzili get his hands on this research in the first place?"

"I'm not sure, but I think it was quite a long time ago – before I arrived. I don't know the detail but Terzili used to be a bit of a lad, so I understand this professor got caught up with drink, gambling and a woman or three. The boss was always pretty good at helping people get out of such situations, you know? In this case, access to the research was the price. I reckon having got it he must have been a bit pissed off. We had to go and find an electrical engineer to help us interpret it, and we only did that because he kept pestering us to understand what we were doing with it."

"How many prototypes do you have?"

"Just three for now and they are kept at this site in a secure location. Only the project development director and I can access them."

"You do know, if we are to sell these we will need to stage demonstrations for customers?"

"Sure. It is why you are here."

Their strolling conversation had brought them to the far end of the compound where two guards were standing by the sheep pen. Belgin nodded to one, who passed the microwave weapon to him, the other took out one of the sheep and tethered it to a post nearby.

"Here is the demonstration. I will use the gun on the sheep for two minutes. Don't worry it will not show signs of pain. We will return the way we have come. By the time we are back at my office, the animal will be dead."

McKee watched with a grim fascination. Belgin took the gun which looked similar in design to an Uzi with a curved plate on the front and took aim. In the next minutes he appeared merely to be looking at the target through the sight. When he decided his task was complete, he passed the weapon back to the guard. They started their return walk.

He continued: "The problem with all this is we still don't fully understand the range and exposure levels so that is where our effort is focused right now. But as this test will show we are close to reaching a conclusion."

When they got back to the office building, they looked back the way they had come. As Belgin predicted, the sheep appeared to be lying on its side. The guard nearby, seeing his boss and guest were looking in his direction, visibly kicked the carcass hard to demonstrate it was now lifeless.

It was dusk when they arrived at Abraham's boat moored on the Canche estuary. All was quiet; even traffic using the airfield at Le Touquet on the opposite bank seemed to have ceased for the night. The craft was no leisure yacht, but an ocean-going motor vessel with crew to match and set sail as soon as they were aboard. The engines provided a throaty roar as they set to work, disturbing some of the bird life that had settled in the nearby reed beds as they moved away. The only discernible features to the casual observer were the twinkling lights of a number of properties spread out on the horizon a distance from the shore.

Although it was dry, the wind from the sea was providing an unwelcome chill which did not encourage anyone to stay on deck who didn't need to be there. A deckhand opened the cabin door as he approached. He muttered his thanks in return.

"Why do they call you Muzzy?" Sunny asked as a means of striking up a conversation.

"It's short for Mustafa. My name is Mustafa Ismail. I am Turkish born, run a kebab business in Britain and the crew are my countrymen so that is the name they are comfortable with."

"So why call yourself Michael?"

"It's a long story. Let's just say, given the circles I mix in, it's easier. You could say Michael Abraham is just an English version of my name."

Abraham gestured to his VIP to go into the warm cabin below.

"Better get comfortable – our journey will be about six hours and the forecast isn't the best," Abraham told her.

He sensed her nervousness.

"Don't worry you will be safe with us, but there is one formality I need you to complete. Take off your clothes."

"All I have with me is in my handbag."

"I'm not interested in that."

Sunny's worst fears were coming true.

"No, I didn't sign up for a cheap fuck," she replied angrily.

He drew a pistol from his pocket.

"I will not ask for a second time. I may only have half your fee, but it's just as easy for me to turn you into fish food."

She hesitated long enough to see the fixed look in his eye and started to comply with his instruction.

"So you're going to rape me? Perks of the job?"

He gestured with his hand for her to get on with it. She got as far as her underwear.

"…And the rest."

She undid her bra and stepped out of her pants and did her best with her arms to cover as much of her exposed flesh as possible.

"If you get close, I will fight," she warned.

He seemed to ignore her defiance.

"Sit down on the couch."

His weapon returned to his pocket and was substituted for a mobile phone. He kept his distance.

"I'm going to take your picture, so look sexy, like you want it. Spread your arms and legs."

"What?"

"Do as you're told, and you won't come to any harm."

She was powerless to resist and readily saw the danger of antagonising her tormentor. In practice, looking sexy when nude in a stressful situation was not an easy ask.

"Good. Thank you. I have to say you are a beautiful woman who under normal circumstances I would be pleased to fuck, but these are not normal circumstances. You can get dressed."

She snatched at her discarded clothes, seeking the empowerment they provided.

"What's all that about? Do you get off at looking at pictures of naked women?"

"No, but I know some that do. The pictures are my insurance if you don't complete our transaction. I have to look at alternative means of recovering my investment."

"Can you get twenty-five grand for a picture of my bush?"

"I would be in a different business if that was the case. No, if you don't come up with the second instalment as agreed before you are ready to leave the boat, I will need to sell you on to one of my contacts, who may have other plans for you. They need to understand your potential. That situation may not be good. An attractive, desirable, *clean* brown-skinned woman without any legal identity in the UK is considered a bankable asset in some places. I have supplied others in the past less fortunate than you."

"You have sold women into slavery?"

Abraham was matter-of-fact.

"And men possibly. I don't know, but only those who are attractive enough. Quite a few are just liabilities with no earning potential who do not make it across the water. Pimping was never my interest – too much effort for too little reward."

Even with Sunny's experience, she was shocked by his attitude.

"How do you live with yourself?" She continued to dress.

"People smuggling is just a business. We don't kill people although some perish on the journey. Our customers freely decide to take the risk of using our service. In fact, many pay us for bussing them to the beach from the city. High turnover, good profits, cash in the pocket as well as the bank – what's not to like about that? We help around fifteen hundred a year, getting them on to inflatables and, until recently, we met them on the other side, helping them off the beaches and into jobs in different cities. We're stopping doing that now as it is getting too difficult for our people on the ground. It's much easier operating in France. All we do is to control a stretch of coast, a one-kilometre strip closest to the jungle migrant camp and put those who sign up at the camp in them. We do three departures, every other night, ten at a time, each paying ten thousand pounds for the privilege. Pascal runs it all for us locally. Together with my fellow directors we only need to get involved in the strategic stuff."

"Strategic stuff?"

"The regulatory aspects – security, banking, buying and transporting the inflatables, keeping the police at arm's length – it's not that complicated."

"Are you bribing the police?"

"On the French side, if necessary, but not with big money. They tend to like a little recreational coke, when it's offered, but the truth is they like the fact we help keep the numbers of refugees in their locality down. They like it even more that the Brits don't end up sending them back if they get to the other shore, so everyone's happy."

Sunny fought to regain her composure and pick up the pieces of her shattered dignity.

"Look, Muzzy, Mike, or whatever your name is. I've taken a bigger risk in paying you to take me to England than you might imagine, much more than twenty-five thousand to put my well-being in your hands. Doing the transaction earlier will leave an electronic footprint that will lead my husband here and it won't take him long to make the link to your vessel. My spending allowance is fifty thousand a week, so if you are thinking of ripping me off by charging me more, don't bother. My new boyfriend is expecting to meet me in London in two days and if I don't make it, he had an email that I sent from Calais with an instruction to go to the police about your friend Pascal, so whoever you are, there are people who will come looking for you if you don't look after me."

Abraham smiled.

"So, we both have some insurance. Issuing threats isn't a great way of starting a relationship, especially when we are locked in a cabin at sea together for the coming hours. I can't think what your husband would make of my pictures. Might remind him of something he's been missing, perhaps. You should remember, together with my associates, we have helped hundreds, thousands to get to the UK safely, most in much more stressed situations than your own. Your passage is a happy combination of circumstances; it is rare as the boss I get personally involved. In fact, this is only happening as I had other business in the locality and my return coincided with your requirements. You have bought a premium service and thus my personal attention. That's why you are not in a dinghy, getting wet with the rest out there. Now you have paid your deposit, we will regard you as a key piece of merchandise to be delivered safely as agreed. We are taking the shortest route north to Dungeness then tracking west along the coast to Brighton. I have my car in the marina car park and will drop you at the railway station on my way home. Given your circumstances I cannot imagine you will be complaining to the local police. Provided the bank confirms your second payment before we disembark you will never see or hear from me again."

"And if not?"

"You won't be leaving the boat."

The encounter had impacted Sunny in a way she could never have anticipated. Although hardened to the realities of her job and despite not being physically harmed, she felt violated, and psychologically bruised by the experience. When she had taken off her top earlier in the day with Tony, it had been her action on her terms for a particular professional purpose. She had been comfortable; in control. This was very different. Her captor seemed detached from everything other than his own reality. Despite her best efforts she felt she was experiencing a sense of shock, a feeling those who have had a near miss in a car accident might understand. Now she just had to stay safe, endure the sea crossing, and hope Tony had posted her letter in Dover. Had she given Mwake enough information to find her? Time would tell. Now the boat was moving into open water and was absorbing the impact and undulation of the incoming waves. She was surprised to observe Mike, apparently a seasoned sailor, was preoccupied with the pitch and roll as they struggled north. Her worries about being attacked dissipated as he looked more concerned with his own welfare. Combined with the distraction of photographing her, he had been careless – failing to search her bag for a mobile.

"I'm going to lie down for a while, until things calm down," he said.

There was no supplementary invitation to her to join him.

"There's a bathroom through that door if you need it. There is a rug on the couch and the toilet is through the door over there. Otherwise make yourself comfortable. I will see you at first light."

Whereas she was pleased to have been left alone, her host had taken precautions, his pistol and phone had gone with him. She hadn't registered that she had been locked in the cabin in the first place but remembered his comment. Given the weather outside, she wouldn't complain. Her first move was to recover her mobile phone. Although no good for calls, at least the camera would work. She would occupy her time exploring the cabin for clues as to his true identity. Shortly after she found one, an old opened manilla envelope date-stamped, addressed to a Mr M Abraham in Buckinghamshire, being used as a bookmark. She took a picture before thrusting it back into her bag, carefully wrapped in her soiled underwear to ward off casual inspection.

TWENTY-TWO

MCKEE'S INDUCTION WITH TURHAN'S operations had continued at the Ottoman Breakers Yard to Duru Hosni, a four-hour drive from Istanbul.

"This is the future for Turhan," announced Hosni with an expansive wave of his arm as he looked out of his office window on the dock at Cakmakli, south of Aliaga, to what was left of the aft section of the *Hawaiian Sun*. He was, in every sense a different character to Belgin; older certainly, but more urbane, expansive, seemingly assured.

"We're doing better deals to acquire ships for breaking. I am negotiating on two prospects at the moment which will mean we will be paid to take them off the hands of the present owners. The *Hawaiian Sun* wasn't a deal I would have done, but now with half the ship stripped, we are turning profit on the associated smelting and rolling operations, producing specialist construction and military alloys as well as refined metals with ninety-five per cent purity for industrial customers – and not just here – South Korea, Canada and Germany are opening up to us. Looking at our contribution to the economy, employment and the environment we are doing more to underwrite the national debt than most home grown-enterprises."

"From what I've been told, you seem to have got a lot done in the time."

"Don't be surprised, what was wrong with this operation when I joined was the financing of the *Hawaiian Sun* – we had all of the debt and precious little of the equity. This is the advantage of being a former customer of Turhan's – I knew better than anyone where the problems were and frankly I doubt whether anyone else could have persuaded my former employers to refinance the deal."

"How did it happen?"

"The motivation was simple. If they had stayed on the sidelines, Turhan would have folded and they would have been compromised by bad debt. Now they will be guaranteed their money and the only additional price has been a two-year extension of terms. Also we have a proper sales team, and our orders for assorted metals and grades are looking positive. Kerim's son, Adnan helps us out from time to time on specific projects. We have the prospect of doubling profits year on year. That in turn will allow us to open up new opportunities. I think vehicle production is the most interesting and even now we are starting to produce axles for military and heavy goods vehicles and coaches."

"I thought Belgin handled the military?"

"He does the sales but brings us the specifications from our customers to improve our products, much like the sort of thing you will be doing, I understand. Armaments are a good example. We have started producing tank armour for the Turkish military using a titanium alloy, stronger and lighter than any armour in production anywhere in the world."

"And precious metals?"

"I'm not sure what you mean. All metal is precious to us, we just have to find the market to give it value."

"Gold?"

"Even within Turhan, we have to retain discretion about some of our operations. I'm not in a position to say more, as we have contractual liabilities to consider. You, of all people, will understand that."

McKee nodded. "I understand about compliance for sure. Managing within the constraints of legal frameworks must be challenging…"

"To an extent," came the reply. "We always have to be aware that what is illegal in one jurisdiction may not be in another, so we have to take a flexible approach. You have yet to spend time with my colleague, Ilkay Vahid. He has the overview of Turhan's new business strategy…" he hesitated, returning his gaze to the dry dock beyond his window.

He continued: "He's an interesting fellow – quite a complex personality I find, but he is the man navigating the world's regulatory schemes…"

McKee nodded some more.

"Not Repcer? I thought as a lawyer that would be his department?"

"Repcer may sign things off and draft the paperwork, but Vahid does the research and makes the recommendations."

He was starting to understand Turhan's operations were not black and white but spanned the full spectrum of grey, illustrated by his next appointment, nearby with Adnan Terzili. They met at a marina on the north side of town. Although separated from the Breakers Yard by a hilly, wooded and semi-urban promontory, the contrast of settings was stark. In the past thirty minutes he had travelled from a dry dock on the fringes of an industrial estate and chemical works to a picturesque harbour on a semi-enclosed bay on the edge of the Aegean, surrounded by whitewashed bars and restaurants fringed with bougainvillea. Finding his host wasn't difficult either, he simply headed for what appeared to be the grandest boat on the marina – a Sunseeker 90 Ocean pumping out dance music, where a party appeared to be in full swing.

As he stood briefly on the jetty taking in the scene, a man in a stripy long-sleeved T-shirt called to him.

"You're Duncan McKee right? Come on board and join the fun!"

He immediately recognised Adnan as Ciller's brother. Despite being younger than his sister by some five years his face seemed older, with what looked like bruised eyes and untamed stubble.

As far as Duncan could tell, Adnan was certainly enjoying himself, surrounded by a posse of scantily clad women who seemed to be in an exaggerated competition to win his attention.

Smartly dressed in a light green suit and white open-necked shirt, McKee felt overdressed for the occasion and was briefly distracted by two of Adnan's followers peeling off to focus their interest on him.

"I hope you don't mind meeting here," he began. "I thought it would be more convenient than expecting you to drag all the way down to my villa at Bodrum, especially as you were visiting the Breakers Yard. My sister was keen that I met you. Will you have a glass of champagne or are you a beer man?"

"Beer's good – especially at this time of day."

"Joint or line? Personally, I like a joint around this time of day. Keeps me cool in the mind, you know? I tend to get a bit hyper if I do a line. The brain starts racing and then I do mad stuff, half of which I then forget," he added, pulling what looked like a tin of loose tobacco out of his pocket, as a precursor to rolling a smoke. McKee's shake of the head didn't seem to slow him down or put him off.

Adnan nodded to one of 'the dusky maidens' who had attached themselves to his guest. She took the hint and disappeared below deck.

McKee was struck by the strangeness of the scene – a noisy shipboard party that would perhaps be held offshore during the day to avoid disturbing the locals and only about twenty guests – all women. Did this man not have any friends?

The beer arrived, which was mercifully cold.

"My sister tells me you are working for her and that I should

251

cooperate with anything you want. So welcome to the firm! I will play the genie from the magic lamp – your slightest wish will be my sternest command." His tone was mocking.

"I think it best if we could talk privately," McKee asked awkwardly.

"Are you sure?" Adnan smiled. "It's not every day you can have a couple of beautiful girls looking after your every need. Don't you want a little time to get to know them better before we get down to it?"

"The thought is appreciated but I have a busy schedule and need to get back to Istanbul."

Adnan saw the need to cut the frivolity and clapped his hands.

"Girls, go and enjoy the sunshine – we will join you later. Come into the forward lounge. If we keep the door shut we won't be disturbed. What do you want to know?"

McKee explained his mission to be an international sales agent for Turhan in the Gulf and also to discover who was behind the family bombing. He asked Adnan to offer his account of the family assassination and his work for the company.

"Our family was broken by the bombing. I was lucky not to be around they day it happened or else that would have been the end of me as well."

"So it was no accident?"

"No – you don't accidentally blow up a minibus in my opinion. But it taught me a lesson not to spend the short time we have on this earth working. Ciller was always more studious than me, she loves all this corporate thing and company bullshit. I prefer chilling out."

"How do you make a living?"

"Income from a small family concern within the Turhan group. In return I have to do a couple of errands a month. For example, collecting a cargo delivery at the airport or receiving a container of some commodity or other to break up and distribute for Ilkay. Now and again, Duru Hosni asks me to help with the odd sales pitch. It helps me to stay grounded. I can tell you, it's much harder than you may think being a playboy and having to keep my girls satisfied. Left to their own devices they're always arguing or fighting about something. Drives me mad sometimes."

"Do you spend much time with the family?"

"I try to see Dad once a month – that was a promise I made to Ciller – and occasionally I see a couple of the family friends, Repcer and Dad's buddy, Canecale, but that's it. Of course, I do a little private business from time to time to help with the cash flow."

"You know the Canecales then?"

"The old gimmer turns up at the *yali* from time to time. I used to know one of his sons, but we fell out. Think he got caught up in some trouble at sea – got his air pipes in a twist with some tart who fell off a cruiser – but I really can't remember."

"What sort of private business?"

"Debt collection, security, enforcement, a bit of cross border trade with some Russian guys into Syria. Pocket-money stuff really, but they're useful people to know. Looks after my personal needs."

He inhaled sharply on the roll up.

"Solokov?" McKee queried.

"He's one for sure."

"Who do you think targeted the minibus?"

"If the cops haven't worked it out by now, I'm sure I couldn't. But I think it's obvious it was someone who had a grudge against the family. You know how it is in business. There's always someone who has a grievance."

"Could it have been the Russians?"

"Who are they? They're not like a football team! It's possible. Dad used to do commodities trades in the former Soviet republics, but no one special springs to mind."

"You mean drugs?"

"Refined – sometimes just seed for processing."

"Is that what you do?"

Adnan shrugged.

"Maybe – agriculture out east can cover all sorts of things – nuts, pomegranates, dates, wheat. Tell you what, though – if the Russians had a hand in it they'd have needed a local fixer like me. Mum only decided that morning to go in a minibus. Very few would have understood the travel arrangements that day and I was glad I wasn't there."

McKee got up to leave. "You've been very helpful. I appreciate your time."

"So soon?" Adnan looked disappointed to be losing a friend. "We can go and join the party on deck. I think you would find it an unforgettable experience."

McKee offered a non-committal smile.

"It's a pity I've got a long drive ahead of me, so unfortunately I won't be able to enjoy your hospitality but thank you for the offer. I am sure we will meet again soon."

McKee's understanding of the Turhan business would be a challenge to relate to London, and he himself had not expected to encounter such complexity in his research. Regardless of their personalities, Belgin and Hosni represented two thirds of the modern Turhan business and their activities seemed to be legitimate if amoral in parts, but Vahid seemed to be in control of a wider, sinister and more dispersed brief.

"What I do is sometimes difficult to explain to the uninitiated," he began when they met a couple of days later following his return from a business trip to Europe.

"On paper my portfolio appears modest but most of my work is looking at new high-potential growth opportunities for the group. For example, I have a watching brief on international commodities markets, where we keep a presence in staples such as wheat, maize, soya, oil and liquified natural gas, but we also dabble in consumer markets, such as personal finance and travel. In fact, our biggest investment in the last year has been in a company called Global Bus that runs an integrated luxury passenger service linking principal cities across Europe from Istanbul to Brussels and on to London. You have probably seen our local ticket office on Istiklal Street, off Taksim Square. Although we recognised a market opportunity, demand has taken us by surprise. We rarely have departures that are not fully booked in advance – our total fleet is around sixty vehicles of which anything up to twenty will be travelling on other sections of the route as we speak."

"Presumably you are big in real estate as well, I should imagine…"

"Actually no. The company has real estate holdings, but they are held for investment purposes only. Kerim and Repcer deal with that sort of stuff."

"How long do you look at a market before going in?"

"It depends on what is involved. Commodities are easier as we just buy and sell. On some lines we don't even have to take delivery, we just trade them online in the spot markets. Financial services takes more organisation. We have set up a small savings bank called Azure that does savings and unsecured loans to people with poor credit histories where we can charge unrestricted interest levels in line with local conditions. Global Bus is an interesting example. We looked at that for two years before making a commitment, largely because that was the time needed to get the necessary logistical support infrastructure such as depots and sales agencies in place."

"And what of the future?"

"Who knows, Mr McKee, maybe you will bring some new deals to us? I have to say as a group we are always interested in metal fabrication as it is our core business. Alongside our armaments trade, getting into building motor vehicles is particularly attractive to us. Here in Turkey we have a number of sites and plenty of labour to call on, if we can produce a product customers want. These days nobody wants petrol cars, so the biggest barrier for us will be to find a quality battery manufacturer who can supply in volume. We could never expect to do that ourselves and it would take us maybe ten years or more to form the right relationships. And now, Mr McKee, my turn to ask some questions. Firstly, what can you offer Turhan and why should we work with you?"

"You will know I was not looking for this assignment. Your colleague, Ciller Terzili approached me. Why? You should ask her. I think it is because of the spread of my international contacts. What do I get? A good pay cheque and perhaps some gratitude for the business once I have delivered some deals."

"You should be careful, Mr McKee – don't get comfortable. Despite Ciller's obvious charms, she is just a figurehead. The power of the Terzilis in Turhan is in decline. Despite what you may have been told, there is no future for a hired hand like you in this business. If you had any doubts you had better understand it is Repcer who calls the shots around here on everything."

Armed with his own dossier and reports from Matheson, which had no doubt been sanitised by Smith on behalf of the Cabinet Office, Oliver Watson had his own fieldwork to do.

He had signed up as a pole-to-pole customer with Global Bus planning to make the return journey to Istanbul in a week.

Unlike most of his fellow passengers who would be engaged in conversation with their travelling companions, sleeping, eating, reading, watching videos, or just queuing for the toilet, Watson would pass the hours watching the actions of the crew and what would happen at each of their calling points en route.

Heading away into Europe with the minimum of fuss it was clear that border and customs officials on the European mainland were used to seeing the Global Bus passing through their territory, so much so that at the first mandatory passport checkpoint, police would check personal identity documentation of passengers, but wouldn't pay any attention to a thorough vehicle check to see if other goods were being smuggled. Maybe that form of inspection was saved for Dover for traffic going in the opposite direction.

Watson had been surprised shortly after leaving the central bus station in Brussels when it was announced their service would be making an unscheduled transfer at the company's private depot just south of the city's ring road.

He called the stewardess to find out more.

"Unfortunately, Mr Watson, sir, this unit has developed a fault and needs urgent maintenance. We will be met by a new fully stocked liner at our depot to continue the journey on to Venice, Belgrade and Istanbul. Once we have transferred all the luggage and cargo, this bus will be diverted back from our maintenance base here to London. I expect us to have around a thirty-minute delay and naturally we will not ask you to leave your seat until we are ready to move on."

"So what's gone wrong?"

The stewardess smiled apologetically.

"Oh I'm not really sure. I think it is probably something minor like a tachograph fault, but these things have to be addressed immediately as they are a safety issue. Although I do understand this is inconvenient, I can say that we will be able to make up time on the rest of the journey so as a first-time passenger you can be reassured that our service is reliable."

"Does this happen often?"

"It's happened to me once or twice in the past, but I would say it's relatively infrequent. Changes happen more on the northern section, especially when we get to Brussels. UK road restrictions require us to use smaller busses than we use on the rest of the route, so we have to maintain the right sized vehicles here in order to cross into the UK. Also, for our customers going all the way south, it ensures you have a more comfortable experience.

"I'm sure as a passenger you haven't noticed it yet, but I should say the quality of the roads vary widely along the route and our larger vehicles absorb a lot more of the small impact damage and vibration, you would feel it more if you continued on this vehicle."

It was late afternoon.

The stewardess's regulation smile brightened an otherwise dull day.

Watson was looking forward to the pending change of coach, the promise of a more luxurious cabin and the start of the airline-quality service Global Bus boasted of in their online advertising.

TWENTY-THREE

HE WOULD HAVE 24 hours in Istanbul before taking the return journey. He had contemplated enquiring whether he would have the opportunity to meet the spook working for the Cabinet Office in order to compare notes on the investigation while he was there, but realised even from his position in HMRC, such a request would be unlikely to be granted.

Instead he contented himself with a boat trip along the Bosporus and a short, guided tour of the Topkapi Palace. As the boat proceeded to the east with a tour guide spouting what he considered to be random, mostly irrelevant statistics about the strategic waterway's use over the years, he spent his time gazing at the opulent villas of the rich and famous along the waterfront on the Asian side and imagined what it must be like to own one of these residences. One such property had a covered terrace looking out directly onto the waterway, he could see a couple sat on a sun lounger looking back towards him. Little did he know he was watching Ciller Terzili and his colleague, Matheson, who were in turn watching his passing. His fleeting glimpse of the city gave the impression of a giant melting pot of people from across the world and a sense of eternity as if the beating heart of the metropolis had not changed with the passing of the centuries. He knew he would need to return on his own time to explore and fully absorb this intoxicating atmosphere.

Equally intoxicating (but not in a good way) was the chaos at the Istanbul bus terminal where his return service was preparing to depart. Recalling joining the outgoing passage at Victoria Coach station, this was pandemonium. In London, it was all very orderly – passengers queued to have their tickets validated and were shown to their seats. Here, it was a scrum of humanity, with whole families, some with what appeared to be their worldly possessions, fighting to access the bus with the hapless driver and stewards trying to stem the tide at the door. Ironically, Watson seemed to be propelled to the front of the queue by the human maelstrom, probably because, compared to his fellow travellers, he had fewer bags and possessions. In the heat of the moment the Global staff showed no interest in checking passports or visas just ensuring each passenger could show a paper ticket with a seat allocation. Having paid the first-class premium, Watson was ushered to the cordoned-off cabin upstairs at the front to one of six seats partitioned away from the jostling crowd. It soon became clear that the majority on board this Brussels- and London-bound bus were not European and from what Watson could tell, few were speaking European languages he could recognise. Given the scene, departure was inevitably delayed with stewards having to remove one or two who had pushed on board but were seatless, as well as convincing some of the passengers their appendages had to be taken way to be placed in the underside storage area. It was with a sense of relief that eventually sufficient calm ensued to allow the bus to start its marathon road trip across the continent. In the vicinity of his seat, the other five premium berths were occupied by a young couple from Guildford, two olive-skinned male students, possibly locals and, next to him, a smartly dressed businesswoman called 'Yasmin Ali' according to the seat reservation docket on the headrest. The latter exchanged pleasantries in the expectation they would be sitting next to each other for the better part of two days and a night. Watson commented on the commotion of the departure. His travelling companion replied: "I travel this route from time to time and leaving Istanbul it is always like this. It's like the passengers think they're not coming back! Most of them will be leaving by the time we get to Brussels anyway." Watson smiled noncommittally, engrossing himself in a book he had brought to while away the hours.

Yasmin smiled as if to say 'I told you so' when they arrived at Brussels the next day. Around thirty of their fellow travellers got off, and the cacophony of their boarding was repeated as they sought to identify their possessions from the hold. Watching the melee, he noticed that the first to recover their bags walked a short distance to another smaller and certainly less luxurious coach and loaded their possessions once more. What was this? A party?

"A lot of South Asians go in for communal travel," Yasmin observed, watching Watson taking in the sight. "I expect they're going to see their relatives."

"Here in Brussels?"

"Or beyond on the coast." She winked and smiled again.

"You mean?"

She nodded.

"Undoubtedly some will take their chances... if they could have avoided the border checks, they'd have stayed on our bus."

The squally weather of the night before had disappeared in the morning light. The sea was noticeably calmer and the English coast clearly visible to starboard.

Sunny had spent a fitful night on the galley settee whilst her captor had retired to the bedroom to calm his upset stomach.

Abraham emerged refreshed with a quick brush and a change of shirt. By comparison Sunny looked stale and crumpled. Although too polite to make the observation, he invited her to use the bathroom while he set up the computer to get a broadband connection.

"OK, Anita, the computer is ready," he announced as she emerged ready for the day. I will admire the view while you get online and do the business. After that I will call for coffee and croissants."

His tone was devoid of the dispassionate tension of the night before, and for a moment, had she not known about his background, she guessed he might be a convivial travelling companion. Yet the fear of being confined with a master criminal hung heavy in her mind. She had realised the scale of personal risk she had taken and how her future prospects where heavily dependent on her colleagues, who might not even be aware of her predicament. One stage at a time. The first thing was to fix the transfer of the second payment. The request to the staged account went through and was authorised. At least she could be certain Mwake would know she was still alive. As she logged off, Abraham's phone lit up, as did its owner's face.

"Excellent, your second payment is confirmed with my bank so I think we can plan to dock as arranged. Just time for breakfast before we land at Brighton Marina. I'll have coffee and croissants sent down."

"Can I go on deck?"

"Unfortunately not. Officially you are not even on board, and I cannot risk you falling over the side. We are still a little distance from shallow water and the currents can be treacherous for even experienced swimmers. Don't worry you will be ashore soon – safe and dry and then I will take you to the station as agreed."

She had to admit breakfast helped her to focus on what was to come. She knew it was important not to drop her guard and didn't challenge his decision, instead attempting light conversation.

"So back to the office for you?"

"My office is at my home – west of London, and yes, I have several other businesses requiring my attention."

"And a family as well?"

"That too."

There was a momentary pause when she thought the subject of family would start a more positive dialogue, but his brief response hung in the air without further equivocation.

They arrived in Brighton Marina around twenty minutes later, berthing in a short-term visitors' slot near the western arm.

"Our arrival will have been observed and one of the security officers will be around shortly," he explained.

"My crew will deal with the administration. For now it is important we disembark quickly and without fuss. I suggest when we get on the boardwalk you link arms with me and walk towards the shops and the exit; that way everything will look normal on the security cameras. When we get to the shops, keep walking to the road we cross over, turn left to the car park, OK?"

Sunny nodded her agreement. All being well, her colleagues would now be watching. Stepping out in the open air was itself a wonderful experience having endured the claustrophobic atmosphere of the main cabin. Climbing out onto the jetty she put her handbag over her shoulder and linked arms with the man who some twelve hours earlier had been her tormentor. Never mind. The end was in sight. The sun was shining, she was still alive and had made the identification critical to the investigation. She thought he too, seemed at ease. Perhaps if she had earned fifty thousand pounds overnight, she would be sharing the spring that appeared to be in his step. When he dropped her at the rail station, she would contact Mwake directly and get back to Colindale.

She could not know that Mwake was indeed close by but having given instructions to his team to continue observations and not intervene, as far as she was concerned, he wasn't there.

It is often said that the value of luck cannot be measured while it is being experienced and it is only with hindsight that it can be truly appreciated. This was the moment Sunny's luck ran out.

Having walked through the parade of shops to the roadside, they turned left heading for the car park and the Malmaison hotel. Looking back it had been difficult to recall the sequence of events that followed in the coming moments. In essence, a black saloon car pulled up next to them, two men dressed in black leaped out and pushed them inside the car. She had been grabbed using the strap of her bag which had broken and dropped into the gutter. The car set off at some speed up the narrow twisting concrete access road that led to the top of the cliff. It had happened so quickly the surveillance team were not immediately aware what had happened. The momentary loss of visual contact was put down to them entering the car park complex. The watcher at the traffic lights at the top of the cliff saw nothing unusual in the queue of traffic snaking its way under Marina Drive to exit for the city centre.

In the car itself, order and quiet was quickly established as the two captives were given a sedative injection.

It was only when the car had reached the A23 some five miles distant, that Mwake realised he had an unexpected problem.

"*Fuck*, how on earth could we have lost them?" he spoke the thoughts of his team.

"I thought Sunny was going to get away from him once they went ashore," said Amelie. "What was all that lovey-dovey stuff when they got off the boat?"

Wetherall interjected: "I've got the watchers team checking out everywhere they could have gone. There's just the top floor of the multi-storey car park and the reservations at the Malmaison to be confirmed before we know for sure they have vanished."

"What's happening down on the jetty?" Mwake asked.

"His boat is casting off."

"Where is it headed?"

"According to the manifest it's heading to Douglas, Isle of Man."

"OK, get the maritime authorities to watch its progress. We can at least be sure Abraham and Purewal are not onboard."

That evening Mwake checked in for his weekly case review with Marshall.

"So one of our investigators and a prime suspect managed to escape our cordon and are somewhere in the UK," Marshall sounded incredulous as he summarised Mwake's report.

"I don't suppose you have any idea how it happened? Should I be reassured Purewal has made it back in one piece? Any leads?"

He was rehearsing how he might explain the situation to his own scrutiny committee.

Mwake shook his head.

"Just a women's shoulder bag with a broken strap and a burner in the bottom found in the street near the Malmaison. There is a possibility it's Purewal's. We're checking the serial number now. If it's hers, we can assume it's an organised snatch and start searching the ANPRs."

"Do I need to be chatting up my friends in Cheltenham again?"

"It would help. My one hope is that Abraham is a high-profile figure, who can't stay off the radar for long. He has a lot of business on his plate right now and I can't help thinking we are going to hear more soon from his contacts."

"I hope you're right. We've come too far with this not to get to the conclusion. I don't want to start making high-level arrests until we have netted the whole show."

"I got some new evidence in the post that Sunny somehow sent from France before she left. It includes a picture of Abraham with Bulent Canecale and Ilkay Vahid, the Turhan guy that the Cabinet Office man is dealing with, as well as a separate image of Kimmerlin, the Calais fixer."

"Well that's something – it must be a rare event that pulls those three together in the same place. Best not to alert the French authorities on the Calais organiser, ahead of everything else – I can't risk an evidence leak at this stage."

"How do you expect to finish this?"

"The first thing is to get the whole story laid out so we can work out what charges we should be putting in place. In the most serious cases we will have to think through the strategy to make the arrests. I am keen to do as much as we can on UK soil where we can exercise sufficient control. If there are others out of reach we will have to think through how we get them. Oliver is finishing off the case file for the original UWO so the reason for the investigation will have been justified. But since then the whole case has expanded and is over budget, which means we must turn in the big result."

With Mwake still in front of him, he called Jane Clark to brief her on the latest.

"That fits with a significant increase in chatter today," she said.

"We picked up a WhatsApp message from a burner to Bulent Canecale in the Netherlands which I was about to send over. It says: *'Hey Unc – new arrangement not good for me. Need a promotion at Izmir. Got Muzz under wraps. Planning on taking over.'* Unusually it is signed *'Celik'*."

"It does seem strange, normally he doesn't sign messages…"

"Perhaps he made an exception in this case as he wasn't using his normal phone," Mwake offered.

"Has Canecale responded?"

"He's forwarded on to another phone in Turkey where we don't have registration details together with an add-on message…"

"Which is?"

"Can't be having this. Must resolve. Confirm."

"And the answer?"

"There is no response for now."

"OK, this could be important Jane. Please call when you have something."

He closed his phone.

"What do you make of that, Jimi?"

"At face value it tells me all is not well in the kebab business. The number of raids we've been doing must be putting them under pressure in the 'above' and 'below the line' activities. Celik Abou is using this to increase his power. In her note from France, Sunny has suggested Abraham is using a cover name, Mustafa Ibrahim shortened to Muzz. Seems more than likely he could be holding Abraham as some sort of bargaining chip in a negotiation."

"Why would he be holding a colleague if he got what he wanted, they would have to be working together in future?"

His phone buzzed again.

"Phil? Jane again. Canecale has heard from Turkey with a one-word reply – *'Agreed'* and he in turn has sent a note to Kotobi – *'Find and delete Celik. Priority. Report'*."

"Sounds like an authorisation for a turf war," said Marshall.

"Jimi, I think you'd better find Celik before Kotobi does. You never know, if Celik knows he's a wanted man, he might just come over to us for protection. That's the sort of witness we will need and be careful, if Celik has Abraham, he probably has Sunny too."

TWENTY-FOUR

ABEL KOTOBI COULD NOT stop smiling.

His ruse to contact Bulent Canecale claiming to be Celik Abou had worked far better than he had expected. He had received a mandate to kill his chief business rival from his biggest customer, just at a time when that rival was going to take his business away.

Talk about turning the tables! Canecale had clearly decided for some reason or other to put Celik in charge of security operations linked to Izmir Barbeque, but such was his lack of trust that he had readily changed his mind at this, the first threat of challenge.

Although he had arranged the capture of Muzz and his 'ho', he had been careful to use some of his people who had not worked on Izmir business and so there could be no association with him at the outset. Now he had the added bonus of planning to rescue Muzz with the rewards that would follow, as well as eliminating Celik.

There was another plus as well. He could use the operation to give tip-offs for police raids on Izmir branches on Celik's territory, providing further vindication to Canecale for the decision to take him out.

How smart was that? This would win him new respect in his community, even from the likes of Levi Gardiner. It was a rare champagne moment that needed to be savoured, and Kotobi knew what was required.

He had a burner phone linked to Canecale for emergencies only. In his book, what he had initiated counted as an emergency, so he called.

"Yes?"

"It's Abel. Got your message and will action. You want Muzz back in one piece?"

"Of course."

"Any message for your target?"

"Tell him he's a cheating bastard. His action makes me think he probably did the Koenigsegg tip-off to fuck us both up. Make sure he knows before you close him down, and dispose of him carefully. Don't leave a trail for the cops to follow."

It was all the approval he needed.

McKee felt a negative vibe from Vahid that had not come from his encounters with either Belgin or Hosni. The latter two had taken his involvement at face value and had appeared relaxed at the prospect of future cooperation. Given Belgin was dealing with the military stuff, McKee had been surprised about how relaxed and open he had been. Vahid was the one supposedly managing the consumer businesses and seemed to be reticent about supplying the most basic information. In a way, given what he had already discovered about the Global Bus operation he might have understood his attitude, but for now, Vahid could not know what McKee's independent research had discovered. It was clear there was more he needed to understand about Ilkay Vahid, but it would have to wait for another day. First there was another piece of the jigsaw he needed to find and review, and until he had some more answers he did not intend to return to see Ciller, preferring to check in to the Severn Hills hotel in town.

The Canecales were in his sights. He noted there were six ferries going to Burgazada from Kadıköy in the centre of the metropolis a day, the trip taking about an hour. Given what he knew and what more he expected to discover, he would make a day of it and take the first crossing. It seemed to him half the city had the same idea. The central embarkation point was chaotic at the best of times. Buying a ticket at the central ticket desk proved to be the easiest part of the operation. Boarding was the challenge. People, livestock, boxes of provisions, white goods, building materials – it seemed something of a miracle that those who were there to travel all seem to be accommodated, although he thought the boat seemed to settle fairly low on the surface of the sea when eventually a deck hand decided it could take no more. Departure was marked with three blasts of the vessel's horn and a significant emission of a grey cloud of diesel fume that seemed to hang overhead, only slowly dispersing despite the gentle breeze of the bright morning. There was no space to sit, although street vendors squeezed around the decks offering the constricted passengers fruit juice and pastries. Every now and then he would be engulfed by the smells of humanity, bad breath, sweat, spices and cigarette smoke interspersed with the somewhat refreshing spray from the sea as they set out on their ten-mile journey. Despite the diversions all around him, McKee was thinking of the task ahead. He had an address for the Canecale residence from London and verified by Adnan. The gamble would be knowing if his target was home. Of course it would save time if he could meet Mersut directly, but he might find he would get more out of his sister if he wasn't there. Time would tell. What he really wanted to know about was the old man's relationship with Kerim Terzili as well as what he knew about the Terzili family assassination and the untimely death of one of his sons and the disappearance of another.

As the ferry approached the island's port, he was struck by how small the island appeared to be with the eclectic jumble of whitewashed town houses and three- or four-storey flats protruding from an almost continuous green band of woodland and shrubbery. Looking up to higher levels, the verdant canopy seemed to become less dense, with patches of grey and brown, a sign of recent forest fires, he assumed. In his vision there seemed to be three significant buildings that stood out, the most impressive being the Greek orthodox church, a castle, and the mosque. Coming from the madness of the city, this place was laid-back, to the extent the arrival of the ferry and its cargo seemed to excite only passing interest and that was in the form of the stall holders at the market next to the quay. Strangely, to his eye, considering the size of the island it had quite a network of streets with cars shoehorned into any available adjacent spaces. He wondered what would happen if all the residents decided to travel to a restaurant or beach from their residence – probably gridlock. The morning was kind to him. As luck would have it he had been the wrong side of the boat when it had docked, meaning he was one of the last to disembark. Considering the congestion getting aboard, most of his fellow passengers had melted away into the town or just absorbed into the plethora of small cafés that seemed to surround the harbour. Following the general drift of the departing stragglers, he found himself walking into the market and beyond that to the street with a rank of taxis. He handed his driver a scribbled note with an address and climbed aboard, his chauffeur setting off at a pace that suggested there were other customers to be bagged before the next boat came in.

As a result he was deposited outside a walled villa some five minutes later, the taxi making a rapid departure kicking up a cloud of dust as it returned the way it had come.

The gate had electric camera-controlled access. He pressed for attention.

"Hello, I am looking for Mrs Cara Yavuz. My name's McKee."

The iron gate clicked open, and he started to walk up the drive towards the front door. Looking up as he walked up the steep gradient, a broad-shouldered woman in a black dress watched him approach.

"Mrs Yavuz? Duncan McKee, Marine Insurance International, London."

The welcome was cool.

"Yes. Ermine has already told me about your visit to Cyprus. I was expecting to hear from you. Come in."

He entered into a grand hallway and through to an opulently decorated dining room with colourful contemporary abstract paintings on the wall and oak parquet flooring. Blinds were drawn over the windows, but a louvre door took them onto a balcony with an elevated view of the Sea of Marmara.

She saw McKee marvelling at the view with a number of small boats and ships out on the water.

"On a clear day you can see all the way to Istanbul from here as well as watching all the shipping heading in and out of the Black Sea. Please make yourself comfortable. I assume you take coffee?"

He nodded his acceptance and she returned shortly with a coffee pot, the rest of the paraphernalia already in position on the table.

"You are here to find out more about Gemlik's family to settle an insurance claim?"

Again, he nodded.

"How unusual. I never realised he got himself insured."

McKee dodged the observation explaining this was a liability bought out by his syndicate which they had now decided to settle.

He felt that she was observing him more intently than her sister had done.

"Ermine has told you our story. I have nothing further to add."

"My interest is to trace the whole Canecale family who may be entitled to share any pay-out and to understand how many are in work with dependents."

"My husband owns a tannery on the mainland at Bostanci, I have a daughter who works in a law office in Ankara and a son at university in Izmir. I look after our home and my elderly father. Apart from Gemlik, I have a younger brother, Bulent, who lives in Rotterdam, I think. I don't know where and I have not had contact for nearly ten years now and that is my story.

You have gone to a lot of trouble to find me. I expect you could have found all of that information without the need for a visit, so why are you here?"

"Procedure, I'm afraid. Forget any documentation, anti-fraud rules we have to personally identify likely beneficiaries. I don't know what else your sister told you, but according to my research there is another member of the Canecale family, Ekrem that I am anxious to find."

She laughed.

"He stole considerable money from the family and disappeared. Nobody knew where he went. I wouldn't be surprised if we was dead by now. There were many who wanted his neck, me included. The best of luck with that."

"Seems odd. Three brothers, one dead, one alive living somewhere in Europe, and the third missing with a lot of someone else's money. Given the circumstances, I think it likely the underwriters will not commit to a final settlement until we can establish where they are or what has happened to them."

"...And we cannot commit to helping you further without understanding your real purpose, Mr McKee."

His attention was drawn to an old man who walked out on to the balcony to join them.

"I am Mersut. If you are a student of the Canecale family you will know who I am. You will know we come from generations of Turkic brigands. We have always lived off our wits by our own laws. We keep our own counsel and, in coming here, you have entered our world and will be subject to our rules of engagement. I have seen you recently at the Terzilis' *yali* when I was visiting. I wondered then about why you were here. If you are truly who you claim to be, why would you be staying there? The Canecales and the Terzilis frequent different worlds. I am surprised you would think we would confide personal information with you under such circumstances. What is your business with Turhan? I doubt whether you are an insurance agent for their business."

McKee stood to offer Canecale his seat and shake his hand, but the patriarch waved him away.

"I will only be staying long enough to hear your answers."

"I am a freelance business development agent, working between London and Dubai. I work for a number of clients. Ciller Terzili has hired me to build new market opportunities in the Gulf and beyond. Given the nature of my work, she has asked me also to look into the circumstances of the mass assassination of members of her family as well."

"As you will know, Mr McKee, I know the pain of personal loss Kerim Terzili feels, and it has proved to be a bond between us in recent times. But the circumstances of our situations are very different. I cannot understand what is in Ciller's mind in hiring you, because it seems to me you have several masters and will be unable to satisfy them all. I admire your bravery coming here to Burgazada. You clearly don't know enough to realise the danger you have put yourself in. We don't encourage visitors and they only get to leave the island with my permission. My best advice is to go away and forget about this. There is no happy ending to be found."

The old man turned and left the terrace sending a signal the conversation was closed.

Cara had read the signal and suddenly appeared agitated.

"As my father says, it is best that you leave. I'm sorry your journey has been wasted. You will not encounter any difficulties leaving the island."

She stood, encouraging her visitor to depart.

McKee obliged but looked perplexed. Mersut had now disappeared, leaving his daughter to show him out. As he stepped outside, she touched his arm. It felt like a plea.

"You must understand, Mr McKee. My father knows how Gemlik died. It was no accident. If you want to find out more, you should be investigating his girlfriend Leeza Leshem, who perished with him."

He was about to draw breath to ask for a further explanation, but in the second that followed, the door was slammed shut behind him. Although tempted to seek readmission, he was now closely observed by a burly gardener with a pitchfork from further down the drive. It was clear he was to be seen off the premises. Outside the gate, he took a piece of paper out of his pocket, scribbled a note and put it in the family post box.

The return ferry crossing provided a good opportunity to reflect on what he had learned.

He was starting to form the impression that most people he had encountered in Turkey so far seemed to have a flexible approach to what was right and wrong, accepting their activities would only ever be governed in part by law.

At least that was his clear view of the Terzilis and Turhan. The most refreshing aspect of McKee's encounter with Canecale was his feeling that he was a criminal, albeit perhaps a semi-retired one. The patriarch had access to money and influence, but it was far from clear how he had acquired both, outside his relationship with Kerim Terzili. He was getting the sense that the Canecale men were in some way or other contractors or stooges for Terzili, running errands that for one reason or another Terzili and Turhan would not want to be associated with. The Canecale women, perhaps not directly involved, knew far more than they were letting on. He needed to update Smith on the situation and agree some next steps – in particular, who was Leeza Leshem?

The next evening he returned to the Terzili *yali* to brief Ciller on his encounters with the three executives running Turhan as well as with Adnan and Mersut Canecale.

She listened intently to his report.

"You seem to have developed a remarkable understanding of the Turhan business in a relatively short time," she observed. "I hope you work as quickly setting up deals for us in Dubai."

"Light armour plating, drones and this new microwave weapon are the three product areas I will be concentrating on. Once we have some clients we can broaden our offer, but first we will need to set up a demonstration event to show what we've got, and Muscat will be the best place for that. Belgin seems positive. Can you deliver or has it got to go to a board meeting?"

"Of course. You will know that when the company was recently restructured it was organised to ensure either my father or I would retain ultimate control alongside our attorney, Repcer. The boys running the divisions know that. I don't choose to engage in all their day-to-day activities that go on but retain a strategic overview."

"So I can proceed with your personal authority?"

She nodded.

"And what about the possible illegal activities that are taking place?" McKee pushed.

"You mean Adnan and his drugs? Canecale?" She seemed so matter of fact. "Let me tell you, I have been at parties in London with some very senior people and seen just as much dealing as my brother gets up to here."

"It's not just drugs though, people? Weapons?"

"International trade is always subjective, don't you think?" she countered. "What is legal in one jurisdiction may not be somewhere else. Also we often operate via third parties. We cannot be responsible for their actions. That is why we have Repcer.

"Many of our partners have profited greatly from their collaboration with Turhan, and you, potentially, more than most."

She smiled provocatively, leaning forward and stroking his hand. McKee ignored the distraction and probed further.

"Ciller, I have to ask you about all this stuff. If I set up deals for you in Dubai there will be diligence procedures to go through, especially with the likes of al-Harriri. He looks for weakness. He will find out everything."

"So what if he does? He might realise we are worthy of respect.

Respect can be a risky concept in my line of work and sometimes carries a health warning."

It was a comment that resonated with McKee when a short time later he took an unexpected call:

"Mr McKee? Cara Yavuz. I have been thinking about our meeting. I am coming shopping in town tomorrow and want to talk with you again. Will you take tea with me, say four o'clock at the Kır Kahvesi in Yildiz Park next to the Value of Luck?" She had picked an unexpectedly beautiful setting considering the central location. The white pavilion next to the Star Palace was set in beautifully manicured gardens with a series of small lakes, winding footpaths and woodland. Arriving ahead of the appointed time, McKee understood the value of the venue – an oasis of calm near Galatasaray University and a short taxi ride from the business district. With all the accoutrements of afternoon tea in place, McKee looked quizzically at the woman.

"So here we are. You wanted to see me?"

TWENTY-FIVE

"OUR STORY IS NOT complete. I couldn't tell you when you visited my home. It is not always easy to talk with my father around. I rang my sister after you'd gone, and she agreed I should tell you. We know more about Gemlik's death than we have shared. It is known he died in a diving accident; except he was murdered together with his companion. He had a business as a diving instructor in Bodrum as well as working for the family firm. He had dived in the area where he was discovered many times before. For safety reasons, even professionals take a diving buddy with them to assist if something goes wrong. He took this girl Leeza with him. Normally he would have been safe. I had spoken to him on the phone the night before he was killed. He had met Leeza by chance the previous day when he saw her jump from a leisure cruiser into the sea by the harbour. The cruiser is owned by a Russian, Solokov, who is known to Kerim Terzili. Gemlik happened to be nearby on his RIB, and she started swimming towards him and asked to come on board. He told me he was amazed by her athleticism but also how attractive she was. She had told him she had been held against her will for two days on the cruiser that had sailed from Haifa but had not tried to escape as they were at sea. She was scared the crew would come looking for her and could she hide at his place until the danger had passed. He had agreed and took her back to his villa. Apart from a bikini, she had no clothes, so he had given her some jeans and a couple of T-shirts. She had asked to make a call to her family in Israel who she said were arranging to pick her up and would pay him for his trouble. He had also taken a call from Adnan Terzili who wanted to meet for breakfast. The next morning the cruiser had left the port and she seemed more relaxed as a result. She didn't want to talk about her ordeal but said she hadn't been hurt and joked it had been worth it as she had kept hold of her precious pendant. Gemlik just assumed she was frightened about being attacked by the Russian and tried to set her mind at rest by asking a favour – would she come diving with him after his breakfast meeting so he could set up some underwater targets for his pupils to recover at their class the following afternoon. She agreed…"

"…And?"

"And that was it. It was the last we heard from him."

"Have you told the police about the call and your theory?"

"No. My father does a lot of business with Kerim Terzili – he wouldn't want to do anything that would cause trouble for Adnan or a potential Turhan customer, without being certain he was right."

"What do you think happened?"

"He must have met Adnan Terzili in the morning before going out on the water with the girl. Maybe Adnan had told him something that resulted in him being attacked, maybe someone from this cruiser had stayed behind, followed him and waited for the opportunity to strike? Maybe, Adnan did it? He has a reputation for violence. Whatever happened, I think this girl Leeza had something to do with it and Adnan was close by."

"Why did Adnan want a meeting that day?"

"Gemlik had acted as a middleman in an arms trade in Africa somewhere. There were some problems with the transaction and Adnan had been asked by his father to meet him to get things straightened out."

"So, if that was the case Adnan wouldn't have killed him, especially as your families were business partners. What about this Solokov?"

"I don't know much about him except he spends a lot of time in Turkey. I heard Kerim bought a mine somewhere out east from him and they fell out. But if that was the case, he would want to damage the Terzilis directly, not us."

"Possibly, but the alternative is by keeping Adnan alive the cops would have an obvious suspect. If he was arrested it would damage the family name more."

"What have the police said?"

"The case remains open. Murder is suspected but not proven which may explain why Adnan was never arrested. They were killed by their air supply being contaminated with nitrogen. Someone must have got onto their RIB whilst they were underwater and tampered with their canisters. The police say Gemlik was negligent and should have checked the gas levels before he went in; alternatively he did it deliberately to commit suicide. It hasn't helped that the body of the girl disappeared."

"Disappeared?"

"The bodies were taken to the local hospital mortuary for further tests, but apparently there was a mix-up. The hospital authorities thought they had authority to release her body to her family for burial. The police are trying to trace the people who came to take her away. At least this is what we have been told."

The effort of recounting Gemlik's story clearly had taken a toll on Cara. Her whole body seemed to deflate with the telling.

"Thank you for listening. I don't care about the compensation – only justice. I have been looking for someone I could talk to about this. Make of it what you will. It is the truth. I feel I can move on now." Matheson duly documented the news in his report to London. It was certain Turhan was smuggling gold in and out of Turkey, but not yet clear where it was going or who was buying. Global Bus seemed to have a pipeline of people travelling to Brussels and London, but who their identities were was not known. The busses were also being used for drug transfers, according to Adnan, but how and where the consignments were being moved was not clear. Turhan was not yet exporting arms but were thought to be dealing in high-tech premium weaponry and armaments including a microwave gun, and finally the deaths of Gemlik Canecale, and half the Terzili family, appeared to be professional hits with a Russian oligarch, Valentin Solokov the prime suspect.

As he sent his note to Smith, he was anticipating the response. Global Bus was about people, gold and drugs. Smith would have others to investigate this further, based on the evidence he had supplied.

He had to focus on Turhan's high-tech weapons trade and any connection between the Canecale and Terzili deaths and Solokov.

Smith spent longer than he had anticipated on Matheson's report from Istanbul. He was confident of his man's progress and yet as soon as the end of his investigation seemed to be in sight another lead emerged. In this case it was Leeza Leshem.

Having entered the name into his database he was surprised at the response. Leeza Leshem was listed as a captain in the Shin Bet, the sister security agency to Mossad and, given her age, must have been something special to have achieved the rank at the age of twenty-five. How come she was the apparent girlfriend of a mid-ranking member of a Turkish crime family and as what he assumed to be a fit martial arts expert, how had she met an untimely death? He would defer to Matheson on the detail but would make his own enquiries into her background.

Another encounter with Avi Weitzman in Old Quebec Street was called for. They met forty-eight hours later.

"Tell me about Leeza Leshem," Smith began.

The Israeli shrugged.

"What about her? You have obviously been researching her background, so you know who she is… *was*."

"What was she doing on a Russian oligarch's ocean-going cruiser that was heading to Istanbul from Haifa?"

"Checking on the owner, Solokov… you know, a man like that has all sorts of connections and buckets of cash to launder. I wouldn't be surprised if at least a dozen countries' security services weren't interested."

"Come on, Avi. You and I work well together, and for all I know will end up collaborating further on whatever this business proves to be."

"We all have our limitations when it comes to sharing intelligence. The best way of summarising it is to say she was monitoring the attempted illegal transfer of technology to a foreign power."

"That sounds like the sort of thing we'd say."

"Well I am trying to talk your language. As you will already know, Leshem was Shin Bet. She was watching Professor Karl Lieberwitz, chair of the School for Advanced Electronics at the University of Haifa who was attending a reception on Solokov's boat in the port. Lieberwitz was detected and subsequently monitored as a Russian sympathiser some years ago, and his department has received several substantial donations from research institutes in that country. Leshem was witnessing payback time. Solokov sailed into Israel to do a favour for his masters, the Russian GRU, to collect classified microwave technology. The package consisted of two parts, the first, an ultra-high frequency data detection system, the second, a microwave radiation gun. Given the university's own security limitations, passing this information through a controlled data file was impossible. The only way it could be done was through a one-time mobile zip. This would mean the files could only be replicated on one machine, would not be able to be copied and would disappear within one calendar month. The two parts of the brief were contained in two separate zip carriers disguised as pendants. Lieberwitz passed these direct to Solokov during the reception and he in turn was going to keep them round his neck until he returned to Russia. His boat, the *Oddessy*, departed Haifa an hour after the last guest departed. It was due to sail to Sevastopol in the Black Sea."

"And what about Leshem?"

"Somehow she was required to prevent Solokov passing on the pendants which was why she stowed away. As you will have seen from her pictures, she was an attractive woman."

"So you think she slept with him to obtain the pendants?"

"I don't know but I think it is hard to imagine she didn't, as when she checked in from Bodrum she reported she had recovered one of the pendants, we think the microwave gun, which is clearly the most sensitive. Assuming the Russians have the other one, I'd not worry so much. They know about this technology already and I suspect our research will only allow them to improve their existing capability."

"How come the *Oddessy* stopped in Bodrum anyway?"

"I don't think we know for sure but believe Solokov wanted a meeting with a local business associate. We think it was because of the meeting, Leshem saw the opportunity to escape. We have recovered her body since. Unfortunately there was no sign of the pendant. The killer was either one of Solokov's people or someone based in Bodrum. They can think themselves lucky she succumbed when underwater. Any assailant who had challenged her in combat would have probably paid the price. I still have a recovery team on the ground there examining potential scenarios so if you have any ideas let me know."

"My man in Istanbul has a line to Solokov. Maybe he can find out more."

"By all means. Apart from the fact we have lost an agent and presently not recovered the documents, we have to plan for the possibility that whoever has the pendant will be looking to sell it on. If that is the scenario, then at some stage the seller will be hawking it around Dubai. The bottom line is we must avoid this falling into the hands of the Iranians at all costs. If Solokov managed to hold on to the other one, you can be sure it ended up in Moscow, which although not good, is better than Tehran."

"But as of now, you don't know where the pendant is?"

Weitzman shrugged.

"If your guy can turn up some more information, we would owe you."

Smith nodded, got up and left. The Israeli could pick up the bill.

Since their first encounter, McKee knew that another meeting with Solokov was inevitable, and it was likely to produce a better outcome if he took the initiative. In calling Solokov he had realised he would be received back on the *Oddessy* with a sense of anticipation which would need to be managed. Sitting in the spacious lounge behind the sundeck above the chaotic hubbub of the quayside with a coffee felt like the most relaxed setting for the difficult discussion to take place.

Solokov opened: "Well, Mr McKee, you are an unusual man. I offer you a substantial fee on the basis of receiving banking instructions and hear nothing. Either you have been busy looking into the matters I suggested or are considerably wealthier than I thought."

"Or, Mr Solokov, I have decided not to accept your offer, my bank reversed your transfer. I might have told you sooner, but I don't believe in leaving such matters to a cell phone call with a poor connection. I noted you had sailed off somewhere, so I checked with the port authority when you were due back, and I am pleased to have caught you before you depart for the Black Sea. If you recall, you asked me to investigate a matter that you already understood, which potentially causes me issues with an existing client and compromises my insurance work. Was your hope that I would be motivated by personal greed, or was it more that you saw me as an obstacle in a complex situation that's going to resolve itself in your favour? I would just be another compromised person obliged to step aside or take your instruction. As I understand it, you've been trading with Turhan and the Terzilis for a number of years. You're buying a supply of registered bullion for cash with no questions asked. Now I am retained by Turhan, we should be capable of talking freely without additional contractual considerations getting in the way. What's not to like about that?"

"It's the price. Mr McKee. Turhan acquire unspecified volumes of the basic commodity at different refinements. I estimate my resources allow them to acquire maybe forty or fifty per cent more volume than they pass on to me. They say it's because of the complexities of logistics and registration. You will know it is the registration that gives the gold the premium value. Bullion is normally registered by national governments not private businesses. They are registering the gold in London through an exclusive nominee. But the nominee restricts the volume of the amount they will register each year. So Turhan acquires more gold than it can register, meaning they are sitting on a stockpile held here in Turkey. There is no point in raiding the stockpile as I don't have the means to register it. Further, when I complain I am told registration has to be rationed in order to preserve the price. As a result they continue to take cash inputs that they hold over. It's bullshit – they just want to control the world supply for unregistered gold. Forget the scrap metal business, the munitions and the narcotics. This is how they really make money. I am being quietly fucked because my money comes from diverse unrecorded trades in Russia so I cannot publicly document my purchases. I have investigated acquiring a nominee to run a competitive trade but the regulatory authorities in the US and UK, which are the only places where licences can be issued, will not accept a Russian corporate entity, despite being welcoming of the prospect of us trading in registered product. It's a phantom market that holds me because I make some level of return instead of nothing. So for now, the only way into this market is through Turhan and unless I can acquire that business my present acquisition activities cannot improve. I will break Terzili in the end but must wait long enough to ensure only I can pick up the pieces. You would have helped me to gather the pieces more quickly than I could have done myself."

"The police think the Terzili family tragedy was the result of an explosive device manufactured in Russia – would you have known anything about that?"

"I agree it's ironic that the Terzilis suffered their tragic loss as a result of an explosion. Ironic as their company manufactures suitable products. They must be crap if a Russian bomb is judged to be better than one of their own, but this is absurd. I am trying to persuade Terzili to work with me. Killing his family, I can see, could be counterproductive."

"You seem to like issuing threats though…"

"This is nonsense. I am sorry for what happened, but I was not responsible."

"I heard you docked in Bodrum last week and by coincidence a young couple died in a diving accident nearby."

"And you think I did it? Please, Mr McKee, I am past the age of dabbling in rough and tumble."

"Apparently the girl had been seen jumping off the aft platform of this boat the day before."

"Tittle tattle. I host lots of girls who like to cool off with a swim in the sea after sunbathing. This sounds like a story you have been fed by your own love interest, Madam Ciller Terzili.

"You have been around these Turks long enough to know their lives are characterised by personal feuds of one sort or another. They are worse than the Mafia. When a person becomes successful, there is always another who loses out. It is another reason why the present management of Turhan is weak and would benefit from the leadership and focus I would provide."

"But you work with them already?"

"From time to time. I would have liked a closer working relationship than we have at the moment, but the Terzili boy has proved useful for various errands in the past. To his credit he is independently minded and had it in his head the Canecales blew up his family to take control of their business. Clearly he's not very bright, drugs rot the brain so I hear, but if he was, I suppose he would not be so... malleable."

"I heard he's engaged in an errand on your behalf now, something about recovering a pendant?"

"It's true, it is a match for the one I am wearing now. I think I lost it overboard in the harbour at Bodrum. I think he has a place nearby. It has sentimental value. I have offered a modest reward for its recovery and Adnan told me he'd look for it. But I have to sail again tomorrow night, so I may have to accept I will be left with just a single one. It makes me realise I should have got it insured." His tone became more reflective as he stared into the middle distance.

"I'm sorry you have decided not to work with me, Mr McKee. I think there is much we could have achieved together, but I am happy for you to keep in touch in case circumstances lead you to change your mind."

TWENTY-SIX

IN A WAY, WATSON was pleased the bus was half empty on the Eurotunnel to Folkestone. It would be much easier to inspect the vehicle there for evidence. The examination would appear to be random, routine and relatively brief. The Global Bus terminus in Slough would be observed while the goods were stripped out and then followed to their destinations. If nothing else, he thought, the action would smoke Michael Abraham out into the open. It would provide a convenient opportunity to find out at first hand something of his complicated financial investments on the Isle of Man and learn why his business appeared to be making considerable rent payments for property in London that it appeared not to use. His fellow passengers aboard would not be inconvenienced – all would be transferred to the train to complete their journeys. In a sense the timing was good, after all, the intelligence he had already gleaned had told him where to look and his HMRC colleagues were ready to act. He too would leave at the unscheduled stop in Kent to supervise arrangements. Travelling to the embarkation point at Coquelles from Brussels tempted him to continue the fledgling conversation he had started with his neighbour in the first-class cabin.

"Did I understand you to say you travel this route regularly?" he asked.

"Once or twice before," she answered. "My job brings me to London now and again and I hate flying. Although this takes a little longer, I prefer it. It's cheaper than the train and occasionally you get to meet some interesting people."

"Sorry I didn't introduce myself sooner – my name's Watson – Olly to my friends."

"Nice to meet you, Olly, I'm Yasmin. I guess you're on your way home?"

"That's right – had some leave to burn that I couldn't get paid for, so decided on the spur of the moment to get out of my comfort zone and see a bit of the continent. I've never done a bus trip like this, so it's all been quite an experience."

"I bet! It's a pity we didn't get to meet on your outward journey. I might have been able to show you around."

"At least I managed a Bosporus cruise and a quick glimpse of the Topkapi Palace. I don't think I'd have managed that if I'd stayed in the queue at the Hagia Sophia."

"You're probably right – tourism is a year-round business in the centre of the city."

"I guess there is no point in me making a similar offer whilst you're in London?" Watson ventured.

She laughed. "Unfortunately not. Like so many in the business world I am no stranger to London, but I'm always interested in trying a new restaurant. My cell phone number is on my card."

She offered hers almost expecting her action to be reciprocated.

"Er, I'm sorry – as I'm off duty I've not got a card to give you," he said.

"Don't worry I'll be in London for the next two days. I've never met anyone called 'Olly' before – I won't forget you," she laughed again.

He would remember her smile. When they arrived in Folkestone he wasn't sure he'd get to see it again.

In the organised chaos that ensued, the Global Bus passengers were transferred to another coach to continue their journey to London. Watson took the opportunity to slip away. The disassembling of the Neoplan took less than a couple of hours helped by the early detection of the gold in the subframe. Once noted the vehicle was rapidly put together once more and its drivers released. With no passengers left to deliver, their admin office in West Drayton had instructed them to take their bus directly to Slough, an action Watson had predicted and appreciated – after all, this would save him time. With a surveillance team ready in Slough, the second disassemblage of the Global Bus frame took place, with the arriving frame cut into sections and loaded in a van. The van was tracked to an anonymous security-fenced compound in Ilford owned by Brodie & Spencer, specialist metallurgists, smelters and registrars. This was the place where the bullion would be produced, valued and authenticated before being transferred to the Bank of England vaults. The quiet efficiency of the operation had impressed Watson. Not only was the bullion being smelted under the noses of the criminal world but then stored for safe keeping in the national bank, apparently with no questions asked. Further investigation regarding the paper trail would be followed to round up those responsible and identify the finished goods owners, but there was no doubt about who was funding the process.

Despite their intimacy, the problem McKee had dealing with Ciller was that he really didn't know her, and she wasn't being open with him. As he was discovering, his skill was always asking her the right question and sometimes deducing from her response what had happened on the basis of what she did not say. The result was their evening dinners were turning into pleasant passive interrogations. McKee had been careful to limit his business discussions with Ciller to the dinner table. He was already finding their relationship was becoming more complex than he had anticipated. Her comment the previous night about respect seemed to be weighing heavily on his mind. He had to meet his clandestine work obligations to

London with his cover in the international insurance and arms business as well as acting as a kind of private investigator and lover to his host. Ensuring he could perform all these roles effectively whilst avoiding conflict and suspicion of his motives required discipline. Of course, the real benefit of performing the roles known to his host concurrently was that it provided the freedom to come and go from the *yali* as it suited without always having to come up with an excuse for his absence. Certainly Ciller appeared confident that he was prioritising her personal affairs sufficiently as a result of his account of meeting Adnan away from the family home.

Armed with Smith's information from London, McKee discussed his latest news.

"Is Adnan's involvement with drugs the reason why he is not directly involved in the family business?"

"Yes, but it's not only that. He's not smart enough to do the trades Turhan expects."

"So he's little more than a courier?"

She shrugged. "Yes, but couriers have some real responsibilities."

"Like moving consignments of illicit drugs around the country as you require?"

"And plenty of other commodities too."

"And yet he has no official role in the Turhan business? Isn't that unusual?"

"Not really, the top team at Turhan manage the business on a day-to-day basis and keep many others in their jobs as a result."

"He seems to have a good lifestyle nonetheless…"

"He is paid up front for what Dad or I ask him to do, and he gets dividend payments."

"Enough to pay for the villa in Bodrum?"

"Duncan, stop playing these games…"

"Did you know the villa down there used to be owned until recently by Gemlik Canecale? I don't think he acquired it as an inheritance – from my research he seemed to move in a month after Gemlik's unfortunate accident, but I suppose the Canecale family agreed to that."

"Property transfers take a long time here. I expect the two agreed a deal long before his accident. Under the circumstances there would have been no need to consult with the wider family."

"I didn't realise they knew each other."

"Naturally, we know the Canecale family. They have often helped us out when we have needed support, especially with some of our overseas ventures."

"Like the arms deal that went wrong in Mali?"

"Yes, he was involved in that, but it didn't work out and he's not worked for us since."

"What happened?"

"He supplied goods – weapons – on our behalf but handed them over without taking all the cash. Came up with some sort of bull about bank clearance delays. If that had been the reason we wouldn't have supplied goods until the bank had confirmed the receipt of funds. We lost over two million dollars as a result."

"So he stole it?"

"No – we checked all that out. He fucked up on the administration. Dad sent Adnan to Bodrum to censure him."

"And then he had his fatal accident."

"I don't know about that. Sometimes there are coincidences. Gemlik didn't die because of us."

"I'm not so sure. The way I see it is Gemlik saw the opportunity to make some serious money for himself on the back of the Mali deal. I think there was no missing two million dollars. I think he hid the money and Adnan was sent to collect. His job was to scare the shit out of Gemlik – a task we could well do when he was high. Gemlik was frightened and turned to the one person he knew that was big enough to get the Terzilis to back off – Solokov. Solokov wanted his mine back from Terzili who had refused to deal and decided to make some mischief. He liked the idea of creating tension between two prominent crime families who operated in businesses he wanted to own. Even though the police investigation showed the explosive used in the Fenerbahçe bomb was of Russian origin, it doesn't prove who supplied it or what their motivation was, although it suggests Solokov may know more than he has admitted. Even if he wasn't directly involved he might have been enlisted to find the answer if Kerim had indicated a wish to sell back the Uzbek mine.

"Remember, it wasn't just Solokov who had reason to create a split between the Terzilis and Canecales. The Colombians were concerned about their businesses in Europe being hit. And Turkey itself probably didn't like the idea of becoming known as a centre of international crime and may have turned a blind eye if they had received intel. It was clearly a professional job although the perpetrators probably expected your father to be on board at the time of the hit.

"There is no doubt Solokov took advantage of the situation. He knew of Adnan's weakness for drugs and women and cultivated his friendship in the name of sharing his sorrow. It's clear he extracted more information about what Turhan was doing in Uzbekistan as a result and, as luck would have it, when the *Oddessy* called into Bodrum on the way back from Israel, Solokov called him to help find Leeza Leshem. He saw Leshem picked up in a RIB with 'Canecale Marine' on the side. He called Adnan with the news, telling him there would be a bonus if he could liquidate Gemlik and Leshem at the same time – which he did the following day and returned a valuable pendant he claimed Leshem had stolen from him."

"So Solokov murdered my family?"

"No. But he may have known who did, and it suited him not to intervene. The piece of the story that is missing is whether Ekrem Canecale was involved. I cannot think why he would flee the country if he didn't think he was the prime suspect. By acting as a friend of the Canecale children and your brother, Adnan, Solokov was smart enough not to involve your father and Mersut as he still saw advantages of continuing doing business with them both. He gambled, rightly, that their pride and independent spirit would stop them telling their fathers. Solokov thinks the explanation of the story is his ace card, which will lead to the destruction of Turhan if he fails to convince your father to sell him the Uzbek mine."

"And the pendant?"

Her brown eyes seemed to drill into his head. Any suggestion of a welcoming smile had disappeared.

"That's the really interesting bit," he continued.

"There were two. Leshem tried to recover them both but escaped with one. Solokov specifically asked Adnan to recover and return the one Leshem had taken. The pendant contained a one-use data file of research about the microwave gun. Adnan passed it to you because he thought it may have a ransom value. You had it downloaded and passed the research to Belgin to develop your prototype. So from that, I conclude that far from being an innocent party caught up in a web of criminal enterprises, you were involved and at least aware of the circumstances relating to your family's tragedy.

"Further documentary evidence suggests that a prototype with only a minor omission in the components is awaiting international patent registration through a company called Yilan of which you are a majority shareholder. Now, what I don't know is why you have the company Yilan, when, as the heir to the Turhan fortune, the money would come to you anyway? I wonder if it is because you are worried about the links Turhan has to international drug and commodity trades and people smuggling. These activities were established by your father, and you have sought to distance the corporate body from them. You chose to do this by putting business in one division under the control of Ilkay Vahid with the brief to launder the profits and close these businesses down. He has already started to do that by cutting funding to the arm's-length business run by Bulent Canecale out of Rotterdam. That resulted in the people-smuggling service that, for some time, succeeded in getting refugees into the UK and into jobs in takeaway restaurants. Now you just provide a 'no questions asked' service to the French coast where other criminal groups dispatch them across the sea to an uncertain future and possible death. Drugs (mainly cocaine) are transported into the UK to order via Global Bus, but are being reduced in volume to preserve market prices. However, the real action is happening on the small island off the coast of northwest England. The Isle of Man with its secretive banking rules is where you receive millions of dollars of illicit earnings that you use to fund commercial property investments in London and other world cities and among your customers is one Valentin Solokov. In the UK, they are fighting financial crime through a legal process called Unexplained Wealth Orders, which, if granted by a court, could allow the state authorities to strip you of your assets. I think Repcer is aware of this, so maybe that is the long-term purpose of Yilan – to make sure your personal fortune is secure."

"You have a strong imagination. Have you any evidence to back this story up?"

He detected a note of bravado in her voice.

"Some. Of course, there are gaps where I've made an educated guess. Put it down to years of working with businesses and governments. But I guess you stay lucky. Firstly, I am just an insurance risk assessor, not a policeman, so it's not my business to collect evidence or prosecute, and secondly, as your lover, any evidence I could be asked to give would be compromised anyway."

"So?"

"So I have fulfilled my promise to find out what happened to your family and highlighted my view that your brother Adnan is perhaps, in some people's eyes, unreliable. I have demonstrated my value as you didn't think I'd be able to find out what was going on, and so I am presenting you with a new proposition. Make me a director of Yilan and together we will make a lot of money selling arms in the Gulf."

"I thought I'd already hired you."

"As a consultant to Turhan but that's not what I'm suggesting now. I need to be on the inside – a partner."

"And if I don't agree?"

"I will leave immediately, and you will never hear from me again."

"Taking your knowledge with you…"

"There is still some honour between lovers and thieves."

"I could always ask Adnan to make our split permanent."

"From what I know, I'd say he's got enough problems without having me on his list. Besides I am the one who can bring you the customers you need."

"So you intend to fuck me in business as well as in bed."

"Quite the reverse – together we will make more money than all of this narcotics crap put together and it will be easier too. Turhan carries a lot of risk which you won't have with Yilan. What we'll be doing is acting as a sales agent for Turhan. We will set up the deals, take the commission and leave the rest of it to Belgin to sort out. Besides, there are fewer people to share the rewards in Yilan. What have you got to lose? One way or another, you have ended up confiding in me, so you might as well ensure you reap the dividends."

She sighed.

"OK, OK – I'm not in a position to refuse. It will take me a few days to organise. I don't work through Repcer on Yilan."

"Why's that?"

"Repcer is my father's man, not mine. Like you, I value trust. What will you do now?"

"I'll get back to Dubai. The customers we need don't do our type of business on the phone. I'll need to get them set up to trade. You and Belgin had better focus on the logistics of a demonstration event. I will call you in a few days to compare notes."

Marshall was relieved to be getting some positive news from Smith. Matheson had delivered sufficient evidence on the illegal supply chain for drugs, people and gold from Turkey to the UK for arrests to be made, as well as the possession of substantial property assets held in London by Turhan, and yet he was frustrated by elements of the process that remained beyond his reach. Turhan's legal operations in the UK – Communi-Kate, HeadingtonMeds, and Flit Hydrogen were small scale and as minority remote shareholdings would not be material considerations. If he moved too soon he would be able to take out around thirty who were operating in the UK but not the main players managing the operations. Watson's work had suggested the high levels of cash coming into the business seemed to be coming from a source in the Isle of Man but getting the information he needed was proving problematic. The authorities had batted back enquiries into Abraham Associated Investments, and the principal, Michael Abraham, appeared not to own any assets in UK jurisdiction. If he was to make progress on this front it would need to be elevated to a political level, which in turn ran the risk of leaks. With the clock continually ticking on the investigation, it seemed the result of the case would depend on Mwake finding Abraham and Purewal alive and not on Turhan's armaments business.

Smith was conciliatory.

"I understand your problems Phil. I'm not sure when we set out on this case any of us realised where it might take us, but I think we can say Cabinet Office resources have provided you with what you needed as an evidence base for the UWO investigation. We take the view that this criminal investigation has taken on a new importance from an intelligence perspective. We need to understand much more about these sonic and microwave weapons. The investigation has already contradicted our own experts, which concluded this technology didn't exist, so now we have to get our hands on it. To do that, I have decided to keep our asset active in Istanbul while we get to the bottom of what is going on. Naturally, if we come across further information that can help you I will pass it on, but from now we will be handling the next moves independently."

TWENTY-SEVEN

"JIMI, HAVE YOU FOUND Celik Abou?" Marshall's tone was more urgent.

"Not yet, boss. Since we last spoke we've been monitoring his apartment and a couple of places where his mates hang out. The flat is quiet and there's no sign at the builder's merchants where he works. I had one of my guys drop in to see what they knew and all he could find out was he'd gone away for a couple of days, probably with some chick. Apparently he's got form with the ladies. We know his car details and I'm waiting a return from the traffic cameras so maybe that will help."

"What else?"

"It's probably a long shot but not so long ago he had a 'clear the air' meeting with Kotobi. Apparently they've been treading on each other's toes for a while. The meeting was brokered by a tropical fruit importer in Bethnal Green, Levi Gardner. He is a community leader and knows the two families well enough to bring them together. Keeps himself to himself pretty much but is legit. He's helped the local police dial down neighbourhood tensions in the past and was active in promoting a local knife amnesty a year or so ago. My hunch is that he may be able to find out something to help us, so I'm going to pay him a visit."

"You've got the time?" queried Marshall.

"Probably not, but I'm pretty sure there's no point in sending a white guy to see him, so I'm hoping I'll be able to make progress faster than I would otherwise do. Do you have any more mobile traffic?"

"No. If Kotobi is out on manoeuvres he's going to be careful. We can only hope he remains confident of his WhatsApp encryption. It seems to be the way he likes to communicate with Bulent Canecale. I'll let you know if GCHQ come through with any more."

The novelty of breakfasts in the steamy surroundings of Old Quebec Street was wearing off for Avi Weitzman, but at least the establishment did a good line in beef sausages which seemed to be healthier to his mind as they were served without an accompanying lake of liquid fat. His half-hearted manner was noted by Smith.

"Never mind, Avi, if we get to the end of this project in one piece I am sure we will have the opportunity to celebrate in some style."

"Well, my friend, I will draw some comfort from the fact you have brought me here again. At least I know our discussions are worthwhile. In fact, I must compliment you on your asset in Turkey – he seems to be a very effective operator. The intelligence you have provided is ahead of expectations."

"I'm pleased you share my view, but to have some material value we need to use it."

"Haven't you got what you wanted already? I thought you were looking to clean out these Turks."

"That's the plan but we want the ringleaders who are outside our reach – the directors of Turhan, not just the lower reaches of their food chain. But I guess the prize is even bigger for you. You want your technology back and cut off weapons exports to Iran."

"The technology matter is correcting our own mistake. Like you, we needed evidence that Professor Lieberwitz was exporting illegal materials, so we had to let him get as far as Solokov – but as we both know things went astray at that point. The issue of weapons sales to Iran is, I'm afraid, a continual battle. As soon as we close down one avenue, another will organise itself but, *hey* that's what we get paid to do. I guess we are here because you have a plan that you need our help with?"

"You talk as though you will only benefit at the margin. What I have in mind could make you the bigger winner."

The Israeli raised an eyebrow. Smith continued: "How would you feel if I could deliver you al-Harriri, Vehrani, maybe even Solokov in one place at one time and recover the sonic gun prototype? My man now has influence over Ciller Terzili and has got her to agree to set up a weapons demonstration event for prospective customers in the Gulf region and beyond. You could arrange a hit for your targets, maybe even arrest and take them to Israel."

"Why would you do this?"

"We want Terzili alive plus evidence of her activities. She is feeling confident with my man by her side and will cut corners to get what she wants. He sells her an audience with some of the big hitters and she'll go for it."

"It's an interesting idea but has its own problems. Firstly, with the possible exception of Solokov, we don't have much interest evoking the judicial system. It's expensive and uncertain. For something like this, we prefer a drone attack. Simple, effective but with the risk of collateral damage, especially for your own asset. Secondly, although it would be interesting to see what Turhan have made of the sonic gun, we would want to know all the plans had been withdrawn. I suspect the prototype Turhan have developed is a product of 3D printing, so at the very least the machine tool used must be destroyed, the original pendant recovered plus any duplicated plans held by Turhan and its associates (including the Turkish patent office) are wiped. A tall order I think, even for your man."

"But achievable, Avi. Turhan see this as a real money spinner. They are not going to share any of their knowledge about this until they have secured the patent and nailed some sales. Now could be the very best time to strike before the global market wakes up to what they've got."

"So what do you want from me?"

"Organise the event logistics – just like you did when we first set this thing up in Dubai. Brief me so I can get McKee to front it. We will take responsibility for getting the key people there and making sure Turhan puts on a show. Then you do what you need to – but save Terzili and my man. I have plans for them both."

"OK, I'll talk to my people. We will expect to see a statement of intent from you – the tracing, recovery and destruction of all the plans relating to the microwave gun. For the avoidance of doubt, I will want some reassurance before the event takes place."

Smith felt strangely empowered by the discourse. The potential prize of arresting Ciller Terzili would be a fitting outcome from what was proving to be a complex and expensive investigation, but for now, he would keep his counsel. Once again, he would need to ensure McKee could deliver.

Sunny had only the briefest sight of the circumstances of their abduction. She knew she had been bundled into the back of a large black saloon, Mercedes or BMW by two athletic men also dressed in black, complete with balaclavas. As soon as she and Abraham landed on the seat, a hood, also black was put over their heads and despite their struggles they were easily overpowered as they were handcuffed. She sensed Abraham was to her right and one of the goons to her left. The car was powerful as she felt the force of the acceleration pushing her back into her seat and the muffled roar of the engine. Hip-hop music was blaring on the radio. Apart from the two figures sweeping them off their feet (literally) and the driver, she had no knowledge of anyone else in the car.

"What the *fuck* is going on? Release us at once!" Abraham's protest lacked the authority it seemed to have minutes earlier.

He continued: "Whoever you are, you're making a big mistake. I have friends in your line of work. When I find out who you are, I'll cut off your balls and send them in the post to your women but let us go now and we'll forget all about it."

His admonishment was cut short by a violent jolt, cough and deep exhalation that Sunny took to be one of their captors landing a punishing blow somewhere in her fellow captive's midriff.

The driver said: "Don't worry, Muzz – we're from the Screamers. Celik wants to make you an offer."

Then there was the sharp pain of the needle in her arm.

The music seemed to take over from Abraham's moans. Sunny had trained for situations like this. What mattered in the moment was to absorb as many of the other sounds going on around her and to try to count to keep some sense of time, and then there was oblivion.

The best thing about oblivion could be said to be the absence of sensory perception. In the case of Sunny Purewal she had no idea how long she had experienced pain and cold. Both were now working together to return her to consciousness. She was still in the dark although tiny chinks of light through the black cotton hood seemed to suggest she was in some sort of office. Movement was impossible. Her arms were restrained behind her back, legs manacled to her chair. A gag had been tied around her mouth. Her head hurt and she was thirsty, a call for help or attention produced nothing more than a guttural vibration in her throat, but the one sense that was not failing her was her hearing. She was becoming party to a strained dialogue in some foreign language she was yet to identify. There were two voices involved, one spoke calmly in lowered tones, the other in a higher, more alarmed pitch. Suddenly the conversation was concluded with a scream of agony and the clatter of something heavy landing on the floor. She recognised the same moaning sound that she had heard moments before she had lost consciousness. Then a scraping noise and a slamming and locking of a door before silence of a kind took over. The silence was the opportunity to listen hard for any background noise that would provide a clue as to her whereabouts. The noises were random – the sound of gushing water, perhaps from a toilet or storm drain, an occasional rush and thud like a lorry dropping a load and the occasional sound of a klaxon clearly warning of something. She had now gained a recollection of what had happened and thought she must be in close proximity to Abraham. This was all she had to focus on for now. She called to him as loudly as she could through the gag, her neck bulging with the effort. It seemed her fellow captive could not hear but, stopping to listen, was sure she could hear a similar grunt of acknowledgement. The uncertainty of the response was countered by the stark noise of a lock being withdrawn, footsteps approaching and then a blinding light in her face as her hood was roughly ripped off.

She was aware that someone was now standing directly behind her. The smell assaulted her nose with a combination of stale body odour and garlic breath.

In shock, her head moved to one side. Her assailant barked instructions.

"I have a gun at your back. Do not attempt to turn around."

Behind the light in her face she was aware of a silhouette of another figure.

Considering she found herself trussed up like a chicken to a chair, she did not see why she was being threatened with a gun, she was intimidated enough already.

"Here. Drink some water."

An arm behind her thrust a bottle to her lips, where she greedily sucked the contents. When she drew breath, the bottle was taken away and immediately returned with half a cheese sandwich to allow her to eat.

Between mouthfuls she spluttered: "Who are you?"

A response was unexpected but freely offered.

"You don't need to know that. But we're known as the Screamers."

The voice started to laugh.

"Remember the name. It's a joke right? We are quite quiet in reality."

She was being fed like a tame animal, but she didn't care. She needed something positive – anything to give her traction in her situation.

Then her interrogation began. Who was she? Did she speak English? Why did she call Muzz Abraham? Was he her boyfriend? What did she know about him? Where were they going when they picked them up? Given the circumstances, it was a challenge to remember her cover, but there was no point in trying anything different at this stage, certainly not before she had been able to get information back about who these people were.

Before anything else she needed to know about Abraham.

"What have you done? I heard you beating him. Does he need medical attention?" she countered.

"He's feeling a bit sorry for himself right now but if he's a good boy he'll be OK, but what about you my beauty? What's your name?"

"Anita."

"Nice name, Anita. What are you doing with lover boy? Quite a lot judging by your pictures on his phone."

"It's not what you think."

"Oh yes and if you're such a great mind reader, what am I thinking?"

"That we are in a relationship."

"Oh your friend doesn't strike me as someone who'd go to all that trouble, I'm sure a quick fuck would have been sufficient – for him anyways. I could imagine you'd have more staying power." He smiled through broken, nicotine-stained teeth.

"He was smuggling me into the country. I don't have a passport."

"Really. So you paid him in kind did you?"

"No, I was forced to do the pictures to ensure I would pay for the passage. Why don't you ask him?"

"I will… but later."

Her inquisitor replaced the gag and the hood. Evidently the pair had retreated as she heard the locks being put into position.

But now she had something to work on. She could hear the groans and muffled sounds of Abraham in close proximity. Although strapped to a chair, it was not attached to the floor. If she stretched out her legs and bent double she could move albeit slowly and erratically. The hardest problem seemed to be the height of the seat which made it hard for her to get her legs grounded sufficiently to move. Fortunately, she had retained a sense of where Abraham was in the room, so she shuffled and scraped her way to get close to him, stopping periodically to call and listen for his response so she could move towards him. Finally her crab-like movement brought her close by, so close in fact that her chair nearly overbalanced as she collided with his leg. At this range, even with the gags, they could communicate – in fact it was easier the quieter they spoke.

"Who are these people? How do they know you? What do they want?" Sunny was aware she sounded just like one of their captors.

"They're a from a criminal gang in south London. I know their boss. A Turk called Celik. We used to do business together – drugs and other stuff, until they started getting careless."

"Who's we?"

"Me and other people I work with in France."

"That's why they were talking to you earlier in Turkish?"

"Right. I am Turkish by birth but have lived most of my life in England. I am estranged from my family back in the mother country. My only contact was with my brother, Bulent, who runs a travel agency in the Netherlands. I started a kebab shop in Green Lanes and built a chain.

"He fixed a family loan to help me expand, which I was going to sell to a US company, FizzyPop. Even got a deposit, but the deal fell through because I didn't pass their financial security checks. I had a lot of debts and warned my brother I would have to delay paying back the loan. I told him I had to get out of Turkey as a result of family business and that they owed me just as much. We reached a compromise. The family would let me pay my debt in another way. I would front a new travel business here called Global Bus that the family wanted to use for people smuggling and narcotics. This business would be financed by one of my father's friends' businesses called Turhan but we would get a percentage that would be taken by my brother as repayments. We smuggled people, gold and narcotics. My role was to sort out the aftersales. In other words what happened to the goods when they got here. I did it by distributing the people to the kebab shops to work, hiring a sales network for the narcotics via the kebab shops and most recently arranging the smelting of gold mouldings for registration via a private bank. Celik Abou was known to me as a local entrepreneur in South London. He acted as the distributor for people and drugs. I managed the gold transfers."

"And we're here because you owe them money?"

"No. I think it's because I stopped doing business. But these are the foot soldiers. Celik is coming to see us so only then will we get the full story."

"Why did they beat you?"

"Who knows? When the boss isn't around they do what they want. The one who fed you was joking about having sex with you before he left. Said he had some meat in his pocket if you were still hungry, but his pal told him to behave."

"How are we going to get out of here?"

"I don't know, but these guys don't take prisoners without a reason. When I know what it is, I guess I'll have to do what they say to get us out. It will probably mean a lot of money. That won't happen if I'm tied to a chair in the middle of God knows where. You could be lucky. They may just let you run. Given your situation, they know you won't be going to the police. Anyway you'd better move away from me. When they come back for us, it mustn't look like we've been talking…"

Marshall called Mwake.

"What's the latest?"

"We have positive evidence about Abraham's links to Izmir kebabs, Global Bus and Turhan and we think he's helping Turhan to launder money from an investment business in the Isle of Man. But that last piece is subject to confirmation. We recovered Sunny's mobile phone with an image that links him to the vessel that took her across the Channel. The camera at the top of the slipway to the marina gave us a licence plate of a black Mercedes to follow, which has gone to a warehouse at Alfred's Way, off the A13 in Barking. We're watching the place now. The Merc is on the move too, heading south of the river. Overall, it seems they are safe otherwise if they were going to be killed they wouldn't have gone to all this trouble.

"No sign of either Celik Abou or Kotobi but one of them will break cover soon and when they do, we'll be ready. In the meantime, I'm seeing Levi Gardiner."

Marshall's next call was to HMRC. Watson also seemed to be making progress.

"We know where the gold goes from the Global Bus deliveries, but we are still trying to track the paper trail. The issue is not the smelting but the stamping and registration. This is where the value uplift occurs. Also, we have requested information from the Isle of Man authorities on Abraham, but there's no doubt we could wrap this thing up much faster if we could pull Abraham in. We can be certain he oversees the process."

"Don't worry, Oliver. We've got him under surveillance. He is linked to a number of investigations, so we'll bring him in when we've completed all our initial enquiries."

TWENTY-EIGHT

LEVI GARDINER HAD A nose for trouble, and he knew it was coming his way as soon as Mwake pulled up outside his warehouse. The investigator moved quickly to put him at his ease.

"Mr Gardiner, I'm Jimi Mwake and this is Amalie De Jong from Four Musketeers Market Research. We work for a private client who has instructed us to do business diligence checks on a couple of your customers, Celik Abou and Abel Kotobi. Your details were passed to us as I understand you know them both. Could you provide references for us?"

Gardiner inspected Mwake's card before responding.

"I don't know where you get your information from, but these guys are not customers of mine, although I have met them socially in the past. I'm not sure what your business is, but you look to me like cops and I wouldn't spend time in this part of Bethnal Green if I were you. Sometimes street crime happens here. Cars get vandalised, people get robbed, some get assaulted, and the police don't do nothing, *nothing*."

"You seem to be doing OK though," De Jong intervened.

"I am careful. I do my job and go home. I go to church on Sundays. I provide free fruit to the local junior school. If you look after the community, they look after you."

"We understand you know Kotobi and Abou. They come from different communities, don't they?"

"How many people do you know who live round here? People from all over the world live next to each other here. One of these guys is Nigerian, the other Turkish, but here we are one community. Their families live close by, but they don't. So I see them from time to time when they come home to see their mamas and I'm not out doing deliveries."

"Together?"

"Not usually."

"But sometimes?"

"Yes, a while back, but when they've been part of a group."

"OK Mr Gardiner – let's cut the crap. We have reason to believe one of these guys is out to kill the other and we're trying to find them to stop it happening before the cops call round to collect the bodies. Do you know where I can find them?"

"No, but I can get a message to Abel."

"OK do it – please call me when you have an answer."

Back in the car and heading back to Colindale, De Jong observed: "You seem pretty confident of getting a response..."

Mwake smiled.

"I'm sure we will. Whatever else, he knows we aren't cops – if we were we would have turned his place over, but he is definitely aware of some sort of trouble involving them. He doesn't know if he can trust us so he was hardly going to give out a number. He will pass a message to Kotobi, so all we can do is sit tight and hope GCHQ come up with something."

McKee called Ciller from his suite in the Burj. After an exchange of the more intimate pleasantries he got down to business.

"The initial discussions have gone well. So far, I have eight governments lined up to get involved, but there is one business critical issue. They want to see the plans of how the technology for the pulsar gun operates. As the tech is so new they want some convincing it is easy to operate, effective and reliable. Although we can get them together to watch a test they are going to need some documentary reassurance and we are going to need something stronger than a non-disclosure agreement to safeguard our position."

"How do you plan to deal with it?"

"I think the safest way to do this is for me to personally review the plans that Belgin is holding on to. I will create new documents that will edit out the commercially sensitive elements. We will put this into a prospectus and market it for a registration fee that can be discounted against future orders."

"You think they'll go with it?"

"Why not? I know quite a few of these people – they want to believe in the product. Our skill has got to be setting the price. It must be high enough to be credible as well as providing an incentive. And remember if this is worth doing it must be done right. There can be no prospect of a potential leak. Get Belgin to assemble all the records for me in the course of the next few days before I get back to Istanbul. I will rewrite the documentation in order to address our customers' expectations."

Under the circumstances, Ciller was pleased McKee was out of town when the monthly Turhan board meeting was held at Repcer's office. The reports from the divisions were patchy. Duru Husni was making good progress with the scrappage and recycling business, but productivity was running ahead of market demand. Margins on conventional weapons sales were being squeezed, which was forcing Belgin to take some losses on new orders – a position that could only be accepted in the short term, and Vahid's 'under the counter' trades were being held back by the present international value of gold.

"Although the immediate situation is challenging, my father agrees with my view that the fundamentals of the business remain strong and our cash reserves are robust," Ciller reported.

"We can be confident of our future prospects as we reduce our dependency of sub-legal trades."

"Or alternatively, the pace of our legitimate market interests is sufficiently weak to mean we must continue with the cash-generating narcotics and commodities lines," said Repcer dryly.

"Not necessarily so, Alper. We have a number of reserve positions that will allow us to continue the downward trajectory of these activities. We have significant new sustainable arms products which could give us a leading position internationally, the pipeline of unregistered gold to activate when global conditions permit and the revaluation of our property holdings to underwrite our operations.

"Asar Belgin is preparing for a major arms trade demonstration event with maybe a dozen of the top global munitions suppliers. This will be important to help us reposition ourselves as a supplier of quality hi-tech products. Duru is looking at developing new alloys for structural engineering applications and we still have shareholdings in a number of high-growth businesses in the UK and beyond to contribute to our earnings."

Vahid spoke up.

"I get that Ciller, but we are going to have to make better provisions for our liabilities. My business carries more risk than the others and is subject to rapid change. Right now, the prospects for our fast-food subsidiary are not good and the remodelling of our people-smuggling operation is adding to our difficulties."

"Why?" she seemed surprised.

"We have some problems with our operating network that has affected the reliability of our services."

"That sounds like a Canecale issue. It's down to you to sort it out," snapped Ciller.

"Maybe I can have a word with Mersut," interjected Kerim, his first contribution to the meeting.

"It's not something Mersut can deal with – it's Bulent in the Netherlands. Don't worry, I can deal with it but you should be aware there could be a bigger hole in my numbers next time around."

Vahid's warning was noted by Repcer.

Wetherall was reaching the end of his shift and getting twitchy as his promised relief replacement had not yet arrived in Barking. He was contemplating calling Mwake to find out how long he would have to remain on station, but suddenly thoughts of the journey home were dispelled. It had turned eight in the evening and in the twilight nearby street lights had come on. The shadow, he knew, often played tricks on the observer, especially those with tired eyes from past hours staring into the empty space waiting for something... anything, to happen to break the monotony. Of course, had he trained in government service, he would not be doing a stakeout on his own, but now, in the brave world of the private sector, bodies were even more scarce than overtime payments. Steeling his eyes through the gloom he took advantage of his pocket binoculars to get a closer look at what was happening. It was the return of the dark Mercedes that he had last seen on the police traffic cameras. This time three figures emerged, one appeared to be supported by the other two but was taken to a side door. A momentary delay, he assumed, as the door was unlocked and then they disappeared inside. He needed to stretch his legs so the opportunity to get a closer look of the Mercedes was not to be missed. Frustratingly, to get close, he had to walk a 50-metre detour to get to a footbridge to cross the adjacent waterway to the car park. As he approached he needed to duck into the cover of nearby shrubs to avoid the piercing headlights of another car, driving in and parking next to the Mercedes. This second vehicle needed no introduction to Wetherall, as he had spent many hours tailing it most recently around Izmir Barbeque shops in Leicester – this was Kotobi – no doubt. He knew he needed to call in but in the moment, his urge to follow his main target was too great.

Kotobi took the same route to the side door as his predecessors, but unlike them entered without delay.

Having waited for what seemed the longest ten minutes of his life, he made his way to the door, not just engaging with the handle but almost embracing it with his body to ensure it opened gradually and silently. The interval provided the opportunity to quickly scan the surroundings. The interior was bathed in a low-level security lighting, little better than the street variety provided outside. It seemed to be laid out haphazardly, a mixture of open space in the middle with unidentified objects covered with tarpaulins and some racking, sufficient to provide some cover as he entered. The offices at the far end had been erected with what looked like flimsy MDF and glass partitioning. This part of the premises was bathed in light, not just the desks themselves but an open area beyond. Frustratingly his position did not give him the clear sightlines he had hoped for and that would only be possible if he was able to break cover. The only thing he could be certain of was Kotobi was here together with a number of others, maybe two or more. It was time to withdraw and report to Mwake.

Wetherall didn't need to take advice at that point, it was too soon to intercept especially when they couldn't be sure how many people were there or what they were doing. His boss would join him shortly to continue the observation.

Kotobi had arrived in Barking to inspect his new acquisitions and the security arrangements. There were three rooms in use in the warehouse. The first consisted of informal living accommodation for his two assistants – in effect a campsite consisting of a couple of steel-framed tents and coking facilities, strategically located next to a communal toilet. Next door was the imprisonment space with Abraham and Sunny tied to chairs and at the far end what Kotobi thought of as the 'interview facility', a room with a camera, IT equipment and a winch with his rival Celik Abou suspended, feet first from it – alive but bound and blindfolded.

His captive started trying to swing his body when Kotobi entered the room accompanied by one of his assistants.

Jailer and inquisitor discussed the situation.

"Any problems?"

"No boss. We picked our moment when he went to his car alone."

"Witnesses?"

"Don't think so. It was in the car park next to a DIY store in Croydon. We were quick. Anybody watching would just assume we were loading some bulky stuff into the boot."

"Any conversation?"

"No. We just made the collection."

"Good – so this is probably the first time he knows who wanted to speak to him?"

"I think he knows – we certainly had a struggle stringing him up."

"How long have you had him there?"

"I guess a couple of hours. Looking in on him he seems to relax when he's left on his own."

"OK, I think you've done well."

Kotobi sat down at the trestle table that housed a laptop and camera. Having adjusted the camera to provide a full view of his captive, he called his customer, Bulent Canecale.

"Hey Unc, how are you doin'?"

"Why are you video calling?"

"I had some of your guys checking up on me, so I thought you'd like to know I'm getting on with biz."

"I don't know what you mean."

"Got that cheating shitbag Abou just hanging around next to me waiting to hear his fate. Take a look… sorry he's upside down right now, seems to have had a rush of blood to the head…"

He nodded to his assistant who removed the hood.

"So as you can see I thought you'd just like to be reassured he'd been put out of business, once and for all…"

"What about Muzz?"

"We know where he is. I think the Screamers roughed him up a bit. He's got a girl with him. They're nearby and OK. My guys are recovering them. So now I've got things under control, when do I get to join the firm?"

"We need to meet face to face to do this. I will want to see my brother and the girl."

"OK, I will hold them until we do the deal."

"There's a flight into the city tomorrow morning from Rotterdam. Make sure you're there to meet it."

The screen went blank.

Abou was trying to speak but his gag limited him to unintelligible muffled noises.

Kotobi moved his chair alongside Celik's head and bent his neck sideways to mock him.

"What is it you wanna say? You're sorry for all those years of dissing me and stealing my business? Or maybe you wanna be part of the deal? Only problem is you had your chance and you missed it. Fact is, you don't have anything to deal with, no collateral, so there's nothing more to say, you are superfluous to requirements. But my mum thinks I'm big-hearted, so I'm listening."

Kotobi took his gag off and learned his ear closer to hear Celik's now quieter voice.

"Don't be a twat. You're making a massive mistake. Unc needs us both. Only by working together can we keep the cops off our backs."

"I would be a twat if I let you go, for sure – you'd be back to do the same to me. Besides I won't have the cops on my back now I've shut you down."

"Yes you have – Unc doesn't have any fixers in London apart from you and me. You told Unc he'd sent people to check up on you. He denied it. Well if it wasn't him or me, who else would it be making enquiries, you thick bastard? It must be the cops. If Unc's coming to see you, you'll need answers."

"Seeing you in your upside-down world makes me realise how pathetic you are. You're done, dude."

"I don't think so. I think you're in much greater danger than you realise. You heard Unc mention the word 'Brother'?"

"'Bruv' is a saying, a term of respect…"

"Get over yourself – you've bagged the guy who owns Izmir Barbeque right enough but he's also Unc's brother. If you've been dissing him as well I think you're in real trouble."

"Bullshit. He's Mustafa Ismail – Muzz."

"In the kebab business here maybe, but in Turkey he is known as Ekrem, Ekrem Canecale. I know coz my dad hid him when he first came to England. He was on the run. Reckoned some Mr Big was after him for fucking up a bombing in Istanbul. His brother is Bulent – 'Unc' and they do some trades. You won't hear Unc ever calling you Bruv. When he used the word he means it literally. How do you think our work supplying the kebab shops happened? It was the brothers working together. You and I were just the middlemen, the little people who did all the running around and took all the risks, delivering people and buying the drugs. Hey man, I'm a Turk, you ain't – Turks are all about family."

"Didn't work out for you then…"

"No, I'm an only child I had to make my own way. But I know how they think. They look after their own even if they think they're out of order. Now let me go and together we can get things smoothed out and get back to making some cash. What do you say?"

"Tell you what I say… fuck off. Unc wants you dead."

At that moment Celik leaned his head over and bit Kotobi's ear hard. The scream was a match for anything heard in the warehouse previously.

"Get him off! Get him off!" Kotobi shouted to his assistant, but Celik would not let go. Panicking, the henchman drew a knife and slit Celik's throat. The act seemed to make the captive bite down harder as he pulled away with part of Kotobi's ear still between his teeth as blood pumped from his neck.

His captor cried, "Aagghh, the bastard's cut me!"

His exclamation was so loud that the attack could not have involved Abraham.

Kotobi grabbed Celik's cloth gag to stem the flow from his gaping wound.

The knife-wielding thug tried to comfort him. "I've done him boss, by halal. It's definitely the last thing he'll do. Inshallah!"

"Get me to a hospital, you idiot. I need this sorting now."

"What about the prisoners?"

"They're not going anywhere. Lock them in and let's get moving."

TWENTY-NINE

THE PLANNED TRIP TO the hospital was good for Sunny and Kotobi in their different ways. For Sunny her brief freedom from the hood had given her a sense of her immediate surroundings and once silence had descended in the warehouse, she started to shuffle her way back towards Abraham – there was more to his story that she needed to understand.

For Kotobi, it wasn't just about getting bandaged up, but a chance to replay in his mind what Celik Abou had said. Who had been making enquiries about him? Could they have been cops as Celik had suggested? Although he trusted Levi not to say anything, his friend had been sufficiently suspicious to alert him. Had he been right to kill his rival? It was ironic that, in the end, responsibility for the murder had been taken out of his hands. On balance, in the interests of his future business it had been a necessary decision. His guys would arrange the disposal of the body after his meeting with Unc tomorrow. And what was the significance of Celik telling him that Muzz was really some other guy, Unc's brother? Could that be another angle to ensure he got his rewards for consolidating the supply chain to Izmir Barbeque? It wasn't clear from Celik's comments whether Unc and his brother actually got on anyway. The best tactic would be to avoid getting Unc and Muzz together until he had secured his own position.

Twenty-four hours after parting company with his bus travelling companion, Watson called Yasmin.

"I just wanted to check that you were OK after all that fuss at Folkstone and make good my offer of dinner."

Yasmin laughed.

"Well I have to say I didn't realise that Brexit would have implications for me as a Turkish citizen travelling to your country. It seemed like the customs authorities were as confused about what was going on as most of our fellow travellers were. Not to worry – everyone was polite and helpful. I ended up completing the journey by train and got a cab to the hotel. I get the impression it is easier getting out of the UK than getting in. It made me feel sorry for those who we saw in France who might be taking their own chances crossing the sea. Dinner sounds nice. Thank you. Where will we go?"

He fixed a table at the OXO tower for 8pm and was relieved she was punctual. The occasion seemed slightly weird. He had extended the invitation from a professional point of view to engage in a sort of a soft interrogation, yet meeting her in this social setting seemed to ignite a strange personal excitement he had not experienced for a very long time.

"And why not?" he had told himself. *Divorced with grown-up children, why shouldn't I enjoy female company when the opportunity allows?* Also, he had no certainty she would be of interest to his investigation which would then allow him complete freedom to manage this assignation however it developed.

These mixed feelings had been stoked by Yasmin arriving, not in business attire but in a slate-grey, figure-hugging Merino wool one-piece, which to his eye was both sexy and demure at the same time. The dress matched well with her long dark hair and light brown complexion.

They dined on roast duck washed down with a bottle of the best claret Watson thought he could get away with on expenses. The conversation had been freewheeling too. Within ten minutes of sitting down he had established it was only her third visit to London and she had come to oversee some asset transfers on behalf of a client. So far so good. Like a good barrister he had time to plan, to formulate more probing questions without appearing to be overly interested.

"You must take it as a personal compliment your client has paid you to come to London and not just used a local agent," he ventured.

"That is one way of looking at it, but I put it down to the fact that my client trusts me and my judgement, so I have the authority to do what I think is right."

"I guess the same must go for your partner."

"Yes, I have more than one – my business partner and a personal partner. I am fortunate that I do not have family responsibilities for now, so I am able to focus on what needs to be done. You?"

"Very much the same."

"What do you do, Olly?"

"I'm an economist, a job much duller than being a commercial accountant or lawyer. I help our government to predict income from taxation, so you can see why I try not to talk about work at the dinner table."

"It must have its moments…"

"Yes, now and again. Like now for instance."

She smiled and raised her glass.

"How long before you go back?" he asked.

"Global have a service out of Victoria to Istanbul at six tomorrow night. I can use the time to catch up on my paperwork and get a little sleep. When I arrive in Istanbul I have to go straight to a client meeting."

"But you're not from Istanbul?"

"No I come from a Turkish city in our far east, Trabzon. I will take a train home once my business is concluded."

"Is it unusual for a Trabzon firm to get an international commission from a major Istanbul-based client?"

"Yes, I suppose, but we are located close to the border with Georgia so it's not unusual for us to get involved with Turkish companies exporting to the likes of Russia, Armenia, Azerbaijan and the rest of the Caspian region."

"So that's what brings you here?"

"Yes, I just have to witness the reassigning of assets from one business to another. It's routine in reality."

"Surely it can't be routine if you have to come to London to do it."

"Well, that is the instruction from my client, so if she says that is what I am to do, then I will do it."

The conversation had moved quickly and before he knew it they had finished coffee.

Yasmin continued: "I must thank you for tonight, Olly. I must say it has been a treat to be entertained by an English gentleman. I will remember our chats in the days ahead. You must visit me when you next come to Turkey."

"I can't wait."

She smiled.

"I mean I can't wait until then. Let's go back to your hotel."

It seemed Watson was in luck.

In Watson's mind, having sex with Yasmin was necessary to relax his subject to tell him more, but he enjoyed it nonetheless. Here was a confident experienced woman who regarded coupling as an integral part of her femininity and seemed at ease with his embrace. She was clearly much younger than him but not put off for all that. For his part, although his hairline was receding he kept himself trim which he now suddenly appreciated as she turned her attention to caressing his flat belly and the rest. Her scent was intoxicating, her skin had a silkiness that seemed to easily adapt to his frame and accommodate his bursting passion.

In the moment, all rational thought of the reason why he had sought her out had been lost. Nothing else mattered other than to enjoy the feeling of being together in every sense of the word. No wonder Yasmin had planned to use the bus trip back to Istanbul to sleep. This night was not just about lovemaking it was about Yasmin taking control. After all, the reality of bedding a relative stranger in a foreign country without any appearance or admission of guilt for her partner back home, struck him as demonstrating her resilience. In the aftermath, in the darkness, despite his better judgement he felt compelled to ask: "Why did you sleep with me?"

"Intuition I suppose, it just felt like the right thing to do. I can't say I thought about it in advance."

Watson couldn't have expected more. He hadn't been fishing for a compliment but somehow wanted to be satisfied she had not targeted him. At least he hadn't had his cover blown.

She had put him to shame in the morning by rising early to shower. Feeling her slipping out of the covers, he followed her to the bathroom. After once more calming his ardour, she pulled free with a word of censure.

"Olly, I haven't got time for this, I have to get ready for my first meeting in the city, I can't afford to be late or else my client will get to hear and then there'll be trouble."

"I thought you said you worked for a woman – surely she would understand…"

"Really? I can tell you haven't had a female boss. I'd say quite the reverse is the case and I certainly don't want to have to explain why I wasn't studying my briefs last night for this meeting."

"Would it help to say you had someone else studying your briefs for you?"

She threw a towel in his direction before concentrating on getting dressed and made up.

"I've just got time for a coffee before I go. Put the kettle on."

He pulled on his jersey and chinos whilst continuing the conversation, asking casually: "So who is this mystery woman, based on your clues I can't believe there are many senior businesswomen in Turkey, from a cultural perspective."

"You're right but it is changing. She is Ciller Terzili, you've probably not heard of her but she heads a family-owned Turkish metals business. They do all sorts of stuff – scrapping ships and smelting sheet metal alloys. They hold investments here in London which is why I'm here."

"Seems to me a big commitment to send you to London from Trabzon."

She laughed.

"You might think so, but the advantage is when you come to the International Metals Exchange in London to do deals, you don't have to arrange any logistics. The commodities remain in the bank vaults, all you do is to exchange ownership documents and authorise cash transfers. Moving the volumes I do, would cost almost as much as the commodity is worth if I had to arrange logistics."

She was back in the bathroom applying her lipstick. He turned his attention to her handbag, found her passport and dropped it into his holdall.

They left the room, albeit separately, a few minutes later. Given the encounter it seemed slightly uncomfortable, even formal to Watson, as she gave him a light peck on the cheek.

"Keep in touch," he said.

"You know where to find me." She winked and departed quickly.

Watson had the idea she would be reaching out to him sooner than she anticipated. For this reason alone, he was sure she would not forget him in a hurry.

Watson took a cab to Canary Wharf to see Marshall, who listened carefully to his update.

"So we now have an overview of the money laundering operation?"

"Almost – it's just the Isle of Man connection we need to pin down – and that depends on lifting Abraham."

"Is this woman Ali connected?"

"She has representative authority from Ciller Terzili. I can't be sure she is party herself to criminal activities here but she may well have wider knowledge of how Turhan manages its investments here."

"Are you looking for an arrest warrant?"

"I think there is a prep stage to go through first."

"Which is?"

"I have acquired her passport, so she can't leave. It was a chance I had to take. Besides I don't think she has broken any laws and if I can persuade her to help us we can take her out of the net altogether. I will know for sure soon, one way or another. When are you going to pick up Abraham?"

"I was ready to do that today but have delayed until tomorrow. Jane from GCHQ has come through with more intercepts that are filling out the picture.

"Kotobi has grabbed him and Celik Abou and is holding them in a warehouse in Barking. I was about to instruct Mwake to move in until I got wind of Kotobi's plan. Apparently he has blamed the kidnapping of Abraham on Celik and apprehended Celik separately. Seems the idea is to present himself as the rescuer of Abraham, remove Celik altogether and offer himself as a new partner for Bulent Canecale's enterprise. However far-fetched the idea might have seemed, apparently Bulent Canecale is flying into London tomorrow to meet him, so we will be watching and waiting. We might never get an opportunity to nab such a big fish as Canecale on our home patch again, so I'm making sure I have full access to NCA resources for the operation."

"Are you sure of the intel?" queried Watson. "Seems like an unnecessary risk for Bulent to take."

"I agree, but the situation must be serious enough for him to be planning it."

"How does this affect Abraham?"

"I can't be sure except if Abraham wasn't involved I don't think the meeting would be taking place at all."

Given their situation Sunny was losing her sense of time. Her focus had been shuffling across the room to get close to Abraham. She would go through periods of intense activity to move her position, stopping occasionally to strain for the sounds of groaning from her fellow captive. On more than one occasion, the force of her movement had nearly resulted in the chair she had been strapped to overturning, and as it teetered from side to side she was really starting to understand that her life was literally in the balance. After what had seemed an eternity, she collided with Abraham's chair and his sudden stunted movement ensured she didn't fall over.

In the darkness there was now silence, a deafening silence that told her they were not being personally guarded but the various workaday noises that they had heard earlier had ceased.

She realised that shuffling towards Abraham had provided an unexpected dividend. Her back was now against a hard surface which seemed to have a curved object like a pipe against it. The pipe had sharp rivets holding it in position and a well-positioned nut and screw provided a perfect tool to lasso the string cord of her hood to it. A fourth attempt with a twisting movement saw her pull the bottom of the hood to her chin. Her facial muscles lifted it high enough for her to duck her head repeatedly and pull it off. Although she had swapped one form of darkness for another this was much better. Her new situation was illuminated by low-voltage security lights that provided clear sight of her immediate surroundings. She was very close to Abraham who was shackled with a metal chain to the very pipe that had partially freed her. To her surprise she had been bound differently to him with her limbs roped together but the perpetual twisting action to remove her hood had started to loosen the tension of her bonds and despite the pain of burning she was succeeding in wearing down the bindings. The first to give way was her cotton gag, followed by her right wrist slipping out from its locked position. Her other arm, waist and fixings followed shortly after, and yet she was still impeded by a metal brace attached to one of her ankles.

She felt the pain of movement having been locked in a stress position for some time, but the relative freedom she gained put her discomfort into perspective. Her first act was to attempt to free Abraham, but his chains and shackles were an altogether more challenging problem. It seemed he had been thoroughly secured first and their captors using whatever items had been left over on her. Without some basic tools he wasn't going to move and there was nothing else in the room for her to try to force the locks binding him. At least she was able to remove his hood and gag.

"Do you recognise this place?" Sunny asked, more in hope than expectation.

Abraham was adjusting his eyesight to take in his surroundings.

"No idea."

"But you know who's holding us prisoner?"

"Yes – as I told you – Celik Abou – he has helped us in the past moving people we've imported away from the coast, I guess you would call him a gang master. He runs a crew called the Screamers. When we started to see how high profile his activities were becoming, I cut him loose as it was causing a risk to my kebab business.

"He was supplying slave labour to the shops and using his people to fence narcotics at the same time."

Sunny could hardly believe what she was hearing. Abraham was talking as though he was a legitimate business that had just discovered it was dealing with a criminal enterprise.

"I don't think he was that good at what he was doing. His organisation is leaky. Someone started informing on him. My business became an innocent party in a series of police raids.

"I sense he's under his own pressure and is trying to spread the tension around to protect himself. I suppose by holding us he will be expecting some form of ransom, but the way Izmir is structured, only I could agree to make payments from the business, which I will not easily do. To get to this position, he has to take responsibility for his own mistakes. Threatening me won't do any good, just delay the time till he is busted."

"Why have we been left alone?"

"Why did they beat me once I was tied up? That's not Celik's style. I think that was his people having fun when he wasn't around. Their purpose was to freak us out. You would hear my pain and I would piss my pants. But I know he will be back for us. As he sees it, we are a new commodity that he will be wanting to get some value from."

"If, as you say, his operation leaks, is there a possibility someone else will know what has happened to us?"

"Who knows? If you recall we were kidnapped by three guys including the driver. Doing a job like that is one for the professionals. Those guys are probably part of his inner circle. I doubt he shared details of what he was planning beyond those involved…

He was interrupted by the sound of a car engine pulling up nearby followed by the slamming of doors – one, two, three. Sunny hastily replaced Abraham's gag and hood, putting on her own head covering and slipping her hands through the loosened knots that had held her. Silence once more descended on the room before warehouse arc lighting came on, followed by incoherent shouting and the sound of blows being landed. Had they been guarded after all? Was this the sound of helpers coming to their aid? Had either been able to see what was actually taking place and, had their situation not been so serious, Sunny and Abraham might have laughed at the comical scene. Kotobi had returned with three members of his gang, two of which had started a noisy fight, utilising fists, a wooden crate and any other projectile that came to hand to assault each other. Kotobi and the colleague not directly involved in the skirmish, contributed to the sound effects, shouting and swearing. The show must have lasted for five minutes until one of the protagonists succumbed, the victor standing with a bloodied face.

The event was just the warm-up act for Kotobi who then announced loudly: "Come on let's get them out of here."

The lock on their door was duly smashed open and their hoods removed directly.

"Hey Muzz, are you OK?"

Kotobi stood in front of Abraham, head bandaged, his 'side kick' releasing Sunny. The two fighting henchmen looked suitably dishevelled as they took some industrial wire cutters to the prisoner's chains.

"Yes, yes, what's happening?"

"Bulent contacted me and told me to silence Abou for tipping off the cops about our business. Then I go looking for him and hear he was ransoming you back to your brother. I did the only thing possible. I nailed the bastard and came to find you. I'll be taking you and your woman out to meet him in a couple of hours and things will get back to normal. I say normal because now the Screamers are no longer in business we have to discuss how we run things, so there will have to be some changes, know what I mean?"

Abraham looked shocked.

"Bulent told you to eliminate Celik and you've done it?"

"Yeah, Muzz, I took it like an order, man, although it hurt me to do it," he said with some irony touching his head wound. He added: "Did him halal style – thought his people would appreciate the trouble I went to as a mark of respect. He's hanging around in the next room."

Abraham wasn't sure if this was Kotobi's warped attempt at levity. He continued in a matter-of-fact tone.

"So here's the deal. You sign the kebab business over to me and I'll return you safely to your bro. I've downloaded all the forms you need to sign from the internet before coming to see you so we're ready to go."

"Wait a minute – that's a chain of more than fifty shops – it's worth millions."

"I know, but I'd say your life and that of your woman were priceless, so I think it's a good deal for you."

Abraham challenged: "It's the wrong deal for you. Besides my Turkish backers, Turhan make the big decisions. They have decided to get out of the people-smuggling and narcotics businesses tied to the Izmir business, so there will be no big money win for you in the takeover. We had planned to stop working with you as well as Celik. Bulent would not have told you to kill him."

Kotobi's confidence was high.

"Well, we'll talk to him about that in a couple of hours. I think he'll want to cooperate when he hears what I have to say. From your point of view I think it's an outstanding offer. I've been getting a lot of heat from the cops recently, so with me in control and Celik out of the picture I'll be happy to let the scene quieten down for a while so I can build it back up in a few months' time. But for now, we're gonna take you to one of our places to get you cleaned up. It's important for me to show I've looked after you, having had such an ordeal with that animal, Abou."

He turned to his other captive.

"And as for you, *lady*, my assistant here has shown me your pictures on Muzzy's phone. I feel we should get to know each other better before we go our separate ways."

THIRTY

CILLER WAITED ON THE veranda of the *yali*, staring across the water, beyond the Maiden's Tower to the imposing silhouette of the Hagia Sofia. She reflected on the tumult of the past years since the untimely death of her mother and siblings, the decline of her father and how Repcer had been so helpful implementing a radical restructuring of the family business. It was a private moment also when she thought of the fortuitous chance encounter with McKee, someone who personally and professionally had made such a telling impact on her life.

Since the administrative reforms had been introduced, Repcer's visits to the *yali* had become less frequent and on the occasions he called, he spent less time chatting with her father. It was a telling indicator of the power shift in the company which was very apparent to her. She wondered whether he father had made the same observation. If he had done, he chose not to share it. It was with some surprise therefore that Repcer arrived unannounced the day after his last conversation with McKee.

"I'm sorry to arrive without warning, but I happened to be passing and decided on the spur of the moment to drop by. I know we aren't scheduled to meet until the board meeting in a couple of weeks' time, but events are moving at pace, and I thought we should compare notes to ensure we can take a coordinated approach when the time comes."

For a minute, Ciller looked perplexed.

He continued: "Vahid has been in touch to advise of potential supply chain problems with commodities in England. Apparently one of our subcontractors has stepped out of line as a result of our service agreements."

"What is affected?"

"Virtually everything with the exception of our strategic commercial and property investments. It's sufficiently serious for him to travel there to get it sorted out. The subcontractor is looking to renegotiate."

"Should we be concerned?"

"Not really. Vahid and associates decided working with these people was too risky and wanted to drop them anyway. I think he's only interested to ensure we don't suffer any collateral damage to our network. He seems to regard it as a chore but says if we don't address this now it could prove to be more serious later on. I will monitor the situation and keep you informed. By the way, I hear from Belgin, McKee is bringing in a deal for us?"

"Yes, I've been really encouraged by what he has achieved to date. We have a strategy to transform our armaments business internationally."

It was Repcer's turn to express surprise.

"Isn't that a matter for the board?"

"Of course. He's working on a report now in Dubai."

"I thought it was a bit strange that he wanted to collect all copies of the microwave gun specification…"

"I think he wants to undertake diligence on the design and testing. He was adamant that, without the necessary technical appraisals, we would not be able to certify and guarantee the product. Belgin seemed to understand his purpose."

Repcer was not convinced.

"So would I if he was conducting the research here."

"We have a patent ready to go which is our insurance," Ciller added with confidence.

"That could be worthless if it doesn't work consistently," the lawyer replied.

"I agree. I know he is concerned about testing the weapon on desert ranges in arid conditions, especially given the calibre of the guests he has lined up for the demonstration."

"The timetable for putting this together seems tight."

"It is why we need him to lead this work. He seems to think most of the necessary admin backup is already in place and what he needs to do now is to restructure it."

"Don't we need a second opinion?" The lawyer was far from convinced.

"If you want that you might as well publish all the details online. He's walking a tightrope between getting this right in the eyes of potential customers but ensuring we're first in the market. That's why he is preparing the demonstration to feature our new lightweight armament alloys as well. He thinks that demonstrating their effectiveness will rub off to our tech offering."

"It all seems like a big risk to me."

"New product development is always a big risk, but we have the prospect of entry to a new market, so we have to take the chance. But let's not rehearse the argument before we get to the board. By then we will have a clear proposal for the way forward."

"Just be careful, Ciller – don't let your emotions cloud your judgement."

She didn't like to be patronised.

"For now, I have instructed Belgin to offer our full cooperation with McKee's requests. I will monitor the situation in the meantime. If I have cause to be concerned, I will call you directly. By the same token I am expecting you to keep an eye on Vahid. If things in the UK go wrong that could be equally serious for us. Perhaps you should be thinking of a strategy to relocate our investments there if necessary."

Repcer nodded his agreement. It was time to get back into town ahead of the evening rush. He hadn't time to engage in niceties with Ciller or her father. His visit would serve as a warning and put her on notice he would be scrutinising McKee's proposals.

She remained on the balcony, watching his car depart before heading to her study to call Belgin.

It had been less than a week since Weitzman had last spoken to Smith. Leaving their last meeting the Israeli had not been confident about his British counterpart's ability to deliver but knew the level of response he might expect would dictate the level of cooperation he would be able to offer.

"My man in Istanbul, McKee, has recovered all the known plans of the microwave gun as discussed and is ready to hand them over."

Smith enjoyed the moment, basking in the surprised reaction of his colleague.

"Is he confident he has them all?" Weitzman added with a slight tone of scepticism.

"I guess so. As you said, the file on the pendant could only be downloaded once before it destroyed itself. It was downloaded to a Turhan computer and, owing to commercial confidentiality, was not copied elsewhere. Turhan reported although the design of the signal pulse emitter was advanced, the direction controller was not fully developed. Their people had to work on that element to complete the device and in so doing claiming its authenticity to be Turkish."

Weitzman ignored the observation.

"So the plans are wiped from Turhan sources and your man has all the originals?"

"Yes, but it is likely there is a backup on the cloud that he hasn't been able to get to yet."

"OK, I will brief my tech people to take that down, but it will be easier working from the documents McKee can supply."

"I am sure you are right, but your people need to get on to set up the demonstration event as we agreed."

"Of course. Turhan expects to demonstrate the weapon. How has it been produced?"

"The pre-manufactured prototype test kits are being produced in Turkey by 3D printing, so you can expect to be able to recover these directly at the event."

"How many have been produced?"

"Only three at the moment, because the design is undergoing atmospheric trials…"

"Which presumably your man is leading? OK. I get it. I'll set Bonnie and Clyde up to make the necessary arrangements. Make sure your man finds a cloud reference that our people can follow."

"There he is."

De Jong pointed to a figure in heavy horn-rimmed glasses at passport control at City Airport.

"First flight of the day from Rotterdam so we must assume he'll be returning later on," muttered Mwake.

"I thought you said he was coming with someone else?"

"Yes, that's what the intel suggested. Now we have an eyeball we will see who he meets in arrivals and follow him from there."

"He's got no luggage so he's walking through now."

The lead investigator spoke into his lapel microphone.

"OK – Hawk One – target is with you. Over."

A voice responded.

"Check. Doesn't appear to be being met by anyone. He's going for a coffee."

"Don't lose him – this is an important connection for us. If he goes to the bog follow him in there."

"Copy."

The arrivals hall was becoming busier as more flights arrived, but the watchers had to wait for the best part of an hour for further developments. Another smartly dressed figure in a light-coloured trench coat emerged from the customs area walking at pace into the growing crowd of people waiting to meet flights. The man was clearly surveying the throng for another person to engage but in so doing bumped into another man in a flower-patterned shirt carrying a notice sign. By the looks of him he appeared to be just another taxi driver collecting a fare, but the collision resulted in him dropping his sign together with what looked like a small carrier bag. The new arrival immediately bent down to collect the sign and bag. The body language suggested he was making an apology and he continued towards the exit. Heading outside to the taxi rank, Bulent suddenly got up from his seat nearby and followed him out. The two made contact and climbed into a waiting car.

Although the pickup had been made, Mwake had been surprised that the vehicle doing the collection, a white Jaguar, was not registered to any address connected with the investigation. There had been no time to attach a tracker, Mwake would be reliant on a watch team from the NCA and street ANPR cameras to monitor the progress of the vehicle.

Meanwhile, Wetherill reported Kotobi and colleagues had left the Barking warehouse and were travelling east on the A13 turning north on to the M25 London orbital motorway.

Mwake and De Jong were following Bulent and his mystery guest as they too headed east to join the same route.

The tension was palpable. Although Mwake could call on the resources on the NCA, he had no clear idea where his targets were going, so he could not instruct colleagues accordingly. He would be on his own with this for a while.

Journey's end for Kotobi proved to be a picturesque country cottage on the Essex/Hertfordshire border. The address showed the property was owned by an expatriate and was available for short-term lets. The frontage was close to a bend in the road and offered poor sightlines. Frustratingly, Wetherill could only confirm the location and the fact Kotobi was definitely there.

Marshall was listening in to Mwake's reports as he drove out of town to meet him when Watson connected online.

"I've had a call from Yasmin as expected. I let it run to voicemail. Are you happy I interview her informally in return for her passport or do you want me to bring her in?"

"It's your call. We are sailing pretty close to the wind on this now. I don't think you can bring her in unless you are really confident she's acted illegally. Also be aware if you formally detain her, her client in Istanbul will get wind of it and could go to ground, so discretion is the order of the day."

Watson called Yasmin and arranged to meet her back at her hotel within the hour. He had rehearsed his lines.

Upon arrival he found her in the lobby on the phone and talking animatedly in Turkish. She had lost a little of the serenity of the night before but none of the passion. As soon as she registered his presence she cut the call to focus on him.

"Oliver, *Oli* – thank goodness. I've had my passport stolen. I can't catch the coach home tonight and I don't know when I can leave. You've got to help me."

"I think we may be able to help each other."

She stopped in surprise.

"How do you mean?"

"When you called I contacted someone I know in the Border Force. They are running some checks which could help."

"Can you call now and find out what's happening?"

"Just sit tight. I know they'll call me when they have news."

"OK, what do you want from me?"

"Tell me what you're doing in London and who your client is."

She looked confused.

"You know... I told you. Why the questions? I thought you were an economist, not a detective."

"It's complicated, but I work for the UK government in

revenue protection. We store a lot of wealth here in London and we need to make sure everyone who uses the facilities pays rent. It is possible some of your trades that you were here to supervise may have escaped our attention."

"Meaning?"

"They are either subject to tax or illegal. Given your profession and expertise, I think it is most likely to be the former. That being the case, I cannot imagine anyone here would want to cause you a delay. Tell me what you've been doing and I predict your passport will reappear and you can be on your way, but if you don't you'll be arrested and taken into custody."

"This is very unusual, certainly not a level of interference I have experienced before."

"It's called regulation. It's just what governments do, but I agree. Most transactions are managed electronically and don't require personal supervision, so it's an unusual response to an unusual situation."

The penny dropped.

"So you targeted me and fucked me to find out what I was doing? And they say the Russians are devious…"

"Meeting you was a strange but lucky coincidence – we call it serendipity."

"I don't want a fucking English lesson from a bastard like you…"

"As a lawyer I can't imagine you would allow your emotions to cloud your objectivity. Besides if our intelligence is correct, you don't want to get caught up in our criminal investigation."

Yasmin confirmed what Watson had suspected. She was working for Yilan acquiring assets from Turhan, as well as assigning gold reserves to a number of Swiss bank accounts. In her explanation it all sounded entirely reasonable and straightforward. In effect, she was manipulating data to a sequence of bank account reference numbers. With no names – just dates and amounts.

Her work in enabling crime was dispassionate, her role supervisory, and yet this amounted to theft on a grand scale.

For Watson, Yasmin's work would be the subject of months of further investigation. Identifying accounts covered by Swiss banking confidentiality might be the easy part. Far harder following the paper trail showing the fluctuating ownership of a passive commodity stored deep in the vaults of Threadneedle Street.

The key information Watson needed was the evidence of instruction from Turhan – the very documentation that demonstrated her authority to confirm the transactions.

Although being in a weak position, Watson respected Yasmin for the way she managed her predicament.

"I have no understanding about whether these standard transactions relate to criminal activity, evidence of my authority is commercially confidential, and besides, if you plan to detain me I will have to give a complete account of my time in London which would compromise your investigation."

"Take it easy. All I need are pictures of the screen from your laptop that you used at the Bank of England to show your authority and the list of the bank account numbers and you'll be able to go – no more questions and no problems."

Reluctantly she opened her laptop to reveal the documents. Pictures taken, she closed it hastily and in the same movement took her passport from his jacket pocket.

"That wasn't so bad was it?" he added.

Yasmin felt deflated.

"And what about confidentiality?" she asked.

"No one will know we ever met after we left the bus. For us both it will be a private, happy but distant memory."

He got up to leave. Being on view in the lobby of the hotel, he chose not to offer her a kiss, merely smiled and nodded his head before turning towards the exit.

"I still think you're a bastard," she said, towards his departing back.

She was probably right, he thought, but he'd managed the situation as best he could and somehow doubted she would want to relate her encounter when she got home.

THIRTY-ONE

BACK IN HIS SUITE at the Burj, Matheson was working hard on arrangements for the Turhan Defence Industries demonstration. Rafiq had taken the earliest opportunity to pass on his files to Weitzman's people. This would be a small-scale, high-level event, designed to attract the major scale freelance traders; the sort who travelled the world as they needed, regardless of political boundaries and jurisdictions. Gathering the top dozen or so would be a reputation boost for him and strengthen his influence with the Turhan board and Ciller Terzili in particular. But to make this happen he would be dependent on help from Mossad. Relying on a secretive organisation from a foreign country whose capabilities were largely unknown to him was a worry, yet his boss, Smith, seemed confident, especially once Matheson had achieved the seemingly impossible outcome of collecting up or destroying plans of the pulsar microwave gun. His excuse had been to revise the specification and testing to improve its reliability in different climate conditions, but in reality he had no idea about how that could happen. Mossad was putting together a report in his name that would answer the question with some technical credibility. All he had to do was absorb enough of the brief to get him through any awkward questions from the participants. His immediate priority was to host Belgin and familiarise the Turk with the venue and agree arrangements for the import of the necessary hardware to be exhibited.

Apart from his liaison with Ciller, Belgin was proving to be the most accessible and easy-going of the Turhan board. Their early cautionary exchanges had become more positive as McKee had demonstrated his knowledge of the international arms industry and Belgin vented his frustrations at the inefficiencies of the Turhan organisation. He saw McKee as contributing a new professionalism to their organisation. On more than one occasion he had told the Scot, "It's time for the industry to take Turhan seriously as a quality armaments manufacturer, not a set of pirates smuggling arms for proxy wars for people who don't want to get their hands dirty."

It was this new-found camaraderie that was giving McKee increasing confidence in the plan. Once McKee had extended the invitation, the Turk wasted little time in travelling to Dubai to discuss the logistics. The plan was to view the venue for the demonstration and discuss logistics. They talked as McKee drove south towards the Omani border.

"The site we're visiting wasn't my first choice for this exercise, but may be better for what I have in mind. It's a range used by the Emirati army mainly for close combat, riot training and urban warfare. I have made a provisional booking at the end of next month. It means you're going to have to revisit the inventory you wish to show."

"What's the problem?"

"There are many – not least my job of guaranteeing the audience you need. But there is one big one that only you can deal with. Based on the design and the prototype, the specification for the pulsar sonic gun is defective and must be corrected before you demonstrate it. Since we were last together I have had the weapon on diligence test with my associates, London-based Defence Assurance Systems. They have indicated the design is substandard

– in particular the defensive sheath that guides the vector for the pulse. In essence, they confirm the pulsar is ineffective over a distance of more than ten metres because the sound wave loses its density and focus. It is at least 50 Hertz underpowered. It needs a secondary guidance emission to focus its wave. So in its present form, the weapon is not lethal and can only stun a target. The length of the stun depends on the mass of the target which explains why it can kill a sheep like you showed me but not a human. My people have proposed how the missing component could be manufactured, but you need to get it made and fitted so we can test it before potential customers get to see it."

Belgin frowned.

"Who agreed to the diligence report?"

"I told Ciller it was necessary, and I would handle it. Defence Assurance Systems are the best with this type of technology. They're locked into a confidentiality agreement, and I removed all originators references from the plans as a security precaution. There was no way of avoiding this. The calibre of the buyers you will meet will insist on the diligence report before placing orders, so it was important to go to the best to test. Do remember, atmospheric conditions in this part of the world are different to Turkey, with air densities and climatic pressures stronger here.

"The marketing adjustments I have proposed will lower the scrutiny thresholds and for now we should only licence this product for the northern hemisphere and North Africa, until we can test elsewhere."

"What you're saying undermines our market proposition."

"Narrows it certainly but at least it gives us something to show and protects our credibility. Otherwise we just look like the sort of freelance opportunists we're trying not to be. Remember, what Turhan is trying to do – that is break into the international arms trade – is not easy. You have had to wait for the opportunity, you cannot postpone and when you implement the demonstration you need to do it with authority and confidence. So Asar, I was absolutely right to do what I have done, otherwise your international business will be dead before it has started. Everything you need to do in the next few weeks is set out in my report and the recommendations relate to specific points in the Defence Assurance Systems review. Both documents are in the attaché case behind the seat ready for you to take back to Istanbul."

"If all this extra work is needed, have we been set up to fail by the Israelis?"

"Who knows? Bearing in mind the initial plans we acquired were originally designed to go to Russia, maybe there is a state-on-state dimension to this. Maybe the plans you worked from were preliminary projections that even the inventors could not have known about until a prototype had been developed. Think yourself lucky you have a route to correcting the problem quietly without embarrassment."

By the time the conversation was concluded they had arrived at the test range, a flat and dusty plateau with a collection of semi-built breezeblock buildings on one side and a four-storey observation tower on the other. It was punishingly hot, and the glare seemed to seep around their dark glasses. They climbed out of their 4x4 and walked forward to survey the scene. The chat turned to the mundane matters of logistics catering and briefing guests.

Given their dialogue, Belgin showed only passing interest.

McKee knew the conversation had confirmed his role as the master of the emerging situation. Belgin would do what he was told.

On the drive back to Dubai he was quiet, already absorbing the reports McKee had provided.

"When are you next in Istanbul?" Belgin asked as McKee drove to the terminal building.

"I won't be back until we have delivered the demonstration," he replied. "There is just as much to do here in the course of the next few weeks as you will have back at your base. Call me when you have fixed the problems. I'll be in touch with Ciller as the plan details fall into place."

Kotobi had chosen the location for the meeting with Bulent well. Spacious fully furnished like an upmarket hotel suite, yet slightly off the beaten track. A short distance from a motorway for easy access and relatively secluded with limited sightlines, mature perimeter foliage and surrounded on three sides by arable fields.

Arriving with his crew he knew he would only have a short time to prepare before his guests arrived. His crew delivered Abraham into the lounge and moved quickly around the house checking windows and vantage points. Kotobi led the way to the master bedroom and after a cursory inspection nodded to one of his team to bring the girl.

"OK darlin', I hope you like the surroundings – it's much better to fuck in a clean room than on a warehouse floor don't you think? We got a lot of businesses on today, but you are top of my agenda. There's the bathroom. You got five minutes to get showered and get back out here. We'll even take the cuffs off so you can get to it."

He pushed her into the en suite and put his foot in the door.

"…And, sorry about that, I don't want you getting ideas about lockin' me out – you know what I mean? For the next half hour you're mine and I want my money's worth."

Once more Sunny had the feeling of dread she had experienced on Abraham's boat. Although she had suffered the humiliation of being photographed, she had survived the incident without being assaulted. This situation seemed very different. What was the matter with these men? They seemed addicted to the prospect of sex.

She took to the shower, planning on spinning out the time as far as she could. Scanning the room she looked for something, anything she might be able to use as a weapon against her prospective assailant. There appeared to be nothing obvious except the cord of the dressing gown on the back of the door. What a gift! Kotobi may have thought he had covered all eventualities, but he'd missed that.

"Come on darlin' my cock is ready for you now."

"Er… yes I'm just getting dry is there a hairdryer I can use?"

"It's out here baby."

Quickly wrapping the gown around her she loosely tied the cord in readiness to attack.

Emerging into the room, Kotobi had his shirt off and grabbed her firmly in his arms enveloping her and pulled her hard to his chest, his hands urgently feeling their way into her gown. Despite expecting his move she was in shock and her planned action to repel his advance stalled as she froze. Circumstances came to her aid by a doorbell and a commotion downstairs together with a shout: "Boss we've got company."

In the moment, his confidence drained away. He threw Sunny down on the bed like a ragdoll, grabbed his shirt from the floor and rushed out of the room, calling to one of his henchmen to lock the bedroom door.

Knowing that the occupants were armed but not being sure how many of them there were, limited the options open to him.

His first move was to send in the postman – the classic surveillance move. The vagaries of Royal Mail deliveries meant the visit of a red uniformed courier at any time of day didn't raise suspicions and his man given the task looked authentic in a red-badged gilet and shorts ideal for a summer's day. Arriving in a red van and parking in front of the gate, his brazen visibility was a great defence. Clutching a bouquet of assorted junk mail, he made his way briskly to the front door ramming the assorted paper into the letter box whilst attaching a small magnetic microphone to a corner of the adjacent window. It was a skilful move by a seasoned operator, attached swiftly with a sleight of hand that only generated the briefest glance from one of the watching Leerys.

The visit by the postman proved to be well timed. Shortly afterwards Bulent and his colleague arrived. They were expected, the driveway gate was open and a slightly flustered Kotobi opened the front door to greet them, smiling his welcome.

"Hey Unc – who's your friend?"

"This is Mr Vahid, my Turkish associate and financial backer. He accompanies me when I have important meetings."

Kotobi liked the sound of that. It was clear he was being taken seriously from the start.

"Come in guys. I was just chillin'. You're welcome to my summer house. Drink?"

Now Marshall and Mwake could listen in on the proceedings in the house.

Bulent opened the negotiation.

"Thank you but no, Mr Kotobi, let's just get down to business and go our separate ways. You have Mr Abraham and his associate here? We will take them with us and provide you with a reward."

Kotobi smiled and nodded. "We did you a big favour guys. Not only did we rescue your people from the pirate Celik Abou, but we took out Abou and cut down his network. So you get a bonus of a streamlined organisation and the security of working with a single team. You know, it got me thinking, I should really be running all your operations over here – the gear, the people, the shops. Understand this boy Abraham and his ho are your mates, but really? You want a fat middle-aged dude like that running your business? He looks like he's had too much of the good life, you know what I mean? He's sloppy, careless. If I'd been runnin' the show, I'd have taken Abou down in an instant, not allowing him to create the hassle he has."

"So you're telling us you have control of Celik's people?"

"Man they don't shit unless they get the order from him. My people have told a couple of his sidekicks they won't be hearing from him no more and they ain't smart enough to do anything for themselves – besides they don't want to mess with me now – know what I mean?"

"If you want to run the show over here, there will be more risk as well as reward. You will have more product to shift so if you can't move it we won't supply and we are aware of the interest the authorities are showing in your activities," Canecale observed.

"Yeah that was Celik's fault. I put a stop to that. Life will be good from now."

Vahid intervened. Throughout the dialogue he had kept his gaze fixed on Kotobi almost as if he was subjecting him to an X-ray. His quiet and focused demeanour unnerved his host, but the gang leader knew he had to keep cool.

"Before we discuss reward, we need to see Abraham and the girl," Vahid said flatly.

"Sure. My guys have them here."

There was a rustling, followed by a muffled banging with doors being opened and slammed shut.

"Here they are, safe and sound."

There were more muffled noises. The captives were not able to speak – so it seemed.

"Alright, leave them in the next room. I must commend you. How many men have you got here?"

"Four and me."

"Bring them into the front room now. If we are going to make a new arrangement I need a picture of each one so I can complete individual security checks before I commit to your proposal."

"All together? A couple of them are keeping watch."

"Yes now. It won't take a minute. Your captives aren't going anywhere."

There were more banging noises and some incoherent shouts. A pause.

Vahid spoke again: "Gentlemen as your boss's main customer I wanted to take the opportunity of this short visit to thank you for your hard work. You have achieved some success in growing our shared enterprise. This success also brings consequences, and it is clear you are attracting more interest from the regulatory authorities. We have to weigh up whether these gains are worth the effort and your boss's initiative to streamline your activities has made us realise it is time to act. I regret we have decided to close your business with immediate effect."

A cough. Now some incoherent shouts – then four more coughs, thuds and moans.

Marshall and Mwake looked at each other, both were imagining the scene but neither reacted, choosing instead to listen closely to developments.

They seemed to be tuned in to a stunned silence.

"OK – don't touch anything. Let's go." The accent suggested it was Canecale talking.

Mwake had been waiting for a signal from Marshall to move in and make arrests, but his boss remained silent until prompted.

"Do we bring them in?" he asked.

"Not yet – put out an *all ports* alert on Canecale and Vahid just in case. These guys are professionals and I suspect they have alternative exit arrangements. We need to see where they are running to."

Their targets had been quicker to leave the scene than Marshall had expected, and the support unit ordered to surround the location were not in position in time, leaving Mwake and De Jong to approach the house. Kotobi's car was still outside but there were no obvious signs of activity and the shuttered windows weren't giving anything away either. Despite listening hard, there was no sound of voices or movement coming from inside. Exchanging nods, De Jong used a ram to smash open the door, rolling clear to avoid any outgoing fire. Again nothing. Weapons at the ready, they went in to be greeted by a scene of carnage in the front room with Kotobi and his henchmen dead, sprawled at crazy angles, their blood oozing into the carpet. This had been no casual act of violence, but a rapidly administered programme of execution, the victims either with head or chest wounds, their expressions of surprise and disbelief testament to the speed and callousness of their dispatch. The French window at the back was open and Mwake ran on, leaving his partner to raise the alarm. Through the garden was a low fence, a wheat field beyond. Despite his quarry being in a hurry, there was no tell-tale trail of trampled corn to follow and no sign of movement on the horizon – yet, following a route around the edge of the field, he picked up signs of broken twigs on the side of the hedgerow which told him they couldn't be far beyond. Despite stopping to listen to the sounds around him, there was nothing untoward to focus on, just the twitter of skylarks, the rustle of wind through the wheat ears and the hum of traffic from the distant motorway. Just a little further on he came to a track and, half hidden by the dappled sun breaking through the leaves of a nearby tree, was a clearing and fresh tyre tracks heading off in the direction of a country lane.

He had lost them.

THIRTY-TWO

MATHESON WAS DOWNHEARTED. HE'D just been advised that HMRC now had evidence to prove Ciller had been involved in money laundering in London and a warrant could be served if she entered UK jurisdiction. Yet the fact she was using a nominee to travel to the UK to undertake the transactions suggested to him that she must have been well aware about what was taking place and that she would be at risk of arrest if she had managed the trades in London personally. He was forced to admit in the time he had known her he had developed feelings for her which at best were unprofessional and at worst offered the prospect of compromising the whole case against Turhan. He had been told that the NCA were closing in on Vahid and some of his associates in the UK and arrests would be imminent. His instructions were to find a way to get Ciller into a British territory to face justice or find other means to shut down the Turhan operation. If the matter was left to his boss, the focus would be on the latter, so it seemed his focus had to remain on the Emirates.

It had been two weeks since Matheson, in his guise as McKee, had last spoken to Belgin, but he had not been overly concerned. After all, the time away from Ciller would help his required exit strategy. The work he had asked him to do would take at least a month and he had stressed he didn't want to hear from him until he had a solution. He had supplied copies of the technical reports to Ciller to ensure the board were sighted on. In the meantime, he spoke to Ciller about arranging the exports of armour and weaponry to the UAE, allowing him to arrange the necessary licences and warehousing near Al Ain, close to the demonstration site.

His efforts were being assisted by the Mossad team led by a couple, who had introduced themselves at his hotel when he had arrived from Istanbul as Bonnie and Clyde. They had joked, given the complexities of the arrangements, theirs were the only names he needed to remember although they would be using a number of aliases in the name of McKee's 'pop-up' consultancy. They had already surveyed the demonstration site, taken care of all the logistics – invitations, transfers, security, servicing, staffing and marquees. Normally, he would be confident – yet he was apprehensive. After all, he was fronting a black op with a team he had never worked with, but Smith seemed happy with the approach. McKee had come up with the running order of the demonstrations, which would run for a little over two hours. Part of his role would be to act as event host, a compere, who would introduce the products and provide a narrative and commentary of the demonstration activity. Due to the technical issues he had raised, Belgin and colleagues would only arrive in Dubai three days before the event, limiting time for rehearsals. By then McKee needed to have all the products in place, except the main feature – the modified sonic gun. Bonnie and Clyde met with him at his hotel suite to provide updates on the arrangements which he in turn was able to feed back to Istanbul. As far as he was concerned, the Israelis were a class act – thorough and methodical in their approach. All he needed to do was to check London was keeping his corporate bank account in funds as Bonnie and Clyde chalked up a myriad of bills for his signature. How ironic the UK should be subsidising the foreign escapades of another sovereign state, but that wasn't his worry. All that mattered was that his promises to Ciller were being fulfilled.

She was still a mystery to him. On the positive, she would call him every day, often about minor matters from her father's state of health to her plans for them both to take a trip on a sailing boat on the Aegean when the business in Dubai was concluded and how she was missing him in bed, yet she seemed to avoid business topics that he would have expected her to discuss. For example, he had been expecting to be called to the Turhan board meeting, if only to provide a report in person about his activities in the Emirates and specifically his due diligence work on the sonic gun, upon which so much of the company's future depended. Yet the first he heard about it was a passing reference to the fact that a board meeting had indeed been held when he was out of the country and his reports were presented and discussed by Asar Belgin. He reached a point where he felt obliged to ask her directly how the preparation arrangements were progressing. Her response seemed casual.

"Belgin brought everyone up to date on what was going on and the board approved your reports and instructed me to offer every cooperation, so that is it. You have asked for my logistical support which you're getting with export licences and shipping product. Belgin has got his entire team working on the sonics."

"And the new prototype will be through in time?"

"Belgin assured the board that it would be, so all that remains is his confirmation."

"I was surprised the board hadn't got further questions about all this?"

"You shouldn't worry – the quality of your documentation has not been challenged. In fact, it is because of this they have been so quiet. It is something that even Repcer could not find a hole in your planning. Personally, I think your work has exposed his lack of knowledge in this market sector and Belgin is a fan. When will you have the confirmations of the attendees?"

"Probably in a week or so. Should be quite straightforward most have an office base in Dubai anyway so they won't have to come far."

"Will al-Harriri be there?"

"Yes, and he is bringing one of his big customers over from Iran so you can be sure the effort will be worthwhile. When will you be coming over?"

"I've not made plans yet. I wanted to know who was coming and what the protocols would be. I had thought you and Belgin would run it between you. It could be an occasion when having a woman present would not be helpful."

"It's madness. The board must be here. At the very least, you and Repcer should be present. You can come with Belgin to supervise the rehearsal."

"I will talk to them, but I can tell you now, Vahid is away in England and Hosni is tied up with a new breakers contract."

"That's OK – you and Repcer will be enough. Let me know when you have fixed your travel plans."

He closed the phone and stared out of his 14th-floor room at the panoramic view of the Gulf, pockmarked at intervals with ships large and small plying their trade. He tried not to think too hard about what lay ahead. His purpose was to make the show happen and get all the necessary people there. Then it was up to others... Smith? Mossad? Somebody else? The countdown was on, just five days to go and nobody was talking to him.

The queue on the M11 at the junction with the London orbital motorway was as slow as ever, but the static situation gave Marshall the opportunity to reflect on the progress of the investigation as he edged his way back to his Canary Wharf office. The UK end of the operation was heading towards a conclusion although the stakes had got higher. He was contemplating the size of the files he would need to assemble to go to the Crown Prosecution Service as the charge sheet was growing ever larger.

Evidence of racketeering, including money laundering, people trafficking, and the import and sale of narcotics was there, with some lower-level arrests already made, and now several murders (some victims known, but others yet to be identified) would be added to the list. He could be pleased with the performance of his team and the quality of collaboration he had been offered by other agencies of the State, but momentum had come at a price. The two gang leaders that he had expected to net had been killed. Perhaps one of them could have been saved had he reacted faster, but there was no point in worrying about that now. At least he knew who their key suspects were and that he had a realistic chance of apprehending them in the coming days. But he also knew his targets had a trump card – Purewal – who was in clear danger, even more so, if her true identity was revealed. His relationship with Mwake was strained as a result. His lead investigator would have moved in within minutes of the shooting starting with some half-baked plan to rescue her, but Marshall had resisted, unsure of the firepower he and his operational partner might face. At least they were certain she had been at the house and had left unharmed for now and his investigators lived to fight another day. The focus would now be on tracking the fugitives' whereabouts before deciding when and how they would be intercepted.

Despite being clear on the identities of his suspects, Marshall knew that the stakes were even higher for Smith. He couldn't be sure what he was planning but had given his word he would not close down the UK operation without informing him first. When he had given the undertaking he had been clear that lives of other people connected to the operation could be at risk, especially his man in Istanbul who had been so helpful in the early stages providing intelligence on Turhan's activities. Although Smith had not said so in as many words, Marshall got the clear impression that he had a strategy for closing Turhan down, although quite how he expected to achieve it, operating beyond UK jurisdiction he could not imagine.

They arranged to meet for breakfast the following day at Smith's regular morning haunt, the café in Quebec Street, near Marble Arch. This time without dietary sensibilities to observe, the two men indulged in the full English experience, washed down with a generous supply of cappuccinos.

"The chances are we will have to nab our targets in the course of the next week depending on how the opportunity presents itself," explained Marshall. "I suspect, even if all goes well, news of our action will get back to Istanbul quickly. I cannot afford to let the opportunity slip, so I want you to be aware this is now a time-sensitive issue. How do you plan to resolve your man's obligations?"

"I'm afraid I can't tell you that other than to say the matter is in hand. I'm glad we've been able to help you out from an intelligence point of view, but you will know we have always had a broader interest in Turhan which has driven our involvement. I understand your issue with timelines and don't expect your circumstances to cause us any problems. Just keep me informed as matters progress."

Smith's response was aimed at providing reassurance, but Marshall was far from convinced. He had already noted that as their apparently joint initiative had progressed the partners appeared to be diversifying from their shared objective. For Smith's part it didn't suit him to acknowledge the deep involvement of Mossad in bringing the investigation to a conclusion.

Vahid, Bulent Canecale, Abraham and Anita were together in a Range Rover driving through the Midlands. There was a strange atmosphere in the vehicle. Abraham and Anita were still in a state of shock having witnessed the cold-blooded assassination of Kotobi and his gang and the apparent calmness of the perpetrator, Vahid, who drove north with a clear sense of purpose. The conversation was left to Bulent.

"So what happened when I left you in France?"

"All was well until we landed in Brighton and then we got jumped by the gangsters."

"Did you see what they looked like?"

"No, they bagged and bundled us in too quickly – apparently they worked for Celik."

"How did you know?"

"They kept talking about him."

"Like they wanted you to know who they were in reality?"

"Yes, I suppose. They took us to some warehouse. I think the idea was to ransom us off but then Kotobi arrived and there was a big fight which he won."

"How did you know? Did you see it?"

"No, we were kept blindfolded most of the time. We only got to see where we were after Kotobi freed us."

"What happened to Celik's people?"

"I guess they split after the fight. They kept one guy back who they were torturing. We heard the screams. And then Kotobi arrived."

"Yeah and he freed us but said he'd linked up with you and was going to take us back."

"And that was it?"

"Pretty much."

Bulent unburdened himself.

"Kotobi was a cheating shit – stupid and greedy with it. He said he killed Celik in response to an instruction from me. The guy tortured in the warehouse was Celik. Kotobi sent me a video. I never ordered him to kill Celik. His death just drew more attention to what we were doing and Kotobi wasn't smart enough to avoid being watched. Celik had a tracker on Kotobi's car which he checked to find out who kidnapped you an hour before he disappeared. He had told me Kotobi's car was in Brighton. How often did Kotobi go there? Hardly ever because it was Screamers territory. And why would he be there at that time? No, it was a pity Celik had to die. He was useful – I could have found him other work in Europe, but Kotobi pushed the decision on us – we needed to close down that business before we all got caught up in it. Bastard! This has been a good day."

Vahid drove on without comment.

"What's next?" Anita was now consumed with adrenaline and the shocking conversation prompted her to ask about her own fate.

It was an opportune time to ask because for the first time, it showed Vahid and Bulent had assumed she was Abraham's girlfriend and Abraham had clearly not advised them to the contrary.

"We're heading to the Isle of Man, then to Ireland and back to Turkey. Now the authorities have a number of bodies that they will be crediting to us, we can assume nowhere in Europe will be safe for a while."

"But they're bound to be watching the ports and airports."

"Yes," said Vahid, "that is why I intend to avoid them."

He put the radio on, filling the car with some anonymous Euro pop music designed to kill the motivation for small talk.

Left to their own thoughts, his fellow travellers watched the passing scenery, wondering about their fate. Surprisingly, considering he appeared to be at the centre of a maelstrom happening around him, Abraham seemed relaxed to Anita's eye. Was it because sitting in a comfortable car going anywhere was a much better prospect than being held captive, trussed up like a chicken by a lunatic? Considering Abraham and Bulent were supposed to be brothers there were no obvious demonstrations of filial bonding she had seen. Those limited exchanges that she had witnessed were short and unintelligible to her ear (she assumed they talked in Turkic). Had she heard Abraham's story during the crossing from France wrongly? Perhaps he was one of those who would call anyone brother – ironic, as that had been a trait of Kotobi's.

Recognising the perilous situation she found herself in, Anita saw potential advantage playing up to Abraham, allowing herself to get closer to him in the car. To help the effect, she pretended to fall asleep leaning into his shoulder, aware that Vahid was watching her in the rear-view mirror. Embarrassingly, the strain of the situation started to overtake her and soon her premediated action morphed into a genuine if fitful slumber.

Abraham's midriff had become a comfortable cushion, and, on waking, she had absent-mindedly put her arms across him in an involuntary cuddle. Feeling him shift awkwardly she woke, slightly flustered and pulled away from him. Looking forward, she saw Vahid watching.

"I'm sorry," she blurted, "I don't know what came over me." The driver smiled, noting Abraham's discomfort as well as her own.

"Don't worry," he said in English. "According to the sat nav we are close to the end of our drive."

Focusing on the view, Anita looked at the scenery – rough moorland in sleety rain, but without any noticeable road signs to help her work out where she was.

The first clue came as their vehicle started a slow descent through a narrow valley and in the distance the sea appeared.

"Where are we?" There was nothing to lose by asking the question, but the answer didn't help her much.

"Wales. We are being collected from a beach around here and then responsibility for taking us to our destination rests with your man," the Turk said.

Abraham added: "The crew from my boat will be picking us up then we'll pay a short visit to the Isle of Man before heading home via Ireland."

"If we're being chased, why are we going to the Isle of Man?" Anita queried.

"Unfinished business. It shouldn't take long, and we can relax once we have left the British mainland. The authorities won't be looking for us over here. In fact, we have made their lives a little harder. We changed the number plates before we left so if they are using the police traffic cameras they will not have been able to find us."

"They're not dumb. They will have traced this car from the hire desk at the airport. Even if they don't have a plate to work from they will know the make model and colour," Anita exclaimed.

"True," said Abraham. "It will take them time. We set up this route as our emergency escape if we needed it: we were always going to be one jump ahead."

"Well you're not really," Anita said. "I paid to come to the UK. I don't want to end up in Turkey."

"I think, lady, you should consider your situation more carefully. Unfortunately you know too much for us to let you go now. Besides, a woman without documentation will be locked up as an illegal immigrant and deported at the first opportunity. You won't find anyone interested in trading information for citizenship. Besides, you are a good-looking woman. A prison is no place for you. With us, you can look forward to a good and comfortable life in the sun in exchange for... occasional favours."

Although repulsed at the thought she knew it was important to play along with the situation, her life could depend on it.

The shingle shoreline where they were met by one of Abraham's crew had been a well-researched location. As they had made their way down the valley the road had become increasingly narrow until it expired at a wooden gate. Although padlocked and chained by the landowner, probably as a gesture to the more adventurous tourists who might pass this way, a handy pair of bolt cutters in the back of their 4x4 made light work of the obstruction. The vehicle itself was parked in the lee of a large rock that would partly obscure its sight from the end of the road. Their luck continued as they set out across the benign waters with Abraham's vessel visible on the horizon.

The fugitives seemed to get a sense of relief as they climbed aboard, Abraham loosing no time telling his captain to weigh anchor before seeing the look of hopelessness on Anita's face.

"Don't worry about being back here. It was not in the script from my point of view either. You may not be where you wanted to be, but you will be safe with us."

"How can you say that with what has just happened?"

Abraham shrugged. "That's just business I'm afraid. Death and taxes – life's certainties, but worth avoiding if you get the chance. Those guys were shitheels – they are not worth bothering about. Many people have probably suffered at their hands, so now they've had some payback. Just put it out of your mind and move on. We're making a short stop at the Isle of Man before heading to Ireland."

"Then what?"

"My friend and driver, Mr Vahid, has arranged a private jet to take us to Turkey. When we arrive you will be able to contact your friend and make whatever arrangements you like and your business with us will be concluded. For you I think the future is positive – you may even get to like our company and, if that is the case, you may not need to worry about staying in England – certainly if you wish to escape from your husband I cannot think of a better place to be. Anyway, you must appreciate I have some business to attend to with my colleagues. I am afraid, for now, the same rules will apply from our earlier trip across the Channel you will be locked in the lounge, but I will arrange for refreshments to be provided in the meantime."

He nodded to one of the crew nearby.

"Bertrand my steward will escort you to your quarters."

It was clear to Anita that her failure to cooperate would result in her being frog marched to her confinement. She didn't want to risk being groped in the process.

Her mind raced. Did her colleagues understand her plight and where she was? If so, why hadn't they rescued her? Her training taught her she could only rely on her own efforts. She would need to think through her options.

THIRTY-THREE

"SO WHAT DO YOU think?" McKee had finished his presentation in his suite at the Burj, his audience of Turhan board members was briefly silent contributing to an air of tension in the room.

Belgin was the first to speak.

"You're some guy, McKee. I have to admit I wasn't sure about you when we were first introduced but having seen the way you approach your work and the effort you have made to create this plan, I can only compliment you on your effort. I don't think we could have pulled together a demonstration of this complexity without your help. The fact that you have most of the elite weapons dealers in the world attending our show when we are relatively unknown internationally is an amazing achievement.

"My operational team reported they are satisfied with the field conditions and the manoeuvres they are expected to perform, and the equipment has proved resilient in the local conditions. My concern is that we have sufficient spare parts available for fitting at short notice, but really that is just an issue of detail."

"Ciller?"

"What is there to say? We hired you to do a job for us and so we can see it is done. I remain concerned about the microwave gun, given your diligence report recommendations, but if you and Belgin are happy with what is proposed, I am content."

McKee looked at Repcer as did his two other directors. He would have preferred to stay aloof but given the importance of the moment was obliged to comment.

"I cannot fault you, Mr McKee, on your preparations. There is no doubt that a successful event will propel our company into the major league of international arms manufacturers, but assuming this happens it will present us with capacity issues. I cannot see we will have the ability to respond to any more than three significant orders within our present resources and so we must be prepared to consider licencing or franchising manufacture elsewhere. If we do that we will run the risk of our patents being compromised. This is going to be difficult for us to control and for me, the only way we can reap the full benefit is to retain your services afterwards to manage the new commercial relationships that will be created. With this in mind I will suspend my view until we have attended the dress rehearsal tomorrow and then, Mr McKee, we will need a further discussion about how we process orders. And now if you will excuse me? I have some other business to attend to. You can collect us from our hotel at ten in the morning."

Ciller frowned at Repcer and interrupted: "What he is saying is that he agrees. The arrangements are good. All we need to do is to watch the dress rehearsal and study your file on our guests ahead of their arrival. Well done. We will all leave you now so we can prepare. You must press on and so we'll pick up tomorrow."

She gave him an almost imperceptible wink as she got up to leave, her two male companions stood to follow her out.

So this was it. McKee had passed the point of no return. He was about to be the ringmaster in the most elaborate sting of his life, so complicated that only a state's resources could be mobilised to deliver it.

As part of the elaborate security arrangements, the three Turhan directors would travel to the demonstration site separately by helicopter in order to experience how McKee's team would manage Turhan's transfers from Dubai airport. The demonstration site was immaculate and Ciller in particular was impressed with staffing and guest management.

Even Repcer broke into a smile at the end.

"This is excellent. There is no substitute for the use of live munitions, even the sonic gun looked good in the hand-to-hand combat scenario. And the guest list is impressive too. I had not heard of many of these people before you profiled them, but of course Solokov is the exception to the rule. Well done. I think we will have to be recommending a bonus payment of ten million dollars for running this event. I am looking forward to the show tomorrow. I am sure you can go one better with this."

Belgin had offered to spend the forthcoming night at the demonstration site with McKee, but he had been persuaded to return to Dubai with his colleagues. It was just as well. McKee was starting to feel the pressure. Bonnie and Clyde, his two senior staffers who between them had brought the whole plan together seemed relaxed when they held their final debriefing meeting.

"Everything is ready for tomorrow. You know what you have to do. Just do your thing and leave the rest to us," said Bonnie.

McKee was not in a mood to be patronised.

"I wish you guys would stop fucking me about. I need to know how this will be brought to a head."

Clyde stared him in the eye.

"You know our people say you are one of the best British agents. This is the chance to show that. All this operation has been predicated in us arresting three of your guests al-Harriri, Vehrani and Solokov. We have agreed to terminate the Turhan team in a coordinated hit as collateral damage. For this to work you cannot know what the plan is in advance. Above everything, your reaction to events as they unfold must be genuine, as it could mean the difference between life and death for you personally. All you need to remember is that the majority of observers will be Mossad, but those involved in the demonstrations will be Turhan people, ex-

Turkish military who are certain to involve themselves if they see a disturbance taking place."

"In other words there's going to be a war tomorrow?"

"Right, and it's not in your interest to be in the way."

Vahid and Abraham landed on a short shingle beach just north of Peel on the island's west coast. The landing point was a short distance from the nearest road, and the two set off to find it, Abraham using his mobile to contact a local taxi company.

They looked a little incongruous walking along the side of the highway a mile or so outside town and registering the surprise of the taxi driver made an excuse they were there surveying building land and didn't want to walk back the distance they had inadvertently walked.

Taxi drivers the world over tend to be curious people and this one was no exception.

"Don't you want me to take you back into Peel?" he asked.

Abraham replied: "Unfortunately there is no time for that. If we don't go straight to Douglas we will miss an important business meeting. We can come back here at our leisure afterwards."

The driver took their destination address and set off accordingly.

Annoyingly, he had not taken the hint his passengers did not want to engage in conversation.

"Is this your first time on Man? People who come this side of the island normally appreciate its quieter setting, although I guess you could say Man is quiet at the best of times. Will you be going to the ferry or the airport after the meeting? If you like I can hang around for you in Douglas and take you back. From my business point of view getting a double fare makes more sense you know?"

"I'm not sure we will need that, thanks – it depends how our meeting goes."

"I get it. It's one of those big international finance meetings is it? A yes or no scenario. Champagne or chips on the quayside. Well not to worry. I feel lucky today and I think my luck will rub off on you.

I'll take a chance. I'll get you to your destination and I will wait at no cost to you. That way if you suddenly decide you need a lift back to Peel or anywhere else around here I'll be waiting."

Abraham had switched off to the cabbie limiting himself to general noncommittal nods hoping that by not providing the oxygen of conversation the driver would just run out of words.

Vahid sat beside Abraham looking bored.

Twenty minutes later the car pulled in outside the Douglas office of the bank. The driver was paid by credit card, smiled and watched his two passengers disappear into the premises. It was a sweet job. Unbeknown to Vahid and Abraham, agent Wetherall had been at the wheel and used his own phone to confirm to Mwake his guests had arrived.

Having shown identification to gain access, Vahid and Abraham were ushered to the manager's office in order to conduct their business.

"Mr Vahid and Mr Abraham, welcome to the bank and I think in your case, Mr Vahid, as a first-time visitor, welcome to the island. We are pleased to receive your visit and hope you will make the most of our sophisticated range of international services. You will understand we pride ourselves on client confidentiality and so we must ask you to deposit your mobile phones in the safe box provided for the duration of your time with us. Naturally these will be returned before you leave the premises. Thank you for your cooperation.

"Now, I understand you must have particular requirements that have necessitated a personal call? We are used to dealing with your affairs electronically."

"Thanks right, Mr Carson. We have some high-level sensitive business to transact that will involve us closing our account in the name of Abraham Associated Investments with immediate effect. This is because our holding company is about to make major changes in its financial arrangements that will require some corporate restructuring and in preparation we must decide to safeguard our assets. Once all our internal issues are resolved, we will seek to reactivate our global investment strategy, most likely with new arrangements for oversight."

"So is this money to be deposited in London?"

"No – Turkbank in Fatih – this is the branch that manages our international transactions. Here is the identifier code."

"Certainly, Mr Vahid. This will take a few minutes to set up. Please make yourself comfortable while I set up the transactions. I will return shortly to run through the authorisation procedure. You are aware we will require to see your passports plus two other identification documents."

"Sure, we are ready."

"Very well, please help yourselves to coffee. I won't be long."

Further down the corridor, Marshall and Mwake monitored the waiting pair in the bank's security room, listening in to their conversation.

"I hope they're not bureaucratic about this, I don't want to have to come back tomorrow."

"I think it's just fine. Once they have clarified this is a Turhan account they'll just get on with it. It's not like it's being paid to an individual."

"Yes but releasing that level of funds in one transaction may mean they have to report it to the Bank of England."

"They can report it to who they like. Legally this is little more than an internal transfer. We are registered accounting officers along with Ciller and Repcer. There are no third parties so there is nothing they can do to stop it. As soon as we have the electronic confirmation that the transaction has been placed we can get out of here. I have received confirmation that the Turhan plane is en route from Dubai to Dublin, so we can expect to be heading back tomorrow night, and *Autumn Breeze* can set sail for Beşiktaş. Then if the authorities are trying to find us they can follow your boat."

"And the girl?"

"Leave her on the boat when we go ashore in Ireland. Tell the master he can do with her what he wants. He will have plenty of time and opportunity to drop her body overboard. By her own admission, she's an illegal. No one is going to miss her."

"What about our other businesses here?"

"Thanks to the carelessness of those assholes you've been working with, the authorities will be looking into your business in particular. The danger for us is that if an investigation is underway they will make a link to Bulent and Turhan, so that's why we need to get our assets out of the UK and lie low for a while."

"But the authorities will take my assets, my home in Buckinghamshire."

"And the Turhan property portfolio in London that's worth much more. That is the price we must pay for our freedom. Given our skills we will soon make it back and more besides, once the dust settles, after a while you can send for your wife and live in a villa on the Aegean – maybe start to rebuild those strained family relationships."

"And Turhan?"

"It depends on what happens when the company gets restructured. There's talk we might get out of the money laundering game altogether. Metal recycling is the big new business that can make us more money for less risk. Armaments is doing well also. It looks like the company is about to do some big deals in Dubai. If all that happens we won't need to be fucking about with smuggling gold from Uzbekistan, running people and narcotics to London or relying on these greedy English fuckers to front up for us. No, for us our most risky work is done. We just need to go home and enjoy the rewards for all our hard work."

Back in the security room, Marshall could not resist a smile. Without any intervention on his part he had collected all the information he needed. He had warned Smith that his investigation was drawing to a close, but circumstances meant that he needed to finish it now.

He looked at Mwake.

"Are the premises secure?"

His investigator nodded.

"OK."

Twenty minutes had elapsed before the flustered bank manager, Carson returned to the meeting room.

"Gentlemen – I am sorry to have taken so long. These major-scale transactions always take longer than we think, by the time we have located and transferred the assets. This scale of funds will take another twenty-four hours to register in Istanbul, but the first stage of the move will begin today crediting Dalabank's London branch. So first, I need you to check the transfer authorisation and see it is correct. Secondly, I need to see your identification as required, and thirdly we have to have the transfer independently witnessed."

The final piece of information came as a surprise to Abraham and Carson noted the reaction.

"Please, Mr Abraham, don't worry. This is a standard procedure, and we normally have an independent person (normally a local notary) we can call on for this purpose."

"Once you have signed the authority I can call him in."

Abraham and Vahid scanned the documentation and signed accordingly.

"Thank you, gentlemen. I will just go and collect the independent witness."

Carson disappeared and returned with Marshall.

"Can I introduce you to Mr Philip Marshall, our duty independent witness. He will examine your passports, complete a visual identity check and then add his signature under your own. Once he has done this, the instruction to transfer will be complete and, assuming he is satisfied with it, will be implemented within the hour.

"May I take this opportunity to thank you for your business and who knows, we may expect to be of service to you again in the future. Mr Marshall…"

"Thank you, Mr Carson. I am satisfied you are Mr Vahid, Director of Turhan International of Istanbul and you are Mr Abraham of Abraham Associated Investments, and you are accounting officers and therefore empowered to make the specified transfer of assets.

"Before I sign the authorisation there is one more form I have to sign first, which I have asked a colleague to bring in now."

He went to the door and gestured for assistance.

"May I introduce you to Mr Mwake, latterly of Four Musketeers Research, a wholly owned subsidiary of the UK National Crime Agency. He has been investigating Turhan International's activities in the UK and has concluded most of its operations are contrary to the prevailing laws here on the Isle of Man as well as elsewhere in the UK.

"Mr Mwake has got an extensive charge sheet to run through with you now, with the most serious being the murder of Abel Kotobi and four of his associates at Field Cottage, Saffron Walden, Essex two days ago. Given the extent of these charges, I would suggest you give up any weapons you may have on your persons now. The bank is surrounded. Your exit routes blocked. We would welcome the prospect of working with you to fully understand the extent of your activities which will help us to secure further arrests. In these circumstances we can petition the examining judge to minimise the inevitable prison sentences. You will now be searched and escorted to Douglas Police Station for formal interview under caution at which time you will be given access to legal advice should you request it. It's been my pleasure to meet you both. In the course of our investigation I have come to believe I already know you, although I am sure I have plenty more to learn."

THIRTY-FOUR

"I THINK YOU MAY have made a mistake, Mr... er, Marshall. I am a Turkish national, merely an associate of Mr Abraham, here to assist in a private transaction of behalf of my company Turhan International. If some crime has been committed maybe Mr Abraham can assist you, but I fear this may be a case of mistaken identity. I am not in the habit of carrying a weapon into a bank in case they might think I'm going to commit a robbery."

He made a feeble effort at humour.

"Don't worry, Mr Vahid, we know all about you and your activities, so I would suggest you spend some time thinking over your situation. You won't be going home for a while. In the meantime, we understand there are two other members of your party at large – a Mr Bulent Canecale and a girl. Where are they?"

Abraham spoke up recognising the hopelessness of the situation.

"They are not on the island. Mr Canecale is a relative of mine who has been holidaying on my boat with his girlfriend. I'm not sure where they are. We are the ones who can help you with your enquiries."

"Very commendable, Mr Abraham, but we know about Mr Canecale and his involvement in your shared endeavour, and you may not have realised his girlfriend is one of our agents and we want her back. So in the interests in resolving this matter it would be helpful if you could put us in touch."

A desert dawn is not only beautiful with the animated star-studded sky moving from black to blue and then shafts of orange as the sun emerges, but also surprisingly noisy with the calls of coucals and sunbirds waking up to start their day. But McKee had no time to contemplate the beauty of the scene that was being steadily illuminated around him. Beyond the field camp was a flat expanse of scrub, either side of an aging concrete runway; to his immediate left, two camouflaged hangers holding the hardware to be exhibited; to his right, water and fuel tanks; and in the middle, some distance away, a control tower. One of the hangers was in the process of being emptied with equipment being moved into the launch positions. The other would be an exhibition hall and reception centre for the guests and was readily identifiable by the temporary viewing platform and cover that had been erected above it. Despite elaborate canopies, it would inevitably get hot up there and for that reason alone the demonstration was not expected to last more than an hour.

The camp where McKee had based himself for the past three days was a hive of activity through the night with Belgin's people checking demonstration equipment tanks, artillery and mortars, signing out equipment and spares from the compound and moving towards pre-determined positions. It was divided into two – the Turkish part, and the Emirati part, which was essentially the Israeli contingent. The arrangement had not aroused suspicion amongst the Turks. They readily understood the need for security and their encampment was next to the equipment stores that would feature in the demonstration, meaning the Emiratis did not need to go near it. Further, McKee didn't need to have much contact with them. He had passed a copy of the plans for the day to Belgin a week earlier. The Turhan man had taken responsibility for briefing his people, and to their credit they had fulfilled their orders completely. Last evening, McKee had thanked him for all the preparation his battalion had completed, their commander had been nonchalant in his acknowledgement.

"My people are all ex-Turkish military they understand what they need to do," he had said.

In fact, Belgin had felt more confident about his team than he had about his colleagues, Ciller and Repcer, to the extent he had chosen to return to Dubai with them to discuss who would be handling the sales pitches to their guests the following day.

That gave McKee his final opportunity to discuss the forthcoming events with Bonnie and Clyde.

Apart from Belgin's people who had sole responsibility for demonstrating the equipment, Mossad effectively controlled all other aspects of the proceedings from perimeter security to hostessing. As a result they had decided what role he should take in the proceedings.

"You must stay at the control tower throughout," explained Bonnie. You will be able to justify this because you will be providing the commentary on the demonstration. If for some reason, you leave this area to go to any other place in the vicinity we cannot guarantee your safety. Do you understand? During the event, it will be difficult to spot individual guests owing to the harshness of the weather conditions, everyone will be wearing protective clothing and anti-glare glasses, so we can't be looking out for you. Also at the end of the demonstration we will be leaving, and you will have no further contact with us."

McKee had grown increasingly apprehensive about the arrangement and had said as much to Smith. He had received an unsympathetic response similar to Bonnie and Clyde. "Just do what you are asked to do. Others will take responsibility for what happens around you."

The first helicopter of the day brought the Turhan contingent of Repcer, Ciller and Belgin.

All seemed strangely relaxed. The concerns and suspicions of recent days had all disappeared. He was sure he had Belgin to thank for that.

Ciller explained that her key target was al-Harriri and his Iranian sponsor, Vehrani.

"I am going to enjoy showing those two the true capability of Turhan. I am going to make them come begging for business with us. Repcer will look after the Russians, Belgin will take the Saudis and Indians. Your people can do the rest."

Most of the guests arrived at Al Ain by helicopter direct from Dubai airport, given their personalised briefing pack and escorted into a hangar where each was greeted by the Turhan directors before touring the exhibition of the hardware and taking refreshments in a large, air-conditioned suite. Conversations took place in several foreign languages as Turhan representatives discussed the merits of their products and the prospective buyers had the opportunity to use simulators to get an appreciation of how their products would respond to the user. McKee moved around the room ensuring the buyers' interests were being looked after. Most of the participants there he had never met, but as they had been invited in his name, being conscious his Turhan colleagues were watching him, he needed to be seen to be engaging them, talking freely, and introducing Ciller as the company's CEO whenever the opportunity arose.

His task was made easier by the fact that the Turhan chief was a beautiful woman, even in formal business attire, in a room dominated by men. All the delegates were keen to meet her, some almost too keen.

Al-Harriri was a prime example. He had not waited for a formal introduction but gate-crashed a conversation she was having with a Qatari sheikh.

"Madam, it is an added pleasure to meet you again. It seems only a few weeks since we last met in Dubai and since then you have been busy assembling this presentation. I am hugely impressed by your efforts. Your company clearly understands what it takes to compete in this challenging market and to my eye you are even more beautiful than I remember."

For a fleeting minute, Ciller looked blank before playing along with the guest.

"Thank you for your kind words. Your attendance today is all the recognition I seek. Turhan is a major hi-tech weapons manufacturer and needs to be better recognised in the market. We seek partnerships. Today is the start of that process. We are not just showcasing our products today but will be unveiling some of the most competitive credit arrangements in order to drive our advantage. My colleague, Mr Repcer will be able to tell you more."

At that moment, Repcer's mobile started buzzing. He nodded, slightly embarrassed and moved to one side. McKee was out of earshot but saw the familiar frown cross the lawyer's face as he closed the phone. Moving back to Ciller, Repcer propelled her away from al-Harriri to the edge of the gathering.

"Vahid, Canecale and Abraham have been arrested by the authorities on the Isle of Man. I've just heard from Abraham's captain. I'm going to send a lawyer from London to find out what's happening. I think we should go home soonest and await developments."

Ciller was incredulous.

"In the middle of our corporate presentation in front of some of the world's most influential buyers? We can't do that. We will be a laughing stock. We are an international corporation and we must act like it. No, find out what is happening over there certainly, and we can discuss what to do, if anything, when our guests have departed."

She returned to al-Harriri.

"Please excuse the interruption. Turhan aims to become a partner of choice for your business. We understand we have to earn your trust if we are to trade."

McKee checked his watch – the time had come. Clyde has made it his business to seek out McKee and to tell him to move to his position.

A tannoy announcement confirmed the demonstration would begin in ten minutes and guests were invited to take their seats on the observation deck.

As the guests filed up to the gantry, McKee instinctively pushed by to catch Ciller by the arm. For a split second she looked annoyed at his move.

"Firstly Repcer and now you, what is going on? Can't you concentrate on the job in hand?"

"I need you to come with me."

"But I have to be with my guests."

"But I need you now."

This time, he was more forceful, gripping her by the wrist and pushing out of a fire door.

A sand buggy was parked outside.

"Duncan, what are you doing?"

"Get in – we need to get to the control tower now."

"You don't need me for that. You're providing the commentary."

"I need you to help."

He had effectively pushed her into the buggy and while she was trying to comprehend what was going on, he had leaped in the driver's side and set off towards the control tower.

"What's happening?"

"Don't worry it will all be OK – just do exactly what I tell you."

Minutes later they pulled up at the control tower and once more McKee propelled her through the door roughly.

She complained and wanted to scream, yet a combination of fear, dust and the futility of her situation meant it only came out as a whimper.

The top of the control tower was relatively low at three floors, so McKee was quickly in position reaching for his notes and starting his smooth welcome on the tannoy.

The first act meant introducing the targets – six tanks, one from Russia, Germany, China, South Korea, the UK and US with detailed technical descriptions of their armour and fire power. After introducing them, they were driven away to a marker position at the far end of the runway, just visible to those on the observation deck with field glasses. For the demonstration, each had been painted in a bright colour so the audience could recognise them. Then, when they were lined up in the distance, two soldiers emerged in front of the audience. One carried a shoulder-mounted launcher, the other a backpack of shells. The pair loaded the launcher, waited for the signal, then fired. The first target tank exploded. The exercise was completed in short order, leaving fire and billowing smoke where the tanks had been. The range, accuracy, speed and ease of loading as well as the ability of the shell to pierce the highest quality armour currently available made its own statement. Then another tank was brought before the audience, this, McKee explained to the audience, was a new hybrid, a US Abrams battle tank refitted with Turhan light galvanised military-grade alloy. It was subjected to worse treatment. Firstly, it received one of Turhan's mobile shells which seemed to bounce off it. Then a large Russian GRAD rocket launcher was deployed to do the same job, delivering such an impact that the compressed air of the explosion momentarily made the armoured vehicle bounce on to one of its twin tracks. The final assault was made by one of Turhan's own drones. The vehicle was driven back towards the observation deck allowing the audience to see the damage sustained. Both shells had been direct hits, yet the only sign of the incident were scorch marks on its body. Unlike the first display, a tank crew had remained inside the vehicle during the attack. Again the tank turned, aiming at the wrecked tanks already destroyed and fired a single shell in their direction to demonstrate it was in full working order before the crew emerged waving to their observers and receiving a ripple of applause from the onlookers.

"Good?" McKee asked Ciller.

The display had lifted her out of her anger. She was enthralled.

"I only wish my father could have been here. This is beyond my expectations."

"Now here is something you won't have seen," McKee whispered in a low voice before reverting to his commentary.

While the guests were preoccupied watching the artillery display, the Emirati team staffing the hanger had left quickly joining a bus moving away from the compound.

Already the gathering had been impressed with what they had seen but, as if to make the point, the Turhan modified tank was moved to a central position on the runway. McKee continued to read his notes.

"We at Turhan are so confident about the quality of our armament, we will now attempt to destroy the tank with an aerial attack with the crew of the tank onboard. As we prepare, the tank is moving into a position a safe distance from the viewing platform to meet the attack head on."

Then a high-pitched sucking noise and a deep bass roar, as an unmarked jet came into sight appearing to be descending out of the sun. He remembered it had a twin tail possibly a MIG-25. Apart from the speed of its approach, the uninitiated may have assumed it was preparing to land, only to see it accelerate possibly no more than 100 metres above the ground before firing a single missile on to the tank. The explosion drew gasps as everything was shaken by the impact. The jet had pulled away as quickly as it had arrived, climbing towards the stratosphere, leaving the tank crew to emerge once more to receive the adulation of the crowd.

McKee continued with his commentary trailing the imminent arrival of the microwave gun. The power of the demonstration had gained the audience's full attention.

As McKee was explaining why the Turhan armour was so good, the jet became visible banking away to the right and lining up to the airfield. One or two of the spectators had seen the sun reflecting off its wings as it turned, and one or two more were pointing out that the tank crew seemed oblivious as it dropped to low-level attack altitude. Suddenly that tell-tale sucking, rushing sound, this time at 45 degrees to the runway before loosing off another two rockets at the hanger where the viewing platform was. McKee's quick reactions made him dive to the floor, pushing Ciller to the ground ahead of him. The force of the impact blew out the windows of the control tower and engulfed the hanger in a wall of flame as the high explosive tore into the structure with a double boom. Then the marauding aircraft was gone climbing to the southwest over the desert towards Yemen, leaving a wall of acrid black smoke and fire in its wake.

There was an eerie silence, no noise of wailing sirens or emergency services here to administer to the victims. Just a rumpled sound of burning from across the runway.

THIRTY-FIVE

MCKEE GRABBED CILLER UP by the back of her blouse collar and dragged her out of the room and down the staircase. As they fell out of the door, the inferno, combined with the heat of the day, created a temperature that felt similar to one of Turhan's smelting plants back home. Fair enough, Bonnie and Clyde had not told him specifically what was going to happen and getting Ciller away from the wall of flame had not been part of the script, for London or Tel Aviv, but despite being hot to the touch, the sand buggy was working, and he was able to escape, just anywhere away from the fire. His ears were ringing, his mind racing – were they the only ones to survive? Where would he go? Surely the explosions that had just occurred would have been seen and heard throughout the area and some sort of alarm must have been raised. Meanwhile he steered the little buggy towards the now burnt-out tanks on the edge of the airfield whilst he tried desperately to get his thoughts together.

"Don't worry Ciller, it will be OK, just stay calm." By listening alone he couldn't tell whether she was calm or not. He thought she was making some sort of sound but was unable to take it in. He was driving just ahead of a rapidly building cloud of black smoke and knew he had to stay clear if he was going to avoid succumbing to the flames coming into view to his left. Ahead was the encampment where the Turhan team were based. There appeared to be no order there, the inhabitants were following his example – getting out, but their departure offered him an escape route.

He could now see vehicles ahead of him heading over rough ground to what he assumed to be a highway, marked out by road signs next to an elevated plain. He didn't reduce his speed and the buggy bounced along over the stony terrain.

The road marked the main route from Muscat to Dubai and he quickly turned north, in a bid to find a safe haven from the dystopian scene. Yet as he headed back in the direction of the city it appeared that the events at Al Ain had stirred up a hornet's nest of activity. First, two heavily armed fighter jets flew past heading to the scene, followed shortly by three Chinooks. Approaching the city limits, a mixture of civilian and army firefighting units were heading in the opposite direction. He still hadn't got his hearing back, but a glance at Ciller slumped in the passenger seat scared him. For the first time, he was aware that she was not fully conscious, and her face was bloodied. He used one of his hands to shake her knee, which proved ineffective at stimulating a reaction. Now his attention was taken by a red flashing light on the dashboard. It was warning that the vehicle was starting to run out of charge. He couldn't know how much power was left in the buggy, but he knew he just had to keep going as far as he could, especially because if he had to stop he could not be sure it would start again. As had happened so many times in the past, fate stepped in as he arrived at the southern terminus of the municipal public transport service. Oblivious to vehicles moving around him he cut in front of a departing bus and stopped. Pandemonium ensued as the accelerating bus screeched and juddered to a halt just behind. People were running from several directions gathering around the buggy shouting and gesticulating (although in the moment, much of it was lost on him). He leaped out to confront them and duly collapsed.

It was fortuitous, he picked the most accessible venue on the outskirts of the city to finish his escape because he had done enough to produce an early reaction from the now stretched emergency services. They were both taken to hospital.

He was woken hours later with a doctor at his bedside shining a torch into his eye.

"Hello – welcome back to the land of the living," announced a man in a white coat.

"That's disappointing – I had hoped you had the passcode for me to get to heaven – I assume everyone would be wearing white up there."

"According to our diagnostics you are made of tough stuff, Mr McKee, so I don't think you are ready to pay a visit just yet." He smiled.

"You're probably right. Besides I suspect it's pretty dark where I will be going when I reach the end."

"I wouldn't be so negative if I were you. You have plenty of cuts and bruises but there's nothing broken, and I think you will mend quite quickly. The same goes for your companion although she has sustained a slightly more serious head wound that will keep her off the cat walks for a while I fear."

"Catwalks?"

"She is a model yes? She certainly has the looks…"

"No, no – she's a businesswoman… as you say an attractive businesswoman."

"Well, we have patched her up, so she will fully recover. In fact, you should be celebrating your good fortune. The explosion at Al Ain has resulted in over a hundred deaths."

"What happened?"

"I think, Mr McKee, that may be a question the authorities might like to ask you. From what I understand a private defence show was taking place and there were munitions close to where the delegates were. Something caused an explosion, and half the airfield went up. Fortunately not the half you were in."

News of the incident at Al Ain made the news around the world with a range of explanatory theories being propounded for its cause.

One of the more stoical reactions came from Marshall who called Smith directly after hearing the news report on the BBC.

"Is it too early to know about the casualties?"

"I think so," said Smith. "But if I were a gambling man I'd say that is the end of Turhan as we know it."

"When will you know for sure?"

"When I hear from my man at the scene. In the meantime, you'll just have to wait for my confirmation."

Within twenty-four hours, McKee had checked himself and Ciller out of the central Dubai hospital and back into his suite at the Burj. It was moments like this he appreciated working for HMG. His booking was held open and for the first time since this business had started, he could feel at ease, safe in the knowledge that the purpose of his mission had been delivered… well almost.

The Israelis had been efficient in their project planning and now, just as it was all over had disappeared into the ether. There had been no opportunity for debriefs or goodbyes. In fact, McKee had been amazed how quickly they had moved out of the theatre, leaving no trace of their presence. Mopping-up operations were still taking place at Al Ain with the Emirati government claiming there would be a full investigation of the 'accident' and the circumstances around it, but this was really for public consumption. Although not present in person, Smith had been heavily involved, with the result that Matheson's alter ego, McKee would effectively disappear. Travel warrants, hotel bookings, the office suite were paid up and closed. The customer record would show a Mr McKee had departed on a flight to Mumbai. Even if the world could now consign Duncan McKee to history, Ciller Terzili could not. For all the meticulous planning, Ciller was a loose end. By the law of averages she should have perished with her fellow directors, Repcer and Belgin. But here she was, cut, bruised and battered, still suffering from the trauma of the attack.

Smith had agreed to allow him to take some downtime in Dubai before returning to London as a reward for collating evidence on Turhan's international operations and helping to eliminate half the Turhan board. God knows what would happen when news of Ciller's survival leaked and the fact it had only happened because he had not followed orders.

The experience had shaken Ciller's confidence to the core. No longer the outgoing effervescent woman he had found so irresistible but a shadow of her former self. Since leaving the hospital she had not shown an interest in going home. News of the disaster had been passed in calls to her father, as well as Yasmin Ali and Duru Hosni, who would assume control of the business indefinitely until her return. The tidal wave of media attention would inevitably follow, but fortunately centred on the demise of Repcer, a high-profile figure in Turkish society. Media reports were naturally filled with conjecture, with most citing the unstable nature of the ammunition dump in the usually high local temperatures as the reason for the explosion. Fortunately no witnesses had been unearthed to offer a different account of the proceedings, but the real circumstances had not been lost on Ciller.

After another day of silence and fasting, her time spent on the balcony overlooking the Gulf shoreline, she started to talk.

"You may not understand, but I have the same feeling I had when my mother and sisters were killed," she said. "Firstly it was a bomb, then this time a bigger bomb delivered by a jet. What is the connection with these two incidents? Me. Someone must have hated me so much they hire a jet to kill me. I can't believe it. In life you meet people, some you like better than others, but this requires a special form of hatred that knows no bounds. That sort of feeling I would have felt if it had been close to me, so how come I feel so shocked?"

"You mustn't overanalyse the situation, Ciller. You have stumbled into the murky world of Middle East politics. Here you don't have to be hot to get bothered. The air is thick with feuds large and small – individuals, companies, nations. The destruction at Al Ain would not have been aimed at you or Turhan. It would have been quicker and cheaper to send a hitman to do the job. Most likely it was a commercial rival worried about Turhan moving into a protected market and wanting to stop the company getting a foothold or it was a rival state wanting to send a signal to the Emiratis. Your problem was that you were in the way."

"Is it known we survived?"

"Technically as far as the state authorities are concerned we are unaccounted for. It certainly makes the situation more manageable in that they don't know how many people were on the site in the first place, but as a fact, they know how many of our guests were killed – ninety-four is the last figure I got. Because the guests were high-profile people, they were the easiest to identify. Many of them were either former or current customers which is a setback; amongst the most important, al-Harriri and his mate the Iranian Vehrani, and Solokov. The Emiratis seemed more embarrassed about this than anyone. It seems their own security monitoring had not picked up the importance of the occasion. I think for their own reasons there is no desire here to take a big public inquiry into what happened, although I think you can be sure their security services will look into this in much more detail – after all there were quite a few Emiratis involved in the hosting operation."

"But how did a jet get permission to overfly and take part in the demonstration?"

"That's one matter they will need to resolve. I think it is clear it did not have official permission to overfly the country, but it could have flown in and out before permission could be obtained. It also presupposes whoever was flying it, had asked in the first place. For all we know it might have been flown from inside the

UAE, which would raise even more questions. No, even if the UAE investigators get to the bottom of whatever happened and who was responsible it really won't be in their interest to make a fuss about it. *No, what matters is you are alive, and getting better.* So long as you are here, Turhan has a future – even though for now it might be different than the one you had planned."

"It will certainly be that. You know that while we've been here Vahid was arrested with two of our associates in Europe, the Canecales for racketeering and murder, so the fact that I am able to continue suggests Allah wants me to feel the pain of bad fortune."

Matheson's response to this news was one of genuine surprise. He had Vahid and the members of the Canecale clan he had come across as likely thieves but, strangely, not murderers.

"When did you learn of this?"

"Repcer informed me just before the demonstration was about to begin. I told him we would find out more and discuss it after the show."

"So you don't know the circumstances?"

"Not yet – just the fact."

"And you have no way of finding out?"

"Not now. Only Yasmin is left and, given Repcer is no longer with us, I can't risk her making enquiries."

"But she could hire a lawyer in the UK, Ciller. Call her and get it done. It might have some bearing on what you do next."

Ciller followed his advice. Yasmin called Protheroes in London and they sent a litigator to meet Vahid in jail in Douglas, the island's capital. Information was then passed back down the line to enable Yasmin to call Ciller with news a week later.

It was not information she expected to hear.

It had been some ten days since Ciller had returned to the Burj from hospital and for most of that time she had chosen not to venture outside their suite, calling on the services of a nurse to visit daily to check and redress her wounds. Fortunately, with smart dressing most of the damage could be concealed by long airy dresses which really were the most practical clothing for a woman in the heat of a Dubai spring. The nurses' daily ministrations were working wonders and now she seemed confident moving within the hotel's public areas. She started her rehabilitation fixing dinner at the hotel restaurant where she had first met McKee. He seemed to spend quite a lot of the daytime hours away from the hotel, indulging in his interests of golf, water skiing and fishing. When she had first suggested eating outside the suite, he readily agreed, thinking this was her way of marking the start of their relationship. His trips away were therapeutic too, refreshing his own joie de vivre.

Ciller had gone to a lot of trouble to make herself look as she used to and she had taken the preparation to extraordinary lengths – booking the same table, wearing the same outfit she had worn that night and bringing the now well-thumbed copy of the book which had been her previous companion. She had invited him to play the game. Although they were sharing the same suite she told him she didn't want to see him before they met at the dinner table.

"I just want to recreate the moment as it first happened," she had said. He duly arrived at the appointed time (7pm) when she was already at the table.

He could remember exactly what he had been wearing but had opted for a blazer and open-necked white shirt.

"Ms Terzili, may I join you?" he asked in mock formality.

"Please but I am concerned we may be joined by someone else."

She saw him frown. That line wasn't in the script.

"I didn't realise the table booking has appeared in the name of Matheson not McKee. I tried to get them to correct it but was told it was some computer fault."

He quickly recovered.

"Oh that will be because when I left for Al Ain I forgot to

extend my booking. I have a guy in my London office called Matheson who rebooked the suite. I guess it's the sort of innocent administrative error that can occur with these things. But wow! Never mind that, look at you! You're a walking advertisement for the benefits of RnR. I think we need some champagne to celebrate your formal return to the land of the living."

The attempt at levity was not sustained.

"Duncan, my world is a mess. I have lost not only members of my family but some of the few business colleagues I have ever been able to rely on. The family business is damaged as a result of my actions. I need to gather my energies to consolidate, and I need your support to do it."

He looked at her quizzically.

"And…?"

"I am worried. On your advice, I commissioned a good London lawyer to assist Vahid on the Isle of Man and I'm pleased I did. He has explained the circumstances of his arrest which disturbs me greatly."

"Didn't you say he got done for murdering hoodlums who were working for him?"

"Yes but that is not a worry to me. In my world that sort of execution is often the way of resolving a serious business dispute and it is clear to me based on what I have been told, his action was justified."

Matheson looked surprised.

"What is a major concern is the extent of the evidence base the British authorities have collected about Turhan's sub-legal activities."

"Sub-legal?"

"Things that are judged to be illegal in England but are not in Turkey."

"OK."

"Vahid has told of one of his inquisitors claiming they had a spy in Turhan's operations in Turkey who had provided them with evidence about the drugs and people trafficking businesses I had been seeking to close down. Vahid told the London lawyer that they had prepared international arrest warrants for Repcer and me but have not served them as they believe we are dead – victims of the Al Ain attack last week. Apparently, according to Vahid, their information is good, and he believes it could only have been provided by an insider. Vahid's view is that the person who provided it had a vested interest. It could only have been my brother Adnan who has been in the pay of Solokov who has a long-standing issue with my family, or… you, who found your way into my heart, my bed, my family and my business… and all for a reason – to break up Turhan International. What could possibly be your motivation other than you being a spy for the British government? When I think back to the circumstances of our original meeting it is difficult to put it down to chance. You knew why I was here originally. In fact, despite my best efforts, when I met al-Harriri last week at the demonstration event, he seemed to think I had changed my looks since our first meeting, again in this hotel and remembered nothing of our conversation. When I rather easily persuaded you to come back with me to Istanbul you disappeared for several days without explanation. Was this the time you were collecting evidence for the British authorities? And was the time you spent investigating the minibus bombing that resulted in the death of my mother and half my family just a means of gaining my trust? And what of your office here in Dubai? I understand it was a service facility on a short-term contract that has now lapsed. So with all of these questions hanging over you, I need to know whether you are coming back with me to Istanbul or going to London? If you are coming with me I need to know that you are more than a good fuck and we can start with your proper name."

"You are right. You deserve an explanation. Come on, let's take a stroll outside along the promenade. I find it much easier to talk on the move."

They left the hotel through a side door and ended up walking directly onto the beach. Before their conversation, Ciller might have melted on to his arm but now in the light of her newly found information, she kept some space between them.

He started the conversation.

"You know, in some ways it's great we are here. We could have been killed last week."

"We weren't because you took us away from the hanger – like you knew it would be attacked."

"If I was a British agent, based on what you have told me, why would I have cared whether you lived or died? We both got cuts and bruises instead of death – that's the value of luck."

"That's bullshit. You were told to ensure I was killed because as a Turkish national outside the UK you couldn't have me arrested and extradited. If you had tried that, Repcer would have run rings around you. Once your dumb bosses wake up to the fact that I'm alive and you are the reason, you'll be finished in your twilight world. They'll kick you out for not following orders."

"Who's to tell them? I can buy us new identities in a day here. If you are serious about leaving a criminal past behind you, there will never be a better time to do it than now. I know about Yilan. You can get money here and we can go someplace else entirely."

"How?"

"Doesn't matter. You are partly right I deliberately failed in my mission because I got too attached to you. I saw you were a good person trapped in a web of criminality. It is ironic that Hosni is in charge. He was the only one of your colleagues not engaged in criminal activity and the only reason for that was he was making too much money in the smelting and fabrications business. I was hired by someone who did have connections to British intelligence but was not needed specifically to investigate the money laundering, people and drugs trade, but the armaments business. We thought you and Solokov were working together to develop the sonic gun. The guy who came up with the plans was a con man who flogged them to the Russians who in turn got Solokov to bring them back to the mother country. But we didn't know that at the time. We couldn't let the technology fall into potential enemies' hands. My job was to get hold of the plans, see how viable they were and to ensure their destruction. On that part of the mission I was successful. The plans were not viable, the prototypes didn't work consistently and all copies of the plans except one set were destroyed. That set survived but given what I found out in the diligence process they will not be of any value to the Russians."

"Did you know our event was going to be attacked?"

"No. Besides, when ordnance is flying around there is always a risk that something will go wrong."

"So why did you grab me and force me to come out of the hanger with you?"

"Because I didn't like the way that al-Harriri was looking at you. He didn't really give a shit about what Turhan had for sale, but he was getting ready to make a move on you."

"That is ridiculous."

"I don't think so. A guy like that lives life on his own terms. If you were to sell to him, whatever price you wanted he would have cut you down by thirty per cent first and then invited you to a private negotiation second. If he failed to get his way, the deal would be off. You are too smart to be bartered in that way... besides we have history now."

She smiled. "Spoken like a true English gentleman..."

"I'm a Scot actually. We are different..."

They strolled casually along the shoreline. Ciller had removed her sandals allowing her feet to sink into the soft sand and benefit from being regularly washed over by the exhausted waves making their final journeys up the beach. For a while they were both silent, taking in the atmosphere created by a growing group of families joining them to enjoy the early evening drop in temperature. If Matheson was allowing the surroundings to lull him into a false sense of security his companion was not. Outwardly calm, she was experiencing a torrent of rage which was something she understood but had not experienced for several years. What her partner was explaining to her gently was in effect an admission of betrayal which, in her mind was deeper than any physical infidelity. She had been a target – hunted, snared, abused and likely to be discarded. She had high ambitions – to use her wealth and influence to fundamentally change the character of her father's business which she knew had been founded as a semi-criminal enterprise with only a veneer of respectability. She had developed a blueprint – she had flushed out most of the old guard who had influenced her father, and his power had been weakened, so she thought. Yet most of those she had entrusted with the future only seemed to pay lip service to her vision and had, in one way or another, deceived her. Her own brother, an addict, had emerged as the servant of anyone who would pay him. Repcer was supposed to be a professional adviser but was in fact changing her decisions by stealth, Vahid, the man charged with cleaning up the corrupt practices instead wallowed in them. The Canecales, probably the nearest thing to an Italian-style mafia family still operating the controls of the illegal businesses, and now, the man who she grudgingly had to admit she loved, committing the greatest betrayal of all – documenting her enterprise for an international criminal investigation. In her private moments she knew she could not avoid being tarnished by the criminal conspiracy. She had sanctioned the financial transfers made by Yasmin that provided the prosecutors with the unequivocal evidence of wrongdoing, but her actions were much more modest than her father's, and anyone taking an objective view of how Turhan traded would have had to concede she was changing the business by increment. But it was a big job, now, in hindsight, too big a job for her alone.

So what to do? She had been branded a criminal – no better than those who had betrayed her. The ability to progress, to transition to a more respectable way of living, would be denied.

True, either in the Emirates or in Turkey she would be safe from any extradition to the UK, but she would nonetheless be a prisoner of circumstance. If she wished to go for a holiday in most parts of the Western world she could be arrested. The man walking next to her for some strange reason had saved her life and in one sense she was grateful, but why? Was it to ensure her public vilification? Would he get some sort of bonus for somehow kidnapping her and transporting her to British jurisdiction? The prospect was too awful to contemplate. Whatever the motivation, the reality was he had condemned her to a life of crime that would stalk her reputation to the end of her days. Compared to the infidelities of her former lovers, McKee's crimes against her were legion. She remembered the price they had paid which she had never wished to publicly acknowledge. Both had their penises cut in a rough form of circumcision made possible by drugging them into submission. The first time she did it in her room she had been repulsed by the amount of blood discharged from the wound. Second time she did it was a cleaner affair in the sea down the coast from Fenerbahçe. Her victims, both of whom had known her intimately were shocked by the premeditation that had gone into the assaults, from the selection of the jungle knife to her skill in making the incision designed to stop any prospect of future intercourse. How their attitude had changed from traditional Turkish arrogance to a childish fear. Retribution directed to a Terzili would result in a far more devastating outcome, which meant both sought anonymity away from Istanbul and a voluntary *omerta* as they didn't want to talk or show their injuries to anyone. In her mind, there would be no way back from this.

The relationship with McKee needed to be ended here and now with a more permanent solution.

THIRTY-SIX

THE SUN WAS MOVING rapidly towards the horizon, the gentle breeze now had an edge to it. McKee had been smart enough not to make much conversation during their walk as he guessed her thoughts would still be on the horrors she had witnessed the previous week. Given her private thoughts it seemed perverse that she should suddenly wrap her arm around his waist and slowly turn him around.

"I'm tired now. Let's go back to the hotel. If you saved me from being fucked by an unscrupulous Arab, then I suppose I will have to reward you in kind," she said.

Matheson obliged, now lost in his own thoughts.

Upon their return to their suite they shared a joint and then made love. Matheson had been hesitant at first, knowing her trust was on the line and aware it was the first time since their shared 'near death' experience in the desert. Was she doing her duty as a businesswoman merely repaying a favour, or did it seem to be something more? Certainly her body was submissive to his touch and yet again he was reminded of her perfect beauty, silk-like skin, the warmth of her body, the softness of her touch, her murmured submission. In their coupling he felt complete, fulfilled as if in Ciller he had found the one – *the* one who instinctively knew how to draw forward his natural responses, satisfy his lust but also strangely nurture his soul. How could he continue to deceive this woman who had him in the headlights of her passion. Although a little weird, she had interrupted the foreplay with a demand to take a picture of him erect and ready to perform. She joked she would look at it every night before she went to sleep. In the moment and the heady rapture, he had readily agreed – anything that added to her enjoyment.

Thinking about it afterwards, he wondered whether her reaction to the sex, was a mark of celebration for her own life being snatched out of jeopardy rather than an expression of love for him, but he had remonstrated with himself for being too analytical. Just accept it as a special moment that he would treasure, regardless of what the future held he thought.

It seemed like a fitting and logical end to their relationship in the Gulf. They had reached a fork in their personal journeys – in one direction was Istanbul and an uncertain future in a criminal enterprise, in the other was London, the civil service and paper pushing in Whitehall – a certain punishment for not following orders. Having delivered on his original mission his head had gone to mush – probably too much sun and the good life – whatever, he had misread the signs if that was what he thought his life chances to be. His would-be partner had recognised the situation and was one jump ahead.

Breakfasting on the balcony she had encouraged him to look at the view commenting on a speedboat chasing another out to sea. She went inside to collect a wrap to protect from the now burning sun.

"Why don't we go out there today? I am sure the concierge could fix it," she called.

At her prompting, Matheson had gone to the balcony rail with a pair of binoculars to take a closer look. His attention had been diverted as he gazed at the horizon, and he had not heard her re-emerge out into the sun and grip his legs from behind.

This was no act of sexual foreplay but the move of a rugby second row forward.

With her man relaxed and off balance, leaning against the rail his body weight seemed light to the touch, the speed and efficiency of her movement transferred his weight first to the balcony rail and then into the void beyond.

She started to scream like an innocent bystander as if shocked by the outcome of her action.

Far below, she saw the body of her lover and tormentor spread-eagled on the terrace with tables, parasols and people instrumental in delaying his impact lying at crazy angles. As she looked down screaming, some were looking back at her while others were either tending to her victim or those caught up in the aftermath.

The impact from the thirteenth floor had delivered the fast and final exit she had sought to their relationship.

It was left to Weitzman to deliver the news about the death of Matheson to his boss, Smith, in London.

"I'm sorry. There is no doubt. I have a contact at the Burj who has confirmed it. Apparently your man jumped from the thirteenth floor. He had no chance."

"Was it an accident?"

"You should know in our world the line between fate and circumstance is narrow. That, my friend is the value of luck."

"Spare me the bull."

"What we know for sure is he went over the balcony of his suite. He had spent the night with Ciller Terzili who was the last person to see him alive. She has told the local police she had been in the shower and when she came out, she saw him fall."

"Really?"

"Well the police will accept it because there is no alternative explanation and certainly no evidence to the contrary. She has given statements and been discharged. I understand she has checked out and is travelling back to Istanbul."

"Damn."

"I wouldn't be so negative about it, John. Firstly, our joint mission was successful, and your personal mission almost succeeded, if your man had followed your orders. So although Ciller is still alive, her organisation is largely destroyed and you still have the international arrest warrant for her open, so she is in effect locked in her own prison in Turkey where she can't do much harm. If she is crazy enough to go somewhere else then you may be able to catch her, so I guess you can say your man Matheson has paid the price for his own incompetence or vanity."

It was an uncomfortable truth for Smith. Operatives like Matheson were, on occasion, able to live the high life at the state's expense but had to live with the risk of failure and, in some cases the consequence of death. It was a professional irony that, in the extreme circumstances, it always seemed to be the best assets that paid the ultimate price. He would report the sad news to Marshall in the knowledge that he wouldn't give a shit, as Matheson had supplied some of the visual and documentary evidence he had needed to nail HMG's targeted felons on the Isle of Man.

Someone who did share Smith's regret was Ciller herself as she contemplated her situation from the relative safety of the veranda at her family's *yali* on the banks of the Bosporus. Her father had got to hear of the problems she had experienced as well as the arrests and deaths that had followed. In reality, he was old, too tired to enquire too much into the circumstances but the permanent absence of Repcer had taken its toll. Father and daughter were united in their respect for the man who, one way or another, had done so much to build the Turhan brand, but that was it – there was no love beyond that.

Ciller sought her father's forgiveness.

"I tried so hard to build up the company to compensate for the loss of the family to make you proud again. I got close to success but have ended up getting it snatched away because of our criminal associations," she told him.

Kerim replied: "I think you have been preoccupied by my past and that of my associates. We were, and remain, traders who do business to meet the needs of our customers. Legal, illegal no one gives a shit. Every corporation in the world is tarnished by acts considered illegal in one part of the world or another. All they do is cover it up and carry on. That is what we must do – we trade to survive and if we are fortunate we thrive. The difference between the winners and losers is the value of luck."

He retired to his quarters leaving her to her thoughts looking out on the teaming comings and goings on the water. What should she do now? She sought solace in her phone, looking at the sculpted nude figure of a man, whose life she had decided to end only a few days ago.

The *Autumn Breeze* had stayed offshore outside territorial waters, waiting for a call from Abraham to send the RIB to Peel harbour to collect them. It had turned four in the afternoon and still no contact had been received. Sunny had remained locked in one of the forward cabins so had no idea how the tense waiting game was playing out above deck. Canecale and the ship's master had been discussing their plan B.

"We both know what the escape plan would be if we didn't hear back from the guys, and their phones appear to have been switched off. I think we should start moving."

The skipper knew the plan also. His instructions were to keep the boat outside UK territorial waters to avoid being impounded.

Reluctantly he nodded and ordered his pilot to weigh anchor and set a course to the southwest towards the Irish coast.

"We should be OK. The Irish authorities won't have anyone out on the water north of Dublin. We'll put you ashore at Rush. From there it's a relatively short run to the airport. Once I drop you I will do one more sweep to make sure we haven't missed a contact from the boss or Mr Vahid. If there is still no contact, I'll head back to Turkey."

"What will you do with the girl?" asked Canecale.

"She's no good to me. There is plenty of time for me to feed her to the fish. Those were my instructions."

"I know that. But the situation has changed now. If Abraham and Vahid have been arrested, the girl might be a useful bargaining chip. It may be better if I take her with me."

"Do you really think she has some use? I've heard she doesn't have a passport, so who will be interested?"

"She's a good-looking woman – that will be enough for the authorities and as we are using the private airport terminal I am happy I can get her on the plane with the minimum of fuss."

"OK Mr Canecale, we'll do that, but be aware I will be monitoring for contact from Mr Abraham. If we hear from him we will have to come back."

"That's understood. Mr Vahid gave me the contact details for the Turhan plane just in case I needed it, so I will check when it is due in Dublin."

The stress of the situation and their dialogue had resulted in them largely ignoring the circumstances of their now 'hostage'. Being locked in one of the forecastle cabins, they had no more interest in her well-being than any other parcel they would be carrying. They had overlooked the fact that their captive had been examining her cell in meticulous detail looking for something, anything she could use to escape. Her examination had revealed a metal plate at floor level fixed by screws that appeared to be lose and at the boundary was leaking small amounts of water. Fiddling with her hand, the leak seemed to grow stronger. Her searches had also recovered some cutlery. Taking a butter knife to the screws she started to work on loosening the plate further until the pressure pushed the plate out of the way and a jet of sea water entered the cabin. She was shocked at the torrent, but even more surprised that, instead of engulfing the cabin, it appeared to be draining away. Quite what she had managed to do she didn't really understand, except she hoped it was going to hamper her captors. The boat had been at anchor offshore but now seemed to be moving at pace which could have explained the force of the water now entering the hull. But it was still not clear where it was going. She had also started to become more aware of the noise of the engine which sounded like it was labouring despite the sea being relatively calm. But still no one had come to check on her and there were only muffled sounds of the crew going about their business.

What more could she do? In fact there was nothing more except to wait for an outcome and wonder about her fate. What she was finding difficult to come to terms with was why her colleagues had not attempted to rescue her. Yes, she knew about the importance of collecting evidence, but in her old guise as an employee of the NCA she would never have been exposed to the level of danger she had experienced in recent days. Now her solitude was complete. Her kidnapping had resulted in the loss of her mobile phone. She would have known her colleagues would have been able to trace her through her early incarceration with Abraham and most likely to the country cottage where they had been moved to but would they have known about the crazy drive to Wales and back to the *Autumn Breeze*? She couldn't help but wonder and hope for the best. She decided to take a nap on the settee and calm her tensions by practising the mindfulness techniques that had served her so well in the past. Her karma was soon shattered by a piercing alarm. Two minutes later a deck head unlocked the door and gestured for her to come out.

Her relief about enjoying some fresh air was tempered by the new gravity of the situation. Bulent was in front of her. Before she could ask what was happening, he announced: "The boat's bilges are flooding, and the onboard pumps can't keep up. We're sinking and have to get in the RIB. Get the life jacket on and follow me."

"But surely we are too far from the shore."

"The alternative is to swim. The skipper has had to issue a mayday and we are relatively close to a shipping lane, so I think it will be OK. He and two crew will remain on board to liaise with the emergency services."

"How come we have just discovered the leak?"

"Who knows? The skipper says it seems to have got a lot worse in the past hour, so we have to go. Get in!"

Bulent was gesticulating with a gun as a means of getting compliance, but under the circumstances, persuasion wasn't required. Once on the RIB, two other crew members had been instructed to bring jerry cans of fuel with them. Sunny now understood what was going to happen. They were going to make a run to the Irish coast.

EPILOGUE

IT WAS NOT VERY often unannounced guests arrived at the *yali*, but the persistent buzzing brought Osman to the intercom to deal with the enquiry. Establishing the identity of the visitor, he consulted with Ciller.

"Ma'am, there is a Mr Solokov here to see you. He says he has important information that he can only impart directly."

For a moment she froze. Solokov? But surely he had died in the Emirates.

"He can only enter alone and on foot. Show him into the basement reception room. Security needs to check he is unarmed and must be present on the door outside. Let me know when the arrangement is complete, and I will go and meet him."

Osman nodded and departed, Ciller moved to check her make-up, before heading downstairs.

"Madam Terzili, thank you for receiving me and I am delighted to see you have recovered from your ordeal in the Emirates," Solokov ventured.

"Appearances are deceptive, as you know, Mr Solokov. I am still recovering from the shock and meeting you has added to my symptoms. I had heard you were one of those who perished."

"Life is a game of chance don't you think? As you can see I have suffered minor injuries but am still capable of walking up your drive unaided."

"I'm sorry I didn't realise."

"No matter. God has decided you and I still have mortal duties to fulfil before we go to the gates of heaven, and I intend to make the best use of my time here on earth. Which brings me to your door…"

"How did you…?"

"Survive? Purely by answering the call of nature. You see just as the show began, I realised I needed a pee and so I went from the viewing deck back down to the basement of the hangar to use the facilities. As I did so, I was surprised to note the exhibition hall was deserted but then I thought all had gone to different vantage points to watch the proceedings. As I relieved myself the huge explosion happened outside, and I was thrown to the floor. Heard an ear-splitting bang and rush of fire but stayed down. I dragged myself up to the ground floor and almost choked in the fumes, but through the haze I saw a hole and open space so I just scrambled as best I could towards it and got out, where I collapsed but at least in a place where the emergency services were able to find me and get me out. Remarkably that basement toilet saved my life so here I am wanting to know what happened and already I have started to make my own enquiries. If someone wants to kill us I think we should have a right to know why. Don't you agree?"

"Well yes."

"You seemed to escape because you went to the control tower. Wasn't that unexpected?"

"Indeed it was, Mr Solokov – one of my senior staff required assistance."

"Ah yes, Mr McKee… I met him. How is he? Recovered I hope."

"Yes and no. He survived the attack but alas has passed away subsequently."

"Now that is tragic. He was very helpful organising the insurance of one of my boats. I thought he had a lot of potential."

"Yes, it always seems to be the best people who get taken from us first," Ciller added. "But these are unusual circumstances that bring you to my door."

"Indeed, Madam, it is. Given these recent terrible events that have affected us both, it seems to me this could be a moment for us to forget past enmities and forge a new alliance. You appear to be short of management to drive your business and my own resources are depleted. Working together we would rapidly regrow our respective market positions."

"My father never trusted you…"

"But your network has laundered money through London for me in the past and it is you who runs the company now. I have disagreed with your father about ownership of a mine in Uzbekistan, but if we are collaborating, that problem disappears. All that matters now is the future, not our history. Besides I am not coming to you empty-handed. I have information of extreme personal value which I will freely offer as a down payment."

Even with a powerful outboard engine a RIB is not always the most stable on the water and certainly not away from the shore in the mid Irish Sea. A skilled pilot would tell you the best way of stablishing the rubber craft in the swell was to maintain a steady speed to minimise the risk of impact with heavier waves, but Bulent was not one of those and he took the tiller with a clear sense of purpose to move as quickly as possible in the direction of the Irish coast. Those onboard with him were seated on the inflatable's walls to add some stability as the engine sought more traction to force it through the water. Under the circumstances, the spray and noise of the engine prevented any real dialogue on the journey, the four of them clutching the safety rope through the pitch and roll. Bulent's determination to press ahead was providing Sunny with the scariest part of the mission so far. All the threats to her that had occurred to date were at least backed by a warped type of logic. She had accepted her part in this journey as it was clear she was 'walking evidence' and at the very least Abraham would not want her found on his boat, but this situation could only be explained if her captors had decided her death, probably from hypothermia should not have been chalked up as another murder. Yet it still didn't quite make sense. Bulent was a criminal, but to her knowledge had not killed with impunity like Vahid, so why should he be desperate to escape capture? Despite the relatively benign conditions, the RIB continued to be buffeted as it precariously ascended the swell. The two crewmen from the *Autumn Breeze* may have been seasoned sailors but looked no less comfortable on their perches, each with one hand clinging to the RIB's safety line, the other to the jerry cans. Bulent appeared to be in his own world, almost oblivious to his fellow passengers and their immediate predicament, willing a vision of landfall to appear on the horizon. Sunny had no idea how long they had been in the RIB, nor how far they had travelled, other than the fact the sinking *Autumn Breeze* was no longer visible on the horizon and that nothing else appeared to be. Whatever the duration of their trip Bulent seemed to draw confidence that they would soon reach a shore. Perhaps it was at that high point of confidence that his concentration slipped. As he steered into the next approaching undulation of sea, he failed to see a large wave emerging from the port side. The engine, already revved, was losing its gravitational pull. The two waves connected at precisely the wrong moment and the RIB capsized. Then came the panic and the confusion. Sunny and the two sailors appeared to be stuck under the inverted hull – the jerry cans gone in an instant and there was no sign of Bulent at all. The shock of the seemingly intense cold sea enveloping her was forcing her body into what felt like a paralysis. Suddenly she felt out of control in an almost out-of-body existence, vaguely aware of what was happening but seemingly unable to influence events. Now the real game of survival began, with the passengers depending on their lifejackets and swimming skills to get them out from under and keep them afloat. Spluttering and gasping for air having escaped the rubber dome Sunny seemed to draw comfort from seeing the sky and feeling the wind on her face. Only one of her fellow passengers seemed to be visible some distance away, shouting and waving at her. Her eyes were stinging and swollen from the salt water and her mind seemed unable to process the wild pirouette of this other person. In an instant, she was picked up by a wave and thrown in another direction. The new view appeared almost as unintelligible to her mind. Another figure, further away from the last, seemed to be swimming away from the RIB. What was happening? If this person wanted to survive surely they would at least be attempting to hold onto the RIB itself. What did they know that she didn't? Was help at hand?

Deep in her soul she had accepted not everyone on board would make it.

"How are you so sure?"

Solokov seemed to mock her with his eyes although his tone was more matter of fact.

"Hey, Ciller I am like you – a commodities trader. *Semplosiv* is the Russian brand of Semtex, cheaper but also more fragile than its Czech equivalent. My people made the sale of the explosive that was used against your family, and it leaves a tell-tale residue in its wake. It was a rare transaction and customers only buy from me if the purchase needs to be untraceable. Your police may not be the cleverest but even they worked out there would be limited sources of supply in Turkey. I had a visit about it. They wanted to know who I might have sold it to. I had explained in my world most transactions are in cash and I couldn't be sure, other than the fact, to the best of my memory, my people had nothing to do with it, but I have a network of associates who may have been involved. The police told me they had recovered two separate sets of prints from scene and that they knew who one set belonged to. Well, you know me, I hate rumour and conjecture hanging over my affairs, so I provided a modest incentive to the investigating officer to tell me who owned the prints and so I got a name – Bulent Canecale."

"Not Ekrem, his brother?"

"I had heard of the Canecales and was aware what they looked like. One of my partners had some sketchy recollection of doing a deal but a surprisingly clear impression if he had made a transaction, the man he did the deal with was an Arab. All the police know is that whether or not he planted it, Bulent had handled it before it exploded. So that is something for your father and his long-time associate to discuss when they next get together. I wouldn't want to see it. There is something not right about watching old men fight. Perhaps it explains why Bulent left the country as well as the long-lost brother, Ekrem. I guess both thought they'd suffer the same fate as Gemlik had they stayed."

Rather than providing comfort, Solokov had told Ciller that in all likelihood the murder of her mother and siblings could never be beyond doubt, but it would be hard to prove the perpetrator. She recalled McKee telling her the same, and that must have been something her father had known, for he had continued working with the Canecales after the bombing. With hindsight, the death of Gemlik Canecale had the same note of question against it. Had Adnan killed him by way of revenge? No one would know for sure. The only link between the two was both enjoyed diving and had been known to be in close proximity when the death occurred. There had been no point in talking to Adnan about it, when he was on one of his highs he couldn't remember anything afterwards anyway.

Perhaps that was the reason why a feud between the two families had been avoided – after all both families had suffered losses in questionable circumstances.

Sunny Purewal realised how she had aged over the past six weeks of the investigation, a time when at one time or another she had been in fear of being assaulted, raped, trafficked and killed, and yet here she was now in a hospital bed attached to a drip with fruit and flowers nearby and a welcoming committee of her colleagues staring at her intently as she took in her surroundings.

"Great to have you back," said Phil Marshall.

"Seems like you've never been away," added Amelie De Jong.

"We thought we'd lost you," observed Wetherall.

"Thanks to you we've nailed the case," said Mwake. "We got all our UK targets and one or two besides. This is the biggest success the NCA has achieved with the smallest team and all thanks to your bravery."

"Bravery? You bastards left me out to dry," she croaked.

"You looked a little damp when we fished you out of the Irish Sea," Wetherall observed with a smile. "Just as well you and another held on to the capsized RIB or we may not have found you."

"And no," chimed Mwake, "your fellow survivor was one of the crew from Abraham's boat. Bulent's body was found floating in the sea a mile away from you, the other sailor never got out from the capsized hull. Still, at least you can look forward to meeting Abraham in court once you have fully recovered."

The irony of the moment was not lost on Sunny. She closed her eyes and drifted into a deep sleep comforted by the knowledge that her ordeal was over.

Smith and Weitzman had an altogether more stylish venue for their follow-up meeting. Gone was the morning workaday location of Quebec Street. The new venue was on the private terrace of Cliveden House, the stately home on the banks of the Thames in Berkshire.

Smith was quick to thank his host for the invitation. Such an assignation on HMG's account would have been out of the question.

"It is my pleasure to bring you here to celebrate a great outcome from our collaboration. Together we have taken down an international criminal enterprise and prevented a significant new arms business from selling weapons to our enemies. It is a great success. Although it will only delay the problem reoccurring I am confident by then I will have retired, and it will be someone else's concern. We must enjoy these moments – we both know they are rare in this world. But before we celebrate success it is important we have reviewed the few aspects of our collaboration that did not work out. From your perspective, your man McKee, while delivering valuable intelligence for the mission should not have got involved with Ciller Terzili. Had it not been for him, she would have been killed with the other bad guys present, but in the end he paid the price for his compassion, colliding with the patio at the Burj from thirteen stories. There was also a problem from my point of view as well. One of our targets, Valentin Solokov, survived the attack by going to the toilet the moment the missile struck the hangar. Such shit luck! But hey! Between us we have taken the rest down. When I reported the outcome to Tel Aviv I had a surprising response. I was sanctioned to arrange hits immediately on Ciller Terzili and Solokov. Very rare this happens as targets who survive our attacks normally act more cautiously and take on more security. However, in this case, I got lucky. Solokov and Ciller Terzili met for tea in Yildiz Park by that ugly contemporary monument, The Value of Luck, the day before yesterday – it looks like they were finally working out how to collaborate over their shared Uzbek mining interest. My man, a Palestinian refugee who I had last used to buy explosive from Solokov to start a turf war between the Terzilis and Canecales, was able to get his moped up close enough to pop them both away so we can draw a line under the whole business."

"You blew up the Terzili family earlier in Fenerbahçe?"

"Yes, we thought we'd done a good job. Got the explosive from Solokov and tried to sell it to Bulent Canecale for use in a bank raid. My man managed to get Canecale to handle it before the sale fell through. It was all we needed to set a trail. The idea was the

Terzilis would take out the Canecales in revenge, but two of the sons fled the country and the third was working near Bodrum and didn't know anything about it. Our idea started to go wrong when one of our own people, Leeza Leshem, restole plans for a microwave weapon Solokov had smuggled out of Israel. It was fate she chose to make her escape in Bodrum, where she was seen to be rescued by Gemlik Canecale. That was when Solokov contacted Adnan with the offer of a substantial reward for helping Gemlik and his new partner to have an unfortunate diving accident. Adnan was motivated by greed and revenge and because Gemlik's death could not be proved to be murder, the whole controversy blew away. Solokov lost his plans that he was selling on to Moscow, we lost an agent and two well-known Turkish crime families experienced filial deaths. So the tension we had expected to create failed to be enacted as we hoped but the result of our collaboration in Dubai has made everything better for us. So now, let's drink to us and a more peaceful world. *LeChaim!*"

They clinked glasses and drank in the view of the parterre and the river valley beyond.

Some weeks had now elapsed since Sunny Purewal had left hospital and been debriefed by her colleagues as the evidence was assembled to prosecute Abraham and Vahid. Apart from appearing in court to give evidence, this was in effect the end of the mission and the time to re-evaluate her career. The choice ahead of her was simple, stay in work and go through the redundancy process, as Four Musketeers Research went into liquidation, or quit and find something more fulfilling to do.

Marshall and Mwake had come up with a redundancy package in lieu of the reward for all her exertions on the investigation and the outcome would give her a lump sum that would provide a life-changing option if she wanted it. Yet the price of acceptance would be separating from her colleagues who had inevitably become closer. Had she still got the grit to start her life again?

Curiously, she needed a conversation with one man she had met by chance along the way during the investigation whose help had proved invaluable. Fortunately Mwake had recovered her phone at Brighton Marina and so his contact details had been preserved.

She would set off for Southampton to see the man who had befriended her undercover identity, Tony Moroney. In one sense it might have been easier to ring in advance, but somehow she thought it best to arrive at his doorstep to take him by surprise.

With hindsight, she was pleased with her decision.

Ringing the bell at 22 Cromwell Road, Southampton, a heavily pregnant white woman answered the door.

"Is Tony in?" Sunny asked.

"Not at the moment," came the reply. "He's taken our eldest son to the football. He'll be back in an hour or so. Any message?"

Sunny smiled, shook her head and said: "Not to worry. Just tell him Anita from Calais called by. I'll phone him sometime over the next couple of days."

As she walked away down the street, she knew she would be re-kindling her career with the NCA.

About the Author

West Yorkshire-based Martin Venning is a project communications and strategic investment adviser working in the property and construction sector with 20 years' experience engaging with businesses in the UK, continental Europe and Asia. He trained as a journalist as part of his undergraduate studies and writes for pleasure.

Find out more at mvenning.net